CRUEL & BEAUTIFUL WORLD

• BOOK TWO •

SUNKEN EYES

L. STODDARD HANCOCK

Cover design by Kit Foster

To my brother and sister, who suck it up and read everything I write even though they'd rather be reading nonfiction.

CHAPTER ONE

Nita maneuvered her way through the maze that was the underground, a gasmask pulled over her face by the chance that President Saevus had cameras around down there. It was doubtful that he did, since the Resistance had been exploring the tunnels for years and hadn't yet been caught.

Not recently, at least. Back when the Resistance first formed the president cared a great deal about their every move, capturing and executing several of them as they tried to escape Utopia through the underground, but every since he found out Godfrey Leon was no longer the one barking orders ... not exactly, anyway, his whole manner had changed. For some infuriating reason, he only saw this one man as a threat.

Nita stopped and sighed as she thought of the current state of Talon's father, the man who was still pulling the strings of the Resistance, especially his son, even though he rarely spoke.

If Talon was actually going to follow through with Dakota's ridiculous plan then he should've been there now, with her and her team, searching for a new route leading to the inside of Utopia. Because there was always a way in.

Nita scribbled her path into the notebook she carried as she turned another corner, frowning when she hit a dead end.

Well, that was it. She had searched every pathway in that day's chosen direction and all led to squat. There were a few doors that looked promising, but all she found behind them was more housing for their ancestors. There certainly were a lot of people down here at one point.

After aggressively drawing a wall into her notebook, she put it away and turned around, heading for the meeting point for her and her team.

On her way there, she only came across one S.U.R.G.E. - Saevus's Utopian Robotic Guardians for the Elite. They were black robots, the size of two fists with fluttering wings, and always ready to kill or capture, the result often depending on the president's mood that day. The Resistance had developed the technology to take them down, but it was not meant to be used when they were trying to be discrete. The president had each robot tracked, so if one went down he would know about it.

As the familiar click of the S.U.R.G.E. approached, Nita pressed herself against the closest wall, pressing a button on her coat that cooled the air around her, hiding her body heat from the passing robot. It continued on without a second glance in her direction.

Once the S.U.R.G.E. was gone Nita continued on, twisting and turning around dozens of corners and silently wondering why their ancestors ever thought somewhere so complicated was ever a practical place to live. Whoever designed it must have really liked messing with people's heads. There had to have been a map at some point, but they had yet to find one. It was likely that all maps had been destroyed when everyone moved upward and the first President Saevus somehow weaseled his way into power.

As always, it was a lot quicker getting back to the meeting point than it was wandering around, since she didn't have to draw her stupid maps in her notebook. She arrived in the room they always used as their starting point, an old communication room of their ancestors filled with rusted machines and monitors, formerly used to keep in contact with the other underground civilizations throughout the country, probably the world. But, alas, it was all dead, cords rotted through and screens fried. But it *could* be replicated. It had -

"Neetles, do you read me?"

Nita lifted her two-way radio and pressed the button on its

side. "Yes, Talon. I'm here," she said, leaning against the nearest table.

"I saw on your tracker you're back in the communication room."

Nita smirked. "Must you always keep such a watchful eye over me?"

"Must you always insist on taking the most dangerous missions when you know I can't accompany you?"

Her smirk quickly flipped into a frown. "As long as you insist on going through with Dax's stupid plan, then I insist on heading it so I can at least make sure it's done right."

Silence.

"It's not too late to back out of this, Talon. It would be nice if you could at least consider speaking to Xander Ruby rationally."

"He's a Guardian, and Guardians aren't rational."

She sighed and took her tracker out of the bag strapped to her hip, bringing up a hologram of the map they had created so far and checking the location of her three teammates. Not one of them was headed back yet, all of their colored dots still drifting off map. She supposed that was promising.

"The others are all still searching so I'm going to try another direction."

Silence.

She sighed again. "We'll find her, Talon. I promise."

"I'm finding it harder and harder to convince myself that that's true."

Nita tapped her fingers on the table she was leaning on, trying to find the right words to say. But there were no right words. They had been searching for Deryn Leon for over five years. This shouldn't have been an impossible task since Utopia really wasn't that massive, especially these days. Yet, here they were. All this time had passed and they were still searching.

Deciding it was best to say nothing, Nita put her two-way away and headed out the door she had just come through. She skipped the immediate path to the right and the one straight ahead, eventually turning left and then another left before she was at a crossroads they hadn't yet explored. Taking out her notebook, she began drawing lines and walked straight.

The first turn she made ended up being a dead end. The second led to a medical facility that she marked for later exploration. When they didn't have a deadline for a suicide mission. But the turn she made next actually seemed promising. There were some tracks there, indicating travel between important locations.

While there were several tunnels branching off of the main track, she kept on her steady path, checking the progress of her teammates every now and then to make sure she didn't stray too far from them in case they all finished around the same time. Not once did she pass a S.U.R.G.E. in this big, open area.

But then, before long, the tracks ended, disappearing right into a wall that must have raised at some point. She searched for a lever but couldn't find one. While staring all around, she spotted a crawlspace high and to the right of the wall. She didn't see a ladder but, checking the wall below it, she found small grooves her feet could fit into, so she used them to climb.

The crawlspace was tight. No bulky men could shimmy through here and she suddenly found herself wishing Dakota was broader so he wouldn't fit, by the off chance this actually led somewhere significant.

But it did lead somewhere significant.

When the crawlspace ended, a ladder awaited her, the midpoint of three meeting pathways. She stepped onto it without a second thought, climbing for a long ways before she spotted a small spot of light.

A manhole cover.

She was in an escape route disguised as a sewer.

Reaching the top, Nita pushed the cover but it wouldn't budge. Noticing something small poking out of it, she gave it a tug. Nothing. Then a twist. An iron key popped out and Nita pocketed it before trying again, lifting the cover just a bit so she could peek out. It was an alley. A quiet, abandoned alley with gray sky straight above it.

Utopia.

With a gasp, Nita put the cover back on properly and locked it with the key. She held onto the ladder with one hand while the other grabbed her two-way out of her bag.

"Talon."

Silence.

"Talon, are you there?"

"Yeah, I'm here. Sorry, I just ... sorry about earlier. You know I -"

"Talon, shut up for a minute, will you?"

He did just that.

"I've found it," she said, feeling more overjoyed than she ever thought she would, knowing that Dakota's stupid plan was coming to fruition. "I found our way in."

CHAPTER TWO

Xander stood in his bathroom leaning against the wall while Deryn was in front of the mirror, fiddling with her blonde wig as she attempted to get it on perfectly.

"What do you think?" she asked, glancing at his reflection in the mirror.

"Hate it," he said. "I'd rather you just kept your usual appearance and stayed -"

"Spread the bangs out more. Stop pushing them off to the side," Luka called from Xander's bedroom. He was lying on his back, sprawled across the bed while flipping through one of Deryn's books, angled so he could see into the bathroom.

"He's being much more cooperative than you are," said Deryn with a smile. She fluffed the bangs around then looked at Xander for approval.

He grunted. "Better. You look less like you with them covering your forehead."

She smiled wider. "Now, was that so hard?"

His face tensed as he looked away from her, breathing heavily. A soft hand entered his. He turned back to see Deryn and her strange hair standing incredibly close.

"It's going to be fine, Xander. Please stop worrying." She leaned in and pressed her lips to his cheek.

Xander pushed the bangs out of her face before kissing her properly.

"Focus, you two!" called Luka, now lying on his stomach with his feet in the air while he flipped another page.

Deryn smiled and rolled her eyes. She gave Xander one last

kiss and returned to the mirror. Then she grabbed the eye drops, which would make her green eyes appear blue, and dropped two in each eye. "Do you think we'll be longer than two hours?" she asked.

"No," said Xander. "Bring them just in case, but don't waste them if you don't have to."

Deryn gazed in the mirror. She didn't look half bad. Definitely not like her, with the hair and the eyes. She also had some foundation caked on to hide her freckles. And lipstick. Nothing too showy, just a shade or two pinker than her natural lip color.

"Oi! Ruby! Your email went off again!" said Bronson, walking into the bedroom holding Xander's portable computer, Quigley just behind him. "Someone really wants to get a hold of you."

Xander groaned. He grabbed his computer and deleted the email without reading it.

"Your other girlfriend again?" asked Quigley, cocking an eyebrow.

Xander punched his arm. Lona Von had grown more persistent over the last few days, and Xander couldn't help but think that his father had something to do with this. Needless to say, he had no interest in seeing her. Especially with their pending engagement.

Finley had found out that this 'arrangement' had actually been made by their parents years earlier. Only it was Odette, Lona's sister, he'd originally been promised to.

Of course, that was only after the Elvira arrangement fell through - thank god - which he'd actually known about at the time. She'd told her father, President Saevus, that she would never in her life marry weak-minded, three years younger than her Xander, and opted for one of the Tash brothers instead.

But since Odette's family had disowned her after she refused to be a guard and ran off with Neo Boyce - a friend of Xander's who was in the same predicament as her - it became about Lona instead.

Following the start of the war with the Outsiders it had been forgotten. Until recently, when Arron Von approached Atticus with the idea, wanting to unite their families once more. Atticus had agreed, so Arron's next step had been to go to the president, who was originally against the idea of his favorite Guardian getting married but had somehow been convinced.

Of course, Xander had tried to keep this information from Deryn, but then the emails started arriving and, with the lack of privacy in their apartment, he was forced to come clean.

Deryn walked out of the bathroom and to the closet. She grabbed an olive-green sweater and put it on over her white shirt. She then grabbed her bag off of the dresser. "Are you ready?" she asked, looking at Xander.

He frowned. "I don't like this."

"I know," she said, walking over to him and taking his hand. "But you already agreed." She smiled and gave him a kiss. "I just want to test this and see what's there while we're out. Then never again."

Xander groaned.

She smiled wider. "Besides, I'm going to have two horribly frightening Guardians with me. What could possibly go wrong?"

"Aannnddd ... you just jinxed us all," said Quigley.

Deryn narrowed her eyes. "It'll be fine. Now, let's get a move on."

They all left the bedroom, Luka marking his page, and went to the front closet to grab their coats. Xander helped Deryn into hers before putting on his own. She then took the wristband she'd been working on for weeks out of her bag and clasped it to her right wrist.

"What is your name?" asked Xander, testing her.

"Allison Darby," she answered. "But you can call me Allie."

"How did you make that thing again?" asked Luka.

"Skill," Deryn and Xander said together.

Luka rolled his eyes, catching Deryn's addictive habit along with the rest of them. He opened the front door and stepped out first.

The others all followed, Deryn holding on tightly to

Xander's hand as they descended the stairs. He stopped on the second floor and let the others go ahead of them. Then he pulled her close and kissed her softly.

"You're really sure about this?" he asked while staring into her foreign blue eyes.

Deryn gulped and nodded. "I need to get out of the apartment and this needs to be done. You've never lived outside before, Xander. You don't know what will be useful."

He sighed and kissed her again. "If anything happens and we're separated then find a tram and get back here. Understand?"

Deryn nodded again. Xander had successfully managed to take a great deal of physical coin out of his account, and then used half of it to pay a woman to open a new account for Ms. Allison Darby. Just yesterday Deryn had successfully linked it to her wristband. An indication that everything was working properly. "Yes. And thank you again for letting me do this," she said while rubbing her hands along his back. They kissed one last time before linking hands and heading down the stairs.

When they got to the first floor, Bronson grinned as he held out his hand to her and said, "Ready, girlfriend?"

Deryn grinned back, hesitantly letting go of Xander's hand and taking Bronson's instead.

"So why is the gay guy playing her boyfriend again?" asked Luka, who was leaning against the wall with his arms crossed.

"Because Ruby doesn't want either of you straight bastards holding her hand," said Bronson, swinging his and Deryn's arms joyfully.

"Deryn's the one who picked you, you fucking idiot," said Xander, knocking Bronson's shoulder as he headed out the front door.

Luka and Quigley followed. Bronson attempted to walk out, but Deryn pulled him back.

"I don't know about this," she said, her voice trembling.

"Relax, Deryn," he said, giving her hand a squeeze. "Everything will be fine. Even though you're stuck holding my hand instead of Ruby's, he's going to be right there the entire time, and you know he's not going to let anything happen to you. Neither will I."

Deryn breathed deeply and nodded. She took one step forward and then another, slowly moving towards the door until she was standing on the last square of tile. She glanced down nervously before stepping through the doorway, landing outside on the cement stoop. With a breath of relief, she headed down the stairs with Bronson just beside her, keeping her eyes on Xander the entire way down.

"Everything alright?" he asked.

"Yes," said Deryn before looking around and taking it all in. She was outside, the fresh air brushing against her face as a cool breeze shot by them. She inhaled deeply. "It's so nice to breathe air that isn't littered with cigarette smoke."

There was a click and they all turned to find Quigley lighting a cigarette. He looked at all of them, his eyes darting around. "Oh, sorry. Are we not doing this?" He quickly put his cigarette out on the nearest wall and slipped it back in his pack.

"It's fine," said Deryn. "I know you're all addicted to that disgusting habit, and at least now I have space to avoid it."

Quigley started to take his cigarette out again, but one stern look from Xander and he was quick to put it back.

Deryn still felt nervous but since there was a light drizzle she was able to wear her hood without looking suspicious, making her feel slightly more secure.

The five of them walked down the street, Xander making sure to stay on Deryn's other side even though the narrow sidewalk didn't really allow it. At least there were few hover-bikes and even fewer hover-cars in the area, so Bronson wasn't at risk when he was the one kicked off the curb and onto the street.

They eventually arrived at the spot where Deryn and Xander had gotten off the tram that very first night they'd found each other. Standing on the curb, they all waited patiently. Except for Xander, who was pacing with his arms crossed.

"Stop being so antsy," snapped Luka. "We're trying to be inconspicuous, remember?"

"I just want this to be fucking over already," said Xander, stopping his pacing but starting to fidget with his coat. He glanced sideways at Deryn, who was staring straight ahead, trying to breathe steadily while squeezing the life out of Bronson's hand.

Suddenly, a red tram hovering above the ground pulled in front of them, ringing its bell as it came to a halt. Xander stepped on first, scanning his wristband then waiting as the others all entered. Deryn was second to last and trying hard to look casual as she touched her band to the scanner. It gave a green light of approval and she moved on, smiling at Xander as she did so.

Once they were all in, Xander purchased a chocolate bar from the attendant behind the counter and handed it to Deryn. She smiled and laughed at the joke, easing slightly as they took their seats in that first car. This time she ate the candy, but the first bar he'd given her she would never eat.

"I miss my bike," said Luka with a frown. "The tram is so fucking annoying."

"At least you Guardians can afford bikes *and* ride them at night," said Bronson. "I actually have to take this shit home every day."

Deryn was surprised that Luka was actually sitting behind Bronson when he could have easily sat with Xander instead. Over the last couple of weeks she couldn't help but notice that he often made a point to be as far from the other man as possible.

She hadn't told Xander about the secret she'd tricked out of Luka, even though he had asked numerous times what it was that made her fall over in laughter the night Luka had his mind control chip installed. She knew it was not her place to say anything but almost every time she looked at Luka she found herself giggling, so she was fairly certain Xander had come to his own conclusions about what had happened.

Throughout the entire tram ride Deryn could feel Xander's eyes on her from the seat just across from her. She turned to him every now and then and smiled to reassure him that everything was all right, but the farther they got from his apartment the more nervous she became. Staring down at her and Bronson's clasped hands she couldn't help but wish it was Xander's hand she was holding. But that would have been too risky. Xander couldn't look like he had a girlfriend if, by chance, they ran into any Guardians.

She wasn't his girlfriend, of course! They had never discussed such a thing, but if they were walking around holding hands then observers would obviously jump to conclusions.

"Why are you blushing like that?"

Deryn was torn out of her daze and whipped her head to look at Luka, who was watching her closely. "I'm not," she said while moving her eyes to the floor.

"Yes you -"

"Our stop is next," interrupted Xander as he got to his feet.

Everyone else followed his lead.

Some girl walked by Xander right then, making sure to knock his shoulder exceptionally hard. He fell against Deryn and barely caught her, as well as himself, before they could plummet to the floor.

"Excuse you!" he said, whirling his head and staring coldly at the girl.

"Oh, I am *so* sorry, asshole," she said while turning to face him. She crossed her arms and gave Deryn a good onceover. "Is this your wife?"

Xander knitted his brow. "Do I know you?"

The girl's eyes sparked. "Are you kidding me?"

He shrugged.

After letting out a frustrated huff, she looked at Deryn and said, "If you are his wife then I suggest you start looking into divorce as an option, because your slutty husband has been messing around with just about every girl in Middle City."

Deryn looked at Xander, who had gone incredibly stiff. She rolled her eyes, pushed him off of her and grabbed Bronson's hand. "I'm not his wife," she scoffed. "He's not even married. And if you believe he is I can only imagine that you're one of the many women he brings home at night."

The girl opened her mouth to say something but, before she could, Deryn continued.

"He lied to you, like he lies to all of them to get them out of his apartment. But what really gets me is how women like you actually expect the men you go home with only hours, sometimes minutes after meeting them to be of any quality. So instead of getting on him for being an asshole - which we all already know he is, that's no shock - maybe you should sit down and take a good long look at your own life choices."

And with that, Deryn grabbed Xander's wrist and pulled him and Bronson towards the front of the tram, leaving the girl standing there with her jaw dropped to the floor.

Quigley followed them laughing, but Luka went right up to her and said, "So, if it's Guardians you're into -"

He lifted up his left sleeve so she could get a good look at his wristband with Saevus's crest on it.

"- I'm going to be at the Pit tomorrow night and -"

"Luka! Get your butt over here!" shouted Deryn from the front of the tram. "She clearly doesn't need another *asshole* in her life!"

"Ah, don't listen to her. I'm only part asshole," he said. "The Pit. Tomorrow night. I'll see you there." Luka took a couple steps backwards and winked before turning and joining the others.

"Trying to milk off of Ruby's sloppy seconds, are you?" asked Quigley, looking highly amused.

"Wouldn't be the first time," said Luka. "It's kind of hard not to hit some of his seconds considering all of the women he's been with. All of Middle City, according to that one." He pointed back at the girl.

Xander's eyes widened. He bared his teeth while shaking his head at his oldest friend, not blind to the way Deryn was looking anywhere but at him.

Deryn's wandering eyes landed on Luka, who seemed to be watching Bronson out of the corner of his eye. She turned to her pretend boyfriend and noticed him eyeing some guy who had just walked to the front of the tram, smiling slyly at him as he did so.

She tugged on his hand. "Hey!"

"Sorry!" he said, quickly turning his attention back to her. She narrowed her eyes, so he smiled and kissed her cheek. "Forgive me, schnookums."

Deryn crinkled her nose. "Schnookums? Seriously? All of the pet names in the world and that's the best you can come up with?"

The tram came to a stop and they all filed out with the crowd.

Along with their group, around fifteen other people stepped off of the tram. The gate to Outer City was now directly in front of them. Everyone headed towards it, forming a line as the S.U.R.G.E.'s scanned their wristbands and two guards on duty questioned them about their business in Outer City.

Deryn was squeezing the life out of Bronson's hand again, having to continually remind herself to breathe.

As the guards approached, Xander kept one hand in his pocket, fiddling with the two mind control chips he had confiscated from Aila and Orson's dead bodies. Just in case.

"Hello, Commander Ruby. Commander Voclain," said a young guard, smiling brightly. "Are you both on a mission today?"

"No, just visiting," said Xander, motioning to the trio of people with them. A S.U.R.G.E. flew over and scanned his wristband. Then Luka's, Quigley's, Bronson's, and finally ...

Deryn lifted her wrist, somehow managing to hold it steady. The S.U.R.G.E. scanned it and then quickly moved on.

It worked. The wristband had done more than just link to her bank account, it was fully functioning for Allison Darby.

"Okay, have a good day then," said the guard, letting them all through without asking any further questions.

The gate was still open from the people before them. As they headed into Outer City, they all took out gasmasks and put them on, Deryn, Bronson and Quigley wearing older models so their faces would be less visible than their Guardian companions.

And then they walked on through, ready to test out their luck at the one place that was as safe for Deryn as it was dangerous. The Black Market.

CHAPTER THREE

Deryn was a little surprised when she noticed everyone from their tram walking in different directions.

"Are we not all going to the same place?" she asked as Bronson pulled her towards a street no one else had gone down.

"Yes, but the Black Market is supposed to be a secret," he said, lifting a finger to his lips. "We can't all enter from the same place at the same time."

"Who is it a secret from, exactly? We're entering with two Guardians."

"The Guardians who actually care," said Luka. "Like my father."

"And here we are!" said Bronson, stopping beside an abandoned building and looking at Deryn. "After you, pudding."

"No," she said simply before walking inside.

"Really? And I thought for sure pudding would be a hit. Never mind, never mind. I'll get it."

He stepped in after her, taking the lead in the dark space and guiding them through what felt like a maze to Deryn. Eventually they came to a large room with a steel trapdoor in the center of the floor. It took Bronson and Quigley working together to get it open.

"It's a long ladder down, boo bear. Make sure to watch your step," said Bronson, giving Deryn a wide grin.

"*No* and I will, don't worry," she said.

Bronson went first, followed by Deryn. Xander, of course,

went right after her. Luka was the last one in, making sure to pull the door shut behind him.

As they headed down the ladder, Xander almost lost his footing several times as he tried to look down at her, but it was too dark for him to see anything.

When Bronson got to the bottom, he waited until Deryn was close enough and then pulled her off of the ladder by her waist.

"I'm capable of getting myself down those last few steps, thank you very much," she said, shoving him. "I'm not fragile, so stop treating me like I am."

"Whatever you say, porcelain doll."

"No one says that! That's not even a thing!" she shouted.

As Xander approached the bottom, Bronson grabbed his waist and pulled him off too.

"Dammit, Bronson! Get off me!" shouted Xander as he thrashed around.

"You try to help people, Quigs, but they're all so damn hostile," said Bronson as he helped Quigley down.

"I appreciate you, mate," said his friend with a smile.

"Don't even think about it," said Luka, kicking outward as he came down those last few steps. He slipped on the last one and smacked his head against the bars.

"That bottom one's slippery, by the way. Might want to be careful." Bronson smirked as he retook Deryn's hand, heading down a hallway with wall lamps lighting their way.

It was a good five minutes before they reached a large, open space. Several people, some recognizable from the tram, walked in from different directions, heading to the edge of what appeared to be a metal cliff and taking another ladder down.

Deryn let go of Bronson's hand and walked to the edge, staring in amazement and what appeared to be a tram graveyard down in a pit. There were old tracks leading into various tunnels, and trams still built with wheels crammed across them, lights illuminating inside of them as people hurried in and out of their open doors.

The Black Market.

"Our ancestors used them to get around," said Xander, who was now standing beside her. "But they stopped shortly after everyone moved up to Utopia. The few people who stayed down here tried to keep them running, but there just weren't enough of them."

"It's amazing," said Deryn. "How long has the Black Market been here?"

"Fifty years, give or take," he answered. "It used to be in a string of warehouses in Outer City, but the former President Saevus shut it down once he discovered its existence. It's for the better. From what I understand, it's grown a lot since then."

"Let's get a move on!" shouted Luka, who was standing near the ladder leading downward. He descended it without waiting for the others to join him.

"Come along, sweet cheeks!" said Bronson, taking Deryn's hand again and guiding her towards the ladder.

"Definitely not," she said, going down first.

He pouted and followed after her. "I'm beginning to think that you're going to say no to all of my suggestions."

When they arrived at the bottom, Deryn stared open-mouthed at the bustling Black Market, her eyes darting around in circles as people sold their goods from booths while customers pushed, haggled, and filed in and out of the red, blue and silver trams.

"Come along, gumdrop. Shopping awaits!"

"No, Bronson," said Deryn as he pulled her into the crowd.

"Ah, why not? They're delicious and sweet, just like *you*." He poked her nose.

She batted his finger away. "I'm beginning to understand why you're single."

"Ouch, honey bear."

"*No.*"

"You women are no fun."

Deryn and Bronson went from booth to booth, looking closely at every item they had to offer. She wanted to be fully prepared when the time came to leave Utopia.

The first item she purchased was a tent, wanting to hit

herself for not thinking of it sooner. She also bought several books on survival, some powders that kept food from spoiling, a canister for water, some socks that heated feet and gloves that heated hands.

While walking through different compartments inside one of the trams, Deryn noticed two bulky men guarding the door leading to the back car.

"Why are they standing there?" she asked Bronson.

He glanced over to see what she was looking at. "That's where they keep the goods that are ... well, let's just say they're harder to obtain. It's invitation only."

"Is that where you get your cigarettes?"

Bronson nodded.

"How did you get an invitation?"

He smirked. "The man who sells them is an old friend of mine. He knows I'm an addict and loves to bank off of that. Speaking of which ..." He glanced around, his eyes not stopping until he found Xander in the compartment across the way, presently putting a chess set into his bag. "Oi! Ruby!"

Xander turned and walked over. "What?"

"We need to restock," he said, taking out his pack of cigarettes and showing him that there were only two left in there. "Keep an eye on my girlfriend, will you?" He winked before looking around for Quigley, who was watching Luka in amazement as he did tricks with some toy on a string. "Quigs!"

Quigley looked around until he located him. Bronson pointed towards the back car. His friend nodded and walked over.

"Did you see what he can do with that thing? It's amazing!"

"Yes, Luka is quite amazing," said Bronson, glancing over Quigley's shoulder and winking at the object of his affection.

Luka sneered in response. He put down the toy and joined Deryn and Xander. "We about done here?"

"I think so," said Deryn. "I just wanted to visit a few more medicinal booths and -"

"Cover us, Luka," said Xander, grabbing Deryn's hand and pulling her into an empty compartment. Once inside, he pulled down the old and tattered blinds, slammed her against the door, pulled off both of their gasmasks and kissed her.

"Xander, this is hardly the place," said Deryn, even though she made no attempt to stop him as he caressed her.

"I know. I just ... don't want you to be mad at me."

Deryn pulled away and crinkled her forehead. "Why would I be mad at you?"

"Because of that girl earlier."

"On the tram?"

He nodded.

Her lips curved into a smile. "You think I'm mad about that?"

He nodded again.

"Well, I'm not," she said with a faint chuckle. "I was fully aware of your history with women going into this. We shared a wall, if you recall."

"True," said Xander, leaning in and kissing her neck. "But hearing and seeing are two very different things."

"Well, I didn't *see* you have sex with her." Deryn put her hands on his chest and pushed him away. "Why are you so concerned?"

"No reason," he said, kissing her lips again. "I just don't want you to be mad." And again.

Deryn brought her hands up to his hair and stroked it while he ran his along her hips, pulling her into him while he grew hard against her.

"We shouldn't do this here," she said between parts of their lips. "I'm a taken girl, remember?"

Xander smiled against her mouth and said, "Taken by me."

Xander froze. *Shit.* That sounded possessive. He hadn't meant to say it like that.

He slowly pulled away. "Sorry."

"It's fine," said Deryn, dropping her hands to her side. "Xander ..." She looked up at him and gulped, unsure of what she wanted to say. "Are my eyes still blue? They've been feeling a bit funny."

He looked closely at them. "Yes, but they have a hint of

green." He reached into her pocket and pulled out the drops, dropping two in each eye. "You still alright here?" he asked as he put the drops away.

Deryn smiled. "Yes. But I don't want to be here much longer. We really shouldn't press our luck."

Xander smiled back and nodded, giving her one final kiss on the cheek before pulling down their gasmasks and opening the door. Luka was leaning against it on the other side and almost fell backwards, but he caught himself and ungracefully turned towards them.

"Finished spending a moment alone with your neighbor's girlfriend?" he asked with a smirk. "I suppose that's alright, since your goal was to act natural and all."

Xander narrowed his eyes, noticing, once again, that Deryn avoided looking at him. None of them spotted the hooded figure turn at the sound of their voices, the gaze behind the hood immediately falling upon Deryn.

"You're a bastard," said Xander.

"As are you."

"I suppose that's why the two of you get on so well," said Deryn.

She pushed past both of them to walk farther down the car, still not noticing as the hooded figure turned away quickly, the men guarding the back car opening the door without hesitation.

Deryn looked in every compartment until she found another one with medicines. She went inside. Luka followed her but, since it was so crowded in there, Xander stood just outside of it, leaning against the wall while staring out the window of the compartment just across from him. While scanning the people out there, he came across a familiar face that definitely looked out of place, especially since he wasn't wearing a gasmask. His jaw dropped.

Xander shook his head about, hoping his eyes were playing tricks on him. But when he looked again the same man was standing there, studying a bottle very thoroughly.

Poking his head into the compartment Deryn was inside, Xander called, "Luka."

Luka walked out. "What?"

Xander nodded towards the window.

Luka looked and gasped. "What's that fucker doing here?"

"Don't know, but I'm going to find out. Keep an eye on her for me, will you? And *don't* let her go out there."

Luka nodded and hurried back inside the compartment Deryn presently occupied.

Xander took a deep breath and headed outside. He clenched his fists while walking up to the man, who was still holding the bottle which he could now see was filled with capsules.

"Didn't expect to see you here."

Soren jumped before looking at Xander. He touched the collar around his throat. "Xander, why are you -"

"I don't think my being here is the oddity. Why are *you* here, Sorey?" Xander looked down at the bottle he was holding, just able to make out the small, black lettering on the label. Hydration capsules. "What are those for?"

"Here you go, sir." A young man who was working in the booth put a well-sized box on the counter in front of Soren. "Half hydration, half starvation. Just make sure you take the starvation ones with real water. All together it's five-hundred coin."

Xander looked at the box, and then back at Soren. He furrowed his brow. "Are you fucking kidding me?"

Soren ignored him and handed the shop boy his money. The boy counted and smiled when he confirmed it was all there. "Pleasure doing business with you."

"I don't know what you expect to do with all that," said Xander. "Is it for when you get your slave back? I highly doubt Veli plans to kill her with malnutrition."

"Veli and I see her future very differently," said Soren, one hand on his collar while the other slipped the bottle he held into his box. "Do not concern yourself with this."

A light triggered in Xander's head. "You're planning on pulling a fucking runner with her, aren't you?"

"I repeat, do not concern yourself with this," said Soren, one hand on his collar and the other reaching into his pocket. "But, whatever I have planned for the future, it's clear that my brother and I no longer see eye-to-eye." He pulled out a small chip. "There are eight others, besides the two I already know you have, and the only time they are not with their owners is when they are with the president." He tossed it in the air and Xander caught it. "I trust that information is worth your silence."

Soren picked up his box and began to walk away. It was only then that Xander noticed a tent poking out of the bag he carried on his shoulder.

"She'll never go with you," he said.

Soren stopped. He glanced over his shoulder at Xander and pressed the button on his collar again. "Which is exactly why I've procured another of those." He motioned towards the chip. "But don't bother telling the president about it. He'll never find it."

"She doesn't even have a wristband."

"An easy fix."

"You're not afraid of living out there?"

"Of course not."

Xander stared at Soren's face right then. *Really* stared. Baffled that such a strict follower of the president would not only consider living outside, but that he would go anywhere in Outer City, a high risk zone, without a gasmask.

"Why aren't you wearing a mask?"

Soren chuckled. A very hoarse chuckle which could barely be heard with his damaged throat. "You know why," he mouthed without bothering to press his collar.

Xander's focus was drawn away from Soren when someone started screaming. He glanced over to see an older man who ran a booth with herbs on the ground, thrashing about while his wife cried beside him. People tried to help, but when someone was affected by the toxic air nothing could be done. It was over.

Xander looked back at Soren, who smirked at him before turning away and heading for the exit.

He followed him with his eyes, his heart nearly stopping

when Deryn walked out of the tram at precisely that moment. She noticed Soren, but played it off well by turning and heading towards Xander. Soren didn't even give the blonde girl in the gasmask a second glance.

Bronson followed her out.

"What was *he* doing here?" she demanded when she reached Xander.

"Being the sick bastard we all love to loathe," he said, motioning to the man who was no longer thrashing on the ground, but completely still. "Where the fuck is Luka? He was supposed to keep you inside."

"Oh! So that's why he was trying to distract us with that damn toy again," said Bronson. "Yeah, we got bored and left, but Quigley will be entertained for hours."

Xander noticed Deryn was looking at him. When he met her eyes, she frowned. "You could've just told me he was out here and I would've stayed inside. I don't know why you and Luka insist on being so secretive all of the time."

She walked past him and looked through the bottles at the booth Soren had just vacated, glancing up every now and then at the woman who stayed at her booth of herbs, crying while her husband's body was carried away.

Bronson came up beside her. "So what are we looking at, cupcake?" he asked, trying to take her mind off of the dead man.

"That name is definitely a no," she said, picking up a bottle of hydration pills.

"Oh, come on! It's sentimental."

Luka ran out of the tram, looking around frantically until he found them all standing there. He sighed in relief.

Xander narrowed his eyes and marched over to him. When Quigley walked out of the tram, he said, "Keep moving, Quigley."

Noticing the angry look in Xander's eyes, Quigley was quick to obey.

Luka frowned. "I only took my eyes off of her for a second."

"Yes, and that's all it takes. She walked right fucking past him, Luka," he said through clenched teeth.

"I'm sorry," said Luka. "I made one mistake -"

"*One* mistake? All fucking day you've made me look bad by reminding her of what an ass I used to be. I thought we were past this?"

"*Fine*! I'll stop making jokes at *your* expense," said Luka mockingly. "Ever since you started fucking Leon you've become so sensitive." He rolled his eyes and went to join the others.

Xander noticed that Deryn had moved on to another booth. He walked forward while keeping his eyes on her, not stopping until he hit the booth Soren had been at before. Looking down, his eyes were immediately drawn to a black bottle that held one single capsule. He picked it up and read the label. LAST RESORT.

A suicide pill.

"One of our top sellers in recent days," said the shop boy with a disconcertingly bright smile.

"How much?" asked Xander.

"Three-hundred coin," he answered. "Dying peacefully and painlessly doesn't come cheap."

Xander grunted but still handed over the money. He slipped the bottle into his bag before Deryn had a chance to look over at him and notice. When he turned to leave, he ran right into someone.

"Sorry," said a man while rubbing his head.

When their eyes met, both sets widened as they were hit with a moment of recognition. *Shit.*

"Moffett?" said Xander, still unsure if he was seeing this Outsider's face correctly. Chace Moffett was very active in the Resistance, and there was no possible way he could've been hiding in Utopia since the start of the curfew without the Guardians knowing about it. Unless one of them was helping him, which he highly doubted. That meant only one thing. Chace had sneaked in.

Without another moment of hesitation, Chace took off

running. Xander could have grabbed him. *Should* have grabbed him. Bound him right there and pulled him into a private compartment in the tram so that he could explain everything and use him to get Deryn out of Utopia. Being a Guardian, he had the jurisdiction to do just that.

But he didn't.

Instead Xander just let Chace go, watching him disappear into the crowd while he just stood there. Because he was not ready to enlist help, not if that meant he would have to let Deryn go. It was too soon.

And then, once Chace was out of view, the guilt kicked in and Xander felt horrible. He could have gotten her out. Maybe today. But he had chosen not to for his own selfish reasons.

Just then, he felt a pair of hands grab onto his arm. He turned to see Deryn smiling at him through her gasmask. "Are you ready?" she asked.

Xander nodded and let her drag him away, watching in disappointment as she, once again, took hold of Bronson's hand.

Things could never be the way he wanted between them. Not in this world. But at least now he had an escape for the day she left, hopefully taking Soren and several others down with him.

CHAPTER FOUR

Later that evening Xander lay in bed, using Deryn's breasts as a pillow while enjoying their post-coital bliss. She giggled when he gave her left breast a kiss, then she grabbed his cheeks and pulled him up until his lips were against hers.

"Thank you again for today," she said. "I know you hated it but I really needed the escape. It felt good to be in the real world again."

"I don't know if the Black Market really qualifies as the real world, but I'm glad you enjoyed it." He paused. "But never again."

Deryn rolled her eyes. "Oh, fine." Running her fingers through his dusty-blond locks, she asked, "So are you going to tell me what Soren was doing there?"

"I'd rather not."

"Did it have something to do with me?"

He frowned and nodded.

"Then I should know."

Xander sighed. He knew she was right, but that didn't make it any easier. "He was purchasing hydration and starvation pills. A shit load of them. And a tent. I think he plans to try and run away with you if they capture you again."

Deryn froze. Her hand tensed in his hair while her eyes became wide and fear stricken. "That's ... sick," was all she could manage to say.

"He's sick," said Xander. "But there is a positive twist to all of this."

"How can there be a positive twist on anything when there's a man out there who wants to kidnap and run away with me?"

Xander grazed his fingers across her cheek and smirked. "He gave me his mind control chip for my silence, and then told me some useful information for obtaining the others. Though he admits he has another for you."

"Oh," said Deryn, her tone suddenly brightening. "That *is* positive. Aside from the extra one to imprison my mind during my kidnapping, that is."

"I'm not going to let them capture you, Deryn," Xander reassured her. "Don't let anything that bastard does worry you."

Before Deryn could respond, there was a knock on the front door.

"That's probably Bronson," she said. "He had me put his cigarettes in my bag and I forgot to give them back to him when we got home."

Xander suddenly found himself feeling very light at the sound of her words. She had called his apartment home. He tried not to smile too much.

"I'll get rid of him," he said, pressing his lips to hers. "Then another round?"

Deryn rolled her eyes but didn't object.

Xander winked and kissed her one more time before getting up and locating his pants. He pulled them on, going commando since he didn't plan on wearing them for very long.

There was another knock as Xander left the bedroom. "I'm fucking coming!" he called as he shut the bedroom door. Bronson might be gay, but that didn't give him free reign to see Deryn naked. Only Xander got to see that.

Just as he reached the front door, the person knocked again.

"Did I not say I was fucking coming?" he shouted while yanking it open. His eyes widened when he saw Lona Von looking slightly taken aback on the other side.

"Sorry, I didn't hear you," she said, scanning him up and down, reminding him that he was shirtless.

"What the fuck are -" Xander gulped and started again, this time without the cursing. His mother raised him better than that. "What are you doing here?"

"You haven't returned any of my emails, so I had to draw the conclusion that either you were lying dead and decomposing in your apartment, or you were ignoring me. I'm afraid to say that it appears to be the latter."

"No offense," he said, crossing his arms.

"None taken. Would you mind terribly if I came in?"

Before Xander had a chance to say no, Lona was walking inside and taking off her coat. She handed it to him and, noticing the shoes by the door, she took hers off and put them beside his.

"Make yourself comfortable," Xander said scornfully as he tossed her coat over the nearest chair. He didn't want to give her the impression that she was going to be here for very long by hanging it in his closet. "You don't take a hint very well, do you?"

"Well, if your father called you three times a day asking if you'd seen *me* yet, you might be a little more persistent. All I'm asking for is five minutes, Xander, just to get him off my back."

Xander groaned but still shut the door.

Lona smiled. "You know, you're much more polite when my father's around. What happened to that overly charming man I encountered on the street not too long ago?"

"*Overly*? I have just the right amount of charm, sweetheart."

"Believe what you want but, from a woman's perspective, you lay it on a little thick." Lona walked towards the kitchen. "Do you have anything to drink?" She started opening cabinets.

"I really wish you'd stop making yourself so comfortable."

She came out with a bottle of wine and smiled triumphantly. Then she grabbed two glasses. "Now, Xander, is that any way to speak to your future wife?"

Xander tensed.

"Don't look so shocked. I *know* you know. That's why you've been ignoring me, isn't it?"

"Don't flatter yourself. I'd be ignoring you even if I hadn't heard the terrible rumors."

"You could do worse. In fact, didn't you used to date Finley

Scout?" Lona smiled almost wickedly.

"I'm not fucking marrying anyone." So much for being raised better than that.

"Why not? Don't believe in it?"

"No interest," he said. "Especially when it's not even my choice."

"Hmm ..." Lona opened the wine and poured. She handed a glass to Xander before sipping hers. "I don't know why you care so much. It's all just for show, isn't it? The president likes to keep the higher families unified, as did his father before him. That's why my parents got married. And I can only imagine that yours -"

"*My* parents actually loved each other," snapped Xander. He chugged down his wine and slammed it on the counter.

Lona poured him another glass. "Maybe they did, but that doesn't change the fact that any initial romance between them was because they were both socialites from Inner City."

"They didn't have an arranged marriage," he said. "They met in guard training, like normal fucking people."

"You and I met in training."

That was true, though Lona was brought in at the age of thirteen and Xander was only months shy of turning eighteen at the time. The encounter they had at Eagle Center was brief. They'd met once, introduced by her older sister Odette, who he'd been friends with at the time. That was it.

"You know what I mean."

"I do," she said. Then, replaying her words in her head, she smiled. "Oh, look, you already have me saying it."

"Not funny," said Xander, making sure to sip instead of chug his wine this time.

"It was a little funny."

"I don't understand why you're pushing this. You should be as repulsed by our fathers' primitive ways as I am. You're barely eighteen. Have some fun."

Lona frowned as she finished her glass of wine. While pouring another, she said, "Let me level with you, Xander. My Guardian initiation is in two days. I know this is hardly shocking but, while I may be a lot of things, ruthless is not one of them. I'll make an absolutely horrible Guardian. But my father says if I marry you and have a child then I won't have to perform the usual tasks that come with being one. So, in layman's terms, you're my out." She took a long, hard sip of her wine.

"I'm not marrying you."

"Why not?" she shouted, slamming her glass on the counter.

"Because I don't want to."

"And why don't you want to? Do you think I'm unattractive?"

"No."

"Do you find me annoying?"

"In this present moment, yes. But, otherwise, no."

"Do you think you would be absolutely miserable with me for the rest of your life?"

Xander gulped and glanced towards his bedroom door. "Yes."

Lona's eyes glossed over. "Why?"

"Because."

"I need more than just *because*, Xander! Why can't you be at least moderately happy with me?"

"Because."

"Because *why*?"

"Because I already have someone!" he shouted, his eyes flaming. Then they softened and widened. *Shit.*

Lona's jaw dropped. "You do?"

Xander held his lips shut tight and bit his cheek.

"But I ... I thought you were a ladies' man?"

He sighed and weakly said, "I was."

Suddenly, Lona's eyes drew to something behind him. Xander turned to see Deryn's bag on his coffee table. It wasn't particularly feminine, but didn't exactly look like something he would carry around either.

"Oh god, she's here, isn't she? That's why you're shirtless. Oh, shit." Lona put down her glass and ran towards the door. She grabbed her coat and swiftly put it on while slipping into her shoes. "I'm so sorry, Xander. I really didn't realize." She reached for the knob.

"Lona."

She turned.

Staring at her very seriously, he said, "Don't tell anyone about this. If the other Guardians find out that I -"

"I know," she said, looking sadly at him. "Your secret is safe with me. But I don't think this is going away."

"Don't worry about that," he said, suddenly thinking about the pill that was still in his bag. "And about being a Guardian ... as long as I'm in charge I'll take care of you. There will be no blood on your hands."

Lona nodded. "Thank you." She glanced back at his bedroom door. "Please just tell me it isn't Finley in there."

Xander chuckled and shook his head. "Fuck no."

Managing a smile, Lona said, "Good." She opened the door. "Goodnight, Xander."

As soon as she was gone, he locked the door behind her. He took several deep breaths before returning to his bedroom. Deryn was sitting up in the bed with the covers held above her chest. When she looked at him, she tried really hard not to smile.

"Sorry about that," he said, taking off his pants again and climbing in beside her.

"So does this make me your mistress?" she asked as he wrapped his arms around her waist.

"As far as I'm concerned, she's the other woman. Not you."

Giving in to her smile, Deryn reached out and stroked his cheek. "So you have someone, do you?"

Xander smiled back and said, "Yeah. I believe I do."

She kissed him then, the two of them falling back on the bed before hastily beginning another round.

When it was over, Xander was quick to fall asleep while Deryn rested her head on his chest, carefully listening to his heartbeat. She didn't have the nerve to say it, but she wished there was some other way to let Xander know how she felt. That he wasn't the only one who had someone. She had someone too, and she was pretty sure if he ever ended up marrying someone else, even if forced, her heart would be broken.

CHAPTER FIVE

"So I've compiled a list of all potential Guardians who may be in possession of a chip," said Deryn, laying out a piece of paper on the coffee table for all to see. "These up at the top in black ink are the ones we have. Soren Tash, Aila Parrish and Orson Yam. The ones just below that in red are the people we know for certain have one. Veli Tash, Wyatt's father Gordon Mackey, and Luka's father Barath Voclain."

She glanced sideways at Luka. No reaction.

"There are eleven total and we still have five that are unaccounted for. That is where the names in purple come in."

"Why purple?" asked Quigley from the armchair he was seated in.

"It was the only other color pen Xander had," said Deryn with a frown. "I wanted green ink for the ones we already have so it would look more positive, or yellow for our possible options since it expresses a sense of hope, but that wouldn't have shown up very well on the white paper, so I suppose purple works as well as anything. It's said to express mystery and that's certainly what we have here."

When Deryn looked up, everyone was staring blankly at her. She blushed and quickly looked back at her paper.

"So why do you have a purple pen?" asked Quigley, glancing over at Xander.

"I have no fucking idea," answered Xander. "I'm surprised I have pens at all."

"I found it buried in the back of the desk," said Deryn. "But that's hardly what's important right now. We *need* to make sure we have all possible names."

Elvira Tash
Stuart Scout
Wenton Pace
Eamon Graham
Arron Von
Atticus Ruby

"My father?" asked Xander, knitting his brow.

"We're covering all our bases, Xander," explained Deryn. "Now, did I forget anyone?"

Xander and Luka looked at each other curiously. "Maybe Dougal's father Mathis," said Luka. "He doesn't hang around the others much, but he tries often enough that I don't believe we should rule him out as a possibility."

"Mathis Fender," repeated Deryn, writing his name with the purple pen. "Good one."

"Put Sewick Blum on there, too," said Xander. "He's not a Guardian but that fucker has his hands in everything."

Deryn wrote the name down. "Any others?"

"No," said Luka, looking at Xander again, who shrugged. "I believe you've compiled a perfectly good list. Though Atticus and Arron are stretching it a bit. Why would he want your position taken from you if he's trying to marry you off to his daughter?"

"Well, if they offed Atticus and then put enough doubt in the president's mind to execute Xander, his widowed daughter would come into a great deal of money, wouldn't she?" said Deryn, setting down her pen. "It would certainly explain why he's trying to push this along so suddenly."

When she looked up, everyone was staring blankly at her again.

"Stop doing that!"

"Here we are," said Bronson, walking over from the kitchen and putting a plate piled with freshly baked pieces of focaccia on the coffee table beside her paper. "A little brain food for everyone while the dinner is cooking. I remembered you were a fan, Luka." He smiled at him and sat down in the only available armchair.

"So what exactly is the plan here?" asked Luka, trying a little too hard to ignore Bronson's smile. "That Sorey fucker said they only ever don't have the chips on them when they're with the president, and we need to take them all at the same time so they don't notice and warn the others."

"Yes, I've already thought of that," said Xander, staring down at all of the names Deryn had written on the paper. "The only time we'll ever really have is during our meetings."

"But those only ever last an hour, if that," said Luka.

"Has Lona had her coronation yet?" asked Deryn.

"It's tomorrow," answered Xander.

"That will last longer, won't it? And it's mandatory."

"Yes," he said with a nod, "but because it's mandatory Luka and I won't be able to get out of it to search everywhere. Meetings are easier."

She shrugged and said, "Why can't I do it?"

Xander froze, his jaw clenching as he stared sideways at her with cold eyes. "Excuse me?"

"Why not?" she asked, furrowing her brow.

"Because it's dangerous."

"So? You do dangerous things every day."

"Comes with the territory."

"And being a runaway slave, that's not dangerous territory?" she snapped. "We already know my wristband works so I'll have no problem getting into Inner City, and I know their worker slaves routines. No one will be any the wiser."

Xander narrowed his eyes and very sternly said, "No. Bronson or Quigley can -"

"They don't know those houses like I do, Xander!" shouted Deryn, rising to her feet. "I've been there! I know half of those people's bedrooms like the back of my hand!"

Xander turned white as he glared at her.

"Sorry to be blunt, but that's the reality." She stormed into their bedroom and slammed the door behind her.

"This seems like our definite cue for alcohol," said Bronson, getting back to his feet. "Would you say this is a wine night?"

Quigley was the only one who nodded.

Bronson didn't even make it to the kitchen before Xander was shooting up from the couch and following Deryn into the bedroom, making sure to slam the door twice as hard as she had.

"Oh, those two. Always fighting for control," said Bronson as he pulled some glasses out of one of the cabinets.

"You and your damn dramatics," said Xander as soon as the door was closed. He pressed a button on his wristband to put a soundproof shield around the bedroom, which he could do more often now that he didn't have to explain every move he made to Luka, who was the one to check his activity every morning.

"You're one to talk," she said, taking a seat on the bed. "Xander, part of the reason I liked being around you in the beginning was because you didn't treat me like I was made of glass. What happened to that?"

Well, he cared a lot more now than he did in the beginning. "It's not that I think you're incapable of doing this without getting caught," he said. "It's just that I don't want you to."

Deryn scoffed. "*You* don't want me to?"

"That's right."

"Well, if that's the only reason then why should I listen?"

"You should listen because I know what's best, Deryn. You're *not* doing this," he said sternly.

"Yes I am. With or without your consent."

"Fuck no you're not!" he shouted.

"Fuck yes I am!" she shouted back, rising to her feet. "Someone needs to do this and I'm the best option! You know I am!"

"We'll find another way!"

"No, Xander," said Deryn, deepening her voice. "I need to do this and you can't stop me!"

"Why?"

"Why what?"

"Why do you *need* to do this?"

Deryn blushed and cast her eyes to the floor. "Because."

"Because why?"

Her voice going quiet, she said, "Because you helped me when I was in trouble, so if there's an opportunity to return the favor then I'm going to take it. Please, just let me do this for you."

Xander sighed. His fists clenched as he said, "I don't want you to get hurt," through gritted teeth.

"I know," she said, taking a few steps forward and grabbing one of his tense hands. "But nearly every day I have to watch you walk out of here, knowing that there is a possibility you won't ever come back. This is a war, Xander. We all need to risk our lives from time to time. And I want to expose those Guardians for what they are. Twisted, manipulative bastards who need to be put in their place! And who better to do that than you?"

She smiled proudly and Xander smiled back.

"Don't tell me you get off on me being a top Guardian?"

Deryn shrugged nonchalantly. "What can I say? I like a man who's clever enough to have fooled the most evil man in our present world into believing he's loyal."

"Does it get you hot?" asked Xander, his smile turning smug as he pressed their bodies together.

Deryn blushed as he hardened against her. "Xander, there are people in the other room."

"So?" he said, kissing her neck. "A shield's up. Besides, they think we're fighting. I'm sure they already expect to be waiting a while."

"Our fight hasn't ended, you know?"

"Sure it has. You're going to do whatever the fuck you want whether I like it or not, I'm going to get fucking pissed, and then we'll have sex and make up. In fact, why don't we skip a few steps and start that last one right now?" His hands slipped down her sides and began to undo her pants.

Deryn grabbed his wrists and held them still.

"Come on, Deryn," he said, licking her ear. "Just a quick fuck. No one will be any the wiser."

Deryn's hands eased and Xander was able to slip his fingers into her underwear.

He smirked. "I knew you were into this."

Within seconds, both of their pants were off and Deryn was pushing Xander onto the bed, quickly pouncing on top of him.

In the front room, Bronson was back in his armchair, slowly sipping his wine while they all waited patiently. "Five coin says they're having sex in there."

There were several seconds of silence.

"Make it ten and you're on," said Luka.

Bronson smirked. Easy money.

CHAPTER SIX

Xander sat on the couch with his head held low as Deryn gathered everything that she needed together. She wore her blonde wig and black clothing, with blue drops in her eyes.

"Xander, it's time for you to go," she said, stopping in front of him.

He stood slowly, staring at the floor silently for a moment before holding out his arms and waiting for her to come into them. Deryn did just that, wrapping hers around his waist and nuzzling against his chest.

"I'll be fine," she promised. "Anyone who poses any danger will be where you are."

"Don't you dare go in thinking like that, Deryn. Some waves are viciously loyal. If one of them sees you -"

"They *won't* see me. I know their schedules. The majority of them use the time their owners aren't around to get the shopping done. They won't even be home. Should we place bets on how many chips I find within five minutes of entering their houses? I know Bronson just *loves* placing bets," said Deryn bitterly.

Xander smirked. That was true. They had found out about his and Luka's little bet the day before when they came out of the bedroom. Deryn's disheveled hair gave them away, even though she had attempted to fix it beforehand.

"I call two," he said.

Deryn smiled. "You're giving your Guardians too much credit. I say four."

"And just what are the terms of this bet?"

She scrunched up her face in thought. "Let's just say that whoever wins is free to call the shots tonight."

"I can live with that," he said, kissing her.

While they were lost in each other's lips, the clock struck six. It was exactly one hour until Lona's coronation and he needed to be there a little early.

Xander reluctantly pulled away, stroking her soft cheek while gazing into those foreign blue eyes. "Wait ten minutes before going. And remember, always take the blue tram in Inner City. It's faster but it only runs until eight. If you can't find a chip then move on."

Deryn nodded.

"And please be careful."

"I will," she promised.

Xander sighed before giving her one final kiss and letting her go. He didn't look at her again until the door was open, trying hard not to notice her terrified eyes as he walked away.

Deryn waited eight minutes before her impatience got the best of her. She took a deep breath as she stood in front of the door, her nerves kicking in. She felt distant, separated from her body as she realized this would be her first time leaving the apartment alone in months. Not to mention the fact that she'd been caught within minutes of leaving the last time. But, luckily, Xander had come for her. He had helped her time and time again and never asked for anything in return.

It was thinking of him that gave Deryn the courage she needed to step forward and forget about her nerves. Because he didn't deserve to be blackmailed like this. This was her chance to pay him back for everything he'd done for her.

Without another thought Deryn opened the door, descended the stairs, and left the building.

She could do this.

That's what she kept telling herself as she walked to the tram stop. Then continued to tell herself as she stepped onto the tram, buying a chocolate bar to remember that this was all for Xander. She munched on it until she reached her stop.

She could do this.

Deryn took a deep breath and stepped outside. She walked up to the gate leading to Inner City, her wristband immediately scanned by a S.U.R.G.E. that dinged and lit up green, letting her pass.

She had created a working wristband out of nothing. She could do this.

Then there was a guard.

"Where are you going today?" he asked.

"A friend's house," she answered, sounding as casual as she could.

"Their name?"

"Luka Voclain."

The guard looked up at her and she smiled. They had decided on the name beforehand. Luka often had women over so it wouldn't seem unusual.

"He won't be home," said the guard. "There's a meeting."

"Yes, I know. He asked me to go there before it's out. So I don't run into his dad." She leaned in and said under his breath, "You know how awkward it is when you still live with a parent. I have access if you want to see." She held out her wristband.

"No, that's alright. Go on through."

Deryn did just that, smiling at the guard as she went.

As a citizen she was required to take a different door than the one Xander would take as a Guardian. A metal slate sucked into the ground and she stepped through, stopping as she hit another slate, waiting for the one behind her to rise again. When she was sealed between the two of them she was spritzed with something. It supposedly disinfected her of toxins, a quick quarantine, but she doubted it was anything real. Just a lie created to keep the fanatics happy.

Once that was finished, the slate in front of Deryn lowered and she walked through the gate. She took a deep breath as she entered Inner City, a place she never thought she'd go willingly again. Yet here she was. It was no surprise that everyone on their list lived here, the majority still in their family homes. Only Guardians who needed to prove themselves lived in

Middle City. Like Xander five years ago. Or Lona today.

Shaking off any nerves she had, Deryn walked in the direction of Luka's house.

She could do this.

When she arrived she scanned her wristband at the front entrance. She had not been lying to the guard when she said she had access. The door clicked and she opened it, stepping into the Voclains house for the first time since being a slave there.

Upon entering, Deryn walked straight to Barath's bedroom, knowing very well where he hid that chip. An unfortunate result from being his slave so many times. She didn't even bother to keep an eye out for his wave as she walked, since Luka had intentionally sent him on errands that would take hours, if not all night. She was happy the simplest house was first. It would help ease her into this.

She entered Barath's bedroom, dropped down beside his bed and lifted the floorboards about a foot inward, revealing a small box hidden beneath them. She grabbed it and located the chip inside, doing her best to ignore the other sketchy items he had in there. Barath had a strange fetish and collected certain samples from his sex slaves. Deryn saw the phial with her name on it now. She was tempted to take it, but knew that would look suspicious. She sighed before closing the box and putting everything back in its place.

On her way out Deryn passed the basement, stopping for a moment to listen to a girl crying down there. While she desperately wanted to help her she knew she couldn't. As horrible as it was, in Utopia's current state the girl was much safer here than she was out there. No one survived long after they escaped. Unless they had a Guardian like Xander helping them.

Clenching her fists, Deryn gulped back tears and somehow managed to walk away. But it wasn't easy, and she would, undoubtedly, never forget that moment for the rest of her life.

Knowing that she couldn't risk being seen going out the front door so soon after entering, Deryn headed to Luka's bedroom, went inside and shut the door. He'd brought her

Element over for her earlier that day, by the chance that she might need it sometime that night, and she found it now under his mattress. She strapped it to her hip, hidden beneath her coat, and climbed out the window, creeping through the backyard and using the back gate to enter a narrow alley behind the Voclains house.

One down.

Taking another deep breath, Deryn walked back out to the street. She located the tram stop and waited a good four minutes before a blue tram arrived. She rode it for two stops, got off and walked a block to the next house. This one belonging the Veli Tash.

Veli's house would be a bit trickier to enter. His wave was very loyal. While she wasn't a sex slave, that didn't stop him from having his way with her frequently, and she was more than willing. It happened sometimes, as twisted as it was.

He also had a girlfriend who practically lived with him, though he'd never call her that. In fact, Deryn could see her through the front window now. She was in the living room instructing the wave to do something. The wave nodded and wandered through a doorway Deryn knew led to the kitchen. And then his girlfriend was leaving.

Deryn leaned against the wall she was near and pretended to fiddle with her wristband as the woman walked out of the house, not locking or setting the alarm on the door before hurrying down the street. As soon as she was gone Deryn looked back at the house. This was her chance.

Without taking a moment to talk herself out of it, Deryn walked to the front door. She opened it quietly and slipped inside, listening to make sure the wave was still in the kitchen. She was.

Deryn tiptoed to the west end of the house. While Veli had never owned her, she'd been brought here often enough by Soren to know where he might hide things. There was one room in particular that she was never allowed to enter with them. She headed there now.

When Deryn got to the closed door, she found it was

unlocked. She very quietly entered the room and shut the door behind her.

Looking around, she saw that it was an office. No surprise there. Now, if she were Veli where would she hide things?

Noticing his chair was slightly turned towards a bookshelf, she headed there, scanning the books until she found one sticking out just a little bit more than the others. Like someone had rushed to stick it back in. She pulled the book out and opened it. A small chip fell to the floor.

Jackpot.

It appeared that her friend Veli had been in a hurry. That was a mistake he wouldn't make twice.

She picked up the chip and put it in her pocket with the four others they'd already acquired. Five down, six to go.

After putting the book back, Deryn left the office. She could still hear the wave in the kitchen so she went right out the front door, doing her best to look like she belonged to any passersby.

As she walked down the block, she passed Veli's girlfriend walking back to his house with a grocery bag in hand.

Gordon Mackey's house was only two blocks away, so she didn't bother with a tram. While Gordon didn't have a wave he did have a wife, but she wasn't exactly faithful. When Deryn was his slave once, almost every day while Gordon was at work she could hear his wife and her lover through the wall of the closet he kept her locked in. They weren't quiet.

While Deryn didn't condone cheating, she hardly felt sorry for him. Not only did he, on occasion, own sex slaves but his current wife was also a trophy. Much younger and prettier than his first wife, and the product of a very public affair that left his son Wyatt so bitter that he changed his surname to his mother's maiden name, Firman. Perhaps the estrangement - even though Wyatt still lived in the house with him, which was big enough that they never saw each other - was why Gordon was so quick to offer his son as a sacrifice for Xander's cooperation. Or he was just a heartless bastard.

Looking around and seeing that the street was deserted, she walked up to the front door. It was locked, of course, but there was a key hidden that Xander had told her about. Because Gordon Mackey was an idiot.

She located it under a not-so-cleverly placed rock and let herself in. Xander also knew the code to turn off the alarm, since he was fairly good friends with Wyatt. She entered it now. Even all the way in the front hallway she could hear Gordon's wife and her lover going at it. She had to admit, they certainly had stamina. Never a dull moment when her husband was out.

There was a table right near the front door with two small drawers. She opened one, not especially surprised to find the chip casually tossed in there on Gordon's way out. At this rate she would be finished even earlier than expected.

Deryn left the house and located the closest tram stop. The first one that came by was red. She let it pass. It was a good seven minutes before a blue one arrived. That would cost her some time. But Xander swore by the Inner City blue trams, claiming they moved faster and made less stops. She didn't really notice a difference but she trusted he was right.

After five stops she got off. Sewick Blum was next on her list. He wasn't a Guardian, just a dubious man the president kept around. If someone needed something sketchy done then he was the one they came to. Which was exactly why Xander and Luka were positive he had a chip.

Of course, not being a Guardian meant that he wouldn't be at Lona's coronation, and if he wasn't home there was a good chance the chip was with him. Still, it was worth a shot and Deryn was going to take it, despite Xander's request that she just skip him. In fact, he thought she was going to. It was Luka who gave her directions to his house, as well as a bar only blocks away that he often frequented.

She went there first, ready to go inside and ask if she could use the bathroom just to get a look around. But she didn't have to, because Sewick was standing outside. Granted, she had only ever seen him a handful of times throughout her years as a slave, but there was no mistaking him. He didn't look like he belonged in Inner City - and that was probably because he didn't – with his shifty eyes, five o'clock shadow, dirty hands and worn-down clothes. He always wore pants with plaid patches sewn on the knees. This was something she vividly remembered about him.

Currently, he was smoking a pipe outside the bar, probably with tobacco despite it being prohibited. Being the president's right-hand conman put him above the law and he knew it. The pretty young girl hanging on his arm probably knew it, too.

Knowing where he was, Deryn continued on. She made sure not to catch Sewick's eye as he stared at her, trying to get a better look at the hooded woman across the street.

Since he'd noticed her, she turned in the opposite direction of his house, planning to circle back around. When she got there, she wasn't exactly sure how to enter. She didn't know this house or this man. Not like the others. It was undoubtedly locked. And alarmed. While security wasn't quite as intense in Inner City because it didn't need to be, Sewick didn't get to his position by being an idiot.

His house was easy to spot. It was as out of place as he was, dirty and simplistic. Nothing lavish like the mansions around it. But there was a side gate she wanted to investigate.

Looking around, Deryn made sure the street was deserted. It was funny how the main streets in Inner City could get so crowded but the residential streets were so quiet.

Once she confirmed everything was clear, she went to the side gate. Unfortunately, it was very much locked and the house didn't have any visible windows.

Well, shit.

As she stood on the side of the house at a loss, she suddenly heard two people chatting and laughing nearby. She pressed against the wall, not especially shocked that her luck had brought Sewick and his lady friend home early.

The side of the house was dark and they didn't see her, at least. He scanned his wristband and used a physical key to enter. The door slammed shut behind them.

After waiting a few seconds, Deryn took a chance and tried the knob. Unlocked. She opened the door slowly, peeking inside through a small crack. The room directly in front of her was empty, laughter coming from farther back in the small house. This was risky, but Deryn knew she needed to take this chance, so she walked in.

His home was absolutely disgusting. Not only did he never clean, actually living in his own filth, but the place wreaked of something putrid. She had to breathe through her mouth just to stomach the place.

Deryn decided right then that she wasn't going to be here long. Just for a quick search through the front room. She saw a desk and immediately went over, holding in a groan as she stepped over stacks of garbage, dirty clothes and rotting food, and quietly searched the drawers.

Nothing. Though she did find a wanted poster for her old friend Nita, the photo taken from a security camera as she ran out of some building. She sighed and put it back.

Then she searched all flat surfaces. There really weren't a lot of options.

The moans had started back in the bedroom. She was getting a lot of that tonight.

Deryn stood there feeling frustrated. She was here, in his house risking her life. There had to be –

And then she spotted it. Halfway down the hallway the moans were coming from. The coat he'd been wearing when she saw him outside the bar. She fell to her knees, crawling forward and skeptically looking down the hallway. The door was open and she could see them on the bed, but their backs were to her. She reached out and quickly snatched it, crawling back out of view and into the living room.

Deryn dug through the pockets, not finding anything. But then she remembered that Xander never put anything of importance in his outside pockets, so she searched the inside. Sure enough, there was a pocket with something small and square inside. She pulled it out, releasing a breath of relief when she saw the chip.

After pocketing it, Deryn tossed the coat aside. She was just about to stand when she saw something under the couch. She moved to get a better look. Then crawled forward, peeking underneath and dragging out a box. Her eyes widened.

It was Elements! Lots of them. A few shallow boxes worth, at least, not to mention several Outsider guns and knives. On instinct, she grabbed two of the nicer ones and stuffed them in her bag. She didn't know what she was going to do with them, since it was too risky to go back through the gate with that many Elements in her possession, but this might be their only opportunity to get them.

As she was shoving the box back under the couch, she noticed a piece of paper squished farther back. She grabbed and un-crumpled it, knitting her brow when she saw it was another wanted poster of Nita. Granted, this one was older with a photo clearly taken from her old home on the outside, but it was still her.

While she found it strange that Nita's were the only wanted posters he had around, she didn't exactly have time to investigate. Putting the poster back where she found it, Deryn stood and quietly rushed out of the house, not stopping until she was several blocks away.

When she finally did stop, her heart was racing. That was the worst of it and it was over. But there was no time for pause. There were still four more chips to find.

Now, more than ever, she believed she could do this.

Finding the tram stop, she only had to wait two minutes before a blue tram arrived. Her next house belonged to Stuart Scout. This one would be easy since Xander had gotten the code to his front door from Finley - Stuart hated physical keys and scanning a wristband wasn't necessary - and, having been his slave, Deryn knew exactly where he'd hide a chip. Stuart wasn't wealthy enough to own a wave and his wife had died a couple of years earlier - suicide, if she remembered correctly - so she went straight to his bedroom. She wasn't surprised when she found the chip right where she thought it would be, locked in his desk with a key he kept under his pillow. Only three left.

Xander had already lost the bet. She had definitely found Barath, Gordon and Stuart's chips within five minutes. Veli and Sewick's were the only ones that had taken some time.

Deryn smiled smugly before heading out the door and walking several blocks to Eamon Graham's house. He had an unlocked window and no wave. She entered quickly, taking a chance by checking the drawers by the front door. The chip was there. Another idiot.

Maybe she would take her time in the last few places so she wouldn't be lying when she told Xander she was the victor with four chips in less than five minutes.

As tempting as that was, she knew she was running short on time, and there were still two chips and five Guardians left.

She tried Mathis Fender's house next and gave it ten minutes. Nothing. He was a long shot anyway.

Wenton Pace's house was after that. He actually owned two houses, the one she was presently inside of and another in Middle City where he had kept his slaves for the past three years after promising his wife he wouldn't own them anymore.

The chip wouldn't be in Middle City though. All he had there was a mattress on the floor, enough food to keep his current slave alive, dirty water and various torture mechanisms. He was a sick bastard, and she considered herself blessed that he had only owned her twice, once in each house.

She searched his house for a good fifteen minutes. Nothing. That actually shocked her. But there were only so many places he could have put the chip, and since it wasn't in any of them she was positive he didn't have one.

That was two dead ends in a row and Deryn was getting nervous. There were still two chips and three Guardians left.

The next house on her list was Elvira Tash's. The one she shared with her husband Soren and the house where Deryn had left him for dead.

She gulped as she stepped off of her latest blue tram, willingly walking to the place where she'd tried to kill a man not even four months earlier.

When Deryn arrived outside of the house she just stood there, staring up at it and not knowing how to feel.

She sighed and checked the time on her wristband.

8:33 p.m.

Elvira and Soren's wave Fontaine went to the store every evening between eight and nine o'clock, and Soren's personal slave would either be with him or locked in his bedroom. The bedroom he didn't share with his wife. Ever.

It was easy to enter their house since a window leading to the living room was always open a crack. That was how Soren liked it, wanting a small gust of cool air.

Deryn went around the side of the house, opened the window a little wider and crept on through. Once inside, she was immediately forced to stare at the spot where she had stabbed Soren in cold blood, a memory that would forever haunt her.

Shaking off her fears, she wandered towards Elvira's side of the house. She'd often wondered if Elvira and Soren had ever shared a bed.

Deryn explored this side of the house thoroughly. She hated being there, but refused to leave until she'd searched every corner. Still, she came out empty-handed. Elvira didn't have a chip and Deryn wasn't surprised. But she'd also dreaded it, because there were still two chips left and only two names on her list.

Atticus had setup his son.

Deryn scowled. First Barath and now Atticus. Guardians had no respect for family, especially their children, the people they should've loved most in this world.

Returning to the living room, Deryn took a moment to stare at the spot where she had last stood as a slave. Nothing here had changed but her life was very different. She had someone who cared for her now. Truly cared for her. Not in whatever sick, twisted way Soren did.

She would do anything for Xander, including protect him from his father. Atticus wouldn't win this. She wouldn't let him.

With a new burst of confidence Deryn left that house, ready to walk the few blocks to Arron Von's, then take the tram to Atticus Ruby's.

Atticus lived in the back of Inner City, at just about the farthest point you could get from the gate to Middle City. That was how the Rubys had always liked it. Xander's great-grandfather fought to keep a gate from being built on this side of the city - to keep the toxic scoundrels out. She certainly had to appreciate the family history of the man she cared so deeply for.

When Deryn arrived at Arron Von's house she immediately walked around the back. Xander had previously asked Lona if she could stop by her father's before her coronation and leave a window open. She'd agreed without question. Deryn wasn't sure how she felt about the girl's blind loyalty to him, but she tried hard to just focus on how the task had been made significantly easier for her.

She found the window that was open a crack, opened it wider, and stepped through. She was in a bedroom, but the lack of personality in it led her to believe that this was just a guestroom.

Arron Von had never owned a slave, so she wasn't exactly sure where to go. He did have a wave but, by the clanks and dings Deryn could hear through the door, it was clear the wave was busy in the kitchen.

Deryn slowly opened the door, peeking out before walking into the hallway. There was a dining room in front of her, garnished with an elaborate meal. Most likely a congratulatory dinner for Lona after her unwanted coronation.

A woman walked into view. Her head was shaved, a signifier that she was a wave, and she hummed as she put down a tray of something. Deryn pressed herself against the wall, only then noticing a staircase opposite her. Once the woman was out of view again, she darted for it and hurried upstairs.

Deryn wandered through the dark, searching doors until she found the master bedroom, which doubled as an office. She went in and shut the door behind her.

The first thing she noticed upon entering the room was a telescope next to the window, which was odd since nights in Utopia's bubble were rarely clear enough to see any artificial stars.

Curiosity led Deryn over to that telescope, making sure not

to touch it as she stared through the lens, straight into the president's grand hall. She knitted her brow, wondering why Arron would be spying on his president, but more curious about the event currently on display in front of her. It was Lona's coronation. All of the Guardians stood in a circle. Lona stood in the center of them with President Saevus, a woman in a lab coat and a strange metal contraption. Her left arm was shaking as she held it out to the woman, glancing nervously at a Guardian who Deryn immediately recognized as Xander. Even with their hoods up there was no mistaking his stance.

He nodded at her and she looked back at her president, staring into his eyes as the woman grabbed her arm, fitting a wristband around it before sticking it in the nearby machine. Deryn turned a knob and zoomed the telescope as the band must have pressed into Lona's skin inside of that machine.

She wasn't sure how it worked. What happened to Lona's wrist's bones? Did they squeeze inward? Even watching, she still couldn't figure it out. But there was blood seeping out the sides of the machine. The president used a handkerchief to wipe it clean.

Lona was biting her lip, trying hard not to cry out in pain.

Forcing herself to look away, Deryn began searching the room for the chip. She hadn't been in there long when she heard footsteps coming up the staircase. In an instant, she was across the room and under the bed, just making it out of sight as the door to the bedroom opened.

The wave walked in, heading straight for the telescope and looking through the eyepiece. Deryn could just make out her feet from the small crack between the floor and the bed skirt.

She heard a sigh, then watched the feet as they headed for a desk. The familiar dings of a code being entered on something locked filled Deryn's ears. Shortly after some rustling, the feet moved again. And then something dropped. A chip. Right beside the bed.

"Lona said someone might be coming but she didn't know why," said the woman quietly. "I know this is why you're here."

All I ask for is one thing in return." She paused and gulped. "Get her out."

The wave headed for the door.

"And work on your stealth. Second story floors are connected to first story ceilings." And with that small piece of advice, she left.

Deryn let out a breath of relief and climbed out from under the bed. She grabbed the chip, put it in her pocket with the others and headed down the stairs, doing her best to be stealthy about it.

The wave was back in the dining room, folding napkins into flowers. She smiled and said, "Much better," without looking up.

"Thank you," whispered Deryn before heading for the room she had entered through.

She climbed back out the window, checking her watch and realizing she didn't have much longer to get to Atticus's house.

Just one last tram ride before her journey back to Luka's and then home. Knowing there was only one house left, Deryn's fast beating heart finally slowed and she was able to breathe again. Though she wouldn't feel completely safe until she was back home.

As she walked the few blocks to Atticus's house she could feel her already fluttering stomach rise into her chest. While she had thought Soren's house would be the one that haunted her the most, she now realized that she had been wrong. It was Atticus's house. The place they had brought her shortly after her capture five years earlier. Shortly after he had ...

She gulped, finding herself unable to even think the word of what had happened to her before she was locked in Atticus's basement, given to him as a reminder even though he didn't want her.

Trying to shake the memories, Deryn focused on how there was one chip and one name left. She wanted to believe that maybe she'd missed something, but she knew she hadn't. While she hated Atticus, she knew Xander was torn over his feelings for him. He wanted to hate him. Because of her. But Atticus was still his father, his flesh and blood, and while he may have hated Outsiders, Deryn never doubted that he loved his son. Until now.

When she arrived at the house, she sighed deeply and entered the code that would allow her to enter. Xander had sent his father's wave out on an errand that evening, so she didn't have to worry about running into him.

According to Xander, there was only one place his father would keep something so valuable, and that was in a small chest in his bedroom.

Deryn searched the room for the chest. She knew she didn't have long until the coronation was over, and Xander needed those chips before the meeting began.

She tore that room apart, searching in drawers, in the closet, under his bed. She checked floorboards to see if they lifted, took frames off of walls, even went through books, but the chest wasn't anywhere.

Then she saw it.

On the windowsill, just visible through the sheer curtains. She ran and opened it, which wasn't even locked, tearing through its contents. Nothing. It was clear.

"Shit."

Had she missed something somewhere?

No. Deryn had searched those houses thoroughly. Xander and Luka must have been wrong. There had to be someone else who could have -

The front door clicked open in the distance. Deryn put the chest back and hurried underneath the bed. Atticus charged into the room a moment later.

He went straight for the windowsill and began searching the chest frantically, eventually coming out with a simple necklace with a flower pendant. He let out a breath of relief and slipped it into his pocket.

Then Atticus was walking over to the nightstand, the breeze from his hasty movements making the bed skirt flutter. She grasped it and held it in place.

Atticus was standing right near the bed, so close that Deryn could smell him. It was still the same. A very crisp smell, like leather with a small hint of lavender. He ruined lavender.

Pulling a bottle of brandy out of the nightstand, Atticus poured himself a glass and drank it down. He sighed deeply before pouring another and drinking it even faster than the first. It was evident where Xander got his drinking problem from.

There was a knock on the door, the *bedroom* door, and Atticus's head turned. He put his brandy and glass away before walking towards it, pausing as he passed the bed, obviously feeling that something was amiss. He stood very still for a long moment. Deryn was sure he could hear her heart beating, thumping so hard it was likely to burst right out of her chest.

Then there was another knock, making Atticus move again. He opened the door.

"Arron. How did you get in here?"

"The door was unlocked," answered Arron with an obvious lie. The front door locked automatically. "I was hoping we could have a moment to talk before the meeting. About Lona and Xander's future together."

"At this point in time I would say they have no future together," said Atticus, refusing to step out of the way even though Arron obviously wanted to enter his bedroom. "Xander has made it very clear that he's not interested."

"But, surely, if you tell him he has no choice -"

"I stopped micromanaging my son's life years ago. I suggest you do the same with Lona."

"I don't understand," said Arron. "You were for this only a few short weeks ago. What's changed?"

"Nothing's changed," answered Atticus. "I wouldn't mind at all if Xander decided to get married, but he's still young. I see no reason to push this."

"But -"

"If you have any further issues with this then I suggest you take them up with Xander. This is his decision and I won't push him into something he seems so dead-set against."

And, with that, Atticus nudged Arron backwards and pulled

the door closed behind him.

Deryn let out a breath of relief, listening until the front door opened and closed before climbing out from under the bed. She put her ear to the front door when she reached it, making sure they were gone before slipping out. Now it was time to meet Xander.

It was only two blocks from Atticus's house to the back of the president's lavish mansion, which might as well have been a castle, impenetrable and towering over everything around it.

Deryn was walking fast but slowed her steps when she saw two figures ahead of her. She was catching up to Atticus and Arron, the former always two steps ahead of his unwanted companion. They turned the last corner. She hurried again until she was right at the edge of it.

"Xander, what are you doing out here?" asked Atticus.

"Just getting some air," answered the voice that made her heart flutter. She'd made it to him. Breathing became a little easier.

Silence.

"Leave me," ordered Xander.

Footsteps started again. Then a gate opened.

After about thirty seconds of waiting, Deryn poked her head around the corner. Xander was leaning nervously against a wall. He glanced up and stared at the corner as she stepped into view.

He was beside her in a flash, pulling her into his arms and kissing her deeply.

"Thank god," he breathed into her mouth before kissing her again.

"Sorry," said Deryn. "I ran into a bit of an issue."

"What's that?" he asked, stepping back just enough to look at her, but still keeping a firm grip on her waist.

Deryn reached into her pocket and pulled out the chips. "I only found seven. There's still one out there."

Xander knitted his brow. "And you were able to check every house?"

"Yes."

"Thoroughly?"

"Yes, Xander," she said, rolling her eyes. "It wasn't there. It wasn't anywhere. There has to be someone we missed."

Xander took a deep breath and pressed his forehead against hers. "No matter. We'll figure it out later." He kissed her again. "Who had the other four?"

"Blum, Scout, Graham and Von," she recited.

He raised an eyebrow. "Blum? I thought you were skipping - "

"Not the time, Xander."

He scowled but didn't push the issue further. "My father didn't have one?" he asked, the relief quite evident in his voice.

"No," said Deryn, thinking it best not to mention how Atticus had almost caught her just now. It would only make him worry over nothing. "You need to get back for the meeting." She slipped the chips into his pocket and kissed him softly. "Expose them as the lying bastards they are. And don't forget to emphasize how they lied to the woman working on the chips to obtain them. That ought to deserve a painful punishment."

Xander smirked. They kissed once more before he forced himself to let her go, heading inside while she hurried to the closest tram stop.

Being on the complete opposite side of the city than Luka's house, it took her nearly an hour on the tram before she reached it.

She went around back and through his open window, dropping off her Element, as well as the two she had confiscated from Sewick Blum. Then she was off, hurrying out of his father's house before his wave could return.

It was only a few blocks to the gate. The same guard checked her information again. When he questioned why she was leaving before Luka was out of his meeting, she gave some sob story about a call she received regarding her dying grandmother, whose time was up. A few fake tears was all it took for him to send her on her way, even letting her go through the Guardian door so there was no quarantine stop in the middle.

After that, it was only one last tram ride and a short walk until she was back at their apartment, falling face first onto the couch as she finally breathed again.

She had done it.

How the hell did Xander do this deception thing every day?

CHAPTER SEVEN

During the Guardians' meeting, Xander's mind kept drifting as he tried to think of who else could have a chip. Looking around the table, it was safe to say that it wasn't anyone here. There had to be someone else. Maybe not even a guard, just someone close to Veli. Possibly his anonymous source for Resistance information. He had to admit, he was more than a little curious as to who it was.

Xander had one hand in his pocket, fiddling with the chips as he waited for his opportunity to bring them up.

"We've covered everything that is on the agenda for tonight," said Elvira looking up from her paper and gazing dotingly at her father.

"Is there anything else that needs discussion before we part?" asked President Saevus, glancing around the table.

And here it was.

Xander stood and said, "Yes, Mr. President. There's something I've wanted to bring to your attention for quite some time now, but first I needed proof."

Luka smirked at him from across the table. He smirked back as he took the chips out of his pocket and dumped them directly in front of President Saevus. He heard several gasps and turned to see every Guardian involved growing ashen. None more than Veli.

"What are these?" asked the president, picking up the closest chip.

"Those are what Veli has been using to blackmail me into doing his bidding. They're mind control chips. He threatened to install them in the wristbands of everyone important to me and then potentially have them commit suicide. The first on his hit list was my father."

Atticus stiffened as he moved his cold eyes to Veli.

"The second was Luka, whose own father offered to do the installation."

Xander couldn't help but chuckle as Barath scooted his chair away from his son.

"The same with Wyatt. I will gladly give you every name involved."

Saevus shuffled through the chips. "So ten of you -"

"Eleven, actually," corrected Xander. "I wasn't able to find the last one. It doesn't belong to anyone in this room, I assure you. Who else do you have working for you, Veli belly?" he asked, gazing down the table at him.

Veli's nostrils flared as he slowly shook his head. "None of your fucking business, you prick."

"Language, Veli," said Saevus in an even tone.

"I also feel the need to point out that the woman in charge of mind control research was told by Veli that her prototypes would be presented to you, Mr. President. So Veli obtained the chips by giving false information."

"Yes, I figured as much," said Saevus. "Give me the names."

"Veli and Soren, of course," said Xander, smiling at the Tash brothers. Soren slyly smiled back. "And I took Aila and Orson's off their bodies in Willow. Barath and Gordon you already know. Other than that there was Sewick Blum, which I'm very curious about, Stuart Scout, Eamon Graham and Arron Von."

Lona's eyes widened. "Father?"

"For obvious reasons, Mr. President," said Xander, "I'm afraid that any union between Lona and me isn't going to work."

Lona frowned but nodded. "Understandable."

"Such a pity," said Saevus. "So let me try and understand this. I've always considered our small but elite society to have the makings of a family. It pains me to know that many of you would be so willing to kill your brothers, your children, and all for the sole purpose of usurping Xander. Possibly even getting him executed."

No one objected.

"Mr. President, I would like to request a seat change," said Luka, raising his hand. "I have little interest in remaining next to my potential murderer."

Barath went red. "It was all a bluff, Luka -"

"Of course," interrupted Saevus. "From now on you may take the seat beside Xander."

Same spot, different side. He would just have to switch with Eamon.

"Veli, I would like you to stay behind, but everyone else is dismissed. Xander, perhaps you might come in early tomorrow and we can discuss the proper punishment for these chip holders."

Xander grinned. "Absolutely."

Lona was the first one out of her chair and darting for the door. Her father was quick to run after her. Atticus, on the other hand, stood up very slowly, avoiding everyone's eyes until the room was practically empty. When Xander left, he followed him.

"Xander, why didn't you tell me about the seriousness of their threats?" he asked as his son headed for the exit.

"Because it was not your burden to carry, Father. I told you it was nothing I couldn't handle and I took care of it, just like I said I would."

Xander stopped in front of the door with Atticus by his side. Luka walked up behind them.

"But you had no problem burdening Luka?" asked Atticus.

"That's right. When I found out his father was trying to expose him as the spy he isn't and had his mind swept, it only seemed fair to let Luka know that it wasn't the man's only plan to kill off his son."

Atticus stared openmouthed at Luka.

"It seems you've missed a lot while locked up in your house," said Xander.

Just then, a loud, earth-shattering scream echoed from the

conference room.

"My president! Please forgive - AHH!"

Xander smiled triumphantly. "And that is my cue to leave. Have a good rest of your evening, Father."

He headed out the door and walked briskly towards the gate, ready to get home to Deryn and celebrate their successful mission.

CHAPTER EIGHT

Back at the apartment, Deryn was going through Xander's drawers. For a while now she would often catch herself packing some of his things in the rucksack she was preparing for when she ran, just in case, but she always lost her nerve and put everything back where it belonged. She didn't want him to notice if things went missing, knowing very well that he would throw a fit. But she didn't want to leave him behind when she ran either. Deryn wanted to ask him to come with her, but she'd never mustered up the courage.

She sighed heavily and was just about to return her favorite gray sweater of his to its drawer when she accidentally knocked Xander's rucksack with her elbow. It landed upside-down on the floor, its contents falling everywhere.

Deryn dropped to her knees and began picking everything up. Her fingers froze when she came across a small notebook. Unable to stop herself, she picked it up and opened to the first page. It was a list of names. They were written on several pages and, after that, nothing. The last name written was Aila Parrish. Before that was Anna Bellamy, preceded by Dougal Fender.

A breath got caught in the back of Deryn's throat. It was the names of his victims.

She slammed the book shut before she could glimpse any names that she might recognize.

Just as Deryn was about to put the notebook back in Xander's bag, she caught sight of something else. A small, black bottle that had rolled underneath the dresser. She picked it up and read the label.

LAST RESORT.

Deryn began to shake, her body burning as she read the label over and over again.

She knew the name. Everyone did.

A suicide pill.

"Oi! Deryn! You here?"

The sound of Bronson's voice calling her from the living room barely registered. And then the front door opened again.

"Bronson, what are you doing here?" asked Xander.

Looking towards the door, Deryn slowly began to rise, her grip on the bottle only tightening as she stepped towards it.

"Just looking for Deryn."

There were suddenly more footsteps, making Deryn freeze.

"The fuck you follow me here for, Luka?"

She began to walk again.

"I'm not going home! Not after my father's whole 'it was all a bluff' bullshit."

Deryn opened the bedroom door, stepping out. Everyone turned to look at her. Her eyes immediately locked with Xander's.

"You alright?" he asked, noticing how pale she looked.

She shook her head.

"What's wrong?"

He stepped forward but Deryn stepped back. Then she slowly raised her hand, exposing the black bottle to him.

"What's this?"

Xander stopped dead as he caught sight of what she was holding. He gulped. "Where did you get that?"

Deryn said nothing.

"Have you been going through my things?"

"Answer the question."

"You answer the fucking question!"

Bronson and Luka slowly stepped backwards towards the door.

Deryn breathed in deeply through her nostrils, her eyes flaring even though tears made them hazy. "What the *fuck* is this?" she said slowly and deeply. "Why do you have a *fucking* suicide pill in your bag?"

"Right, so, Xan, I'm going to be heading to the Pit," said Luka. "Feel free to join me if you can." He couldn't get out that door fast enough.

"And I'm going ... just not here," said Bronson, turning on his foot and following Luka out. Neither of them wanted to be present for the obvious bomb that was about to explode.

"That is none of your fucking business," said Xander as soon as they were gone.

"It is so my *fucking* business! Now, why do you have this?" she asked again, her voice growing shrill with every strained word that fell from her mouth.

"Don't worry about -"

"Why?"

"Give it here, Deryn." He held out his hand and stepped forward, but she hurried back into the bedroom.

"Why?" she cried.

"You have no right to -"

"WHY?"

"It's for the day you fucking leave me, *alright*?" shouted Xander, his face going red, his eyes wet and angry.

Deryn's jaw dropped. She sobbed loudly and darted for the bathroom.

Xander followed her. "What are you doing?"

Deryn opened the bottle, went over to the toilet and held it above the water.

"What the fuck are you doing?" shouted Xander, running over and trying to pry the bottle from her hands. "Let go!"

Deryn swung her free arm and slapped him hard across the face. When he flinched, she yanked the bottle from his hands and dropped the pill in the toilet. She flushed it and tossed the empty bottle hard against the wall, shattering it.

"No!" shouted Xander as he watched his salvation whirl down the toilet. "What have you done?"

"How dare you, Xander!" shouted Deryn. "How dare you *ever* purchase that pill!"

"Why do you care?" he spat, tears spilling from his eyes.

"You're leaving! You're fucking leaving, Deryn, and you're never going to see me again! It shouldn't matter what I do!"

"It matters!" she cried. "How could you do this? How could you leave me after everything?" *Hiccup!* "After everything we've been through, you were just going to give up? Like none of this ever happened?"

"No, you don't understand!" shouted Xander, rubbing his eyes. "This was for you! I was doing this for *you*!"

She whimpered. "What?"

"I wasn't just going to fucking off myself, Deryn! I was going to off *them*! All of them!"

"Them ... them who?"

"Every Guardian who ever touched you! I was going to kill them, and then I was going to take that damn pill before the president had the chance to capture me! To torture me to death, or worse!"

"No." Deryn shook her head frantically. "No, that's not what I want. I don't care about vengeance, Xander. Not if it means I lose you."

"You're already going to lose me," said Xander coldly.

"No." Deryn ran forward and threw her arms around his waist. "No, no, no! I ... I can't lose you, Xander. I *need* you. I do. If you die I want to die with you!"

"Deryn, don't you dare talk like that."

"Xander, please."

"You're spouting all this shit now, but what about when you're back with Triggs, huh? Will you still be thinking of me when you're fucking him?"

Deryn pulled away and looked sadly at him. "What?"

"That's the plan, isn't it?" said Xander, his face tense. "Leave here and go back to him. Because you love him, right?"

She didn't answer.

"I've never once heard you say that things have changed," he said with disdain.

"They ... they have."

"Really?"

"I don't ... I mean, I'm not ... Dax and I ... I *do* love him but -

"

"But what?"

Deryn's heart ached as she gazed into his golden-brown eyes, unable to speak the words she so desperately wanted him to hear.

"Say it, Deryn."

Silence.

"Say it."

She whimpered.

"Say you're fucking mine!"

Before Deryn could respond, Xander's lips were on hers. He picked her up and slammed their bodies down to the floor, the same spot where they had shared their first kiss. He tore off her clothes ravenously while she did the same to him, and then he was thrusting into her on the cold, tile floor.

While Xander pounded her hard into the spot that meant so much to him, he couldn't stop himself from muttering possessive claims over her.

Deryn cried beneath him, hugging her arms around his neck and still struck mute. When it came to words, at least. Her moaning was loud and hoarse, Xander causing her to burn from the inside out.

It wasn't long before Xander was coming inside of her, his movements slowing as he realized that he hadn't even tried to make her come with him. For the first time while having sex with Deryn, he'd been selfish. Completely and inexcusably selfish.

Hearing the sound of her whimpers now that her moaning had stopped, the realization of what had just happened suddenly overcame him. Had she even wanted this just now, or had he just taken her?

Was he no better than the rest of them?

"Deryn ... what have I done?" He cried as he nuzzled into her hair. "I'm sorry! I'm sorry! I'm so -"

Suddenly, Xander felt Deryn's soft hands cupping his cheek. She pulled his head back so he was forced to stare into her swollen eyes.

"Xander, I ... I'm yours."

"I don't want to possess you -"

"It's not about possession," she said while stroking his damp cheek. "It's just how I feel. I'm yours and you're mine. Simple as that."

Gazing down at her, Xander cried harder as his heart suddenly felt light.

"I've known for a while now that I can never go back to Dax. Not like that."

"Why?" he asked.

"Because it's you I want, you fucking idiot!" Deryn attempted a smile.

Xander attempted one back and sniveled. "I love it when that foul language comes out of your mouth." He traced her lips with his thumb. "When they don't sound angry, at least."

Pressing their foreheads together, Xander took several moments to just lay there and breathe her in.

"Come with me, Xander," said Deryn suddenly.

"What?" he asked, pulling back so he could look at her once more.

"Come with me," she repeated.

"Deryn, you know I can't."

"Why not?" she asked. "It's too dangerous for you to stay here and I want you with me. Please come with me."

"It might be dangerous for me here, but it'll be even more dangerous for both of us if I go. The president will never stop looking for me. No Guardian who's ran has ever escaped him for more than a few weeks. He can track us with our wristbands and you know what happens when we take them off. We die."

"Yes, I know," she said, grabbing his hand and stroking his wristband. "I'll find a way to take it off safely."

Xander shook his head. "I can't go. I won't risk your safety like that."

She sighed and wrapped her arms tighter around him. "Then I'm staying here. Indefinitely."

Xander chuckled. "What? That's insane."

"Well, apparently *I'm* a bit insane, so I suppose it makes sense."

"You can't -"

"I'm not leaving without you."

Xander smiled. He leaned down and kissed her. "You're not staying."

"Watch me."

CHAPTER NINE

L uka sat at a table in the Pit, drinking straight from a bottle of whiskey the girl at his side had bought for him. She smiled and took a sip of her fruity cocktail, rubbing his thigh and scooting her chair closer to his.

"Evening, Luka."

He looked up to see a familiar man with chestnut brown hair and striking deep-blue eyes standing over their table.

"Fancy running into you here," said Bronson, his smile triggering something inside of Luka that he didn't quite understand.

Luka pushed the feeling back and rolled his eyes. "Th'fuck you doing here?"

Ignoring him, Bronson turned his smile to the girl. "Oh, hello. I remember you. From the tram the other day, right?"

"Oh. You're the one with the girlfriend," she said with disdain.

"Yes, right. Off and on, that is," said Bronson, taking a seat beside her. He grabbed the bottle out of Luka's hand and took a swig. "Weren't the two of you supposed to meet here yesterday? Don't tell me this is a budding romance?"

Luka scoffed.

The girl didn't seem to notice. "I was unable to make it yesterday, so I came tonight in hopes of running into him."

"And it looks like tonight is your lucky night!" said Bronson brightly.

"Guess so." She smiled at Luka.

"Whatever. I'm taking a piss."

Luka stood and wandered towards the bathroom. When he came back a few minutes later, Bronson had moved incredibly close to the girl, rubbing her arm while whispering teasingly in her ear. She quivered and leaned into his touch.

"Th'fuck you doing?" asked Luka, slumping into his chair. He took the bottle back and chugged.

"I was telling Tami here how terrible it was of my girlfriend to speak to her like that. We were just discussing a little revenge."

Bronson raised his eyebrows suggestively, causing Tami to let out a small moan and bite her bottom lip.

"What do you say, Tami?" he asked, leaning in and brushing his lips against her neck. "Should we go upstairs and put her in her place?"

Luka cocked an eyebrow. "'Scuse me?"

Bronson took some money from his pocket and handed it to her. "I can't be seen going upstairs with you. Go ahead of me, get a room and have the person at the desk send someone over to give me the room number. I'll follow shortly. If we're lucky, maybe Luka will join us." He winked at Luka.

Without hesitation, Tami stood and ran off to get a room.

When she was gone, Bronson laughed. "Oh, come on, Tami. Don't make it so easy."

"Seriously, th'fuck are you doing?" asked Luka, taking another swig from his bottle.

"Proving a point," said Bronson, tearing the bottle from Luka's hands and taking his own swig.

"And what's that?"

Bronson gulped down his whiskey and put the bottle back on the table. "I just stole your girl for the night. Do you even care?"

Luka shrugged. "A dime a dozen. I'll find another one."

"And that's my point," said Bronson, watching closely as Luka picked up the bottle again. "You don't care about your damn conquests because you're bored."

"What?" asked Luka, knitting his brow and taking another sip.

"You're bored, Luka. Sure, you can go out and fuck any girl you want, but I doubt it's given you any satisfaction in a long time. Am I right?"

Luka shrugged again. "I've yet to find one pussy more exciting than another. Sex is sex."

"So why fuck them at all, when you can get just as much fulfillment wanking your own cock? Why waste your time?"

"Does it matter?" asked Luka, putting down the bottle.

"It might."

Luka groaned. "Well, I'd rather have someone there than no one."

Bronson grinned. "Is that all?"

"What are you getting at, anyway?"

"Oh, nothing. Just that you and Ruby had the same problem."

"Huh?"

"He wasn't satisfied either, so he went and got himself a girlfriend. But, somehow, I just don't see you going down that road. What you need is something else. Something different."

"Something like *your* cock?"

Bronson's grin widened.

"Not interested."

"Your actions over the past couple of weeks say otherwise."

Luka huffed. "Look, I was drunk off my ass that night. I never would've let you do that if -"

"Drunk or not, I know you remember how hard you came that night."

Luka blushed and turned away from him.

"Admit it. I satisfied you more than any girl has in a long time."

"No."

"You know I did."

"No," he repeated. "I'm not gay, alright?"

"I know," said Bronson with a smile. "But that doesn't mean you're not curious about what I'm offering."

Luka blushed brighter.

"Excuse me."

Bronson and Luka looked up to see a young boy standing beside their table.

"Some girl asked me to give you this." He handed Bronson a folded piece of paper and smiled before disappearing.

Bronson opened it and held it out for Luka to see. "Room five." He tossed the paper on the table. "It's all yours. I highly doubt Tami will care which one of us goes upstairs. She seems pretty easy going." He stood up. "I'm going to the alley for a cigarette. You're free to join me if you'd like."

Bronson walked outside, leaving Luka alone to stare at that damn piece of paper. He picked it up and twisted it in his hands, glancing all around as women everywhere kept eyeing him, but only because he was still wearing his dark-blue Guardian trench coat.

Luka groaned. "Fuck this."

He slammed the paper down, taking one last swig from his bottle before following Bronson out. When he entered the alley, the other man already had a lit cigarette in his mouth. He smiled and offered one to Luka, who took it and leaned against the wall beside him.

"I meant it when I said I'm not fucking gay," said Luka, lighting his cigarette and taking a drag.

"I know you did."

"But you're right. I'm bored. And I have no interest in going down the same road as Xander."

Bronson smirked. "Sounds right."

"I'm not going to fuck you."

Now Bronson laughed. "Not yet." He tossed his cigarette down and put it out with his foot.

"No, not *ever*. I'm not - Th'fuck you doing?"

Bronson had dropped to his knees and was undoing Luka's pants. "Just a little gift from me to you. The last one you're getting without returning the favor."

"I'm not - Oh, shit!"

Luka bit his lip to hold in his moans as Bronson engulfed his cock in his mouth. In the fucking alley. Outside of the Pit. Where anyone walking by could see.

Yet the exposure of it all was part of what he found so gratifying. It wasn't long before he was coming, feeling even more satisfied than the last time Bronson had done this for him.

When Bronson was finished, he zipped Luka back up and got to his feet. He kissed Luka then, happy that he wasn't immediately pushed off.

Bronson pulled away and grinned. "If you want that again then you're going to have to work on your attitude."

Luka gulped.

Bronson chuckled. "Oh, come on. Pay for us to get a car and we'll go get your shit out of your psychotic father's house."

He walked towards the street. Luka hurried after him. "So you'll pay for some strange girl to get a room for the night, but you won't pay for a fucking car?"

"Yeah, I used Ruby's money for that. He really needs to find a better hiding place."

~

Xander leaned against the arm of the couch while Deryn sat between his legs, both of them naked with nothing but her favorite blanket covering them. She had his notebook in her lap and was currently writing names down.

"So we have me, Bronson, Quigley, Del and her whole group, and I think we should write Luka's name in here, too."

Without waiting for a response, Deryn started scrawling the name *Luka Voclain*.

After the two of them had calmed down a bit, and Xander had successfully made up for his selfishness earlier, she'd asked him about the list he kept with the names of his victims. He supposed it was always meant to be a sort of tribute to them, and he'd wanted to keep it all on record in case the war ever ended. So he could find and help their families. Anonymously, of course. He knew they would never accept help from a loved one's murderer.

Once she'd heard that, Deryn insisted on writing down the names of people Xander had helped over the years. It just didn't seem right that he only had the bad things he'd done on record.

"Who else?"

He thought. "There was this Resistance member we captured that I helped escape last year."

"Their name?"

"I'm not sure, but he trained with us."

"Was he our age?"

Xander shrugged. "Hell if I know."

Deryn rolled her eyes and said, "Typical," before writing down *Unidentified Resistance Member.*

The front door suddenly burst open and Luka marched in carrying a suitcase. "I'm moving in," he said, kicking off his shoes and heading for the guestroom without even so much as a glance at them.

Deryn's eyes widened as she pulled on all corners of the blanket to make sure she was fully covered.

"I brought your Element back, Leon!" he called from the other room. "And those extras. Where'd you get those, by the way?"

Xander looked at her and cocked an eyebrow.

"Sewick Blum," she answered. "I'll tell you later when I'm *not* naked."

Not even ten seconds later, Bronson walked into the apartment holding several pairs of shoes. He dropped them by Luka's other pair. "I've never seen a man with such an obsession with shoes before." He went over and took a seat on the couch. "So I know this is hardly ideal for the two of you but -"

"Fuck, Bronson!"

Bronson looked at Xander and raised his eyebrows. "Hmm?"

"Ever heard of fucking boundaries?" spat Xander, clutching the blanket tighter around them while Deryn blushed.

Bronson scanned them up and down. "Oh. Are you naked under there, Deryn?"

She furrowed her brow and nodded.

"Obviously!" shouted Xander.

"Sorry," said Bronson. He slowly turned so he was facing the other direction. "So I know this is hardly ideal for the two of you but -"

The front door burst open again and Quigley walked in. "What's everyone up to?"

Luka walked back into the living room and crossed his arms. "Do you have any other sheets? I hate your silky shit."

"No!" shouted Xander.

"Seriously? There are no extras?"

"You're not living here, Luka!" shouted Xander, trying to turn around and look at him without exposing Deryn.

"Why not?" he whined. "The president won't get me another place for at least a couple of weeks. You know he's always slow with that, and I can't stay with my father anymore. You should've seen the fit he threw just now."

"It was pretty pathetic," said Bronson, turning back around.

"Ruby, are you two naked?" asked Quigley.

Luka knitted his brow and walked closer to them. "Oh, shit."

"Everybody, get *out*!" demanded Xander in a booming voice. No one moved.

"Get out or I'm going to stand without the fucking blanket!"

Luka screamed and ran into the guestroom, slamming the door behind him.

"Wait, Ruby, I feel this is important," said Quigley. "Is Deryn standing without the blanket, too?"

"Fuck no!"

He shrugged, "I'm out," and left the apartment.

Bronson didn't budge, continuing to smile at them. "I have to admit, I've always been a little curious -"

"If you don't get out then I'm going to stand, Bronson," said Deryn, putting her hands on the top of the blanket.

Bronson shuddered. "Alright, alright! I'll go." He stood up. "Just keep your disgusting lady bits covered."

When Bronson was gone, Deryn put her face in her hands. "We really need to talk to all of them about boundaries," she said.

Xander smiled and kissed her cheek.

She turned to meet his lips with hers. "You know you have to let Luka stay here."

He groaned. "I know. But I'm not getting him new fucking sheets."

"Yes you are!" called Luka from the other room.

Xander groaned louder. What a horrible turn of events.

CHAPTER TEN

Xander and Luka stood with their arms crossed, staring intently at the bushy trees in front of them.

"Do you really think she'd like one of these?" asked Luka, cocking his head to get a better look.

"She seems like the type, doesn't she?"

"I guess. You have to like trees if you're an Outsider, right? It's, like, in their rule book or something." Luka stepped forward and began walking through the assortment of Christmas trees. "So how do we pick one?" he asked. "We never had one in my house."

"Yes, you did. In the living room," said Xander, staring around blankly.

"Really? Huh. Guess I never paid attention."

"Our wave always bought ours," continued Xander. "I believe certain ones are meant to be more attractive than others."

Luka crinkled his nose. "They're fucking trees. They look the same."

"Are you two still over here?"

They both turned to see Bronson standing behind them.

"What's the problem?"

"Oh! He's common, I'll bet he knows!" exclaimed Luka, looking brightly at Bronson. "Are certain trees more attractive than others?"

Bronson knitted his brow. "Umm ... yeah. Are you serious?"

They both blinked.

Bronson rolled his eyes. "You want to find a bushier one,

with the least amount of bald spots."

They blinked again.

"See how that one's all thin and has that big bare spot?" He pointed. "You want to avoid that."

"Huh ... makes sense," said Xander, looking at Luka and nodding.

"I thought these all grew in Inner City's conservatory," said Luka. "Are they not bred to be genetically perfect?"

"Why would they waste their time doing that?" asked Bronson. "Haven't you ever heard that the beauty is in the flaws?"

"No," said Luka. "There's nothing beautiful about bald spots, whether it be trees, women, or your men, or something."

Bronson smirked. "To each their own."

"How about this one?" asked Xander, bringing them back to the topic at hand.

Bronson walked up beside him. "Well, it's good, but ..."

"But what?" he asked, truly wanting to understand.

"But it's about a foot taller than your ceiling, mate."

Xander shrugged. "So? Can't we just cut it shorter?"

"I mean, I guess, but I don't know if it would look right on the bottom. And that sort of takes away from the fun of it."

"How is this fun?" asked Xander. He and Luka both looked at Bronson expectantly.

Rolling his eyes again, Bronson said, "Pick whatever tree you want, Ruby. It's obvious that this tradition is wasted on you. But let me be in charge of picking the ornaments. At least let *that* be fun for Deryn."

"You mean we're supposed to ornament the tree *ourselves?*" asked Luka with wide eyes.

"Who else?" said Bronson. "You don't have a wave anymore, remember?"

Luka paled at the realization.

"How about this one?" asked Xander, walking over to a smaller and very spirited tree.

Bronson nodded in approval. "That one's good."

Xander looked around and waved his arm to get the seller's

attention. A young woman walked over, looking nervous as she approached the obvious Guardians.

"Have you decided?" she asked.

"Yes, we'd like this one," said Xander, "and the large one over there, as well." He pointed at the one he had been looking at before.

"Who's the large one for?" asked Luka.

"Who else do I know?"

Luka thought about this. "Oh. Metal hand. Got it," he said recalling Adelaide 'Del' Norris, the believed to be deceased but very much alive wife of President Saevus.

"Don't call her that!" snapped Xander.

"Alright. That's seventy coin for the small one and a hundred for the large."

"Fucking rip off," said Luka, crinkling his forehead. "They're just going to be thrown out in a few weeks."

"Oh, come on, Luka," said Bronson. "Where's your Christmas spirit?"

"It's an ancient holiday. My father doesn't like ancient holidays so we rarely celebrate." Luka looked at Xander. "Are you sure we had a tree?"

"Every year. I remember because I always thought it was funny you never had lights on yours. Ours always had lights. Can you deliver the small one?" Xander asked the seller.

"Yes, but it's extra."

"Obviously," he said. "Bronson, give her your address."

After that was done and Xander told the seller they would be back for the big tree, he and Luka followed Bronson around Middle City's Shopping District to pick ornaments. He ended up choosing several that needed decorating, knowing very well that Deryn would enjoy the art project. Even though her perfectionism would, undoubtedly, bring her a great deal of stress. She seemed to relish in stress, though. None of them could deny that.

Once the ornaments were chosen, along with a few other Christmas decorations for around the apartment, they met up with Quigley, who had just finished having lunch with his ex-girlfriend. Then they all went back for the tree, trying to figure out the best way to get it to Del without anyone noticing while they walked. Luckily, not many people wandered onto the old street where she was hiding out, and Xander and Luka were able to carry it to the back entrance unnoticed while Bronson and Quigley stood guard. Xander did his special knock and a short while later a small chunk of door was removed. Brown eyes peeked out at him.

"You've never come here in the middle of the day before," said a woman whose voice was much higher than Del's. "Is something wrong?"

"No, but I have no time to come later. Luka, go back around the corner, will you? I'll meet up with you at the bookstore in a bit," ordered Xander.

Luka put his half of the tree down and did as he was told. As soon as he was gone, the door opened and a young raven-haired woman named Miki stood on the other side.

"I brought you all something," he said, motioning towards the large tree.

Miki smiled and helped him carry it inside. She was an Outsider around his age, probably a little older, but her family had gone into hiding just weeks before President Saevus sent guards to their village, so she'd successfully avoided recruitment. Which was why the Resistance often sent her into Utopia, either as a spy or to purchase supplies. She was doing the latter when the curfew came into effect and she was left stranded. All of the Resistance's usual exits were now heavily guarded and monitored by S.U.R.G.E.'s. It was almost as if the president knew of them the entire time.

"Thanks, Xander," she said. "Sometimes this place gets so dreary. It'll be nice to have a little Christmas cheer to brighten it up."

Something crashed in the other room. "Ah, shit!" Miki's usual partner on her missions to Utopia, a young man named Kemp, charged into the room, looking rather red in the face. "This isn't working, Miki! We don't have enough parts for it to stay together!"

Xander looked between them and cocked an eyebrow.

"We're trying to build Ronan a little play area for Christmas," explained Miki. "But we're sort of lacking in materials."

Kemp shook out his hand, then sucked on his wounded thumb. He looked over and stared at Xander for a moment. His eyes widened. "What are you doing today?"

"I don't know. I guess I'm Christmas shopping."

Kemp and Miki exchanged a look. "Could we come with you?" she asked.

Xander laughed. "No."

"Why not?" asked Kemp. "Del doesn't want us going out without a firm purpose."

"Like buying food," explained Miki.

"But if we're with you -"

"No," repeated Xander. "Besides, I'm not alone."

"You and Luka, right?" asked Miki.

Xander nodded. "And two others. Not Guardians but -"

"Do they know about us?" asked Kemp.

"Sort of." Bronson did, at least. He wasn't sure what Quigley knew.

"Then what's the problem?"

Xander thought it was obvious, but he supposed he would have to spell it out for them. "It's dangerous," he said. "The other Guardians are watching me even closer than before."

"Why?" asked Miki.

"None of your business."

"Oh, Xander! I didn't know you were here." They all looked to see Del walking down the stairs with a big smile on her face.

"He brought us a Christmas tree," said Miki, motioning to the tree they had placed sideways on the floor.

"Oh, how lovely," said Del. Xander handed her the bag of ornaments he'd also purchased for them.

"And Xander just invited us to go out holiday shopping with him," said Kemp.

Xander's eyes widened. He slowly turned his head and gave Kemp a cold glare.

Kemp just smiled. "Would it be alright?"

Del thought about this for a moment. "You'll be with them, Xander?"

"Apparently," he said, never taking his eyes off of Kemp.

"And is Luka with you?"

"He is."

"Well ... I suppose that would be alright. If you all promise to be extra cautious."

"We will! We just need to grab our coats!" exclaimed Kemp, he and Miki already running up the stairs.

"Make sure they have fucking hoods!" Xander called after them.

When he looked back at Del, she was smiling. "You didn't actually offer, did you?"

"What do you think?" he said with a sneer.

"I think they need this. So *be* nice." She rubbed his arm affectionately before grabbing one end of the tree. Xander grabbed the other end and the two of them headed upstairs.

In the main room, Xander helped Del move things around so the tree would fit while two men played chess on the board he had given them a few days earlier. Ronan, the youngest member of this little group, was in the back room napping. The man named Ulric looked up at him and smiled, but the other man, Anan, a boy really as he was only seventeen, simply sneered down at the board without giving Xander any sort of acknowledgment.

When Kemp and Miki came back out they were both wearing their coats, hoods already up. The two of them were not necessarily recognizable - in fact, he was pretty sure they'd successfully managed to stay under the Guardians' radar - and they probably didn't need the hoods, but better safe than sorry.

"We'll wait to decorate the tree until you're back," said Del.

Suddenly aware that things were going on around him, Anan looked up. "Where are you two going?"

"Out," said Kemp.

Anan looked at Xander. "With *him*?"

"Not my fucking idea," said Xander.

"You're *really* letting this happen right now, Del? Like, *seriously?*"

"I am," said Del. "I trust they will be safe with Xander."

"But -"

"We should get going," said Miki, practically skipping towards the stairs.

Kemp trailed after her with just as much bounce in his step, while Xander groaned behind them.

When they got outside, he led them out of the alley and towards the bookstore where he was supposed to meet the others.

Inside the bookstore, Xander immediately spotted Bronson flipping through a book like it was the most foreign thing in the world to him.

"Hey, Ruby! You reckon our girl would like this one? The shop girl told me it's the most complicated book here, and I can't make heads or tails of it so she must be right."

"Who's your girl?" asked Kemp.

Bronson looked up and only just then noticed the two people standing with Xander. "Oh, Ruby, you've brought friends. But, uhh ... who are they?"

"More fucking fugitives," said Xander under his breath.

"Oh, lovely!" said Bronson, beaming at them. "Welcome to our club. Though, I'm not a fugitive per se ..."

"I fucking hate Christmas."

They all looked over to see Luka standing near them now, being pushed around by the busy crowd.

"No book is worth this shit. Who buys real books anymore, anyway?"

"It's *retro!*" exclaimed Bronson.

Luka looked at Miki and Kemp, blinking several times. "Don't I know you?" he asked.

"Excuse me, Miss." Bronson tapped the shoulder of the passing shop girl. She looked at him and blushed. "Thank you so much for finding this book for me, but my friends and I are in a bit of a hurry and the line's rather long. Any way you can wrap it up for me?"

He gave her that charming smile of his and she melted.

"Of course. I'll be right back with that." She took the book, keeping her eyes on Bronson as she walked away, nearly tripping over some child in the process.

Bronson turned to see everyone staring openmouthed at him, none more than Luka. "What?" He shrugged. "I'm good looking. Why wouldn't I use that to my advantage?"

"Get me out of here!" Quigley struggled to push through the crowd to get to them.

"Seriously, how do I know you?" asked Luka, once again staring at Kemp and Miki.

Xander rolled his eyes. "Where was I just now, Luka?"

"The place I'm not allowed to mention."

"Right. And I just came back from there with two people in tow. Now, how is it that you think you might *possibly* know them?"

Luka knitted his brow. "Resistance?"

"You're an idiot."

"Here's your book." The shop girl stopped in front of Bronson, handing him a bag with the wrapped book inside. She was also holding a small and flat device, which she used to take his payment. "And, um ... here's a little something extra." She then touched her wristband to his, transferring her information. She winked and scurried off, trying to swing her hips seductively but instead tripping through the large crowd and nearly falling on her ass.

"Let's get out of here," said Xander.

He led the way out the door, which was actually pretty easy to get to since the crowd pushed them along like a wave in the ocean.

"Air!" shouted Quigley, throwing his arms up and breathing it all in.

"It's not as bad as last year, since no one from outside the city can get in to shop," said Bronson, searching his wristband's records until he found the shop girl's number. "Anyone want it, or should I just delete?"

"How is it that you end up with some girl's number every

time I'm with you?" asked Luka.

Bronson smirked. "No need to be jealous, Luka." He pressed delete and the number was gone. "I get plenty when I'm not with you, too."

Quigley was looking at Kemp and Miki. "Who are these people?"

"Friends of Ruby's," said Bronson.

"Oh, Ruby, I didn't know you had friends!" Quigley said brightly. "Other than your three charming companions for the day, of course -"

"Whoever said you were my fucking friends?"spat Xander.

"- and, um ... Allie. Allie?" He looked around at everyone.

"Who the hell is Allie?" asked Bronson.

"Your girlfriend," said Quigley.

Bronson thought about this. "Oh. Oh, right! Allison Darby. My girlfriend."

"Who are you all talking about?" asked Miki.

"*My* girlfriend," repeated Bronson with a smile.

Kemp and Miki exchanged a look.

"So what is it the two of you need?" asked Xander. "Might as well get your shit out of the way first."

"Well, we need to go to the hardware store and the toy store," said Kemp.

"Ooh, toy store." Quigley sucked air in through his teeth. "Think I'm gonna have to skip that one."

"Bronson, we'll need to use your abilities there," ordered Xander.

"*What?*" whined Bronson. "Why can't you just show your damn guard wristband to get us to the front of the line? It works just as well."

"Not at Christmas. People have tackled me for trying that before."

"They really did," confirmed Luka. "It was fucking embarrassing."

"So you're just going to pimp me out for front of the line privileges?" Bronson pouted. "I feel so cheap."

"I'll buy you a fucking ice-cream cone then, so quit your

complaining," snapped Xander.

"*Oh*, it had better be a double scoop," said Bronson with narrowed eyes.

They all went to the hardware store first and were able to get in and out of there pretty quickly. Kemp and Miki bought a lot of large items, so they asked to store them in the back and planned to come back later.

The toy store was as horrific as they expected. Luckily, there was indeed a young shop girl who was more than happy to help Bronson with whatever he needed.

"The power you hold," said Kemp as they left the store. "Is that teachable?"

"It's all about confidence," said Bronson. "You're good looking enough. You'll try the next one."

They went into a candy store next, Xander, Luka, Quigley and Miki all standing back while Kemp failed miserably at flirting. Luckily, Bronson was there to pick up the pieces and got the job they needed done.

Glancing sideways, Xander couldn't help but notice the way Miki's hands curled into fists as she watched Kemp talking to the female candy store worker.

"Don't tell me you're jealous over Kemp?" he asked.

Miki blushed. "No. Of course not. We're just friends."

An obvious lie.

"Seriously?" said Quigley. "You're, like, way better looking than he is."

Miki smiled. "I'm not jealous."

"Of course you're not," said Xander with a smirk.

"You know, it's mostly men who work in the gaming store across the way," said Luka. "If we go there next, it could be up to you to get us to the front of the line. Wanna see if he reacts?"

"No," Miki said quickly. She bit her lip. "Maybe. Let me think about it."

In the clothing store they went to next, Kemp was much more successful in his flirting, and even managed to get their items purchased without Bronson's help.

As they walked out of the store, Miki suddenly said, "Let's go to the gaming store. I'm sure Ulric would just love a dartboard."

It seemed she'd thought about it, and Miki definitely didn't need any confidence training from Bronson. She had it down, and Kemp wasn't happy about it.

"You know, Miki really isn't bad to look at," Luka whispered to Xander as they left the store. "I doubt Kemp is ever going to make a move. Do you think I should give it a go?"

Xander couldn't help but notice the way Luka glanced sideways at Bronson, almost like he was making sure he'd heard them. He had, of course, because he was right fucking there.

"No," answered Xander.

He then guided everyone into a nearby alley so that he could smoke a cigarette. Bronson, Quigley and Luka all bummed one. Surprisingly, Miki asked for one, as well.

"So are you all done then?" asked Xander.

"I guess we are," said Kemp.

"Does that mean you're not coming to the Black Market with us?" asked Quigley.

Xander's nostrils flared as he turned slowly and gave Quigley a cold stare.

"Black Market?" repeated Miki, taking a drag of her cigarette. "What are you going there for?"

"I found a guy who has a record player," said Bronson, watching Xander with a smile. "We're picking it up for someone."

"A record player for music?" said Miki. "Oh, I love music! Could we go, Kemp? Please?"

"I don't know," said Kemp. "When Del gave us permission to come out, I don't think she expected us to ever leave the Shopping District."

"You can't come," said Xander. "You don't have working wristbands to get you through the gate."

"We know how to get there from the underground," said Miki. "S.U.R.G.E.'s never go on this route because they don't know it's there."

Xander shook his head and firmly said, "No," even though he was incredibly curious. "You already got what you came for. Time to go back to your cave."

"Oh, please don't make me go back there yet," said Miki with puppy-dog eyes. "I want to hear music. It's been so long."

"Aw, she wants to hear music, Ruby," said Bronson, putting his arm around Miki and hugging her tightly against his side. "How can you deprive her of that?"

Both Kemp and Luka narrowed their eyes at the two of them touching.

"Please," Miki said again, now giving him a pouty lip.

Xander groaned. "Oh, fuck you all. Let's get this over with."

Miki squealed. Xander put his cigarette out on the wall and the others followed suit. They all left the alley, Miki and Kemp taking the lead.

They walked several blocks, zigzagging through the crowds at first, then taking several side streets, all narrow between tall buildings that shielded them from the artificial sun, which was actually out that day. Even when it was sunny, the streets still smelled like rain on pavement, unable to dry completely in the secluded metal bubble.

Miki and Kemp kept their eyes on the dumpsters they passed, eventually stopping by a green one with a red streak across the side.

They looked around to make sure the coast was clear, then pulled out a vent beside the dumpster. Kemp directed everyone inside while Miki led the way. The path was small and dark, and they had to crawl to get through. Bronson's broad shoulders barely fit. Miki let everyone know when they reached a ladder, then warned them that it was a little wobbly so they would need to climb it one at a time. She went down first and called out once she reached the bottom. Quigley was next, then Luka, Bronson, Xander and Kemp.

Once they were all down, Miki and Kemp guided them through a long, *long* passageway. Which made sense, considering the Shopping District was nowhere near Outer City or the Black Market.

But then they reached something. Small passenger cars only big enough for two people, and with wheels on what looked like old tram tracks. Very primitive but still effective.

Miki climbed into the first one. "Xander, you can ride with me," she said. "Kemp, you show Luka how to drive one. Follow in the back."

Kemp nodded as Xander stepped into the car. He watched as Miki pressed a green button in its center.

"Hold on," she instructed, using a long knob to drive them forward.

Xander watched as best he could in the dark, noticing that several buttons were involved to drive the small car, but it didn't seem to be too complex. She gave a brief description as they moved through narrow caves, eventually coming to a halt when they reached a large space that looked a lot like the place they had just left.

Miki and Xander got out, then she redirected the tracks and pushed the car around until it was facing the opposite direction on an adjacent track.

Luka and Bronson appeared shortly after, the car jerking a lot as Luka attempted to come to a complete stop.

"Ugh, now I have a headache," said Bronson, swaying around as he climbed out of the car.

"Oh, come on. I wasn't *that* bad," said Luka with a sneer.

Kemp and Quigley were right behind them. Once all of the cars were facing the opposite direction, they continued on, only walking a short distance until they reached another ladder.

Miki climbed up first, lifting something at the top that let in a small shaft of light. "It's clear," she called down to them.

They all headed up, eventually coming out of a manhole in a rocky hallway with wall lamps. And just around the corner was the Black Market.

"Clever trick," said Luka as they descended the ladders leading to the tram graveyard.

"Outsiders appreciate our ancestors and their technology," said Miki. "Unlike your president who couldn't care less about the world before Utopia."

"You mean the world that destroyed itself? Oh, that's right! Our ancestors did that!" Luka smirked and Miki grimaced.

"This coming from the Guardian who likes to climb trees every time we have a mission outside," said Xander, rolling his eyes. "Relax, Miki. He's just jealous because you know what it feels like to go swimming. Not to mention, how to swim."

"In a lake or ocean? Oh, that's right! I've done both," said Miki, giving Luka her own smirk.

Once they reached the Black Market, Bronson led the way to the booth that was holding the record player for him. It was a rare item, and Xander had him ask his cigarette guy to find one for him. For an extra fee, of course.

They reached the booth in question inside of an old, silver tram. It was empty at the time and the man behind the counter had them close the door. The wall had been torn out so he actually had two booths, and an entire rack filled with records.

"I love vinyl," said Miki, going over and smelling them. "Do you have Billie Holiday?" she asked the man.

"Dunno," he said as he unlocked a chest, pulled out an old wooden record player and put it on the counter.

Xander's eyes lit up as he looked it over, rubbing his hands along the smooth wood. "Does it work?" he asked.

"Aye," said the man.

"Hey, Ruby! You said the song's called *Blackbird*, right?" called Bronson, who was shuffling through the records.

"Yeah," said Xander, trying to ignore the way Miki was suddenly looking at him.

"Here it is!" Bronson held up an album with a simple white cover. "Wanna listen to make sure?"

Without waiting for an answer, Bronson walked over to the record player, put on the record and set it to play the proper song.

Xander listened closely. "Yes, that's it."

"Hey, Miki! I found that Billie Holiday bloke for you!" called Kemp, holding up an album.

Miki, who was still watching Xander, walked over to him and took it. "Billie Holiday was a woman, Kemp."

Xander put the record player and the album into one of his shopping bags. Just as he was about to pay the man, Miki ran up to him with four other albums in hand. "Anyone who likes the song *Blackbird* might enjoy these, as well," she said, handing them over.

Xander took the albums and shuffled through them blankly, not knowing who any of these people were.

"They're not exactly like it, but the Triggses have several albums that belong to a friend of theirs, and those are all among them."

Xander looked up and stared at her curiously. "Um, thanks."

Miki gave him a half-smile. "We're not idiots, Xander. We all know who that's for, and we'd love it if you brought her to our place for Christmas."

Xander didn't respond.

"Just think about it," said Miki. She turned to the man behind the counter. "I don't suppose you have another record player back there?"

"Not a working one," he said, digging around under the counter until he came out with a very worn and dusty record player.

Miki took a close look at it. "What do you think, Kemp? Is it salvageable?"

Kemp walked over and took a look. "I don't know much about these things but we can try. Ulric's good with ancient electronics. He could probably get it going."

She smiled and nodded. "This can be your Christmas present to me, Xander. And, let's say, five records. I'll pick while you pay the man."

"Excuse me?" said Xander, cocking an eyebrow.

She wandered towards the records, and said, "Well, I'm not exactly bringing any money in right now, am I?" Her back was to him as she scanned the shelf. "Oh! Christmas music!"

Xander grunted, but still paid the man for ten records and two record players. He didn't even get a discount for the one that didn't work.

Soon after, they left the Black Market, starting the long

journey back to the Shopping District where they still had to pick up the items they left in the hardware store before it closed.

"I just realized something," said Bronson as they walked. "I never got my ice-cream cone!"

CHAPTER ELEVEN

The following morning, Deryn hummed to herself as she decorated one of her ornaments at the dining room table. Xander had already left for his Guardian duties, but Luka had the day off and was still holed up in his bedroom.

His door suddenly opened and, without looking up from her task, Deryn said, "Morning, sunshine. I left some coffee for you in the kitchen."

"Thanks," said Luka, wobbling over to the coffee.

Deryn continued to hum while Luka poured himself a cup. He leaned against the counter and watched her while she sprinkled glitter over a glass orb. The glue she had put on it made the glitter look like snowflakes. Deryn smiled proudly.

She stood and went to hang her new ornament on the tree. While rearranging a few of the other ones so they were placed properly to be the most visually appealing, Deryn said to Luka, "I'm going to need you to take me to the Black Market today to find a tree topper, as well as a few presents for Xander and the others."

Luka let out a loud, "Ha!" and said, "No. Unfortunately for you, I didn't wake up with a death wish."

"It's nonnegotiable," she said. "It's safer for me than the Shopping District and Bronson has already agreed to come along to play the part of my boyfriend. Now we just need a Guardian escort."

"No," Luka said again.

"I suggest you go and take a shower because Bronson is going to be here in twenty minutes."

"No."

Deryn turned towards him and frowned. "Now, Luka, don't make this difficult."

"I'm not taking you to the Black Market," he said while sipping his coffee.

Taking a few steps forward, Deryn kept her stern eyes focused on him. "You know, it would be a real shame if I let it slip to Xander exactly what it was you admitted to me the night I fell out of my chair. You know. About when Bronson took you home."

Luka stopped drinking his coffee mid-sip. He gulped. "I was fucking drunk, alright? If you tell him then I will gladly use that defense."

"Oh, and were you drunk in the alley the other night, as well?"

Luka froze. "What?"

Deryn smiled wickedly. "I didn't think so."

"Am I seriously being blackmailed by the Outsiders' fucking princess?"

"Looks like it," she said. "Get in the shower, Luka. Now you only have seventeen minutes until we leave."

Luka narrowed his eyes. "If I wasn't so proud right now, I'd be pretty fucking pissed."

Deryn smiled wider as she took his cup from him.

"You've been spending too much time with Xander." Luka went into his room, grabbed some clean clothes and headed for the bathroom.

When he came back out, Deryn was already wearing her wig and had her eyes colored blue. She and Bronson were waiting by the door with their coats on, hoods up, and gasmasks strapped to their hips.

"I can't believe you fucking told her about the alley," hissed Luka while going into the closet and putting on his own coat.

Bronson smirked. "Sorry. She knew she'd need blackmail to get you out of here, so how could I just sit on such valuable information?"

Luka remained in a bit of a mood all the way to the Black

Market. He mainly stood back while Deryn did her shopping, picking out a tree topper in the shape of a gold star before searching for gifts. She wanted to get something for Xander, Bronson, Quigley and even Luka. Xander had also mentioned an invitation to visit Del and the others in hiding on Christmas day, and she was seriously thinking about it.

The invitation had come from a girl named Miki, who Deryn didn't know. But she did know Del, who had often visited Eagle Training Center during Deryn's time there. And she knew Kemp and Anan, who were from her village Redwood. It would be nice to see all of them again, and if she went she would need gifts for them, too.

Most of the gifts were easy enough, since she didn't exactly have the option of going all out. But, when it came to Xander, she wasn't sure where to begin. He was born rich and already had everything.

"Why not just get some lingerie?" suggested Bronson. "He seems to really like your nakedness."

"I guess that's always a good failsafe," said Deryn. "But I was really hoping to get more creative than that."

"Then make him something, but lingerie is pretty much your only option if you're dead-set on paying money."

There was one compartment on the inside of a tram that sold women's lingerie. They went to it and Deryn glanced around nervously while Bronson picked a few things out for her.

"How about this black one?" he asked, holding it up.

Deryn looked at it and bit her lip. "I don't know," she said, her voice quivering.

"No," said Luka, speaking for the first time since they got there. "Get the green one over there." He motioned with his head. "It's festive. If you want to impress him then that's the one."

"Why thank you, Luka," Bronson said brightly. He grabbed the green negligee and pushed Deryn into a small dressing room, which was pretty much just a curtain hanging in the corner of the tram.

When she had it on, taking the gasmask she'd been wearing off so she could get the full effect, she called Bronson to come and have a look.

"Va va voom," he said while poking his head inside the curtain.

Luka rolled his eyes. He wandered around the small space and took a look out the door at the rest of the tram before heading back in, not noticing when someone spotted him.

"Excellent choice," said Bronson, walking over to him while Deryn changed back into her clothes.

"*You*!"

Luka and Bronson both turned to see an angry-looking girl pointing at Luka. Then she moved her finger to Bronson.

"And *you*! You assholes!"

They both cocked their heads and stared at her blankly for a moment. Then it clicked.

"Oh, right!" said Bronson. "You're the broad from the Pit. Did you not enjoy your room?"

"I've never been more humiliated in my life!"

"Really? Never?" asked Luka, lifting an eyebrow.

"Fuck both of you!" she shouted, giving Luka a shove that caught him off-guard.

He stumbled back and tripped over a rack of nighties, sending him flying into the curtain Deryn was behind.

"What the -" She pressed herself against the mirror, wearing nothing but her bra and pants as Luka landed on the floor. "Dammit, Luka!"

He gazed up at her, his eyes immediately freezing on the large and glossy scar marking her side. The one Finley had given her. Then he saw the others. Noticing his wandering eyes, Deryn grabbed her sweater and quickly covered herself.

"Get out!"

"Sorry," he said, blushing bright crimson as he got on his hands and knees and crawled out of there. When he was back on his feet, the girl was pounding her fists into Bronson's chest.

"Uh, could someone please get this mental bitch off of me?" said Bronson, trying to grab her wrists.

"What the hell is going on out here?" shouted Deryn, coming out from behind the curtain, now fully clothed, her gasmask back on. She immediately locked eyes with the girl. "Why in heaven's name are you hitting my boyfriend?"

"*You!*"

She said that a lot.

"Do I know you or something?" asked Deryn.

Luka cleared his throat and muttered, "Tram," to her.

She knitted her brow. "Is this the girl who slept with Xander?"

He nodded.

"And then you tried to sleep with after?"

He nodded again.

"And did you?"

He shook his head. "Though I did plan to."

"Then why did you leave me in a room all night by myself?" the girl shouted.

"As I recall, I wasn't the one you were expecting to join you up there," said Luka. "You're the one who decided to switch men halfway through the night."

"Wait, switch men? Which men?" asked Deryn.

The girl crossed her arms and motioned angrily at Bronson. "*Your* boyfriend."

Deryn looked at him and crinkled her forehead. "Seriously?"

Bronson looked ashamedly to the floor.

"Was this the alley night?" she asked, glancing between him and Luka.

Neither answered.

Deryn rolled her eyes. "You and your games, Bronson!" She marched back over to the dressing room and grabbed the green negligee. Then she went to the register, purchased it and put it in her bag. "The woman in me simply cannot defend the two of you any longer." She looked at the girl and said, "Have at them," before pushing past her and going off to look for any last minute purchases.

There was nothing else she wanted inside the tram but, just outside of the second to last car, she found a vendor selling mistletoe. The romantic in her simply had to purchase some.

"I'll take two of these," said a familiar voice from a booth to her left.

Deryn's heart stopped. She used her peripherals to watch closely as a hooded man handed over some money, taking two bottles of a vicious-looking green liquid in return. She couldn't see him at first, but then he turned to take a good look around, making sure no one was watching him. She gulped.

Chace.

He was an old friend of hers, around the same age and from Redwood. They were 'recruited' at the same time, quarantined together, trained together, and Dakota had often referred to him as his 'second best friend'. She being the first, of course.

He had escaped the day her father and the other Outsiders stormed into Eagle Center and was now active in the Resistance. At least, that was what she'd heard.

His face was the same as Deryn remembered but, even in the coat, she could tell his body was much leaner, and his eyes were haloed by two dark circles. He was very pale, almost sickly, and something just didn't seem right with him.

There was an iffy feeling forming in the pit of Deryn's stomach, so when Chace moved she bolted. She headed back inside the closest tram, glancing over her shoulder and not noticing as she ran right into one of the burly men guarding the back car.

"Sorry," she said, having to tilt her head way back to look into his eyes.

He made a throaty sound and nodded at her, then stepped aside and held the door open. Deryn stared beyond it blankly for a moment before looking back at the man. He motioned towards the door and said, "Third compartment on the left."

Well, this was interesting. Deryn was about to turn away when Chace walked right by her, staring curiously into the open door. In a panic she stepped through, jumping as the door shut behind her.

While Deryn knew Xander would kill her for going anywhere near the third compartment on the left, she had to admit she was mildly curious as to who was back there. And just who was it they were expecting? Surely not her.

Deryn pushed back her fears and took a confident step forward. The first compartment on her left was empty but the one on her right was selling what appeared to be voodoo items. The vendor had a bone through the base of his nose and gave Deryn a look that sent shivers down her spine. She hurried past him.

The second compartment on the left had a man selling cigarettes, cigars, pipes, chewing tobacco. Everything Deryn hated. He must have been Bronson's friend. On the right, there seemed to be some shady business deal going on with a lot of shouting. When they saw her, a woman quickly slid the door shut.

Finally, Deryn arrived at the third compartment on the left. It was a bit dark in there, since the shades were drawn, and a lone person sat behind a counter, writing something in a notebook. There were many artifacts here, all from the outside. A secondhand shop of sorts.

Unable to make the person out since they had a hood pulled over their head, Deryn stepped into the entrance of the compartment.

Without looking up, the person said, "Hello, Leon. I was wondering when you were going to turn up."

Deryn froze.

The man finally looked up and she was met with the familiar eyes of another fellow trainee from Eagle Center, Neo Boyce. He was not an Outsider. In fact, Deryn was fairly certain he and Xander were friends growing up, but he hadn't been mentioned even once over the last few months. He definitely wasn't a Guardian but, given their group's track record, she very much doubted he was on the side of good.

"Shut the door, will you?"

Deryn took a step back, but someone suddenly pushed her from behind and she went stumbling towards the counter.

"I got it, darling," said a woman's voice. Deryn turned just in time to see Odette Von shut the door.

"I believe you remember my wife Odette."

Correction. Odette Boyce.

Deryn put her hand in her sleeve and pulled out her knife.

Neo and Odette looked at each other and exchanged a laugh.

"Relax, Leon," said Neo. "We only want to talk."

He and Odette both took out knives and guns, and put them on the counter. And not Elements. Ancient, Outsider guns.

"We won't even ask you to do the same," said Neo.

Odette took a seat, smiling at Deryn as she patted the empty chair beside her. "Don't worry. We don't bite. Well ... only each other." She looked at her husband and winked.

Deryn stayed standing and kept her knife at the ready, but she did pull off her gasmask. "How did you know it was me?"

"Come on, Leon," said Neo. "We trained together for, what, two or three years? Maybe we just recognized you, even with the blue eyes and blonde hair."

Deryn rolled her blue eyes. "We barely knew each other. And there have never been any wanted posters of me."

Odette looked at her husband and smiled. "Still sharp. I guess the rumors were false."

"What rumors?"

Ignoring her, Odette said, "A friend of ours saw a strange girl here with Xander a couple weeks back. Said there was something almost disturbingly familiar about her, so I went to investigate. Didn't take long since Luka was keeping you busy with his silly tricks with that toy. I watched you for less than a minute before I realized who you were. You can change your coloring all you want, or wear a stupid gasmask, I still know your face. And so would Soren if he was paying you any mind. You're lucky he was distracted by Xander."

"Who is your friend that saw me?" asked Deryn.

"That's hardly important," said Neo. "We're here to talk business."

"Business," repeated Deryn, finally taking a seat but keeping her knife in her hand. "What kind of business?"

"While we do make quite a bit of money selling the many items you see around you," said Neo, "our primary moneymaker is smuggling."

Deryn raised her eyebrows. "Smuggling."

"Smuggling people," finished Odette. "In and out of Utopia."

Deryn's jaw dropped.

Odette reached out and nudged it shut for her. "We've been doing it for years but this lockdown and curfew have really worked in our favor."

"I don't understand. Why -" What was it that Deryn wanted to ask? "Why are you doing this?"

Neo and Odette exchanged another look.

"Just after the battle at Eagle, my mom tried to force me to become a Guardian. I hadn't even wanted to be a guard, so I fled," said Neo. "Knowing that Odette's dad was trying to do the same, I went to her and she agreed to come with me."

"We went Outsider. It was our only option to evade capture and execution. We were in hiding for over a year before our families gave up," said Odette. "It was during that time that we started the collection you see around you. Scavenging through ancient cities we came across."

"When we were sure our families weren't looking for us anymore, we came back to Utopia and began selling our items in the Black Market to make a living," explained Neo. "We would often hear stories about people unable to get outside to their families. Obviously the Resistance got in and out, but they weren't exactly keen on sharing their secrets. Not unless someone from the outside sent them in for someone."

"We already had our own route we discovered when we wanted to come back in, so we began helping them," said Odette. "Before long it became a business."

"And, as a runaway slave, we're fairly certain you're in need of our services."

"While I'm sure Xander has been really useful in keeping you alive," said Odette, "I highly doubt he has a clue on how to get you out."

Deryn's knife hand finally easing, she glanced back and forth between them. "I don't have any money."

"But Xander does," said Neo with a growing smile.

"I could never ask him to do that."

"Why not?" asked Odette. "Do you think keeping you alive has been free for him?"

Deryn sighed and looked down at the knife Xander had taught her to use. She grazed it with her fingertips. "I'm not interested."

When she looked up again, Odette was watching her closely. "Is this about Xander and you sleeping together?"

Deryn turned bright-red. "W-what? I don't know -"

"There's no need to pretend. I already overheard him and Luka talking about it."

With a heavy sigh, Deryn stood. "Thanks but no thanks." She turned towards the door.

"Leon, wait."

Deryn glanced over her shoulder to find Neo's joking exterior suddenly gone, and replaced with a serious and grim expression. "You can't stay here," he said. "Your dad is waiting for your return to attack and you know it."

"I don't know that."

"Then maybe you know this," said Odette. "My sister, my *baby* sister, was forced to become a Guardian the other day, and I need this war to end before she has to do something she'll never forgive herself for."

"If you love your sister so much then why'd you leave her behind in the first place?" asked Deryn, looking Odette square in the eye.

Odette went red. "I was young, and I truly didn't believe my father would force that upon his favorite daughter. But I was wrong and Lona is living with the consequences."

"So the two of you need me to leave. Is that what you're saying?"

Odette looked at Neo. He nodded at her and said, "Yes, that's what we're saying."

"And you had the nerve to try and charge me," said Deryn,

putting her hands on her hips. "You two are unbelievable."

Neo and Odette both smiled and said, "Thank you," in perfect sync.

"While I feel for your situation, I'm not going to leave Utopia unless Xander comes with me."

Neo laughed loudly. Odette gave him a sharp look and he quickly sucked it back. "Sorry, but Xander's not going anywhere. Or, rather, he shouldn't. He's the bastard's favorite. If he runs then they'll hunt him down and you can bet his death won't be a pleasant one. And if you're caught with him ... well, I can't imagine your death will be much better. Xander knows this. He's not stupid."

Deryn sighed. "I know it's dangerous, but there are Guardians who want him dead. I won't leave him behind."

Odette stared at her curiously again. "Are you two in love or something?"

This time Deryn didn't even blush, but her eyes grew dim, her heart heavy. She knew she loved Xander, but in love? That was something she simply wasn't ready to admit.

Without saying anything, Deryn turned to leave again. She put her hand on the door.

"Leon."

She looked back at Neo. He tossed her something and she caught it. It was an old key.

"If there comes a time when you need to get out of Utopia quickly, then go to Cherish Lane. It's a small street, only three blocks from Xander's apartment, find the oldest house and use that key to get inside. In the room to the left there's a bookcase. Push it aside and you'll see a tunnel. Don't forget to close it behind you."

"There will always be a hover-bike waiting. We make sure there is in each of our tunnels," added Odette.

"If you take it all the way down then you'll come out in the compartment right next to this one." Neo pointed to his left. "An alarm lets us know whenever someone enters it so if we're not here we won't be long. And then we'll take care of you."

Odette smiled. "But keep in mind that there are no package

deals. If two of you show up then we'll charge for two."

Deryn smiled back. "You're still charging me even though you need me to leave?"

Odette shrugged. "Girl's gotta eat. It's not like Xander will miss five-hundred coin. That's the price, by the way. Two-fifty each. Really, it's a steal, considering we're risking our lives for you and all."

"And are most fugitives able to come up with that sort of money?"

"Most fugitives don't have a rich Guardian aiding them," said Neo with a smile. "It's a case by case basis."

Deryn rolled her eyes. She pocketed the key and opened the door.

"See you soon, Leon!" Odette called after her.

"And tell Xander we said hello!"

They both laughed as Deryn walked through the tram car, not looking inside any of the other compartments as she headed back through the door. Without stopping, she walked right out of the tram and towards the ladder leading to the Black Market's exit. When she was up, she walked to the hallway they'd come in through and plopped down against the wall.

Deryn's eyes misted as she took the key out of her pocket and stroked it with her fingertips. She had an out. A way to get to her father, Talon and Dakota. As much as she hated to admit it, she truly believed that Neo and Odette were legit. Xander would be suspicious, of course, but that wasn't saying much considering he'd been suspicious of his own best friend.

Before long, Deryn zoned out staring at that key. She barely noticed when someone sat beside her, but she didn't have to look up to know it was Luka. He was giving her those pitying eyes she hated so much, probably thinking about the scars he'd seen for the first time.

"Don't look at me like that, Luka. The last thing I need is *you* feeling sorry for me."

"Where'd you disappear to?" he asked, turning his head so he could avoid looking at her completely.

"Nowhere."

"What's that in your hand?"

"Nothing," she said, making a fist and putting the key in her pocket.

"Right." A long moment of silence passed between them. "So ... those scars of yours. The ones on your side."

Deryn's breath hitched.

"You got it from these weird black flames, right?"

She nodded.

"I know those flames. I used to have them on my Element. The scars never heal and leave you in constant pain." Luka's face strained, his hands fidgeting with the hem of his coat. "Are you in constant pain?"

Deryn glanced sideways at him and sighed. "I suppose I am. But I've had them for so long that I think I've gotten used to it."

"Who gave them to you?"

"Finley."

"*Oh*," said Luka. "Makes sense."

"What does?"

"Why Xander's been acting so harshly towards her. Don't get me wrong, he's never exactly been nice to her, definitely fucked her and left her on more than one occasion but, even so, they were still friends. He may be an asshole, but he cared about her. Now ... well, it doesn't really seem like he does anymore."

"Good."

Luka bit his cheek. "It's not like I'd ever defend Finley or anything, and I don't know when she gave those to you, but she's changed a lot since first becoming a Guardian. She's miserable. And lonely. Some people just aren't cut out for this business."

Deryn frowned. "It certainly sounds like you're defending her."

"Yeah, well, we both have shit fathers who put us in shit situations. Guess I have to feel some sort of kinship with her."

Luka reached into his pocket and pulled out a pack of

cigarettes. Deryn crinkled her nose. "Don't tell me you've picked up that horrible habit, too?"

"Really takes the edge off," he said while lighting one.

"Does it?" asked Deryn, taking it from him and bringing it to her lips.

"Oh, no!" shouted Luka, quickly grabbing it back. "Xander's already going to kill me for bringing you here. No need to add torture before he finishes the job."

"Maybe he'd like it if I picked up the habit. That way, he could do it more often."

"And it's remarks like that that make me wonder if you even know him at all."

Deryn's eyes misted again. Maybe she didn't really know Xander, but she wanted to. She wanted to know everything about him. But she needed time. Something she was running out of. Especially if he wouldn't come with her when she left.

"Holy shit, are you crying?" asked Luka, looking panicked. "No, no, no! What did I say?" He tried to replay his words in his head.

"N -" *Hiccup*! "N-nothing!"

Luka sighed. He looked around uncomfortably as he lifted his arm and patted her on the back, knocking her forward.

"What are you doing?" asked Deryn.

"Being comforting," he answered, continuing to pat.

"Well, you're doing an awful job of it." She chuckled through her tears.

"God, the two of you are so alike sometimes ..."

Deryn grabbed his arm and moved it so he was rubbing smooth circles on her back instead. "That's how you comfort people, Luka."

"Hmm ... I can see how that might be more pleasant," he said with a smile. He put his hand back in his lap and took a drag of his cigarette. "So are we done here?"

"Where's Bronson?"

"Dealing with that crazy broad. Oh, wait! Is that why you're so upset? Because your boyfriend almost cheated on you?" He smirked.

Deryn smiled. "What do you mean almost? He *did* cheat on me. You were there, remember? In the alley?"

Luka's face dropped. "You better shut your fucking mouth."

Deryn laughed. "Don't worry. Your dirty little secret is safe with me." She zipped her lips.

"So if we find him, *are* we done?"

"I don't know," said Deryn with a sigh. "I was really hoping to find Xander a better present. I mean, obviously he won't mind Bronson's idea but ... well, it's not very clever. But what do you get someone who already has everything?"

"Let me sleep on it," said Luka, taking another drag. "I'm sure we can come up with something. But, either way, wear the outfit."

Deryn smiled and rolled her eyes. "Men are so easy."

Noticing Deryn was still looking a little down, Luka lifted his arm and rubbed her back again.

"Aww, are we hugging?" asked Bronson, suddenly coming up beside them. "Mind if I join?" He squished between them, threw his arms around both their shoulders and squeezed them together.

"I'm really not much of a toucher," said Luka, struggling to get out of the three-way hug.

"Yes, I've noticed," said Bronson, squeezing him tighter.

"Let go."

"This is what we call hugging therapy, Luka. It's good for you."

"Let g -"

"Just accept it."

Luka huffed as Bronson continued to hug him, Deryn laughing on his other side.

"So are we ready?"

"Yes," said Deryn, standing up as soon as his grip on her loosened. Luka put out his cigarette.

As she began to walk, Bronson hurried to catch up to her, throwing his arm around her shoulders. "What's wrong, kitten? You're not upset over that other girl, are you?"

"Somehow I think I'll get over it," said Deryn.

"So you're not breaking up with me?"

With a smile, she wrapped her arm around Bronson's waist and rested her head against him. "No, Bronson. You can still be my outside boyfriend."

"Yay!"

"What happened with that girl, anyway?" asked Luka, appearing beside them.

Bronson shrugged. "Dunno. I just said whatever to get rid of her. I actually think we might have a date tomorrow. She's probably going to be waiting a while."

"Bronson, you're awful!" shouted Deryn, giving him a playful shove.

He laughed. "What? Gotta keep the mental bitch happy in the moment."

Arm still around Deryn, Bronson threw his other one around Luka and pulled him close.

"What are you doing?" asked Luka, trying to pull away again.

"Your father never hugged you as a child, did he?"

"Of course he didn't."

"Hmm ... figures."

Stopping his struggle against the firm grip, Luka decided to just give in and let this happen. Really, it wasn't all bad. It was actually kind of nice to have people in his life who were trustworthy. And Bronson and Deryn were just that. They weren't out to get anyone, except for those who had wronged them or the people they loved. They were just ... nice. And that was something new and unusual for Luka. He was starting to understand why Xander was so drawn to them. It was because people like Bronson and Deryn made him feel almost normal in their crazy world.

CHAPTER TWELVE

"What do you think?" asked Deryn, stepping out of the bathroom and letting Xander, who was sitting on the bed, look her over. Currently, the song *Blackbird* was playing on the record player Deryn had unwrapped about an hour earlier. She had it on repeat, but the song made her so happy that Xander couldn't even get angry about it. Annoyed, definitely, but not angry.

"You look fine, Deryn."

"Really?" she asked. "You don't think it looks like I'm trying too hard with the red?" She looked down and tugged at the ends of the sweater she was wearing.

Xander chuckled. "Since when is being festive considered trying too hard?"

"Okay." Deryn finally let go of the sweater. "And you're sure my hair looks alright up like this?" She fidgeted with the twist she'd made.

"Yes." Xander stood and walked over to her. "All of you looks alright." He reached her and wrapped his arms around her waist, pulling her close and giving her a tender kiss. "You look beautiful."

Deryn tensed in his arms. He opened his eyes to see her staring at him, her expression almost fearful.

"What?" he asked.

Deryn gulped. "Nothing. It's just ... well, you've never said that to me before."

"Said what?" he asked. "That you're beautiful?"

She tensed again.

Xander smirked. "Do you not like it when I say that?"

"N-no," she muttered. "It's fine."

"Then why are you looking at me like I just told you I murdered a puppy?"

"I-I'm not."

"Yes you are."

"No I'm not," she said a bit more confidently. "I just ..." She sighed. "No one's ever said that to me before."

Xander raised his eyebrows. "No?"

She shook her head.

He smiled and kissed her forehead. "Well, you are."

She blushed.

"Stop being so fucking bashful and just take the compliment."

Deryn smiled softly. "That mouth of yours."

She pulled away, but Xander grabbed her wrist and yanked her back, crashing his lips into hers and kissing her with an incredible vigor that sent delightful sensations to the south end of her body.

"What was that you were saying about my mouth?" he asked between parts of their lips.

"Nothing," she said while smiling against him, running her fingers through his soft hair.

Before either of them had time to consider the time crunch they were in, Deryn's pants were off and Xander's were undone. He slammed her against the wall, lifted one of her legs and thrust into her.

Xander put his free hand behind Deryn's head so that the hairstyle she'd worked so hard on wouldn't get ruined during their spontaneous moment of passion. Their lips did not part once during their quick fuck, and when Deryn came Xander couldn't help but do the same.

While catching their breath, Xander stroked Deryn's cheek, keeping his eyes open as he kissed her tenderly. "I think this is when you look the most beautiful," he said with a smirk. "After screaming my name."

Deryn blushed and gave him a playful shove.

Xander chuckled and kissed her again, relishing in the sweet taste of her tongue as it pressed against his. Not once did he close his eyes, wanting to see the serene look on her face as she got caught up in these moments of theirs. It was no wonder the words that next fell from his mouth flowed so naturally.

"I love you."

Deryn's lips froze. She slowly opened her eyes, eyelashes fluttering as she gazed back at him, looking both horrified and delighted at the same time. The mixture of emotions was a bit much for her and she ended up bursting into tears.

"Oh, shit. Deryn, no, I'm sorry," said Xander, trying to wipe the tears from her eyes. "I don't know where that came from. Don't be upset."

"I-I'm not," she said while shaking her head profusely. "Are you taking it back? Please don't take it back."

Xander smiled and kissed her cheek. "Relax. I'm not taking it back. I meant what I said."

Deryn nodded, tears still falling from her wide eyes as she leaned forward and pressed her forehead against his. "Xander, I ... I'm not ..."

"Ready," he finished. "I know. I wasn't expecting you to say it back."

Deryn sobbed, her hands running up his chest and clinging to his sweater. She hadn't told him about Neo and Odette, or how she'd been offered a way out. But the closer she got to him, the more she dreaded leaving. She loved him. She knew she did. But saying it made it too real and, as soon as those words escaped her lips, she knew that leaving him behind would no longer be an option.

After cleaning themselves off, Xander and Deryn walked out to the front of their apartment hand-in-hand.

"You know, you two really need to remember to put up a soundproof shield," said Luka, who was reading a mechanical book Deryn had gotten him on the couch. "You have a roommate now, remember?" He looked up at them and winked.

Deryn blushed, but Xander put his arm around her waist

and said, "Heat of the moment, Luka. If it bothers you that much then put one up yourself."

"Doesn't bother me at all," said Luka, looking back down at his book. "I've heard you having sex before. Even been in the same room once or twice. I just thought it might bother *her.*" Without looking up, he nodded towards Deryn.

She blushed brighter and walked over to the kitchen counter with her head held low to pick up her bag. "Are you ready, Luka?"

"Yeah, whatever," he said. "Still don't know why you're dragging me to this."

"Miki and Kemp invited you," she said.

"Only because they wanted to invite Bronson so he would cook, and Quigley's his best friend, Xander was already invited. It would've been rude to skip me."

"I don't know whether that's true or not but, either way, we're not leaving you alone on Christmas."

"Why not?" he asked. "I've spent the majority of my Christmases alone. I'm used to it."

Deryn frowned. "Well, then I would say it's about time you started a new tradition. Now, stand up. We're already running late."

"Running late has nothing to do with me. I was out here waiting at the precise time you instructed. Not my fault the two of you can't control yourselves." He put down his book and stood. "Alright, let's get this over with."

They all put on their coats and shoes, and Deryn put some drops in her eyes to make them blue. She wasn't wearing her wig that day since they weren't going through any gates. It was also snowing so a hood would be completely normal. She found it funny that it snowed in Utopia every now and then. It never snowed outside, not near here, but her father had seen it once on one of his trips exploring the north. He'd promised to take her one day. She secretly hoped he would be able to keep that promise.

Once her eye color was changed, the three of them headed out the door. Bronson and Quigley were already waiting outside of their apartment with bags of food.

"'Bout time," said Quigley. "I thought we were leaving at eleven on the dot."

Deryn blushed again, keeping her eyes on the floor.

"Uh oh, Quigs. I know that blush," said Bronson, grinning widely. "She and Ruby must've had a quickie." He looked at Luka. "Did they forget to put up a shield again?"

"What do you think?" said Luka, already taking out a cigarette and lighting it. He only got in one drag before Bronson was taking it from him.

"I'm out," said Bronson, who obviously had no intention of giving it back.

"Fucking moocher," mumbled Luka, taking out another.

The five of them headed outside, where a hover-car Luka had ordered was already waiting for them. Deryn sat near the window with her back to the driver. She gazed out of it, clutching tightly onto Xander's hand. She hadn't been in a car since the slave trade - even though the van wasn't a hover vehicle - and felt a bit strange about it. While she may not have been chained in the back anymore the ride felt just the same, minus the clammy but strong hand holding onto hers.

"You alright?" asked Xander, rubbing her knee.

Deryn smiled and nodded. She didn't want him to know that she was actually really nervous to see everyone. While she hadn't been particularly close with Del, Kemp or Anan, she still knew them. This was almost like a practice for when she saw her family and Dakota again. They would ask her questions, of course, and she needed to find the best ways to answer them, and without making everyone feel horribly uncomfortable around her.

That was her greatest fear. That they wouldn't act normal once they knew everything she'd gone through, babying her, walking on egg shells.

The car stopped a block from the Shopping District and the five of them got out. Xander went to the driver's window and scanned his wristband to pay the man while Bronson took hold of Deryn's hand, swinging their arms to and fro to try and ease her nerves.

"Come on, cupcake. Show me a smile," he said as he put an arm around her.

Deryn gave her best attempt, but it still wasn't very good. When Xander rejoined them they all walked a block together, then separated so they wouldn't look suspicious walking into a back alley as one big group.

Xander took Deryn along with him, refusing to let her out of his sight. The streets were pretty deserted, considering it was a holiday, but the two of them still stayed in the shadows, keeping their faces hidden under hoods as they walked hand-in-hand, Xander positioning himself protectively in front of her at all times.

When Xander and Deryn arrived at the abandoned store, they sneaked around the back and he asked her to do the knock signaling their arrival. To make sure she remembered it.

Deryn took a deep breath before lifting her fist and doing the complicated knock Xander had taught her. As soon as she was finished, she stepped back and grabbed hold of his arm, hiding behind him as the door creaked open.

"You're late," said Del, smiling widely as she stood aside so the two of them could enter.

Deryn moved her hand down to his and squeezed tightly as they stepped forward. Once the door closed behind them, she took off her hood and faced Del.

"Hello, Del," she said, attempting to smile. The butterflies that seemed to have permanently made a home in her stomach had never felt so large before.

Del had tears in her eyes as she pulled her into a hug. Deryn's body was shaking as she slowly raised her arms and hugged Del back. She really wasn't used to all the hugging, much like Luka. The only people who had touched her like this in years were Xander and Bronson, and she was still adjusting to that.

"Thank the heavens you're alright," said Del into her ear. "Your dad and brother will be so happy when they're finally able to see you again."

"You've seen them?"

"Not in a few months, but yes. The Resistance took me in after I fled my husband. Your brother's the one who fought for me when the majority wanted me out. I owe him my life."

"And my dad? You've seen him, too? He's alive?" asked Deryn, hoping to finally get the answer she'd been seeking for months.

A strange look flashed in Del's eyes. It was almost like sorrow, but something else. Something not quite right. But, still, she looked at Deryn and sincerely said, "Yes, he's alive."

Deryn knew there was more to the story, but she wasn't ready to find out what that was yet. Not until she saw her father again, and witnessed whatever that strange look meant for herself.

"You made sure to prep the others before we arrived, didn't you?" asked Xander.

"Yes, of course" said Del. "They all know not to speak of anyone who crosses their paths today. The safety of the two of you is the most important thing to us."

"The *two* of us?" repeated Xander, cocking an eyebrow.

Del pulled away from Deryn but kept a hold on her, raising her hand to tuck a curl that had fallen loose from Deryn's twist behind her ear. "Well, it's the most important thing to me, and I'm sure everyone else wants to get Deryn back to her family as much as you do." She looked at Xander and smiled. "Are you ready to go upstairs, dear?" she asked while taking Deryn's hands.

Deryn looked over her shoulder at Xander and bit her lip.

"Need a moment?" he asked.

"Can we wait for Bronson and the others?"

Xander smiled and shrugged.

"We can do whatever you want," said Del, releasing her hands. "Would you like it if I went upstairs and brought Ronan, our littlest member, down first? He's definitely easier to handle than the big ones."

Deryn smiled and nodded. "Yes, that would be lovely."

"I'll be right back then."

As soon as she was gone, Xander wrapped his arms around Deryn's waist and pulled her close. "A bit nervous, are we?"

Deryn plopped her forehead against his chest and said, "You have no idea." She sighed and breathed him in. "By the way, I've never asked before. Who does Ronan belong to?"

Xander tensed. "What?"

"You said there's a small child here but you never said if he belonged to someone? Is he an orphan?"

"No."

"Then who -"

A knock on the door interrupted her. It was very similar to the knock created for Xander to get in, but wrong.

"That's not fucking it!" called Luka's voice from the other side. "It's like this."

More knocking.

Wrong again.

"Yeah, that's definitely not it," said Bronson's voice. "Except for the end. Maybe my knock's beginning and your knock's end?"

He tried that. Even more wrong than before.

"No, no, no. You're both idiots," said Quigley's voice. "It's like this."

Halfway through his incorrect knock, Xander shouted, "For fuck's sake!" He let go of Deryn, went over to the door and threw it open. "You're all fucking idiots," he said while pulling them inside.

"Xander, we heard a lot of incoherent knocking," said Del, walking down the stairs with Ronan in her arms. "Is everything alright?"

"Yes, fine," he answered. "I'm just forced to rely on a bunch of fu -" He looked at Ronan and gulped back his foul language. "Not the sharpest knives in the drawer," he finished.

Deryn's eyes lit up when she saw the small child. He looked at her with interest before brightly saying, "Hi! Deryn?"

Deryn smiled. "Yes. Ronan?"

He nodded. "Uhuh. Unky Tally talks about you a lot. He says the two of you went on all sorts of aventures!"

With a chuckle, Deryn said, "I suppose we did." Childhood adventures, at least. One time they traveled the whole three miles to the lake *without* an adult. "But I haven't seen him in a very long time."

"But soon, right?" asked Ronan, squirming so Del would put him down.

"Yes, soon," said Deryn, her eyes following his descent to the floor.

Ronan took her hand and started pulling her towards the stairs. "Did you know Unky Tally and Aunt Neetie are going to get married? When the war is over."

"Talon and Neetles?" said Deryn, perplexed. They'd barely known each other before. Only through her, whenever Talon was able to sneak into Eagle Center to see her during her training days. All of her female friends would crowd around them to flirt with the older boy. She had never understood the appeal, but Nita had sworn he was dreamy.

Deryn looked back at Xander nervously as she and Ronan ascended the stairs. He laughed before briefly introducing Del to Bronson and Quigley. Then he followed her.

Ronan was still chatting animatedly as he walked into the main room on the second floor, dragging Deryn along with him.

Everyone looked up as they entered, Deryn stopping dead in her tracks as she stared around the room nervously. Xander came up behind her and put a hand on the small of her back, keeping her steady.

Miki was out of her seat first, hurrying over to Deryn. "Hi, I'm Miki," she said, holding out her hand. "It's great to finally meet you."

As Deryn shook, Miki tugged her in and hugged her. When she pulled away, Kemp was right there to claim the next hug. Xander couldn't help but find amusement in how uncomfortable Deryn looked. But this was good for her. She wasn't used to people anymore and once she escaped Utopia and found her way back to the Resistance she was going to be surrounded by them. She might as well get used to it now.

As soon as Kemp was finished, Anan was standing right there, staring at her strangely while keeping his hands firmly in his pockets.

"So it's really you? Ruby, he ..." Anan gulped. "He rescued you?"

"I never said I rescued her," said Xander.

Deryn looked back at him and said, "But you did."

"No. I *found* you. You rescued yourself."

"But you found me right when I was in danger of getting recaptured, and you've taken care of me ever since. It counts."

Xander smirked. "Whatever you say."

"Are you going to hug me now, Anan?" asked Deryn, looking back at him.

Anan blushed before opening his arms and leaning in. "I'm really glad you're alright," he said.

"Thank you." When they pulled away, she really looked at him. "God, I can't believe how tall you are. What happened to the little munchkin I used to give noogies to?"

"I'd like to see you try and give me a noogie now," he said with a laugh.

"Don't tempt me."

Pushing everyone aside so he could get off of the staircase he was more or less stuck on, Bronson strutted forward, raised the bags he was carrying and said, "Should we start cooking?"

Deryn smiled and nodded. "Anan, this is Bronson, head chef today. I'm going to be his sous chef."

"Nice to meet you," said Bronson, shaking Anan's hand. Suddenly, his eyes fell upon Ulric standing a few feet away. His jaw dropped. "I know you. Y-you're Ulric Franklin."

Ulric smiled. "I am."

"Holy cannoli, Ruby didn't tell me you were here!"

"Oh, isn't that adorable. Even his wordplay is food related," Miki whispered to Deryn.

"Am I supposed to know who he is?" asked Xander.

"*Yes!*" snapped Bronson. "He's traveled farther than any other Outsider, trying to remap the world. He takes pictures everywhere he goes and put together a few books. I used to have *all* of them." He hurried forward and shook Ulric's hand urgently. "I am *such* a big fan. Would you mind being a line cook so that we could discuss your time in the ancient city of Las Vegas? It has always fascinated me."

Ulric chuckled and said, "Sure. I've been told I'm an excellent chopper."

"Could I be a line cook, too?" asked Miki. "I would love to learn some of your cooking tricks for days we're not graced with your presence."

"Of course," said Bronson, walking towards the kitchen.

"Me too! Me too!" shouted Ronan, grabbing Deryn's hand and pulling her along.

"So did you open your presents yet?" Miki asked Deryn a short while later as she grated cheese.

Deryn smiled. "Yes, I opened them this morning. Thank you for helping Xander pick out some records for me. I haven't listened to all of them yet. Just *Blackbird.*"

"*All* morning!" Xander called from the other side of the room.

"Seriously," said Luka. "I thought those round things had multiple songs on them."

Deryn chuckled. "I suppose that means they're already sick of it."

"Hold out your hand."

Deryn watched as Bronson poured a bit of salt into Ronan's outstretched hand. He lifted him up and held him over a pot on the stove.

"Alright, kid. Toss it in."

Ronan did just that, laughing joyously as Bronson praised him.

Luka walked over and started picking at the grated cheese. Deryn slapped his hand away.

"Awesome job! High five!"

They all watched as Bronson and Ronan smacked hands.

Miki sighed. "He really is adorable, isn't he?"

"Ronan?" said Deryn. "Absolutely."

"Not Ronan. *Bronson.*" She smiled. "Such a shame that

someone so pretty will never go for me or you. Luka has a chance, though."

Luka choked on the cheese he'd stolen, despite Deryn continually slapping his hand away. Miki didn't seem to notice.

"Do you think he's ever been with a woman?"

Deryn blushed.

"He was only with women until he was, like, nineteen or something," said Luka.

Miki looked at him curiously. "Really? That wasn't that long ago, was it?"

Deryn knew the answer, but she smiled and looked at Luka expectantly.

"Six years," he said with a slight blush. He stuffed one last handful of cheese in his mouth and hurried away.

The whole time they cooked, Xander kept a close eye on Deryn from the other side of the room, wanting to make sure she was all right. She kept giving him a reassuring smile but, even so, it was clear that Miki's girl talk was making her uncomfortable.

Once the turkey was in the oven, Ronan wanted to show Deryn and Xander the play area downstairs that Santa Claus had brought for him. Xander had to admit, it was pretty noble of Miki and Kemp to give credit to a fictitious man after all the hard work they had put in. He'd always known stories of Santa Claus but never actually believed in him. Few people did in Utopia. It was just an ancient fable that Outsiders liked to keep alive.

Ronan ended up dragging Luka downstairs too, and they all played in the small, fort-like play area for a while before deciding it was time to head back upstairs.

"Xander, wait," said Deryn, grabbing his hand just as he began to ascend the staircase. "Would you mind if we stayed down here a minute longer?"

"Sure," he said, looking up at Luka and Ronan.

"I'll take the kid up," said Luka, letting Ronan take him up instead.

"Everything alright?" asked Xander as soon as they were

alone.

"Yes," she said with a nod. "It's all just ... a bit overwhelming, I suppose. I only need a minute." She pulled him close. "Just you and me."

Xander smiled. He stroked her cheek while staring into her eyes, which were sea-green again, and only then remembered the ring he'd found in Willow. It would be a nice surprise when they returned home.

Putting a hand on his arm, Deryn leaned up and kissed him, her heart still aflutter from the words he had said to her earlier. That he loved her.

Upstairs, Anan was pacing around the room, his eyes constantly drifting to the staircase. "What's taking them so long?" he asked, whipping his head towards Luka, who was flipping through a picture book Ronan had really wanted him to read.

Luka shrugged. "Dunno. Why do you care?"

"I just ..." Anan bit his lip and thought carefully about his words. "I just don't like Deryn being alone with a Guardian, alright?"

Luka's eyes glanced up from the book and stared hard at Anan. Then he smirked. "So how uneasy would you feel if I went down there, too?"

Anan turned red.

Luka laughed. "You do realize that the two of them are alone all the time, right? I mean, she's only been living in his apartment for nearly four months." He smiled wider. "And now I live there, too."

Bronson chuckled from the kitchen and Quigley looked plenty amused from where he was playing chess with Kemp.

Anan's face quickly went from red to white. "That's where she's staying? With *him*?"

"And me!" Luka said brightly.

Without another word, Anan was darting for the staircase.

Luka followed him with his eyes. Once he was out of view, he looked at Bronson, smiled and said, "That kid is in for quite the reality check."

Not even ten seconds later, Anan was running back upstairs, panicked and out of breath. Either he was in really bad shape, or something had shocked him.

"They're ... they're ..." He gulped. "They're kissing down there! *Kissing*!"

"Yeah, they do that a lot," said Luka, looking back at his book. "Try living with them."

"Yes!" Miki, who was still helping Bronson in the kitchen, suddenly threw her hands up in victory. "I totally called it! Pay up, Kemp!"

"Oh, hell," said Kemp. He reached into his pocket, pulled out a silver coin and tossed it to her.

Anan looked at Miki, who was smiling brightly at her new coin. "You *knew*?"

"I suspected," she said. "Del did, too!"

He moved his ever-growing eyes to Del, who was sitting next to Luka on the couch with Ronan in her lap. She shrugged. "I've known Xander his whole life. I could tell there was a new presence affecting him."

Just then, they all heard a creak and turned their heads to find Xander and Deryn stepping off the stairs. Both looked around curiously.

"What's with the tension?" asked Xander, his eyes immediately falling on Anan, who looked like he was seriously contemplating slaughtering him.

"The noogie recipient went to find you downstairs," said Luka, finally closing the picture book and smiling at his friend. "I don't think he liked what he saw very much."

Still looking at Anan, Xander raised his eyebrows. "Really now? And just what didn't you like about it?"

"You dirty Guardian," spat Anan through gritted teeth. "How dare you ... how *dare* you kiss Deryn!"

Deryn's cheeks flushed.

Luka chuckled. "They've done more than kiss. Perhaps you'd like to hear the story of why we were late."

Anan's fists clenched. He growled as he lunged forward, heading straight for Xander.

Before Anan could strike, Deryn leapt in front of Xander and held out her hands. "Anan, stop!" she shouted. "You have no right to be acting this way!"

"Move out of my way, Deryn," ordered Anan in a strained voice. "He's had this coming for a long time."

"Why?" she asked, putting her hands on her hips.

"Because he's a Guardian!"

"So? It's just a title. Obviously he's defected or he wouldn't be here."

"You don't know tha -"

"Yes. I. Do," she said firmly. "It's because of Xander that I'm standing here now. That you're *all* standing here now. Every last one of you would have been captured if he hadn't warned you about the curfew."

"*And* found a safe place for us to stay," added Del, who had jumped off the couch the moment Anan started going for Xander and was slowly edging towards him.

"How?" he asked, looking over Deryn's shoulder at Xander. "*How* did you know this place was safe? I've always wondered, but Del would never let me ask, so I've just been waiting for the day Guardians seep out of the walls."

Xander gazed back at him and smirked. He put a hand on the small of Deryn's back and moved so he was beside her instead of behind her. She tried to protest but he was adamant. He wouldn't let her protect him like this.

"Four years ago, when I was still trying to earn back the president's trust, he had me snoop through old, private files the government keeps on all Utopian families, trying to find any information on members of the Resistance that might help us capture them. Really tedious work." He cringed at the memory. But he supposed it was better than what he was doing now. Killing people. "While researching, I came across the deed to this place. It belonged to a family that died out with no will and I simply remember seeing that it was a registered residence as well as a business. I didn't feel it was important enough to correct, so I ignored it."

"So that's it?" said Anan skeptically.

Xander shrugged. "Not exactly the malicious story you were hoping for, I know, but that really is it. It was just a coincidence."

Anan didn't look happy, but he at least seemed satisfied with the answer. "And you two?" he said, pointing at Xander and then Deryn. "What are you?"

They looked at each other.

"What? Like, a definition?" asked Xander.

"Yes."

Still staring at each other, they both knitted their brows.

Huh.

They had never really talked about it before. Luka, Bronson and Quigley often referred to Deryn as Xander's girlfriend but, while he never bothered to correct them, he had never called her that himself.

"Xander and I are ... well, I suppose we're involved," said Deryn, her voice quivering.

"Involved?" repeated Anan. "What the hell does that mean?"

"Why must we label it?" asked Xander. "It means what it means. You name it, we've done it."

Deryn blushed again but she didn't scrutinize him. A surefire sign that she wasn't feeling like herself. It was as if all the hard work she had put into getting herself back to normal meant nothing when other people were around.

Anan sneered. "You fucking -"

"Miki, will you please take Ronan into the back room," pleaded Del.

Miki nodded and headed over to collect him from the couch.

"How dare you!" Anan lunged forward, but he wasn't especially aggressive about it. Xander only had to shove his shoulder to send him back a few steps.

Luka was on his feet in a second, Element aimed intently at Anan.

"No weapons!" shouted Del as Miki took Ronan into her arms.

Luka slipped it away but when Anan went for Xander again,

this time with his fist raised, he immediately reacted by charging forward, grabbing Anan and flipping him over his shoulder so he landed hard on his back.

"Wow," said Bronson from the kitchen, leaning on the counter and watching Luka with lust-filled eyes. "That was hot." He caught Miki's gaze just before she ducked into the back room with Ronan and she nodded in agreement.

"Get off me!" screamed Anan as Luka pinned his arms above his head.

"Not until you take a breath, you fucking dick," said Luka venomously.

"Luka, where did you learn to do that?" asked Xander.

"I taught myself," he answered. "You never know when you're going to find yourself weaponless and, if you do, you might want to know more than how to throw a punch."

Xander smirked. "Noted."

"How could you do it, Deryn?" shouted Anan, still struggling beneath Luka even though his efforts were futile. "How could you do this to Dax?"

Staring down at him, Deryn's jaw slackened.

"He's waited for you!" Anan's face was livid as he took several sharp breaths.

Xander expected Deryn to turn away from him, like she always did when put in an uncomfortable situation, but she didn't. Instead she kept his gaze, stepped forward and crouched down beside him.

She sighed. "I haven't seen Dax in over five years. We're not the same people anymore. It's impossible to fight on either side of this war and come out unchanged."

"But *he's* a Guardian," he spat, motioning his head towards Xander. "They're murderers!"

"Oh, and I suppose members of the Resistance are so innocent?" hissed Luka, tightening his grip.

"We only kill who we have to!"

Luka let out a loud, "Ha!" Then he said, "Two years ago there was a member of the Resistance, I can name him if you want?"

Anan said nothing.

Luka smiled. "Everett Jensen. I know you know him. During a raid he killed a guard by the name of Helena Mack."

Xander blinked. He remembered Helena. Sweet girl, never should have been a guard. Much like Lona. He recalled Luka being troubled by her death but never thought too much about it. At one time he'd suspected that maybe they were dating. Luka always denied it but it was after her death that one night stands became a regular habit of his.

"Helena hated being a guard," continued Luka. "*Hated* it, but her family needed her to do it, for the money. In her two years of service she never killed anyone, other than the people the president had us torture for information. But they hardly count. They're already dead, and they know it." Continuing to pin Anan's wrists with one hand, Luka moved his other hand down and gave his face a tap before grabbing his chin. "So tell me something, Anan. Was what Everett did justified? *Or* was it murder?"

Anan spat at him. "She was a guard. She deserved it!"

Unable to control his anger any longer, Luka lifted his hand and swung it hard against Anan's cheek.

"Luka, that's enough. Let him go," ordered Deryn.

"Not until he admits that there are fucking shades of gray! Neither side is good! The Resistance is just the lesser of two evils and we're both mentally fucked in the head! That's war!"

Deryn looked down at Anan, but he showed no signs of budging on this. She sighed. "Please, Luka."

Luka looked into her pleading eyes and huffed. "Only because this is your fucking holiday." He let go of Anan and stood. "Don't ruin this for her," he said, giving him a light kick. He returned to the couch and sank into it.

"Best Christmas *ever*," Kemp whispered to Ulric. Both had moved incredibly close to the action and were watching with a fixed fascination.

"Reminds me a lot of my house. Right, Quigs?" Bronson looked back at his friend, who was still sitting beside the chess board.

"Unfortunately, yes," said Quigley, finally standing. "Which is why I always dragged you over to *my* house."

Deryn held out her hand to help Anan to his feet but he refused it, choosing to get up on his own. "What's happened to you?" he asked. "You never would've associated with the likes of *them* before."

Deryn narrowed her eyes. "Stop talking about them like that. Xander and Luka have both done a lot for me."

"Yes, I'm sure *he* has," he said with disdain as he motioned his head towards Xander. "Twisted your mind so you actually believe you have feelings for him."

"What was that?" Xander's fists clenched as he stepped forward.

"You heard me," spat Anan. "A girl like Deryn would never go for a sociopath like you if her mind hadn't been seriously fucked with."

Deryn's jaw dropped, her eyes filling with tears as that feeling of insanity washed over her.

"You little fucking -"

"Stop right there," said Bronson, running forward and stepping between them. "Ruby, take Deryn downstairs."

"Just as soon as I deal with this piece of -"

"No, now," ordered Bronson, glancing at Deryn.

Xander looked and saw that she had burst into tears. He grabbed her hand and pulled her away, putting his arm around her shoulders as he led her carefully down the stairs.

As soon as they were gone, Bronson turned to Anan and crossed his arms. "Listen to me, you little shit. Believe it or not, Deryn was actually excited to come here today. It's important to her and I won't have you ruining it."

"Piss off!"

Bronson glared at him. "Do you seriously not know what she's been through? Do you not care?"

Anan went white and quickly cast his eyes to the floor.

"Let me spell it out for you. She was raped. She was tortured. She had to slit a man's throat just to escape and not a day goes by that I don't see her eyes glaze over as she gets sucked back inside those memories. Yet somehow, in this twisted world, she's managed to find a bit of happiness. With Xander. And you will *not* take that away from her. Not on Christmas."

"But ... it's Xander Ruby," said Anan, finally looking up at him. "I have a hard time believing that, after all this time, he suddenly feels remorse."

"What do you mean 'after all of this time'?" asked Bronson. "He has *always* felt remorse."

"I doubt -"

"Quigley and I are Outsiders," admitted Bronson glancing sideways at Luka, who was watching him closely. He had neglected to mention that to him.

"You are?" asked Anan.

Bronson nodded. "We met Ruby just under three years ago. He recognized our forged information in a second and instead of turning us in he helped us. Got us some legit forgeries, gave us a apartment in his building. And he's continued to help us. For *three* years."

"I don't understand," said Anan. "If you're Outsiders then why are you here? Why are you living in Utopia?"

Bronson looked at Quigley, who frowned and said, "My sister. She didn't like it outside and moved back before the war started. But her Outsider roots were no secret, so we came to find her."

"And did you?" asked Luka, who had never heard any of this before.

Quigley quickly turned away.

"We did," said Bronson. "She was hiding underground with some tunnelers, but ... well, we lost her about a year ago. Her group was discovered. Some escaped but most were killed or captured. We still don't know her fate."

"And does Ruby know this?" asked Anan.

"Of course he does," said Bronson. "He's tried to help us find her, but he doesn't know what she looks like and we don't have a photo. All of our belongings were burned years ago with our village. We've described her to him but, apparently, a million slaves fit her description."

"She was pretty," Quigley said weakly from across the room. "If she was captured then she's probably going through the same shit as Deryn." He paused. "I almost hope she's dead."

Bronson took a deep breath. "The point is that perhaps you should ease up on Ruby a bit. He's done a lot of bad. He *still* does a lot of bad, but he's also desperately seeking redemption. And he cares a great deal for Deryn."

"He loves her," said Luka. When everyone stared at him, he shrugged. "Why do you all look so surprised? Guardians are capable of love, you know?"

"Anan, perhaps you should go downstairs and apologize," said Del, stepping forward and putting a hand on his shoulder.

"I don't want to," he said under his breath.

"Come on, An," said Kemp. "It's a holiday and we all want to have a good time. This is the closest any of us have gotten to a real Christmas since the war began."

A pause.

"If you don't apologize then they'll probably leave and take the food with them," said Kemp, looking down at his stomach. "And I really want to taste that turkey. I don't know where turkeys run wild outside but they certainly aren't around here."

"More than likely extinct, since I've yet to see one on my travels," said Ulric.

Bronson smirked. "I suppose I should get back to the kitchen then."

"I'll get Miki and have her put on her Christmas record. Ulric got her record player working last night." Kemp smiled as he ran towards the back room.

"Go, Anan," said Del, giving him a small shove.

He groaned and headed downstairs.

On the ground floor, Xander was leaning against an old counter in the main room of the former store while Deryn sat between his legs, her back pressed against his chest.

"You alright?" he asked, kissing her temple.

Deryn smiled softly. "Yes. I was already aware that reactions like this are unavoidable when it comes to you and me."

Xander burrowed his face into her hair, giving it a whiff. "You stood up for me."

"Of course I did. You've been wonderful to me, Xander. Don't let someone like Anan make you doubt yourself."

He smiled and kissed her temple again. "So we're *involved*, are we?"

Deryn turned her head slightly so she could look at him. "What would *you* call it?"

"I don't know," he said. "I suppose I never really thought to define it."

"Well, maybe it's time we did."

Xander put his head on her shoulder as he began to seriously think about this. Then it hit him. His head shot up as his stared straight in front of him, eyes widening. "Holy fuck. I'm in a relationship."

Deryn raised her eyebrows. "Are you?"

He nodded. "It seems that I am."

She smiled and kissed his cheek. "I might be flattered if you didn't sound so unsure about it."

"Not unsure," he said. "Just surprised." He smiled back at her and kissed her lips.

"One might think you'd have figured that out before you told me you loved me," she said, kissing him again.

Just as they began to melt into each other, someone cleared their throat. They both turned to see Anan standing there but looking a good ninety degrees in the other direction.

"Something we can help you with?" asked Xander.

Anan shrugged, still keeping his eyes focused elsewhere. "No. Just ... sorry," he said with a sigh.

Xander raised his eyebrows. "And just which one of us are you apologizing to?"

"Both," said Anan, finally glancing in their direction. "I don't think I'll ever like you, Ruby, but I get the whole 'gray' thing Voclain was talking about. And you've helped us. A lot."

"I don't need the apology," said Xander, glancing towards Deryn.

"I was getting to that." Anan took a deep breath. "Deryn, I

..." His eyes grew very wet, immediately spilling over. "I'm really glad you're here, alright? And I'm sorry we weren't able to get you out sooner. I've gone on several of the rescue missions Talon and Dax had for you. We tried. We really did and -"

"Anan, I know," said Deryn, using Xander's knees to help push her to her feet. She walked over to him and put a comforting hand on the crying boy's shoulder. "You all did your best, but the point of the slave trade was so that none of us were ever in one place for too long, especially me. If there were rumors about the Resistance looking for me then they moved me early. They made it impossible."

Anan nodded and used his sleeve to wipe away his tears. "I'm just really glad you're safe. And ..." He gulped. "And happy."

Deryn smiled. "I am happy."

Once that was settled, the three of them headed back upstairs. Now that everything was out in the open, Deryn stayed relatively close to Xander for the remainder of the day. Even though it had all been sorted out, he could still tell that she wasn't entirely comfortable.

After dinner, Deryn gave them all the small presents she'd picked out for them. Xander had found out about her little trip to the Black Market the same day she had gone. She had never been very good at keeping secrets. He had given Luka a good punch after but, of course, Deryn knew exactly what to do to calm him down and used that to her advantage.

They knew it was time to leave when Ronan couldn't keep his eyes open any longer. He dozed on the couch, eventually reaching his tired arms in the air. "Mommy, bed please."

There was a slight pause as no one moved. Deryn looked at Miki first, realizing very quickly that with her tan skin and dark eyes, there was no way she could be this fair child's mother. At least, not biologically.

And then, after a long moment, Del stood and picked him up. Without a word, she carried Ronan to the back room.

The silence continued while she was gone, everyone sipping on their wine. It was funny how he hadn't called her mommy all night, until he was half-asleep.

When Del came back, she sat in the same seat and didn't say a word.

"Who's the father?" asked Luka after the continued silence started to get to him.

"I think that's obvious," said Deryn quietly. "Ronan looks about four and Del disappeared five years ago." Not to mention the familial green eyes, more muted among the Saevuses than the Leons but the color was just the same. She now wondered how she hadn't realized it earlier.

"Well, *maybe* she disappeared because she had an affair. I don't know," said Luka. "But it's obvious you asked the kid to be quiet about it all night for my benefit. I'm sure Xander already knows and who cares if three Outsiders know."

Xander rolled his eyes. "Don't jump to conclusions. She didn't want me telling anyone."

"I didn't have an affair," said Del, picking up her wine with her good hand and finishing the glass. "Collin and I had been trying to have another child for years. He was determined to have a son, an heir. But it never happened. And then, one day, it did. I found out right after my husband declared war on the Outsiders and I ..." She paused and took a breath. "I didn't tell him. I knew I had to leave, before he ruined my new child the same way he's ruined Elvira, making her into someone who could kill my best friend." She looked at Xander and gulped. "Penelope had been like a second mother to Elvie, and she murdered her in cold blood."

"So when you left, is that when he did that to you?" asked Luka, pointing at her metal hand.

"Luka!" snapped Xander.

"It's fine, Xander," said Del. "Luka is on our side now, there should be no secrets." She paused and looked down at her robotic right hand. "No, Collin didn't do this to me. Elvira did." A tear ran down her cheek. "When I left, he sent her after me. To kill me. But she couldn't do it. She still had a piece of the sweet little girl I once knew inside of her back then, so she let me go, only taking my hand with his family ring still on its finger to prove to Collin that I was really dead." Wiping her tears with her good hand, Del took a deep breath. "She doesn't even know she has a little brother, and I really hope she never finds out."

"Then why are you here?" demanded Luka. "In Utopia. With Ronan."

"Because no one is looking for a ghost," she answered. "At most, people just think I look a bit like the late Mrs. Saevus. Before we got locked in here, we had eyes on Elvira at all times. That was Ulric's job. She's the only one who might ever recognize me, and Ronan came because he wanted to. He doesn't like the Resistance's base and he wants my job someday. I know that seems ridiculous coming from a four-year-old, but he's adamant."

"That's not ridiculous," said Deryn. "For as long as I can remember, I wanted to follow in my dad's footsteps and become an explorer. I hated being tied down to one place."

"Then you and Ronan are kindred spirits," said Del. She sighed. "This was the first time I brought him with me. It was a foolish choice and every day I wish I could take it back."

"You and Ronan will both be fine," Xander assured her. "Everyone's already agreed. The two of you will be the first ones out. Once I find a way."

"No. The six of us go together or not at all," insisted Del.

Deryn's mind suddenly drifted back to Neo and Odette, who she finally had a purpose for. She needed to find a way back to the Black Market. To tell them about the six people trapped here that needed a way out far more than she did. And, hopefully, she could work out some sort of deal on the prices, because there definitely wasn't enough money in Xander's sock drawer for all of them.

CHAPTER THIRTEEN

"**D**eryn, what's taking so long?" asked Xander as she moved around in the bathroom. "Considering you said you had to give me my present at nighttime and *alone*, I already have a pretty good idea of what it is."

He grinned in anticipation.

Then Deryn walked out wearing nothing but a green negligee. She leaned against the doorframe.

"Fuck ..." he said, his eyes slowly trailing up her, taking it all in. And then he noticed what she had in her hand. "Is that a cupcake?"

Deryn grinned. She dipped her finger in the chocolate frosting and licked it off.

Xander laughed. "Deryn, stop acting like you're nice or something. It's *creeping* me out."

"What? Me being nice is creeping you out?" said Deryn, walking over seductively. She crawled onto the bed, slowly moving towards him until she was close enough to rub some frosting on his neck and lick it off.

Xander shuddered. "Fuck, you're good at this."

"I learned from the best," she said, putting some frosting on her finger and holding it out to him.

As he was sucking on her digit, he noticed that she had mistletoe pinned in her hair. *Damn.* That was hot. "Is this homemade?" he asked, taking the cupcake from her and examining it carefully.

"It is," she said. "You can shove it in your mouth if you

want. I have extras."

Xander smirked. He peeled off the wrapper and stuffed the whole thing in his mouth. Deryn laughed and pressed her palms against his chipmunk cheeks.

While he chewed, she went to the bathroom and came back with a plate full of cupcakes.

By the end of the night, the entire bed was covered with cake and frosting, but Xander and Deryn were licked clean.

The mistletoe had fallen out of her hair at one point, and Xander was currently holding it above their heads, forcing her to lean her exhausted head up from his chest and kiss him. Well, maybe not *forcing*. At this point it was safe to say that Deryn was more than willing.

While keeping their kiss going strong, Deryn slowly reached up and tore the mistletoe out of Xander's hand.

"Hey!" he shouted, pulling away from her lips. "What'd you do that for?"

Deryn shrugged and put the mistletoe on the nightstand. Resting her chin on her hands, she smiled as she gazed at him.

Xander stroked her cheek. While staring into her sea-green eyes, he suddenly remembered. "Oh! I have something for you."

"Another gift?"

"Sort of." He rolled off the bed, walked over to his rucksack and dug through it until he located what he was looking for. "I found it in Willow." He walked back to her and held out the ring.

Deryn looked at it, blinking several times before taking it from him. The band was gold and shaped like a lion with a green stone in its center. "It's beautiful."

"It's the same color as your eyes. And, you know, Leon, lion."

Deryn smiled. "Really?" she said. "It's the exact same color?" She held it up so he could compare.

"Pretty damn close," he said, leaning down and kissing her.

Just then, his stomach grumbled. Xander looked down at it and frowned. He supposed they'd burned off all the calories from the cupcakes. "Hot chocolate?" he asked.

Deryn smiled. "Sounds perfect."

Xander gave her one more kiss before heading for the kitchen. He was a little surprised to see that the balcony door was open. Bronson and Luka were smoking and chatting out there. It was a bit odd, considering it was well after midnight and Bronson would be unable to go back to his own apartment. Then Bronson leaned in and kissed Luka, the two of them quickly melting into each other.

Xander's eyes widened. *Shit.*

He turned away and hurried back into his bedroom. When he got there, Deryn was staring at the ring and frowning. She looked up at him.

"No hot chocolate?" she asked.

Xander shook his head. "Definitely not." There was no way in hell he was going back out there.

"That's fine," she said, holding out her arms so he could come into them.

Xander did just that. Then he touched the ring in her hand and asked, "What's wrong?"

"Nothing," she answered too quickly.

"You're lying."

Deryn sighed. "It's just ..." She took the ring and slipped it on. "This is the only finger it fits on." She held up her left hand to show that it was on her ring finger.

Xander gulped. "Oh. It doesn't fit on the other hand?"

She shook her head. "No. That's my dominant hand so it's a bit larger. The ring won't even go past my knuckle."

"But it fits perfectly here," he said, reaching out and fiddling with it. He was right. Perfect fit.

She frowned again and took it off.

"Deryn, I ... I don't want to marry anyone."

"I know," she said. "I'm not asking you to -"

"I know," he interrupted. "But it's just ... this fucking war. I don't think marriage is fair to people."

Deryn turned and looked at him with hopeful eyes. "So you're not against it completely?"

He shook his head. "Of course I believe in marriage. Not arranged marriage, but when it's out of love I'm not against it."

She drew her eyes back to the ring.

Xander pulled her body against his and turned her head so she was forced to look at him. "Deryn, if I ..." He gulped. "If I ever married anyone it would be you."

Her breath hitched. "Really?"

He smiled and kissed her. "Obviously. I told you I loved you earlier and I meant it. You're *it*. I know you are."

She smiled back, her eyes brightening.

Reaching behind her, Xander opened the drawer on his nightstand and pulled out a necklace. A locket, to be precise.

"This was my mother's," he said, undoing the clasp. "She had two necklaces she wore regularly. This one and one with a flower pendant that my father has."

He took the locket off the chain. Then he grabbed the ring from Deryn's hand and slipped it on before clasping it around her neck.

"You're giving me your mother's chain?" she asked, her eyes wide in disbelief.

Xander smirked. "It's just a chain. The locket is my memory. This is yours now."

She looked down at the ring dangling from her neck and twirled it between her fingers.

"Consider that a promise," he said.

"A promise?"

He nodded. "That if this war ever ends, and we both make it out alive, then I'm putting that ring on your finger. And then everyone will know that you're mine."

Deryn reached up and stroked her thumb across his cheek. She wished everyone could know now. That she was Xander's and he was hers.

Her heart grew heavy as she realized the day he spoke of might never come. There was still the chance that only one of them, possibly neither, would survive this. Or that President Saevus would win. If that ever happened she could not die, could not lose Xander forever without telling him how she felt.

"I love you," she said.

Xander's mouth fell open, his golden eyes dancing as he gazed back at her. "You're not just saying that because I said it?"

Deryn smiled and shook her head. "It's just how I feel. I love you, Xander."

Not wanting her to see his eyes tear, Xander put a hand behind Deryn's head and pulled her in for a passionate kiss. "I love you, Deryn," he said between parts of their lips.

They both laughed softly as they fell back on the bed, once again getting lost in each other for hours that just never seemed long enough.

But Xander and Deryn were not fools. They knew from the beginning that this could never end well. And now that love was involved ... well, that just made things even more complicated.

CHAPTER FOURTEEN

Bronson yipped as Luka grabbed him by the arm and flipped him onto the floor. Even though Luka was a good three inches shorter than him and quite a bit leaner, he still did this with ease.

Luka stared down at him and flashed that cute grin of his. "Hey, you two were right," he said, glancing over his shoulder at Xander and Deryn. "It *is* fun to use him as a test dummy."

Xander grunted and looked elsewhere.

Luka's face scrunched in curiosity. "What's wrong with you?"

"Can you show me now?" asked Deryn, stepping forward and holding out a hand to help Bronson off the floor, doing her best to change the subject. Xander had told her about what he had seen on the balcony when they'd woken up that morning. Well ... when they'd woken up that *afternoon*. It had been a late night.

Xander wasn't exactly upset about Bronson and Luka kissing, but he was confused. Luka had always really liked women. And he meant *really* liked them. A lot.

Deryn tried to explain that maybe Luka wasn't gay - Bronson still insisted that he wasn't - and that he was just attracted to the person. Bronson was great, even Xander couldn't say anything bad about him.

Of course, Deryn had insisted that Xander keep his mouth shut about this. If Luka wanted him to know then he would tell him. And considering how confused Xander felt about the whole situation, it was irrefutable that Luka was feeling that same confusion hundredfold.

At least Xander found slight relief when they'd left their bedroom and found Bronson sleeping on the couch. His excuse was that he and Luka got caught up talking about the whole him being an Outsider thing, which he'd apparently confessed to calm Anan down. And Luka had wanted to know more about Quigley's sister to see if he could help. It probably wasn't a lie, he just happened to leave out the part where they'd kissed pretty heavily.

When Luka put his hands on Deryn to show her the movements she needed to take, Xander suddenly became very alert. Feeling Bronson watching him, he turned and met his gaze.

Bronson rolled his eyes. He'd always felt that Xander's jealousy was ridiculous since Deryn was clearly smitten.

"Bronson, can I try now?" asked Deryn.

"Why can't you try on Ruby?"

Deryn looked at Xander and smiled.

"Fuck no," he said.

"Why not?" she asked with a pout.

"Other than the obvious?"

She nodded.

"Bronson's bigger than me," he said. "If you can't flip him then I'll let you try on me."

She raised her eyebrows. "Really?"

Xander smirked. "Well, only if we're naked."

Deryn rolled her eyes. "Looks like it's you and me, Bronson." She got into position. "Ready?"

Bronson grunted before mumbling, "Whatever."

Deryn attempted the moves Luka had shown her. While she was able to get Bronson off the floor, she ended up doing more of a half-flip, where he rolled around strangely on her back while she wobbled from foot to foot. When he finally fell she fell with him, missing the spot where Luka had laid down several pillows for them to practice on by a good two feet.

Xander and Luka were laughing hysterically from the sidelines. Deryn looked up at them and grimaced.

"It's not funny!"

"It was pretty funny," said Luka.

Deryn got back on her feet and said, "Xander, I'm going to need to try on you."

"Fuck. No."

"But I need to try with someone smaller first just to get the feel for it, and Luka's instructing me."

"Did I not just say fuck no?"

"Xander, stop being difficult!" she yelled, crossing her arms and blowing a strand of loose hair out of her face.

"I already told you I would be more than willing if -"

"We're not getting naked! Now, get in position."

"Hey guys, what's going on?" asked Quigley, who was walking down the stairs.

Xander turned and gave him a onceover. He was about the same height as Xander, maybe an inch taller, but fairly thin. Probably around the same weight.

Xander smirked. "Ah, Quigley. Perfect timing."

~

Xander leaned back in his chair at the president's table with his arms crossed. He didn't like the way Barath Voclain was watching his son. With his peripherals, he could see Luka leaning forward in his new seat and staring intently at his fidgety hands, definitely aware of his father's watchful eye.

Noticing Xander staring at him, Barath moved his head slightly towards him and scowled. Xander just smiled.

"That's all we have on the agenda for this evening," said Elvira as she closed the hologram on her computer and glanced at her father.

"Very well," said President Saevus. "Is there anything else anyone would like to add?"

"Mr. President," said Mathis Fender, raising his hand. Saevus nodded. "I was just wondering why no further attempts have been made to look for my son. It's been over three months now and -"

"Your son is hardly worth our time," Saevus said coldly.

Mathis's face flushed. "But, sir -"

"You've always been of great assistance to me, Mathis, but Dougal holds little value here. He was a dreadful imbecile -"

Xander's mouth twitched upward.

"- and I have been informed on more than one occasion that he was nothing but a burden on missions. Perhaps his disappearance was a blessing in disguise"

"Here, here!" shouted Xander.

Luka glanced at him and rolled his eyes. *Damn*, that Deryn habit was spreading rapidly.

"A perfect example," said President Saevus, motioning a hand towards Xander. "While some of my oldest followers' children prevail by my side, proving their worth to be far greater than their predecessors -"

Atticus's face remained firm but his head sank slightly.

"- others simply do not live up to expectations." His desolate eyes drifted down the table to Lona, whose fear was far more evident than Atticus's as she cowered in her seat. She'd recently been called upon to do a bit of torturing for the president. It hadn't gone well.

"She's young, sir," said Xander. After the promise he'd made to her, he couldn't help but feel the need to be somewhat protective, especially when she was being called out in front of everyone. "Give her time."

"Perhaps you'll be kind enough to take Lona on a real mission once the New Year is upon us," said Saevus, moving his desolate eyes to Xander.

"Certainly, Mr. President." He looked at Lona and smirked. "I would be happy to break her in."

Lona gave him a small smile. She, of course, knew his implications were a joke, but her father didn't, which became very clear when he stood up from his seat and shouted, "You most certainly will *not!*"

Xander smiled innocently. "But the president said -"

"No! You will not be ruining my daughter before she finds a *proper* man to marry! Do you hear me, Xander?" Arron turned redder with every word he spoke.

"Dad, he was joking," said Lona, flushing from

embarrassment. "Surely Xander's been at this table long enough for you to recognize when he's trying to get a rise out of someone."

"And it seems I've succeeded once again," said Xander. "Mr. President, are we finished?"

Mathis raised his hand again. "But what about my -"

"Yes, we're finished," said President Saevus. "Arron, I will need you to stay behind. I do not care for outbursts at my table, and you'll be punished appropriately."

Arron went white as he slowly sank back into his chair.

"Everyone else is dismissed."

Xander stood and headed for the exit with Luka at his heels.

"Luka, wait!"

Luka groaned. Xander glanced over his shoulder to see Barath running after them. He stopped walking, forcing Luka to do the same.

"What are you doing?" Luka muttered under his breath.

"Curiosity," said Xander with a shrug.

"Xander, if you wouldn't mind, I'd like to speak to my son *alone*," said Barath, looking at Xander with disdain.

"I do mind, actually."

Luka groaned again and turned around. "What do you want, Father?"

"A chance to explain."

Xander huffed. "Your son is no fool, Barath. Even without the so-called *empty* threat you made to Veli, you still tried to have him exposed as a traitor."

"I wasn't trying to expose him!" shouted Barath. "I know Luka would never betray the president. But *you*. You I don't trust, Xander. And the way the two of you carry on together, I simply thought he might know something to expose you."

"If he knew something to expose me, then he'd undoubtedly be a traitor himself, wouldn't he?"

"Not if he was unaware of it!" shouted Barath. "You can't be trusted. I know you can't, and I'm going to prove it." He moved his eyes back to Luka. "And when I do, Luka, you *will* be coming home."

Luka stared firmly at his father and said, "I won't," his voice as cold as ice.

He turned and headed for the door, this time with Xander on *his* heels.

Wyatt was standing there waiting when they arrived. "Where're you two headed?" he asked.

"Nowhere," said Luka, his mind clearly still on his father.

"Wanna go to the Pit? Feels like it's been ages."

"I'm busy," said Xander, who really did have a night planned with Deryn.

"I'll go," said Luka, who quite obviously needed a drink.

"Would you mind if I came along?"

They all turned to see Lona walking towards them.

"What are you still doing here?" asked Xander.

"The president wanted me to stay behind and help punish my father." She smiled. "It was easier than I expected."

"S'alright with me," said Wyatt, looking at Luka.

He shrugged. "Whatever. Just don't get in my way when I get piss ass drunk."

"As long as you don't get in mine," she said.

Xander walked with all of them through the gate to Middle City before mounting his hover-bike and heading home.

"Deryn!" he called as soon as he got there.

The door to their bedroom opened and she walked out, smiling as the small black dress she wore fluttered with each step. Bronson had purchased it for her that afternoon, and it did not disappoint. Her hair was in ringlets and there were subtle signs of blush and mascara on her face, but nothing too extravagant. She wore simple black flats, since they had all agreed that heels were not a good idea for her. But, of course, the best detail about her was the chain she wore around her neck with the gold ring dangling from it.

"Wow," said Xander, wrapping his arms around her waist as she reached him and giving her a kiss. "You look beautiful."

"So do you," she said, grinning madly and kissing him again.

"Just let me change and then we can go," he said, but he made no attempt to move. Her lips tasted positively divine right now.

Eventually, she pulled away and pushed him towards the bedroom, giving his ass a little tap to hurry him along.

"Don't tease me," said Xander with a wink.

When he got to their room, he immediately began looking for his gray sweater, which he knew was Deryn's favorite. But it wasn't there.

"Deryn, do you know where my sweater is?" he asked, poking his head back into the living room.

"Which one?"

"The gray one."

"Oh," she said. "No, I haven't seen it."

An obvious lie, but one he would worry about later.

Xander ended up grabbing a light-blue sweater instead and pulling it on. After changing into a clean pair of black slacks, he headed back to the front room, where Deryn was already wearing her coat and holding his for him. He put it on, took her hand and led her out the front door. Then they went out of the building.

Xander hadn't bothered to put his bike away, knowing very well that they would be using it. Luka's chip was now permanently installed. The two of them put on their helmets and rode off into the night.

It wasn't long before they were parking his bike in the alley behind the restaurant where Bronson and Quigley worked. They knocked on the back door and waited for an answer.

"Ah, there you are!" exclaimed Bronson, throwing open the door. He ushered them into the busy kitchen and fixed Deryn's hood to cover her eyes, which she hadn't bothered to change the color of that evening. "Quigs!"

Quigley appeared pretty much out of nowhere and said, "This way."

Xander and Deryn followed him out of the kitchen and through a door that didn't head out to the main part of the restaurant. After leading them down a short hallway, he opened another door and let them go in first. It was a private dining room, lit up with candles while soft music played. The small table was set for two with silver plates and goblets, and was covered with a lacy white tablecloth. Deryn smiled as the candlelight hit the dark walls, making small golden specks twinkle on them like stars.

"Beautiful," she said as Xander removed her coat for her. He then removed his and handed them both off to Quigley.

"Hubba, hubba, Deryn," said Quigley, finally getting a good look at her in the black dress. "You sure you want to keep wasting your time with this jerk? Because I'm totally and completely available -"

"Enough, Quigley," said Xander, shoving him towards the door. "I'm not paying the ridiculous price for this room to have you bothering us all night."

"But I'm your server!"

"Then serve wine."

Quigley smiled. "Yessir!" He saluted and left.

When Xander turned back around, Deryn was pulling out her chair. He hurried over and did it for her. "Not even going to try and let me be a gentleman tonight?" he asked, giving her shoulder a kiss as he helped her scoot in.

"To be perfectly honest, I don't really know what that means. I already told you I've never been on a real date before."

"Which is precisely why we're here," he said, taking the seat across from her. He reached under the table and caressed her knee.

"Is *that* gentlemanly?" she asked, giving him a sly smile.

"Knee is fine," he said. "But if I move slightly upward ..." His hand drifted up her thigh.

Deryn smacked it away. "Not here, Xander!"

He laughed and beckoned her with his finger. She leaned across the table and met him in the middle for a kiss.

The door opened. They both looked to see Quigley enter with a bottle of wine. He grinned. "Already at it?"

Other than Quigley's few interruptions, Xander and Deryn had a fairly private and romantic evening. Bronson had already chosen the whole menu for them. There were seven courses, including both a cheese plate and something sweet for dessert.

Deryn liked the cake he'd made so much that she asked if she could bring several slices home with them.

When the meal was finished, Quigley left Xander and Deryn completely alone, the two of them laughing and kissing as they finished off the last of their bottle of wine.

At one point, Xander stood and held his hand out to her. Unsure of what he was up to, Deryn went along with it, giggling as he pulled her into his arms in one swift movement, holding her close and swaying to the music.

Deryn wrapped her arms around his shoulders and nuzzled her head against his chest. "You certainly know how to make a girl swoon."

"Yes, my mother taught me at a very young age how to treat a lady."

"She taught you well," said Deryn, tightening her grip on him. "Thank you, Xander. This was perfect."

"Don't mention it," he said, lifting her chin and kissing her.

They stayed like that until Quigley came in to let them know the restaurant was closing.

When they walked back through the kitchen it was pretty much empty, other than a busboy doing dishes. Bronson was already gone.

They hurried home, locked the bike in the garage and headed inside. When they got to their apartment, Deryn immediately noticed Luka's shoes by the front door.

"Oh, Luka's home. Do you think he'd like some cake?" she asked.

Xander shrugged. "Maybe. But he's probably passed out drunk off his ass."

"I'll wake his drunk ass then."

She walked towards his bedroom and opened the door. "Hey, Luka - Ah!" Deryn ran away from the door as quickly as she could and clutched her heart. "Holy shit!"

"What?" Xander hurried over to Luka's room and looked inside.

"Fucking hell, Xander! Th'fuck you doing?" shouted Luka. He was currently throwing a blanket over him and Lona, who he seemed to be in the middle of fornicating.

Xander raised his eyebrows and leaned against the doorframe. "Th'fuck am *I* doing? That's my future wife you currently have your cock in."

"Get out!" he shouted, attempting to throw a pillow, which barely made it two feet off the bed and slightly veered left.

Yes, Luka was definitely drunk. If it wasn't obvious by the dazed look in his eyes, then the sloppy way he threw that pillow ought to be proof enough.

"Carry on," said Xander, pulling the door shut as he left. It seemed Luka wasn't gay. While drunk, anyway.

"What's he doing?" Deryn said angrily while pointing at the closed door.

"I would think by now that you would recognize sex when you saw it."

"But ... but ..."

The front door opened and Bronson walked in.

Deryn gasped, her face instantly flushing.

Bronson kicked off his shoes but didn't walk any further once he saw the look on her face. "Something wrong?" he asked.

Deryn shook her head frantically. "N-no. Why would anything be wrong?" She kept her head low to hide her redness, and walked towards the kitchen to put the cake away.

Bronson watched her curiously before moving his eyes to Xander, asking the same question silently.

Xander shrugged. "Don't mind her. She had a lot of wine."

Bronson still looked suspicious, but he nodded all the same. "Luka around? I need to ask him something."

"N-no," muttered Deryn from the kitchen.

Bronson looked from her to Xander. He cocked an eyebrow.

"He's not back yet. Went out drinking with some other Guardians."

"Mind if I wait?" asked Bronson, pulling out a cigarette as he headed towards the balcony.

"Actually, we're planning on fucking pretty loudly in a

minute here," said Xander coolly. "It might be better if you waited in your own apartment."

"Since when is *that* a problem?" said Bronson with a smirk. "I've heard you fucking before. It's really not -"

Luka's door began to open. Deryn ran across the room in record speed and tried to pull Bronson towards the balcony with her. When he wouldn't budge, she eventually had to give up and go out there by herself. She was lucky Lona had been too distracted to see her earlier, and she wanted to keep that going.

Lona stepped out of Luka's room, carrying her shoes and looking a bit dazed as she rubbed at her obviously aching head. She blushed when she saw Bronson, immediately trying to brush her fingers through her tangled batch of sex hair.

"Oh, hi."

"Hi," he said back without his usual smile.

"Fuck!" shouted Luka, running out from behind her and nearly knocking her over. He used the wall to brace himself as he tried to make a dart for the bathroom, but he only made it about two feet before he toppled over and began vomiting.

"My fucking carpet!" shouted Xander, giving Luka a shove once he was finished.

Luka's eyes remained glazed for a moment as his back hit the wall, but then they began to focus and he noticed the third set of feet in the room. He followed them up and saw Bronson staring down at him. Bronson was biting his cheek and trying hard to hide the disappointment he obviously felt. Luka said nothing, unmoving from his spot on the floor as he continued to gape at the other man.

"Right," said Bronson, looking away and glancing at Lona. "Nice meeting you." He walked off to join Deryn on the balcony.

"I should go," said Lona, looking embarrassed as she headed for the door.

Xander followed her. "Lona Von. What will your father think, his precious daughter being *ruined* like this?"

Lona scoffed. "I was *ruined* quite some time ago. Was that

your girlfriend who walked in on us?"

"It might've been."

"I assume if I asked to meet her -"

"That I would say fuck no? You assume correctly."

"Of course." She lifted her shoes and said, "I accidentally wore these across the carpet. I hope you don't mind."

"Luka just vomited all over it. A little shoe dirt is the least of my worries right now."

Lona nodded and glanced over Xander's shoulder at Luka. "Who is that guy who went out to your balcony?"

"Neighbor."

"He looked upset."

"Not your concern."

She nodded again before putting her hand on the doorknob. "Have a good night, Xander." She opened the door and left.

While Lona was still obviously intoxicated, she was definitely in more control than Luka. Speaking of which ... Xander turned around and found Luka on his hands and knees, shaking as he used his shirt to try and clean up his vomit.

"I'm sorry about the carpet," he mumbled as Xander walked back over.

Xander sighed. "Don't worry about it."

Luka closed his eyes and took a deep breath. "I should go outside." He tried to stand but his legs were too weak.

Xander grabbed his elbow and pulled him to his feet. "No. Get some rest, Luka. We have business to take care of tomorrow, remember?"

"But -"

"*No*," Xander said firmly. He used his grip on Luka to lead him towards his bedroom. "Goodnight."

Luka nodded, looking sadly towards the balcony before stumbling to his bed. Xander shut his door and went outside.

When he got there, Deryn was leaning over the edge, her arm linked with Bronson's as he did the same. Her hood was up and covering her face.

"Everything alright out here?"

"Yes," said Deryn over her shoulder.

Bronson wiped his eyes before turning around and calmly saying, "I should head home."

"Okay," said Deryn, looking at him worriedly before following him inside. Xander took her hand as she passed and followed after. "Do you need anything?"

"No," said Bronson as he slipped into his shoes. "I'm fine. It's just late and I'm tired."

"I know but -"

"I'm *fine*, Deryn. I'll see you tomorrow."

She nodded, the frown never leaving her face as he opened the door and left.

When Deryn and Xander were alone, they both released heavy sighs.

"Do you want to just go to bed?" he asked, aware that the mood of the evening had been somewhat tainted.

Deryn bit her lip, getting lost in that pretty head of hers for a moment before eventually shaking it. "No. We shouldn't let this ruin our evening."

Xander grinned.

"But forget what I said before. You need to talk to Luka about this. Find out what he's really feeling. What he did tonight isn't fair to Bronson and he should know now if Luka doesn't feel the same."

Xander's grin immediately fell. Oh, hell.

CHAPTER FIFTEEN

The following evening Xander and Luka sat on top of a bunch of crates in an alley behind some dirty bar. A small black box currently rested on a higher crate, spurting out the muffled voices of Veli, Soren, Barath, Eamon Graham, and Sewick Blum.

The two of them had been following Veli for the last few hours, and this was the first place of importance he had gone. Shortly after he went inside, Xander had sneaked into the back and paid an attractive barmaid to plant a microphone on him. And now they were playing the waiting game, just hoping that some topic of interest would come up.

"Damn, they're all so fucking boring," said Luka, unable to stifle a yawn. "Promise me that when we're as old as these assholes we won't have such lackluster lives."

"If we ever get that old," said Xander, well aware that the oldest, Barath, only had twenty years on them, and Soren, the youngest, had three.

Luka stiffened. "Why would you say that?"

"Just being realistic."

"*I'm telling you, whoever that piece of shit sent into my house* stole *some of my old Elements!*" said Sewick.

"*You have so many of the damn things, how could you ever know?*" asked Eamon.

"*I know!*" shouted Sewick. "*I know every last fuckin' weapon I 'ave and two of 'em are missing! Older ones! That don't need to be registered to work!*"

"*What would Xander need with unregistered Elements?*" asked Veli.

"*Maybe he wants to kill the assholes who tried to blackmail him,*" said Soren mockingly.

"*Shut it!*"

"*Or maybe he doesn't even have them,*" said Barath.

"*Yeah, tha's what I thought!*" said Sewick. "*Maybe whoever went through just took 'em, so I had our li'l puppet search the Black Market to see if anyone was sellin' 'em.*"

Silence

"*And?*" asked Veli impatiently.

"*And nuttin. They weren' there.*"

"*But there's a good chance Xander had to hire some street scum to fetch the chips for him,*" said Eamon. "*I mean, who does the little shit even know besides Guardians?*"

"*Whores,*" said Sewick. "*Lots 'n lots o' whores.*"

They all laughed. Xander sneered at the box. Those bastards laughing at his expense ...

"Who do you think their puppet is?" asked Luka.

"No fucking idea." But Xander would bet good money their puppet had the last mind control chip, which Veli had somehow convinced the president didn't exist.

"*What about those two neighbors of his?*" asked Barath. "*He and Luka have been seen a lot with them lately. Especially that one who always looks like he's brooding.*"

Xander laughed but Luka immediately tensed at the mention of Bronson, the obvious brooder between him and Quigley.

"Something you want to talk about, Luka?"

Luka took a deep breath and said, "No."

"*Yeah, he goes to the Black Market a lot,*" said Sewick. "*I'll 'ave our puppet keep an eye on 'im.*"

While Xander did feel slight concern for Bronson, it was also a relief that he finally had a legit reason to keep Deryn from sneaking out with him again. He looked over to see Luka shift uncomfortably.

"Seriously, Luka, if you have something you need to fucking get out -"

Luka whipped his head in Xander's direction and narrowed his eyes. "Yes, because when you talk to me so compassionately like that I really want to tell you shit."

"Well ..." He gulped. "You can."

Xander went to Luka in a moment of weakness when he found out Deryn had been raped by his father. He supposed he could do the same.

Luka turned his head back straight and stared blankly at the wall. "I'm not an idiot, Xander. I know what you're getting at." He paused. "Did Deryn tell you?"

Xander creased his brow.

"I knew it! I knew she couldn't keep her mouth shut, even after I took her out of the fucking apartment!"

Xander's interest peaked. "Did she blackmail you?"

"Of course she did! She's *your* girlfriend! Two ends of the same stick."

Xander smiled proudly. "She didn't tell me anything." And he was slightly angry about that. "I saw you and Bronson kissing on my balcony the other night."

Luka's eyes widened.

"Pretty fucking horrifying. I believe my eyes might still be bleeding."

"Funny."

"So ... you like men?"

Luka's face crinkled in disgust. "No."

"Then why would you kiss one?" Xander definitely wouldn't.

"I don't know," said Luka. "But I *don't* like men."

"Are you sure?"

"Even though I was drunk off my ass last night, I'm well aware that I was enjoying myself while fucking Lona."

"But ..."

"No buts! I like women! Simple as that!"

Xander smirked. "But ..."

This was fun, and Luka was turning redder by the second.

"I don't know, alright?" he shouted. "I like being around Bronson! There, I admit it! And I haven't been fucking anyone else lately because of him. I didn't even mean to fuck Lona. I was drunk and feeling sick at the bar, so I went back to your place and I didn't even know she'd followed me till her bike was parked next to mine. She then followed me inside and she wouldn't leave. I knew you were going to be home soon so I ushered her into my fucking room so she wouldn't see Deryn and then she started taking off her fucking clothes. I said no, alright? I said no and I tried to push her away, but then she pulled my pants down and started sucking my fucking dick. So I caved! I fucking caved and now I don't know what I'm supposed to fucking do about it!"

"Well, first, how about you take a *fucking* breath," said Xander, who was trying to process everything he'd just heard.

Luka did just that, taking several quick but deep breaths to try and calm himself.

Once his breathing grew steady again, Xander pursed his lips and said, "Forgive me if I sound like a woman here, but maybe you should just talk to him."

Luka glanced sideways at him. "I don't know if I want to. It would've been much easier to ignore all this confusing shit if he wasn't pursuing me the whole damn time."

"So you're just going to pretend like you never kissed him?" Possibly more. Xander really had no idea and he wasn't about to ask.

Luka shrugged. "Maybe."

"Well *that's* not going to be incredibly awkward for the rest of us."

Luka had just opened his mouth to speak when they heard Veli's voice through the box say, "*About time you got here.*"

"*Sorry,*" said a vaguely familiar voice neither of them could place. "*I got held up.*"

"*Is it ready?*" asked Veli.

There was some shuffling, followed by a loud *clang* as something was put on the table.

"*Excellent,*" said Veli.

"*This'll get that asshole talking.*"

"Am I that asshole?" asked Xander.

"Dunno," said Luka with a shrug. "Probably."

"*And did you bring any news of the Resistance?*"

Xander's eyes widened. "It's the rat."

"Scandalous," said Luka, leaning in closer. "About time something interesting happened."

"*No. My source says they're planning something big but she doesn't have the details yet. All she knows is that it has something to do with Deryn Leon.*"

Everything in Xander's stomach shifted at the mention of Deryn. And this person had called her by name. Not Godfrey's daughter or Talon's sister or toxic bitch or slave.

Who the hell was it?

"I swear I know that voice," said Luka.

"Yeah," said Xander with a light nod. "Me too."

"*And she's still willing to feed you this information?*" asked Veli.

"*The Resistance often lacks communication. She knows I've been trustworthy in the past, so she'll never question me.*"

"*And that's why I like keeping you around,*" said Veli, his smile obvious even without a visual. "*Find out what they're planning and meet me back here in two days.*"

"*Yes, sir.*"

Footsteps.

Xander paused for only a moment, his heart feeling heavy as he thought of a rescue plan for Deryn being ruined. And then feeling heavier as he thought of her leaving. Still, he had to try. He had to help her. To keep her safe.

Xander turned off the small box, put it in his pocket and said, "We're moving."

He jumped off his crate, followed shortly by a skeptical Luka. "What do you plan to do?"

"I don't know," said Xander. "But I'm going to find out who that was."

They both pulled their hoods on as they excited the alley, joining the large group of people smoking pipes outside of the dirty bar.

Xander kept his eyes fixed steadily on the door, waiting for a familiar face to exit.

Then a man came out. His hood was up but something about him just seemed out of place. He walked in their direction and Xander stepped backwards. He grabbed the man's arm as he passed, flinging him into the alley and against the wall. Luka moved in front of them, blocking the view from any passersby.

The man's hood fell slightly back and Xander suddenly found himself looking into the surprised eyes of Chace Moffett.

"Moffett?"

"Ruby!" shouted Chace, reaching for his gun. An Element, to be precise.

Xander grabbed it before Chace had the chance and tossed it aside. He took out a knife and pointed it steadily at his throat. "What are you doing here?"

"I don't know."

Xander raised his eyebrows. "You don't know?"

"Looks to me like you're betraying your friends," said Luka, still holding his position but glancing back at them.

"No, I ..." Chace gazed at Xander, his eyes void and distant.

"Th'fuck is wrong with him?" asked Luka.

When Xander turned his head to look at Luka, Chace took the opportunity to knee him in the groin. Xander flinched and Chace took off running down the alley. Before he got too far Luka charged after him, tackling him to the ground and giving him one hard punch that knocked him out cold.

"Seriously, Luka, where did you learn this warrior shit?" asked Xander, catching up to him.

"I *seriously* just taught myself."

"Do me a favor and teach Deryn more than just that flipping thing, will you?"

"Yeah, sure," said Luka. "But what the hell we gonna do with this shit?" He lifted Chace by the hair.

"Take him home with us," said Xander, giving Chace a kick before reaching down and propping the man's left arm around his shoulders. Luka did the same on his other side. "We'll just pretend he's passed out drunk. And keep your hood up. The last thing we need is to be seen here."

Luka nodded and adjusted his hood. Then they walked back towards the street with Chace in tow. When he started to come to, Luka swung his fist and knocked him out again.

"Act natural," said Xander.

As soon as they stepped out of the alley, Luka became very nervous. In an attempt to 'act natural' he suddenly found himself bursting into song.

> *"Oh Utopia, only trains those*
> *Heroic, loyal and stunning,*
> *While the wine and the whiskey flows,*
> *We flee Eagle without the running,*
> *The other trainees sleep all night,*
> *Playing it safe, boring and true,*
> *But the legacy boys drink till light,*
> *They are much cleverer than you.*
> *Guardians!*
> *Future Guardians!*
> *We are so much better than toxic Outsiders!*
> *Utopia!*
> *Loves its Guardians!*
> *Send them all back and put up dividers!"*

"Luka!"

Luka glanced at Xander. "Hmm?"

"*What* are you singing?"

"It's that song, remember? The one you wrote when we used to sneak out and drink while in training."

"Yes, I remember the song. But *why* are you singing it?"

Luka shrugged. "I dunno. It's the only drinking song I have memorized. Every other one I've ever learned has been while already drunk so I always forget them by morning."

"How about you just don't sing, alright?"

"Oh, fine. You're no fun."

Sans the singing, the two of them stopped onto the corner where the tram would be arriving shortly. Being nothing but deadweight, it was hard to keep a firm grip on Chace and they had to keep adjusting themselves.

While they were waiting, Veli and the others walked out of the bar. Xander and Luka kept their heads low as they walked right by them, heading for the Tashes car. Xander had placed a tracker under it so they would always know where it was headed. But, knowing the hour, he assumed they were heading home before curfew. A part of him still wanted to follow them and see if they were up to anything else, but getting Chace out of there and questioning him was far more important right now.

As Veli climbed into the car, Xander caught sight of a brown bag he was carrying, a ruffled green leaf poking out of it.

A plant.

That must have been what Chace brought them. Now he just needed to figure out what sort of plant it was.

The tram pulled up right as Sewick started looking around. He must have recognized that something was amiss but, before he could place it, Xander and Luka had boarded the tram. Chace woke up once during the trip, but Luka lifted his fist and whacked him so discretely that even Xander almost missed it.

When they finally got back to their apartment, they struggled to carry him up the stairs, Luka taking his legs while Xander walked backwards holding his arms.

Xander opened the door to the apartment when they got to the top. Deryn, Bronson and Quigley were all sitting on the couch. They smiled at first, but then jumped out of their seats the moment they noticed he was carrying someone. Bronson sighed in relief when Luka walked in carrying the other end.

"What happened?" asked Deryn, running over to the body and pulling back the hood so she could get a good look at the person. She gasped. "Chace? Xander, why -"

"We caught him feeding Veli information on the Resistance," said Xander, swinging Chace into a chair. Luka already had electronic binds ready for him. Xander attached one set to his wrists behind the chair's back, then another to his ankles.

"What?" said Deryn in disbelief. She knew something had seemed off when she saw him in the Black Market, but a traitor? "That's impossible. Chace is the most loyal person I know. He would never -"

"Well, he did." Luka went into the kitchen, poured a glass of cold water, and returned to where Chace sat unconscious.

"Shall I?" he asked Xander, who nodded. Luka then tossed the water in Chace's face.

Chace jerked and his eyes popped open. He looked around the apartment frantically. "Where ..." His eyes landed on Xander. He gulped. Then they drifted to Deryn. He blinked several times. "Deryn?"

Deryn sighed and stepped forward. "Yes, Chace. It's me."

"W-what are you doing here?"

"I could ask you the same question."

"I ... I must go! I must report to Veli the moment I learn the location of Deryn Leon!" Chace wriggled around chaotically in his chair. "I must report to him! I must let him know that Xander Ruby is a traitor! *Traitor!*"

Deryn's jaw dropped. "Chace, what's wrong with you?"

"*TRAITOR!*"

"What did you give Veli earlier, Moffett?" asked Xander, leaning in closer.

Chace shut his mouth and sucked in his lips.

"How long have you been working for him? What's he planning?"

"Don't you have any more of those mind control thingies?" asked Bronson from behind him.

"No, I had to hand them all over when I ratted out Veli," said Xander.

At the mention of mind control, Chace's face tensed in a strange manner. He let out a muffled cry, his lips opening slightly as blood poured from his mouth.

Xander grimaced. "What the hell?"

"He's trying to bite off his tongue!" Luka stepped forward and pried Chace's mouth open. He held on firmly while Chace continually tried to bite him. "Someone knock him back out!"

Deryn was the first to act, running to her room and coming out with her Element aimed. She used a stunner on Chace. His body went limp and Luka was able to step away.

"We need to make sure he doesn't bleed out!" said Deryn as she hurried into the kitchen. "Xander, do you have anything to help heal his tongue?"

"I don't know. How bad is the bite?" he asked, looking at Luka.

Luka grunted before pulling back Chace's head and checking. "It's severed a good amount on the left side but it's fixable."

"I have this paste that works sort of like stitches for cuts," said Xander, joining Deryn in the kitchen. "It's in a silver tube."

She searched the cabinet she knew he kept all of his medical supplies in and located the tube. She tossed it to Luka, who grunted again but went to work on applying it.

"Is there anything that will help with the blood loss?" she asked.

Xander scrunched his face in thought. He slowly searched the cabinet.

Meanwhile, Luka had finished reattaching the tongue. He wiped his bloody and slobbery fingers on Chace's clothes, but still felt disgusting. Chace's stunned head hung low as all of him, especially his lips, paled.

"This should work," said Xander, finally locating a small bottle filled with a red liquid. "Not right away, but faster than if he doesn't drink it." He went over to Chace, Deryn at his heels, and lifted the man's head so he could pour the liquid down his throat.

Checking his heartbeat, Deryn sighed in relief. He was okay. "Xander, move him to the couch."

Xander nodded. He undid Chace's binds, and he and Luka carried him over to the couch. They laid him down with his head on a pillow.

Deryn put her favorite blanket over him. She looked sadly at his pale figure and said, "This isn't Chace."

Xander looked at her curiously.

She lifted the unconscious man's right arm and showed them that he was wearing a wristband, even though he was an unregistered Outsider. She checked the slot on its side and popped out a small chip, which looked exactly like several others she'd collected recently. A mind control chip.

Xander took it from her. "Well, I guess that answers the

question of who had the last chip," he said. "It never even crossed my mind that it might be in use."

Luka grunted once more. Without a word, he hurried off to the bathroom to wash the rest of the blood off of his hands.

"So are we stuck up here, then?" asked Quigley.

Xander looked at the clock over the mantle and saw that is was already a quarter past midnight. Curfew must have hit during the whole tongue fiasco.

"Looks like it," he said. "You can take our bed. We're probably going to be up for a while." Xander glanced at Deryn, who was sitting on the edge of the couch with Chace's hand in hers. Her eyes were fixed on his face which, even though a great deal of color had returned to it, still looked pained and sickly. He hadn't been in good health for quite some time.

"Ah, sweet!" said Quigley, jumping up and running into Xander and Deryn's bedroom. There was a big *plop* as he leapt onto the bed. "Dude ... this is *so* comfortable!"

Looking at Bronson, Xander asked, "Aren't you going to join him?"

Bronson smirked. "Nah. I've been banned from sharing a bed with Quigley ever since I accidentally groped him in my sleep a few years back. During our fugitive days when we were lucky to even have one bed."

"It was *not* alright!" shouted Quigley, the door to the bedroom suddenly shutting.

"You can sleep in my bed," said Luka. "I'm not going to sleep, anyway."

Bronson stared at him skeptically. "But what if you change your mind?"

"Then I'll sleep on the floor."

Luka went to his room.

Bronson followed him with his eyes, looking unsure for a moment before glancing at Deryn.

"Could you please, Bronson?" she said, not even having to look up to know his eyes were on her. "I really just need a moment."

Bronson breathed in heavily and said, "Alright," before

following Luka in and shutting the door.

"So is he mad at him?" asked Xander as soon as he was gone.

"No. I think reality just finally set in."

Deryn kept her eyes on Chace and Xander kept his eyes on her.

"Are you okay?" he asked.

She nodded. "How long do you think Veli's had control over him?"

"I don't know. I'd say he's been talking about his contact for at least six months."

Deryn sighed. "And how many times has Veli given information from his 'contact'?"

Xander thought about this. "I think five. But only three of those times did the president follow through."

"And did people ..." She gulped. "... die?"

He knew she meant people in the Resistance. "A few, yes."

"Chace will never forgive himself."

"We could lie to him."

She shook her head. "No. It's better to know the truth."

Xander took a seat on the armchair that was aimed towards Chace's face. He held out his arms and, without looking, Deryn went over and settled in his lap.

For an hour they sat there waiting for Chace to awake.

"I'm going to make some tea," said Deryn as her eyes began to droop.

She stood and went into the kitchen. While she fiddled around in there, Xander leaned forward on his knees, thinking about how great it would be to have a cigarette right then.

He had just started searching his pockets for one when Chace stirred. Xander looked at him right as his eyes opened. Chace blinked several times, bringing the world into focus again. Then he saw Xander.

"Evening, Moffett."

Chace's eyes widened, and then he was screaming. His hands searched for his weapon, but Xander still had it, which he showed Chace in hopes of calming him down. But this only made him scream louder.

"Th'fuck is going on?" shouted Luka, running out of his room with his Element raised.

Becoming even more panicked by the appearance of a second Guardian, Chace spun off of the couch, jumped to his feet and bolted. Reaching the front door, he pulled at the knob, but it was very much locked.

"Chace! Chace, it's alright!" shouted Deryn, hurrying towards him and holding out her hands defensively. "Please, calm down!"

Chace turned and looked at her. "Deryn?"

"Yes, it's me," she said.

"You already saw her," said Luka. "Remember?"

Chace shook his head frantically. "N-no. I ... I don't remember anything. Where ..." He looked around. "Where am I?"

Xander stood and slowly walked towards him. "Welcome to my home, Moffett."

"Chace, what is the last thing you remember?" asked Deryn.

"Deryn, what are you doing here with *them*?" Chace looked from Xander to Luka. Then from Bronson to Quigley, who were standing in their respective doorways. "How many people are here?"

Deryn looked over her shoulder. "This is it. Sorry if it's a bit overwhelming, but Bronson and Quigley got stuck here after curfew."

"Curfew," repeated Chace. "What curfew?"

"You really don't remember any of it?" asked Luka, crossing his arms. "Nothing after Veli installed the mind control chip?"

"Mind control chip." Chace's eyes widened yet again. "Who installed it? Veli Tash? I don't even remember the last time I saw him. How long has it been?"

Luka's face dropped. He darted for the balcony, slamming the sliding glass door behind him. Bronson stared after him but didn't follow.

"Please just have a seat and we'll explain everything," said Deryn in a calm voice. She motioned to the couch.

Chace looked at it, but then his eyes drifted to Xander's hand. "I want my gun," he said.

Xander scoffed. "I don't think so."

"Xander, just give it to him," demanded Deryn.

He looked at her and raised his eyebrows.

"If it makes him feel more secure then he should have it."

"How about we all just put our weapons down where everyone can see them?" suggested Bronson.

Now Chace scoffed. "What do I look like, an idiot?"

Xander had to hold his tongue. "Fine." He tossed Chace's Element to him. Chace stumbled before catching it. "If you try anything, Moffett, I can assure you that I will react twice as fast."

"This isn't mine," said Chace, staring quizzically at the Element.

"It is now."

Xander went back to his armchair and Chace headed for the couch. But then he stopped and looked at Deryn. *Really* looked at her.

"It's really you?" he asked.

Deryn smiled and nodded. "Yes, it is."

Staring nervously at the floor, Chace fidgeted and said, "I really didn't think this was how our reunion would go. Should we ... should we hug?"

Deryn chuckled softly. "Yes, Chace, I'd like that very much."

Chace slowly moved towards her, looking nervous as he lifted his arms. He didn't go the full distance, so Deryn had to close that last gap.

While they hugged, Chace's trembling body began to ease. "It really is you. Deryn, you're ... you're alive. God, you're alive!"

Chace's grip on her tightened as they cried in each other's arms.

"Oh, this is sweet," said Bronson, watching them with a wide grin.

Xander felt the opposite, of course, but he knew better than to voice his opinion. Still, he didn't like Chace touching her like that.

"Yeah, yeah, whatever," said Quigley, yawning. "I'm tired. Night, all." He went back into Xander and Deryn's room and shut the door.

Bronson turned to go back into Luka's room but, after a momentary pause, he veered towards the balcony instead.

"You should really take a seat," said Deryn, finally pulling out of their hug. "I'll grab us all tea and then we can talk."

For the next few hours, Xander and Deryn explained everything to Chace. Well, not everything, but the most important details were all brushed upon.

Xander had been hoping to use Chace to spy on Veli, but with his loss of memory they all came to the conclusion that it would do little good. And quite possibly get Chace killed. He was not even sure where he'd been staying for the past six months.

"Well, this ended up being a fucking waste," said Xander.

Deryn gave him a warning look. "No it hasn't. Chace is safe. That can hardly be considered a *waste*."

Xander looked at her and said, "That's not what I meant. We should've realized his memories would be erased and found a way to get him to talk without him biting off his tongue."

"There was no way. You know that."

"Whatever," said Xander. "I'm still pissed. Moffett here gave them some plant to use against me and we have no idea what it is."

Deryn noticed Chace look to the floor ashamedly, quite obviously embarrassed by this whole ordeal. And he still didn't look well.

"At least tell me you remember who your source for information is?"

"I have an idea," Chace said quietly.

"Then maybe we can still find out what they're planning for Deryn, then come up with some lie to tell Veli when you meet with him in two days."

Deryn's brow furrowed. "He most certainly is not keeping that meeting, Xander! How can you even consider putting

Chace back in that sort of danger?" she asked angrily.

"Comes with the territory, sweetheart," said Xander. "He's in the Resistance, and we need him to keep playing the part of mind controlled puppet for as long as we can."

Deryn huffed, but she stopped arguing. She knew he was right. "Chace, you should get some rest. We can continue this discussion in the morning," she said while looking at the clock. "The curfew will be lifted in a few minutes. I'm going to send Quigley home." Deryn stood and headed for their room.

Xander went to the balcony. When he got there, Luka was huddled on the ground while Bronson stood above him smoking a cigarette.

"Something wrong?" Xander asked Luka.

"Oh, *nothing*," he scoffed. "Just that I'm going to lose my fucking memories when all of this is over."

"You don't know that."

"Yes I do. You're going to die saving Leon, I'm going to lose my memories, and then I'm going to spend the rest of my life thinking I was betrayed by my oldest friend."

"If that's your greatest fear then I'm touched."

"Not funny," said Luka, burying his head in his knees.

Xander crossed his arms and sighed. "I feel there is a simple solution to all of this."

"And what's that?"

"Don't lose your memories when the chip is removed."

Luka looked up. "What?"

"I'm *ordering* you not to lose your memories, Luka. And since I'm the one who installed the chip, you must listen."

"I don't think it works like that," said Luka, sneering.

"Why not?" asked Xander. "Veli intended for Moffett's head to be wiped clean, and I intend for yours to remain as is."

Luka looked down and sighed. "You better hope that works. I really don't want things to go back to how they were before."

"I believe it will." Xander turned his eyes to Bronson, who looked as skeptical as he felt. "It's time to go. Curfew's almost over and Deryn's kicking Quigley out of our bed."

When they got inside Quigley was standing by the front

door, rubbing his groggy eyes. The clock chimed four o'clock. He waited a moment before unlocking and opening the door.

"Ready, mate?" he asked, glancing at Bronson.

Bronson nodded and followed him out, taking one last look at Luka before shutting the door behind him.

"Chace, you should get some rest," Deryn said again. She looked at Xander. "I really don't think we should leave him alone after he lost so much blood earlier. I'll stay up and watch him."

"Like hell you will," said Xander. "You already look exhausted."

"I'm fine."

"No, Deryn, go to bed. I'll stay -"

"I'll do it," said Luka.

The other three all stared at him.

"But you have Guardian duties in four hours," said Xander. "You need to get at least some sleep -"

"It's fine," said Luka. "I can't sleep right now, anyway." He was already sinking into the closest armchair. "Moffett, go to sleep. And *don't* start dying on me. I really don't feel like dealing with that shit."

Chace looked skeptical. "No offense, but I would really feel safer on my own."

"Too bad because I've already made myself comfortable. Now lie the fuck down," ordered Luka.

"Are you sure about this?" asked Deryn.

Luka nodded. "Really, I'm fine. I'll wake you before I leave."

Deryn nodded back and said, "Goodnight then." She looked at Chace. "Do you need any extra blankets or pillows?"

"No," he said. "These pillows are fine." He grabbed one off the couch and gave it a good fluffing.

"If you say so. I'll see you in a few hours."

Deryn walked towards the bedroom with Xander just behind her. When the door shut, Chace looked curiously at Luka and said, "Did they just go into the same room?"

"Looks like it," said Luka as he picked at his fingernails.

Inside of the bedroom, Deryn gasped. "Oh, shit!"

"Ah, love, you know I can't contain myself when you curse," said Xander, wrapping his arms around her waist.

She smiled. "Don't get any ideas."

"If you're not trying to seduce me then what's with the language?"

"We just came into the bedroom together."

Xander cocked an eyebrow.

Deryn rolled her eyes. "Well, we never exactly mentioned to Chace that we're *involved*. Sometimes I forget that we're a secret outside of these walls," she said with a sigh.

Xander kissed her forehead. "Not forever."

"I hope not." Deryn smiled and puckered her lips. Xander happily kissed them. He would have to take note of Chace's reaction when they told him they were *involved* later, and then expect that tenfold when brother Leon and Trigger found out. God, he hoped he would be there for that.

CHAPTER SIXTEEN

"**D**id you find anything yet?" asked Deryn, looking over Chace's shoulder as he flipped through one of the books Xander had, coincidentally, grabbed from her old house in Redwood on plants.

"No," he answered. "I really don't think it would be anything in this book. Plants have changed since our ancestors wrote it. I was thinking it might be one of mine but I'm not sure how I would've smuggled it into the city."

Chace had always loved plants. He used to study and breed them when they were children in Redwood, and he'd apparently continued his work after joining the Resistance. Some of his plants were lethal, others were for nutritional purposes and many, the majority, were simply colorful and fragrant.

"There are a couple maybes in here, but I'll need Ruby to verify the leaf for me when he gets back."

Deryn crinkled her nose. "You know, it would really be handy if one of us was an artist."

"I'm an artist in the kitchen!" called Bronson, who was currently throwing ingredients into a pot. "Does that count?"

"Only when we're hungry," said Deryn. Her stomach growled right on cue.

An alarm triggered, informing them that someone had entered the building. It turned out Chace knew a clever trick that connected to Xander and Luka's wristbands, giving them their own unique alarms when they were scanned upon entrance. There was also one for Bronson and Quigley, and another for all strangers who attempted to enter. This current alarm was Xander's.

Sure enough, Xander walked through the door a minute later, Luka right behind him.

"Any luck, Moffett?" asked Xander.

"Maybe," said Chace, flipping to his first marked page. "Come see."

Xander looked at the open page. "No. The leaves were sharper."

Chace flipped to another page.

"The leaves were greener."

Luka reached into his bag and pulled out a different book. He tossed it to Chace. "Merry Christmas."

Chace read the title and gasped. "This book is forbidden in Utopia. It has every lethal plant known to man. Where'd you get it?"

"Don't ask," said Luka, sinking into an armchair. "Hundreds of laws were broken, a few innocent lives lost. A truly messy ordeal. Dismembered limbs, heads hanging by nothing but a thin slice of skin ..."

"Chace, he's joking. His dad has a library," Deryn said quickly when she noticed the sickly shade of green he was turning, similar in color to the plant on the page he currently had open. "Stop messing with him, Luka."

Luka smirked. "You would think he'd have a stronger stomach after being involved in a war for five years - Ouch!"

Xander had walked by and smacked Luka on the back of the head. He then sat next to Deryn, automatically putting an arm around her waist. Chace tried really hard not to stare but in the two days he'd been there he hadn't exactly gotten used to the idea of them being together.

And then Xander leaned over and kissed Deryn's cheek. Chace couldn't hide his grimace.

"If you don't like it, Moffett, then stop staring," snapped Xander.

"Sorry," said Chace with a slight blush.

"Whatever. I need to get our supplies ready." Xander stood and headed for his and Deryn's bedroom.

"How do you know so much about plants, anyway?" asked Luka.

"Living outside we had such little information about everything growing around us, so I began studying plants at a young age."

"*I* discovered ancient poison oak," said Deryn proudly.

"Yes, by falling out of a tree and landing right in it," added Chace with a laugh.

Deryn shoved him playfully. "No one ever said the life of a scientist was easy."

"Food's ready!" called Bronson from the kitchen.

Deryn got up to help him prepare the plates. But then she noticed there were only four. "Aren't you eating with us, Bronson?"

"No," he said while biting a piece of asparagus. "I have plans later."

Luka glanced in their direction. Bronson pretended not to notice.

Xander walked out of the bedroom carrying Deryn's smaller bag, which was more practical for the evening than his rucksack. He grabbed two of the finished plates, went to the couch and dropped one in Chace's lap. "Eat quickly, Moffett. Veli moved your meeting up an hour -"

He pulled Chace's wristband out of his pocket and snapped it back on the man's wrist.

"- and we don't know how much time we need with this source of yours."

Xander ate his food while standing. Deryn brought a plate to Luka, but didn't grab one for herself just yet. She stood behind Xander, wrapping her arms around his waist. "He looks really nervous," she whispered. "You swear you'll take care of him?"

Xander glanced over his shoulder and into her worried eyes. He smiled. "I already said I would. Relax, Deryn. We'll be fine."

She nodded and kissed him.

"Ready, Moffett?" he asked.

"I guess so." Chace stood and carried his plate to the

kitchen, though he'd barely taken two bites. "Sorry," he said to Bronson. "It really was good."

Bronson smiled brightly. "It's fine. You can warm it up later. When your stomach isn't quite so twisted." He wrapped the plate in some tinfoil and put it away.

"Thanks," said Chace, turning around just in time to see Xander lean in and kiss Deryn as she took his plate. More grimacing.

"I know, it really *is* nauseating," said Bronson. "But they're happy." He paused. "Well, as happy as anyone can be considering their tragic lives."

Chace nodded lightly. "I'm trying to understand."

"Let's get a move on, Moffett!" Xander called while heading for the door.

Chace followed after him, pausing momentarily by Deryn. She gave him a hug and said, "Good luck. Have faith in Xander, alright? I promise he won't let anything bad happen to you."

He nodded, though didn't look entirely convinced. Then he went to the door, put on his shoes and coat, and followed Xander out.

"Why isn't Voclain coming with us, again?" asked Chace as they headed down the stairs.

Xander cocked an eyebrow. "Why? You trust him more than you trust me?"

Chace thought about this. "No, I suppose not. I never really knew him during training."

"And you knew me?"

"No. But you were a presence. He wasn't."

Xander could understand that. Luka was a bit of a loner back then. They'd known each other since childhood and had always been friends, but as teenagers they had drifted apart. Aside from the occasional night where they'd sneak out of Eagle Center to go drinking.

Their friendship only really rekindled after becoming Guardians. A sad reality. But Xander always had more in common with Luka than he ever did with Wyatt or any of his other friends, and - while he'd never admit it aloud - he really did like having him around. So did Deryn.

"Luka isn't coming because I don't want to draw attention to us. And, if there comes a time when I need to reveal myself to protect your ass, I want Luka as far away from this as possible."

"Why would you need to reveal yourself?" asked Chace nervously.

"If things go sour, Moffett. And, if that happens, you're going to need to suck it up and pretend I've reset your mind control chip. Understand?"

Chace took a deep breath and nodded.

"In fact, why don't you suck it up right now? If Veli sees you like this then we don't stand a chance."

They reached the bottom floor and Xander let Chace take the lead, his hood up while he trailed him from the shadows. Chace studied Deryn's map earlier and had a fairly good idea of where they were and where they needed to go.

They were walking to the house of Chace's supposed source so Xander could follow him more discretely than if they took the tram.

It was quite a walk but, eventually, they ended up on one of the many reasonably deserted streets of Middle City. Even in Utopia's prime, Xander could tell that this wasn't the nicest of places. He didn't understand why anyone would choose to live someplace so dodgy. The city had an abundance of empty houses that the residents of this street could have taken and registered.

Chace walked up a few steps to a door while Xander stood beside the stoop, still in the shadows. He did a special knock and someone answered. A woman Xander recognized as Sable Bai.

Ah! Now it all made sense. Dodgy place, dodgy woman.

Chace hadn't given him a name before, claiming he wouldn't know her, but while Xander didn't know her personally he knew enough to understand that she was hardly the epitome of sophistication. She was the instigator of many shady dealings but the Guardians had always let her be, knowing very well that she was loyal to whoever paid the most. President Saevus wanted to hold on to this trump card, for the day Sable knew enough to bring down the entire Resistance.

"You," she said, eyeing Chace questioningly. "You come alone?"

"Yes," Chace said coolly, his previous anxiety nowhere to be found.

Xander was mildly impressed.

"You know the rules," said Sable, holding out her hand. Xander took this moment to duck into the alley beside the house, climbing inside through a window that Chace had said was always open a crack.

Chace handed over the Element he had strapped to his hip. If Sable thought it was strange for him to have such a weapon, she didn't voice it. Instead she just smiled, showing off her two gold front teeth, and led Chace inside.

"I assume you've come here for info on Deryn Leon," said Sable, leading Chace into the main room of the small house. Xander, who was watching closely from a dark hallway, had to hold in a moan of distaste as he glanced around. The entire place was cluttered with old wanted posters, moldy books, dirty plates and empty bottles.

"Tea?" asked Sable, holding up a kettle from a hotplate.

Chace eyed the dirty mugs beside it and said, "No thanks." Good call. "And yes. I was hoping you found out more information on what the Resistance is planning."

"Aye," said Sable. "I did. But it'll cost ya."

Chace took a few hundred coin in paper money out of his pocket - donated by Xander's sock drawer - and handed it over. "I believe this will cover it."

Sable ran her fingers through the bills and counted. She smiled, showing off her gold teeth again, and some silver ones way in the back.

"Funny, isn't it? How after all these months, you still haven't found a better way to contact your own people than through me."

Chace knitted his brow. "I'm sorry?"

"I contacted 'em today, through the radio. Spoke to that Laramie Triggs. Didn't wanna give me the info so I gave 'im your name. Funny thing. He said you been missin' since before the curfew. Now, if that's true, then how the hell are you in front of me now?"

Without so much as a flinch, Chace looked her in the eye and said, "No one's supposed to know of my presence here, Sable. Least of all you. But, like you said, the curfew went up and I lost my means to contact the Resistance. So here I am. Now, if you let me use that radio of yours, which I can see right now shoved under the couch, I can straighten this out with them and we can continue business as usual."

It was a decent lie. One Xander would never believe, but he had a feeling Sable just might be that stupid.

There was a long pause as Sable studied Chace, searching for any sign that he might be lying. There was nothing.

Then a drop of sweat dripped from his forehead, Xander catching the glint of it in the light. A clear and vivid sign that something was amiss. But Xander was a trained Guardian. Surely this woman wouldn't notice something as minute as -

"Is it warm in here, Moffett?"

Shit. Apparently, slimy criminals and Guardians were trained similarly.

Sable started to lift her gun but, before she could strike, Xander stepped out of the hallway, lifted one of the unregistered Elements Deryn had taken from Sewick Blum's house, and fired.

Sable screamed as she went flying backwards, slamming against the wall. Then there were strings of light binding her to large hooks she had used to hang pots. She continued to scream as Xander stepped towards her.

"Ah! It's R-Ruby! What're you gonna do? You gonna turn me inside out? Like Oscar Venner?"

Xander cocked an eyebrow. "My reputation precedes me."

"Did you really turn someone inside out?" asked Chace, taking several nervous steps backwards.

"No," said Xander. "Just a rumor. I was a young Guardian

back then. I merely tortured Venner into a confession. The president then had him skinned alive. Elvira volunteered." He looked into Sable's eyes and waved his Element in front of her. "I really wish you hadn't made this difficult." His Element stopped dead, pointing straight at her head. "Now, tell me what the Resistance is planning for Deryn Leon."

"I don't know anything!" she screamed.

"You're lying."

"I'm not! I swear! I asked but they wouldn't tell me anything after I mentioned *him*!" She nodded her head towards Chace. "All I know is they're planning something soon. Very, very soon."

Xander frowned. "I believe her. Fucking waste."

"Yeah, that's right! So there's no reason to kill -"

"There is if you plan on telling anyone about this."

"I won't!" she cried.

"She certainly is frightened of you," observed Chace.

Xander smiled proudly. "Just the way I like it. I'll tell you what, Sable. I'm going to let you live. But I have many people working for me, some just as slimy as you are, and from now on one of them will be watching you at all times. If there is ever a moment where it seems like you might betray me then that's it for you. Finished." He ran his Element across her neck like a blade. "Got it?"

Sable gulped and nodded.

"Good." He grabbed Chace's Element from her hip, where she'd strapped it, and handed it back to him. Then he turned and walked to the couch, grabbed the radio she somehow used to communicate with the Resistance and stuffed it in his bag. "Find your own way out of those binds. If you can!"

Xander headed for the door, Chace at his heels.

"Care to venture a guess on what they have planned?" he asked on their way out.

Chace shrugged. "I dunno. But they've often toyed with the idea of doing something during the president's New Year's speech. I just don't know what that would have to do with Deryn."

Xander sighed. "Still, we should keep our guard up."

"But if they're trying to help Deryn -"

"Endangering her is more like it," snapped Xander. "Any rescue attempt could very well expose her. We need to get her out without drawing attention. Somehow, I don't think your Resistance friends understand that."

Chace nodded. "Yeah. Sometimes Talon and Dax can be a bit dumb, especially when it comes to her."

Xander nodded. "Well, onto our next stop. You did alright here, Moffett. But now for the hard part."

Chace gulped loudly.

Xander opened the door and ushered him out, but he shut it behind him and exited through the window, Sable shouting nasty words at him as she continued her struggle to remove her binds.

CHAPTER SEVENTEEN

"Please, Luka?"

"No."

"Please, please, please?"

"Did I not just say no?"

Deryn frowned. He was really making this difficult, and it wasn't like with Xander where she could just suck on his neck to get what she wanted. The only method that ever seemed to work with Luka was blackmail, and with everything between him and Bronson out in the open she was lacking dirt.

"Level with me, Luka. What exactly would I have to do to get you to go to the basement with me?"

Luka smirked. "Well, I wouldn't be completely against you getting naked -"

Deryn huffed.

"- but I really don't feel like being killed by Xander tonight," he added with a chuckle. "You've already seen me in my bra," she said, crossing her arms.

Luka's face dropped. "That was an accident."

"Still, imagine if Xander were to ever find out about that. Accident or not, I'm pretty sure he wouldn't hesitate to -"

"Are you blackmailing me again?"

Deryn smiled. That wasn't her intention but ... "I suppose I am."

Luka sneered. "Oh, fuck you. We're not staying down there for long."

"That's fine. I just want the distraction. So I don't ..." She gulped. "... think too much about everything that can go wrong."

They went to the front door, put on their shoes, and left the apartment with Luka in the lead. They hadn't even gone down two flights of stairs yet when Luka put his arm out to stop her. Deryn froze when she heard a knock. Poking her head underneath Luka's arm, she noticed a man she didn't recognize standing outside of Bronson and Quigley's door. No alarm had gone off, so someone must have buzzed him in.

He glanced up at Luka and gave a half-smile.

The door opened. "You're late," said Bronson in a playful tone.

"Sorry," said the man. "I got a little lost." He stepped inside. "I think that Guardian who went out the backdoor in our kitchen that one time is on the staircase."

"Oh?" Bronson poked his head into the hall and looked up at Luka. "And so he is."

Luka seemed pretty much frozen, so Deryn lifted her head over his shoulder and said, "We were just heading down to the basement to distract ourselves. Right, Luka?"

He said nothing.

"Luka?" She pinched his side.

Without reacting, he said, "Right."

Bronson nodded. "Have fun then." And the door shut.

"So you know him?" asked Deryn as soon as Bronson was gone.

"He's a waiter at the restaurant he works at," Luka answered impassively. "He was being a bit flirty."

"Oh," said Deryn, biting her lip. "Well, maybe we should get to the -"

Before she could finish her sentence, Luka sank down and sat on the step, his eyes still fixed on Bronson's front door.

"Alright then." She took a seat beside him. "I suppose we can sit for a while."

So much for keeping herself distracted.

CHAPTER EIGHTEEN

Xander followed Chace into the crowded bar, his hood up as he avoided eye contact with everyone he passed. When Chace got to a back hall where there were several doors, he paused for a moment and looked around blankly, eventually settling on the one guarded by a large man. The man opened the door for Chace without question and shut it behind him.

Once he was safely through, Xander slipped into the bathroom and locked the door. He pressed a button on his wristband and a holograph appeared in front of him, giving him a nice view from the small camera Chace had pinned to his chest.

Unlike the last time he came here Veli was alone, sitting at a large table and drinking whiskey out of a glass with ice. "Where have you been?" he asked while motioning for Chace to take a seat.

"What do you mean?" asked Chace, choosing a chair at the opposite end of the table. "I'm here right on time."

"Yes, but you haven't been back to the apartment I set up for you since our last meeting. Why?"

"You've been spying on me," said Chace in the same cool tone he'd used with Sable. Xander smirked. He really was masking his fear well.

"Of course I have. You are an important investment of mine and I'm not about to let you run loose in a city you're not welcome in. Now tell me, where have you *been*?" Veli repeated, his voice growing impatient.

The view slightly altered, indicating that Chace had leaned back in his chair. "I met a girl the other night and I've been staying with her. As I recall, these *terms* of yours don't require that I sleep alone every night."

"Hmm, and here I always believed that you were a good, rule abiding man," said Veli with a sneer. "Very well. If you insist on making this difficult then I must demand that you never see this girl or any other again. Is that clear?"

"Crystal."

"Now tell me what information you got on the Resistance."

"Nothing. When they wouldn't give my source information, she used my name. It didn't go over well. I paid her off but I doubt the Resistance will be willing to share information with her so freely again."

"So your worth to me has dwindled?" said Veli.

"Perhaps. There are other people I could try, but she was the biggest idiot."

Suddenly Chace's gaze, along with the camera's, drifted to something in the corner. Xander looked closely to see it was a plant with familiar ruffled green leaves. Oh, this was too perfect. There was no way Veli could ever be that -

"Why do you have that here?" asked Chace, nodding towards it. "The toxins will sometimes let loose in an enclosed environment, and this room just might be small enough to -"

"It's fine," said Veli. "I'm transporting it somewhere and thought it would feel less threatened outside of the bag."

"Transporting it?" repeated Chace. "You should have removed the toxins and used them already. It looks like it's been ready to strike for days now."

Veli raised his eyebrows. "I thought you injected its leaves with that solution to freeze it in this stage? If that changed or you were unable to do so then you should have -"

"N-no," stuttered Chace as he realized his mistake. "N-nothing changed."

Xander winced. *Shit.*

Veli continued to stare at him curiously for a moment before his eyes narrowed. "You're hiding something from me.

Tell me what it is."

Chace said nothing.

"*Tell me!*"

Well, this charade was over. Knowing that, Chace pulled out his Element, aimed it at the plant and blasted it to oblivion.

"FUCK!" shouted Veli, jumping out of his chair with such force that it fell backwards. He lifted his own Element and shot a blast at Chace.

Xander turned off the hologram, marched out of the bathroom and straight to the large man guarding the door. He held up a stack of bills and said, "Entry for one."

The man took the money and smiled, gladly stepping out of Xander's way.

When he got inside, Veli didn't have a moment to react before Xander was aiming his Element at Chace's heart, hitting him with an electroshock that made him fall back, appearing dead to the untrained eye.

"Must you always make things so difficult, Veli?" asked Xander, kicking Chace's lifeless body.

Veli's eyes narrowed. "Xander. What are you doing here?"

"Trying to find out more about your plot against me." Xander looked at the pile of ashes that used to be the plant and smirked. "But that doesn't seem to be a problem now. Unless the plant's toxins are currently leaking in the air and we're both dead." Looking back at Veli, he noticed the unfamiliar, older model of Element he held. "Is that from Sewick's collection?" He lifted his and smiled. "Mine too. Now put it on the table so I can destroy it."

Veli laughed. "Why would I -"

"Because if you don't I'll tell the president about this." He kicked Chace's lifeless body. "If you keep this up, Veli belly, I won't hesitate to let him know how you had a key member of the Resistance under your thumb for all this time. I'm sure he would just *love* to hear all about it. Stop messing with me, Veli. You should know by now that you'll never win."

Xander smirked before throwing Chace over his shoulder.

"I'll clean up your dirty work."

He created his own exit into the alley by blasting a hole in the wall with his Element, winking at Veli as he stepped through. His hover-bike was already waiting around the corner for him with the passenger car popped out. He dropped Chace into the seat, mounted his bike and took off for home.

When he got back to his building, he parked his bike in the garage and waited for Chace to regain consciousness. Not even a minute later, Chace was popping up, eyes wide as he gasped for air.

"What the hell, Ruby? I thought you'd killed me!"

"Yes, that *was* the point. You thought you were dying and Veli thinks you're dead."

Chace stared down at his hands, which were tingling as the feeling slowly returned to them. "I've seen something like that before. Several times. After some of our battles with Guardians we would get ready to bury our dead and, by some miracle, every now and then someone would just wake up. Like it was nothing. That ..." He gulped. "That was you?"

Xander shrugged. "Probably. A few other Guardians know of it, but I doubt they use it like I do."

"So you really have been helping us. For all these years. Since the beginning?"

"No."

"Then when?"

Xander shrugged again. "There wasn't exactly a defining moment. I saw an opportunity to save someone once and I took it. Then I kept taking it whenever I could." He paused and took a deep breath. "What was the plant, Moffett?" he asked, holding out his hand to Chace, who looked at it reluctantly. It took a moment, but he eventually let Xander help him out of the sidecar.

"It's one of mine. I don't really have a name for it. I made it by accident. I used to jokingly call it the priest plant, because when someone inhales its toxins it causes them to confess all of their secrets. Or sins, I guess. But then ... then my test subjects started getting sick," he admitted, stifling a sob. "It was a fluke and I burned every last one of them. It's the only way these plants can be destroyed, and I don't know how the hell I got one in here." He rubbed his hands down his face. "I must've grown it somewhere."

Xander shuddered. "I suppose that's something we should figure out."

He led Chace out of the garage and into his building. When they got to the third floor, they suddenly came face-to-face with Luka and Deryn, who were still sitting on the stairs. Luka was staring intently at Bronson's door while Deryn rubbed his back. Xander's fists clenched on instinct.

But then Deryn's eyes lit up. She stumbled down the stairs and into his arms, instantly causing him to forget any jealousy he had just felt. Then she was out of his arms and hugging Chace. The jealousy immediately returned.

"Thank god you're both alright! So did everything go according to plan?" she asked, looking at Xander hopefully.

"Actually, nothing did," he answered. "Chace has been exposed to his source by the Resistance ,who believe he's missing, and then when things went sour with Veli I had to pretend to kill him."

"So we have no new information?"

"No," said Xander. "But the plant's destroyed, so I suppose we can call this a win." He looked at Chace and winked.

Chace actually smiled.

"So why are you sitting out here?"

"Oh." Deryn blushed. She looked at Luka out of the corner of her eye. "Um ..."

The door three floors below suddenly opened and a cheerful hummer entered the building. They all turned towards the stairs, waiting until Quigley appeared moments later. He jumped a little when he saw all of them. "Uh ... hi, guys. What's going on?"

"Nothing!" Deryn squealed.

"Alright then." He went over to his front door, scanned his wristband and slipped in the key. Then he turned back to see them all watching him. "Did you want to come in or something?"

They all started to say, "No," but then Luka pushed forward and said, "I will."

Deryn grabbed his arm but he pulled away and went over to Quigley, who was just opening the door.

"Go with him, Xander," Deryn whispered harshly.

"What? Why -"

"Just go!" she snapped, pushing him forward.

Xander ran to the door. He was just in time to enter with Quigley and Luka, and to see Bronson pulling away from some man on the couch, his lips still pink from the obvious kissing he'd just been engaged in.

"Quigs, you're home early," he said while staring at his roommate. Then his eyes moved to Luka and Xander. Luka stared at him straight on, but Xander opted to stare elsewhere.

"And you brought guests. Fan-fucking-tastic."

"Sorry. I didn't know you had company," said Quigley, going over to the table and putting down his keys. He glanced sideways at Bronson and smirked.

"Aren't you going to introduce us to your *friend*, Bronson?" asked Luka, the scorn in his voice blatantly obvious.

"Fucking hell," Xander muttered to himself.

"Okay," said Bronson. "Warren, you already know Quigs. And this here is Luka and Xander. The Guardians who live upstairs."

"Hello," said Warren quietly, who seemed to recognize that something was amiss. "Nice to meet you."

"Likewise," said Luka, walking over and taking a seat on the couch right between them.

"Oh, this is beautiful," Quigley whispered to Xander as they watched from the sidelines.

"So how long have you worked at the restaurant, *Warren?*"

"Umm ... just over six months," he said, his voice cracking.

"And did you know you liked Bronson here right away?" asked Luka, putting a hand on Bronson's shoulder.

Bronson flinched and muttered, "Un-fucking-believable," under his breath.

"Uh ... well, yes. I suppose I did. But I only found out he

was gay maybe two months ago."

"Really?" said Luka, raising his eyebrows. "I knew the moment I met him, mainly because he couldn't stop eye-fucking me. Is that how you found out, *Warren*? Because you could feel him staring at you? Imagining what it would be like to fuck you?"

Warren blushed. "Why do you keep saying my name like that?"

Luka cocked his head. "Like what, *Warren*?"

Xander and Quigley chuckled, but when Bronson gave them both a sharp look they shut their mouths quickly.

"Why do you look so nervous, *Warren*? Do you not like being this close to a Guardian?"

Warren shuddered. "N-no. It's ... it's fine."

"Is that right? Would you like to see my wristband then?" said Luka, already pulling up his sleeve. "You can touch it if you want." He grabbed Warren's hand and put it on the area between skin and metal. "Fascinating how it just burrows in there, isn't it?"

"Luka, that's enough!" shouted Bronson.

Luka looked at him, feigning innocence. "What?"

"You *know* what?"

"Well, forgive me for being curious about what pussy piece of shit you brought home. One look at my wristband and I'm pretty sure I just scared him out of his granny panty's."

Warren looked away and blushed.

"Well, at least he knows what he wants!" shouted Bronson, jumping to his feet.

"And who says I don't?" shouted Luka, doing the same.

"Oh, I'm sorry, is the jealous asshole in front of me now not the same person who fucked some girl in his bed three days ago? The same bed he didn't want *me* to sleep in when I got stuck up there after curfew!"

Luka turned bright red. "I didn't mean to do that, alright? I was drunk and -"

Bronson laughed. "You're *always* drunk, Luka! You were drunk the first time you let me suck your cock! And slightly drunk the second!"

Xander quickly turned away. Oh god, he didn't want to be here right now.

"That excuse only holds valid for so long!"

Luka stared at the floor, taking several deep breaths as he clenched and unclenched his fists. He looked up, stared Bronson straight in the eye and said, "I'm not drunk now."

And then he walked confidently to Bronson's bedroom. Bronson stared after him, mouth agape and his body quivering.

"Are you coming?" shouted Luka, who was presently out of view.

Bronson glanced sideways at Warren, and then at his bedroom, and then at Warren again.

"Come on, Bronson, we *all* know what you want to do," said Quigley, leaning against the wall. "I'm tired. Can you please just go into your damn bedroom already and do what you've been whining about for a month now?"

Bronson glanced at Quigley, and then at Warren again, and then at the door ...

Luka reappeared in the doorway. "I'm not going to wait in here forever." He disappeared again.

Bronson looked at Warren one last time, cleared his throat, and muttered, "Sorry." Then he was off to his bedroom, shutting the door behind him.

"Don't be too loud! You know I gotta be up early tomorrow!" Quigley called before going into the kitchen to grab a snack.

And then it was just Xander and Warren.

"Well, this is awkward," said Xander, unsure of what else they were supposed to talk about. The clock chimed and they both looked at it. "Only a half hour till curfew. You might want to ..."

Xander motioned towards the door. Warren stared at it for a long moment before jumping up, putting on his coat and darting out of the apartment. Less than thirty seconds later, the door opened again and Deryn walked in.

"What happened?" she asked, looking at Xander. "Where's

Luka?"

Quigley laughed from the kitchen.

Deryn followed Xander's eyes towards the closed bedroom door. Her jaw dropped. "*No!*"

"*Yes,*" said Quigley, emerging from the kitchen with a sandwich and taking a big bite. "I'm a little shocked, myself. I really thought Luka was never gonna cave." He laughed again.

"Let's just go," said Xander, taking Deryn's hand and pulling her out of the apartment.

Chace was still waiting for them on the staircase. "Everything alright?" he asked.

Xander smiled. "It's your lucky night, Moffett. *You* get a bed to sleep in."

"Where's Voclain?"

Xander shuddered and Deryn giggled. "We'll tell you when you're older," he said before leading them upstairs.

It had been a long fucking night.

CHAPTER NINETEEN

"Why do you keep smiling like that?"

"Hmm?" Xander looked up to see Wyatt staring at him as they stood in President Saevus's parlor. He sucked his smile back. "No reason."

The truth was he couldn't stop thinking about the night before. It had been New Year's Eve and they'd all gone to Del's hideout, mainly to drop Chace off since Xander's apartment was getting a bit crowded, especially now that Bronson was staying over. Luka swore that they weren't having sex. They were going to that one night, but Bronson stopped them before it got too far. He knew that Luka wasn't ready to take that step, and he wasn't going to push him. Xander didn't bother to ask what it was they *were* doing every night then, because he really had no interest in the answer.

But the night before ... He couldn't help but smile again. The curfew had been raised an hour for the evening, so they all drank quite a few bottles of champagne until midnight. Deryn got a bit drunk, and it turned out champagne made her frisky. The moment they got home, she pulled Xander into their bedroom and they proceeded to have some of their greatest sex to date. Granted, she was hung-over and miserable that morning, but, dammit, it was worth it!

"You're smiling again."

Xander's eyes focused and he looked at Wyatt.

"Could you stop it? It's creeping me out."

His smile immediately fell. There it was again. Creepy ...

"If you fucked as loudly as he did last night then you'd

smiling too," said Luka, who was looking a bit hung-over himself. "Seriously, Xan, you've never made the walls rattle before. While I don't normally care, a soundproof shield was necessary."

"Sorry," said Xander, smiling once more. "Forgot you were there again."

Luka rolled his eyes. "Sure you did."

"Who you fucking, Xander?" asked Wyatt.

"Just some girl I met last night," he lied. "Who I will definitely be fucking again tonight." And he was pretty sure he still had some champagne somewhere ...

"Hi, Luka," said Lona, walking up to them.

Luka blushed. "Hi."

"How was your New Year's?"

"Fine," he said, glancing elsewhere. He spotted Finley standing by herself and hurried over to her.

Wyatt looked confused, but Xander had to fight off another smile.

"Did I do something wrong?" she asked, looking sadly at Xander.

And the smile formed. Poor girl. If only she knew. "He just doesn't want you to get the wrong impression."

Lona rolled her eyes. "Please. I was fully aware of what he was like before I followed him home that night."

A light finally triggered in Wyatt's head.

"Then why do you look so upset?" asked Xander.

Lona blushed and cast her eyes to the floor. But, before she could answer, President Saevus entered the room with Elvira at his heels. He glanced around with his green eyes - the one part of the man that reminded Xander he was distantly related to Deryn - until he located Xander. Then he beckoned him with his finger.

Xander stepped forward and stood beside Elvira.

"Are we all ready?"

"Yes, Mr. President," everyone answered.

President Saevus turned in a swift motion, his steps smooth and elegant as he headed for the elevator. All of his Guardians followed.

As they entered the elevator, Xander could feel Elvira's eyes on him. "Something on your mind?" he asked as he pressed the button for the twentieth floor.

"You look different," she said after a momentary pause.

Xander turned and cocked and eyebrow. "Do I?"

"Yes. I've noticed for a while now. The change has been gradual but it's there. What is it?" she asked, her voice filled with accusation.

"New skin regimen. Leaves me positively glowing."

Elvira scoffed. "Rumor is you've found yourself a girlfriend."

President Saevus glanced over his shoulder at Xander, who was quick to scoff right back at her. "Yes, I'm sure Veli's been spreading all sorts of rumors about me. I assure you, nothing's changed, Elvie dearest. I'm still utterly heartbroken that I never got my chance with you."

The elevator reached the twentieth floor and President Saevus stepped out first. Elvira moved ahead of him but Xander was faster, scanning his wristband so the door to the balcony slid open for his president. She sneered at him while he continued to smile.

Several of the lesser Guardians hurried ahead of them, running to the other side of the large balcony where they checked on the walkway that had been built so their president could step out and over the citizens of Utopia. It extended all the way to Middle City, high above the gate, and seemed to be ready.

Luka was the one to scan his wristband and activate the walkway so it moved beneath their feet. The other Guardians all stood aside while President Saevus stepped forward, Elvira and Xander always just behind him. Even from where they were in the center of Inner City, they could hear the roaring crowd anticipating their arrival. Elvira fidgeted beside him. She wasn't a fan of heights and the walkway put in place for this every year was always crystal clear beneath their feet. Xander smirked and took heavier steps, making her tremble beside him.

"Stop it," she snapped, punching his arm with too much oomph for it to be considered playful.

As they reached the end of the walkway, taking their places on a platform floating above the city, Xander scanned the crowd.

Once everyone was in place, President Saevus lifted his arms. Silence was instantaneous, giving Xander an uneasy feeling. No bustling city should ever be this quiet.

Two giant holograms appeared on either side of them, showing the president's face about one-hundred times larger than Xander really cared to see.

President Saevus's wristband was designed to make his voice project and he started to speak.

"Today is a sacred day for all of us, for it is the day that marks another year. Another year where we are in power. Over five years since we first took back this great city from the toxic monsters who dared to believe that we would let them poison our city. Our families. Our children. Elvira."

President Saevus nodded to his daughter. She smiled and walked across another walkway that led to a smaller platform where a dozen people were standing on gallows with ropes draped around their necks. Elvira stopped beside them and waited.

"You have all been judged," continued President Saevus, speaking to the people on the gallows, "and every last one of you will no longer be allowed to taint the world with your toxic breath."

He nodded and Elvira used her dagger to cut the rope, causing the floor to collapse beneath the prisoners, leaving every last one of them kicking and fighting for their lives. It wasn't long before all kicking ceased.

President Saevus smiled, but then his ears went on full alert and his eyes landed on someone in the crowd. "You there." Everyone in the crowd looked at the person he pointed to. A teenage girl. "Bring her to me."

The crowd lifted her up and she screamed as they tossed her over to the patrolling guards. There was a cable dangling from the platform and they tied the loop at its end around her wrists, pressing a button that sent her flying upwards. When she landed hard on the platform, Veli and Soren lifted her, bringing her to the president.

"Was that a whimper I just heard escape from your lips?" asked President Saevus, his voice steady.

"N-no, my p-president," she said, looking absolutely terrified. And rightfully so.

"Oh, but I believe it was." He looked over his shoulder. "Xander."

Xander stood at attention.

"You know what to do."

He nodded. "Yes, Mr. President."

Xander took out his Element and aimed it at the girl, doing his best to hold back the pain he was feeling. He knew *she* was watching, and he hated that she had to see him do this, but there was no other choice.

With the press of a button, a string of light shot out and decapitated the girl, the quickest and least painful death he could offer her. Her body was quickly tossed aside, her head kicked with it.

Xander turned back to the crowd.

And then he spotted *her*. Barely a dot, but he knew it was her, standing where she'd promised. Towards the back of the Shopping District plaza everyone was crowded in, disguised with her blonde wig and blue eyes, Deryn stood between Bronson and Kemp. Chace, Miki, and Quigley were all there, too.

He still didn't know how she ever got him to agree to her coming here. It was right around the time the champagne hit her, so he assumed her frisky behavior had something to do with it. Still, he hated this. What if she was the one who had whimpered?

"You alright?" asked Bronson, putting his hand on Deryn's back.

"Yes, I'm fine. It ... It had to be done. She was as good as dead, right?" She looked at him hopefully.

He smiled halfheartedly. "Yes. He didn't have a choice."

She nodded and looked back at the platform, keeping her eyes on Xander while listening to President Saevus speak.

"Quigley, stop looking," snapped Bronson. "She's not one of them."

"Just making sure," said Quigley, his jaw tightening. The Outsider sacrifices were the only reason he had come that day. Just in case one of them might have been his sister.

"... and we will not stop, *will not* have won until every last Outsider has perished! No longer able to spread their toxins!"

"Can you believe him?" Miki whispered to Deryn. "He truly believes everything he does is for the greater good."

Deryn nodded. "You do have to wonder why it is he believes that."

"He's just crazy," Miki said simply. "I doubt it delves much deeper than that."

Deryn glanced around the crowd to make sure no one was listening to them, but everyone was too engulfed in the president to be even slightly aware of their surroundings. And then she caught sight of someone. It was a man a short distance away in a gasmask, an air of familiarity around him that she couldn't quite place. Something in the way he stood.

Deryn adjusted her position for a closer look, hoping to see the man behind the gasmask. She then froze, her heart slowing as she recognized the way he leaned on his right hip. She moved towards him.

Someone called for Allison Darby behind her but she didn't care. She had to get closer. To see if she was right. And then she was mere feet away from him, separated by only two people.

Her eyes drifted over him. The frame was slightly bulkier than she remembered but it was the same, arms crossed as he stared up at President Saevus with disdain. Long, dark hair was tied back and hidden beneath a hood, a few strands falling loose over his covered face.

Deryn couldn't breathe as she stared at this familiar man, her heart feeling heavy but also like an incredible weight had been lifted off of it.

Dakota.

And then he was moving, walking out and away from the crowd, headed towards an alley. Deryn followed him.

Dakota stopped near the edge of the crowd and looked to the left of where President Saevus was still speaking. There was a loud screeching noise and Deryn followed his eyes, noticing several figures on hover-bikes coming towards them, hovering higher than the standard two feet, with S.U.R.G.E.'s on their tails.

And then there was a loud BANG.

Everyone screamed and ducked, Deryn looking up for a brief moment to see that the walkway connecting President Saevus and his Guardians' platform to his tower in Inner City had been destroyed. Xander's eyes were still steadily fixed on her.

Deryn turned back around and spotted Dakota leaving the crowd while everything became chaos. She ran after him.

Up on the platform, Xander could see that Deryn was nowhere near the others. How had she gotten so far? She'd seemed to be following something but he couldn't for the life of him see what it was.

"Luka!" he shouted. Luka ran to his side. "Get down there!"

Luka nodded. Just as the Resistance members on hover-bikes reached them, he jumped off of the platform and grabbed onto one of them. Out of panic, the woman driving it began to lower her bike, eventually getting close enough to the ground that Luka was able to jump off and run into the crowd.

"Mathis, Eamon, Wenton, Soren, get down there with him!" ordered Xander. "Veli, Wyatt, Gordon, Finley, find hover-bikes and hack them so you can begin an aerial attack! Everyone else disperse to where you're needed!"

Everyone nodded and took off, some taking turns using the cable to get down to the ground, and others trying the same tactic as Luka - though less smoothly.

"Are you alright, Mr. President?" asked Xander.

Saevus's face was stiff as he stared into the panicked crowd, his green eyes flaming. "How dare they," he said in a voice that sent chills down Xander's spine. "How dare they interrupt my speech. What are they after?"

"I don't know, sir -"

Just then, a hover-bike swooped by, one hand dangling as the rider tried to grab Xander by his hood. He ducked out of reach just in time, looking up to meet the angry eyes of Laramie Triggs hidden behind a gasmask.

"Get him, Neetles!"

Another hover-bike swooped overhead and grabbed for him. President Saevus seized a piece of broken walkway and swung it at her, knocking her bike off course.

Xander stood up straight and looked into the president's angry eyes. "Sir, I don't know -"

Another bike came for him, and he ducked again. *Shit*.

Back in the crowd, Deryn was still chasing Dakota, but he was having much more success getting through the chaos than she was.

"Dax!"

She kept screaming his name but he couldn't hear her, continuing to march on without realizing how close he was to the person he sought. He was heading for an alley between two tall buildings. Deryn knew he was trying to leave, but why?

"No," Deryn said quietly as he got through the thickest part of the crowd. "No!"

She broke into a run, pushing and shoving and knocking people over, doing everything she could to break through.

"Dax!"

He was getting farther from her, his legs moving quickly.

"Dax!"

He had almost reached the alley.

"*DAX!*"

Dakota froze. Deryn kept pushing, not stopping until she was through the worst of it. She sighed in relief. He knew it. He still knew her voice.

Dakota turned and looked around frantically, his eyes darting everywhere as he searched for the owner of the voice he knew so well.

Then he saw her.

Deryn's heart skipped a beat as their eyes met. Hers were still blue and she tried her best to will them green. But there was no need. Even through her disguise he saw her, because he knew her.

His mouth moved in the shape of her name but she couldn't hear him through the pandemonium.

Deryn gave him one soft nod. Dakota took several skeptical steps forward. He kept glancing back at the alley. It was obvious there was somewhere he needed to be but, still, he moved towards her.

"Deryn!"

Deryn heard him this time. She stepped forward but Dakota stopped suddenly and held out his hands.

"No! Deryn, look out!"

A string of blasts went off around her, sending Deryn flying into the air. They weren't damaging in any way and not designed to kill, only distract. Still, she fell hard onto the ground, her eyes hazy as her head shot up. Everything was spinning, but she refused to let this consume her. She couldn't lose sight of him. Not now.

"Deryn!" screamed a faint voice in the distance.

Whether it was Dakota's or someone else's, she didn't know. Her mind was too muddled to tell. Her ears were ringing as she slowly got to her knees.

"Deryn!" the voice called again. She put her hand on her head to try and focus.

"Deryn?" repeated another voice from just beside her. A terribly hoarse voice that shouldn't have been able to work at all without the assistance of a collar.

Deryn's heart stopped. She slowly turned her head, her eyes widening with fear as they fell upon the familiar face of Soren Tash. He was gazing back at her, also on the ground and squinting as he tried to get a good look at her.

The moment he recognized her was all too evident. It was the eyes. Even when blue, he knew the shape of them, having gazed into them countless times before while he imagined he was falling in love with her.

Deryn gulped. She scrambled to her feet. As she moved away from him, Soren's face grew angry. He jumped up and lunged for her, his fingertips grazing her wrist. But, before he could clutch on, someone knocked him from behind and he fell over.

"Shit, Sorey! Th'fuck you getting in my way for?" shouted Luka, jerking his head at Deryn, reminding her to move. "Dammit, Voclain! That was *her*! Get out of my way!"

As Deryn tried to run, someone grabbed her from behind. She turned quickly to see Bronson's face hidden beneath his hood.

"Let's go!" he shouted.

"But -"

"No buts, Deryn! We have to go *now*!"

Deryn turned back and scanned the crowd one last time. As Bronson pulled her away, she finally caught sight of Dakota. He was still searching for her. His eyes found hers and he tried to push to get there, but the crowd was just too thick.

"I'll find you!" he called over the roar of people. "I'll find you, Deryn! I'll find you!"

Deryn nodded, crying hysterically as his brown eyes faded into the distance. Bronson was pulling her and he was not stopping.

"Where's Xander?" she asked.

"Still on the platform! He's their fucking target!"

Deryn gasped and looked up at the platform. Xander and Elvira were fighting off the people on hover-bikes, President Saevus fighting right there beside them, shooting powerful blasts at anyone who had the misfortune of crossing his path. Several Guardians had made it onto their own hover-bikes, hacked to rise as high as their enemies and chasing them down.

"He'll be fine!" shouted Bronson, tugging on her arm. "Quigley and the others are waiting for us! *Let's go*!"

Deryn nodded. She had to force herself to tear her eyes away from Xander, knowing exactly why they had come for him. It was because of her, and what he had said to Dakota. That he knew where she was.

Deryn and Bronson finally reached the others, who were waiting for them. Kemp and Miki had tried to reach some of the Resistance members to tell them to pull back, but with no luck. Everything was too much of a mess.

With one last look at Xander, Deryn gulped before following the others out of there. This was her fault. Any death that took place throughout all of this was on her hands.

Xander ducked as another hover-bike flew at him. There had to be a good five people coming after him and another five attacking anyone who got in their way.

"What do they want with you?" demanded Elvira.

"Fuck if I know!"

Right at that moment, Laramie and Nita pulled out of the crowd of people fighting on hover-bikes, each reaching down and grabbing one of Xander's shoulders, pulling him high into the air.

"Get off me!" he shouted, successfully pushing Nita off but having to grab onto Laramie's bike so he wouldn't fall.

"Where's Deryn?" Laramie demanded as he flew him over the crowd.

"Seriously?" shouted Xander. "Where's your brother because I'm going to kick his ass for this?"

"Where is she?" shouted Nita, who had suddenly reappeared.

The other Resistance members on hover-bikes started dropping to the ground as Laramie and Nita kept their grip on him. Then they were abandoning their bikes and disappearing into the crowd.

"Safe!" was all Xander said. "Or she was! Who knows after everything you just did!"

When they moved so they were only about ten feet from the ground, Xander let go of the bike but, before he landed, Nita had him again, keeping a firm grip on his arm as she carried him towards an alley with Laramie shooting at any Guardians flying after them.

Nita dropped him into the alley where several of their comrades were leaping into a manhole. She and Laramie landed smoothly. "Where is he?" she asked as Laramie bound Xander's wrists and ankles. "He should be here."

"I don't know," he said, looking around frantically.

"But we need to move before someone follows us!"

"Neetles, I know! But we didn't exactly plan for him not being here!"

Xander rolled his eyes and used a laser in his Guardian wristband to cut through the binds. "Great system you've got here," he said, getting to his feet. "Tell Trigger that he needs to cool it. I already told him she'd be back with him soon enough."

Laramie and Nita aimed their guns sharply at him.

Xander smiled and held his hands up innocently. "I'm not going to attack. I've noticed your weapons have gotten fancier." He motioned to the guns they held, not the primitive firearms of their ancestors but something similar to an Element, only sleeker.

Just then, Dakota came running into the alley.

"Where have you been?" demanded Laramie.

"I saw her!" he shouted. "I saw Deryn!"

"Did you?" asked Xander, cocking an eyebrow. "Let me guess. Blonde hair with bangs, blue eyes, and makeup to cover those stubborn freckles of hers?"

Dakota's eyes widened.

"I told you she was fine you fucking -"

BANG!

The four of them dispersed in different directions as a gust of fire shot down the alley, blasting a hole through the metal building behind it. Xander looked and saw Soren marching towards them.

"My knight in shining armor!" said Xander while climbing back to his feet. He stepped between Soren and the three Resistance members. "The president will want them alive."

"Don't get in my way, Xander! I'm going to kill this ... this little shit!"

BANG!

He was aiming for Dakota, but Dakota didn't give him another chance to strike before he was heading for the same manhole his comrades had disappeared through. Laramie and Nita jumped in first, then he took one last look at Xander before following after them and pulling the cover shut behind him.

"No!" shouted Soren, running over and pulling at it. But it had locked behind them. Soren attempted to blast it open with his Element, but no damage was done.

Xander stared blankly at the spot they had just been. So they were planning to take him through the underground. How would they ever manage that without getting caught by a S.U.R.G.E.? And then he recalled the strange satellite guns they had in Willow that took down the robots. Hadn't he seen something fitting that description poking out of Dakota's belt?

Pressing his back against the building, Xander used it to lower himself to the ground. A shadow flew overhead and he looked up to see President Saevus riding a hover-bike he had somehow acquired.

The president descended towards him and Xander frowned. This was going to be bad.

CHAPTER TWENTY

"I'm telling you, it was her! It was her! It was *fucking* her!" Soren shouted at his brother as all of the Guardians gathered with the president in his conference room. "And I would've had her if Luka hadn't tripped me!"

"It was an accident," spat Luka. "You got in my way while I was trying to get to that damn Trigger."

"So you both had two of Leon's closest allies in your grasp and failed," said the president. He closed his eyes and sighed deeply, a sight that had everyone on edge. "You have disappointed me today. *All* of you." His eyes shot back open, landing right on Xander. "And *Xander*. You were their target."

Xander kept the man's gaze, took a deep breath and said, "It seems that way, sir."

"Why?"

"They were asking me about the location of Deryn Leon."

"But why *you*? Would not any Guardian suffice?"

Xander took another deep breath. "If you recall, during our mission in Willow I had an encounter with Dakota Triggs. I may have implied to him that I knew where she was."

The president's nostrils flared. "And *what* was your reasoning for doing that?"

"We are out a prisoner, sir," explained Xander. "We have no one in our possession to hold over Godfrey Leon anymore. I thought if Triggs believed I had her then he might agree to an exchange. His life for hers. But he claimed to not believe me, and then Aila showed up and fucked the whole thing -"

"He's lying!" shouted Soren, pointing at him accusingly. "President Saevus, surely you can see that he's lying! He was speaking too calmly with the Resistance when I arrived! Something's wrong with -"

"You *dare* call me a liar?" snapped Xander, lunging forward and standing up straight so he was glaring into Soren's eyes. "You and your brother have been getting on my last nerve, Sorey! If you spent half the energy you use fucking with me on serving our president then maybe it wouldn't have been so easy for me to take your seat!"

"Xander, you're already on thin ice," said Atticus, stepping forward and grabbing his son's arm. "Maybe it's time for you to just back off and -"

"No!" shouted Xander. "No, I will *not* back off, Father! I will *not* give in! I have been nothing but loyal to the president for years, while this bastard plans to run away with a toxic slave the first chance he gets!"

All color drained from Soren's face as his brother moved to his side.

"How *dare* you," spat Veli. "My brother would *never* run away with that toxic trash. He's already agreed that her execution is eminent."

"Really?" scoffed Xander. "Is that why I saw him buying a box of hydration and starvation pills, as well as a tent at the Black Market a couple weeks ago? Not to mention the mind control chip he claims he has stashed away for her."

Soren's face tensed. "You fucking little -"

"If this is true, Xander, then why didn't you bring it to my attention sooner?" asked the president.

"I'm sorry, Mr. President, but he offered me a deal for my silence. He's the one who gave me information on the mind control chips and told me how many there were."

Veli looked at his brother in disbelief. He slowly backed away until he was no longer by his side.

"I was going to inform you of his plan the moment we recaptured her," said Xander. While he hadn't intended to throw Soren under the primitive, wheeled tram just yet, it was important for him to direct President Saevus's anger elsewhere. His punishment was inevitable, but maybe now it would be slightly less severe.

Several silent moments passed that were absolutely deafening. Xander had always prided himself on how well he read people, but President Saevus was the one person he'd never been able to figure out. He knew he was angry, that was simple enough, but there were always many more layers to it. Disappointment? Definitely. But did he feel so horribly betrayed that he would want to shed blood for this?

Just as Xander's mind began to wander, the president grabbed Elvira's knife from the holster on her hip and tossed it at one the guards, hitting him straight in the heart.

Xander noticed Lona move to help him, so he quickly held up his hand to stop her. The president had made his decision. This man was suffering the fate that should have been Xander's, and there was nothing any of them could do about it.

"Elvira, take your husband home and locate his chip and pills and anything else he has gathered together," instructed the president, turning to his most trusted Guardian while the guard continued to die on the floor. "Once you locate everything, the two of you will return here. Neither of you have escaped punishment for your failures today."

"Yes, Father," said Elvira with a nod. She took Soren's arm, guiding him out of the room as if he were her prisoner.

"Guards, move my table off to the side."

The guards quickly obeyed.

"Xander, stand in the center of the floor, remove your shirt and drop to your knees."

"As you wish, Mr. President," said Xander. He took off his coat and shirt, then kneeled and awaited further instructions.

"I am disappointed in you, Xander. You've been keeping secrets from me, not just about your encounter with the Resistance, but about Soren, as well." President Saevus turned and looked around the room. "Every last one of you will be punished for your failure today. And Xander." His head slowly moved back in his direction. "You will suffer the pain right along with them."

Xander kept a calm face and said, "Yes, Mr. President." He had to fight the urge to scan the room and count how many Guardians there currently were, because he really had no idea. At least twenty. Probably more. His insides cringed.

"Mr. Voclain, step forward."

Barath obeyed but the president held up his hand and said, "Not you. Luka."

Luka's eyes drifted to Xander as he stepped out of the crowd. "Am I first, Mr. President?"

"No, Luka, today you will be last. Until then, I will need you to use your Element to whip Xander every time I do the same to one of my subordinates."

His eyes still on Xander, Luka took a deep breath and asked, "Why me, sir?"

"It seems only fitting," answered President Saevus. "Xander deserves punishment, and who better to administer it than his one true ally."

"But -"

"Do not argue, Luka," said Xander, staring sharply at him. "The president has made his decision. I *must* be punished."

Luka bit his cheek and nodded slowly.

"Show no mercy," instructed President Saevus from beside him. "Veli, you will have the privilege of going first."

"Yes, Mr. President." Veli walked over, dropping his coat and shirt as he moved, and then kneeling beside Xander. They glanced sideways at each other, Veli not even trying to hide his joy.

The president and Luka moved so they were standing behind them.

"Ready, Luka?"

"Yes, sir."

They each raised their Elements, aimed them at their respective targets and shot out a whip of blue light.

CHAPTER TWENTY-ONE

"Where are they?" Deryn frantically paced around the living room, her wet and swollen eyes never leaving the door as she tried to will Xander and Luka to appear.

"Deryn, please just sit and calm down," encouraged Bronson from the couch. "Xander and Luka will be fine. They -"

"No!" shouted Deryn. "No, I will *not* calm down! This is my fault! They were after Xander because of me, and the president will be angry. He'll be so, so angry." She sobbed, stopping her pacing for a moment to steady herself while her body shook uncontrollably.

Quigley walked out of her and Xander's bedroom carrying her radio. He placed it on the coffee table and switched it on.

Static.

"If you're worried about the president killing him for this it's really not necessary," said Bronson. "Xander's his favorite. He would never -"

"There are things far worse than death, Bronson," Deryn said weakly. "While Xander may be strong there is only so much one person can take before they break."

Suddenly, the static on the radio became smoother, and then someone was speaking. *"Attention all Resistance members,"* said the familiar voice of Talon. *"Today, the first of January, we administered an aerial attack on the city of Utopia during President Saevus's infamous New Year's speech. While we were unable to retrieve what we went for, we ended up with something much greater. Deryn Leon ..."* A pause and a breath. *"... my sister has escaped. She was seen inside the city's walls and in perfect health. That being said, we would like to take this time to offer a reward of ten-thousand coin to anyone with information leading to the return of -"*

Before he finished speaking Deryn marched over, picked up the radio and threw it hard against the wall. Her face was red and her breathing erratic as she stared hypnotically at the shattered remains on the floor. Her fists were clenched so tight that her nails burrowed into her skin, drawing blood that trickled down her fingers.

Bronson sighed and stood. He went over to her, rubbing her hands until they relaxed. While she cried, he opened her palms and wiped them on his sleeve. "Who saw you?" he asked, guiding her over to the sink so he could clean the cuts properly.

"Dax," she answered in a strained voice. "I wasn't able to reach him but I ... I saw him." Deryn paused. "Xander was right. He does look angrier." She laughed through her tears, but it wasn't long before her smile faded and she was thinking of Xander once more. "When I saw him I was so happy but ..." She closed her eyes and whimpered. "... but now all I can think about is the price Xander will pay for Dax's actions. I can't lose him, Bronson. He's everything to me."

"I know," he said, releasing her clean hands and using his thumbs to wipe away her tears. "You're not going to lose him. Please, just sit down and we'll wait for him. Alright?"

Deryn nodded. Bronson put an arm around her shoulders and walked her to the couch. Quigley had picked up the remains of the radio and was currently trying to fix it. He glanced sideways at her and smirked. "Happy New Year, am I right?"

Deryn chuckled halfheartedly. "Seriously."

~

Deryn.

Xander closed his eyes and let her image take hold of him. It was the only way he could endure the pain. His teeth clenched together so tightly he thought they might crack, but he had to keep her name from slipping through his lips.

If it weren't for her then he would have given up already.

Which was exactly what the president was trying to make him do. To see if he was breakable.

Another flash of a whip.

Xander tried to hold in his screams, but the faint sound of someone in agonizing pain kept ringing in his ears. It must have been his cries, but he was dead to them now. *Sixteen.* That was how many times he had been whipped so far, and through the haziness in his eyes, he could make out at least ten unrecognizable figures still waiting for their punishment.

"On your knees, Xander," he heard the muffled voice of the president say.

Xander moved his aching body, his shaky arms nearly giving out as he tried to push himself to his knees. About halfway up, they buckled and Xander collapsed. His throat stung as he coughed, blood spurting out of his mouth and onto the floor beneath him.

"President Saevus, please, he has suffered enough," said the familiar voice of his father as one of the blurry figures stepped forward. "I will take on the rest of his punishment. You may even double it if that's what you -"

"No!" shouted Xander as he jerked his head in the direction he was fairly certain his father was in. "No, you will not take my punishment away from me! This was *my* failure, I deserve this!"

Deryn.

Closing his eyes, Xander envisioned her face once more, giving him strength to pull himself to his knees. He stayed there on shaky legs while the next Guardian appeared beside him.

"Xander, you don't have to do this," said Atticus, his voice strained.

"Yes I do, Father." He opened his eyes again and looked over his shoulder at President Saevus. "I'm ready."

The president smiled wickedly. "You heard him, Luka. Continue."

Xander and Luka locked eyes, Luka's beginning to water as he unsteadily lifted his Element. He gulped, pressing a button and releasing a flash of blue light.

Xander clenched his eyes, his teeth, his fists, his entire body as he tried to hold himself together. He could do this. He could fight the pain. During his first years as a Guardian, he had trained himself to become numb to it. The only reason he felt it now was because of the extremeness of it all. He had never been whipped this many times before.

Xander closed his eyes.

Deryn.

And then he saw her again. Only this time she was different. Looking at him and smiling happily as they stood in the center of the bustling streets of Utopia. He looked down at their clasped hands, noticing the jade ring sparkling in the sun on her left ring finger. Luka was there, laughing with Bronson and Quigley while the latter had his arm linked with a girl who greatly resembled him. His sister. Or Xander's version of her. Del walked up, holding Ronan's hand. She wrapped her arm around Xander and hugged him in a way that felt so familiar. It was just like how his mother used to hug him. Even Talon and Trigger were there. For Deryn, not for him. And her father. Godfrey Leon.

And Deryn ... She was right there, always looking at him in a way that made his heart feel light. Like nothing could ever hurt him, ever touch him. She lifted her free hand and stroked his cheek. "I love you, Xander."

"I love you, too."

And then she was leaning up, standing on tiptoe to kiss him in front of everyone. This was what Xander wanted. A future. With her. In a world where they had won, and they could be together without having to hide. He loved her. He loved her so much that it hurt. But it was a pain he could endure. A beautiful pain that he could never get enough of.

This pain consumed him, taking him over and bringing him to a blissful state of unawareness. A euphoria where there was nothing but this feeling. And then someone was calling his name, sucking him back from this place he had found and never wanted to leave.

Xander opened his eyes and glanced sideways. Luka was there staring at him. He was kneeling beside him hunched over, signifying that he had just taken his own punishment. He looked a lot worse than the others.

"How ... m-many times did he whip you?" Xander asked in a shaky voice.

"Three," answered Luka. "For my failure in catching Triggs."

"Th-that's not f-fair."

Somehow, Xander had managed to stay on his knees through the last of it, but, being brought back to this state of consciousness so suddenly, he felt his legs give in and he fell forward. Luka lunged and caught him before he hit the ground.

Lifting his eyes, Xander could now see that his father was standing where Luka had once been, clearly the one who had struck him these last three times.

President Saevus held his hands behind his back as he continued to gaze at them. Xander met his eyes, his breathing heavy as he tried to convey that he did not fear him. Which was true. The only thing Xander feared anymore was losing Deryn, and he would be damned if he died before saving her.

Several silent moments passed while Saevus and Xander continued to stare at one another. Finally, the president moved his eyes to Luka and said, "Take Xander into the parlor and lay him down. Not on his back, of course. Everyone else is dismissed." He walked out first.

The Guardians all began to vacate the room, Veli smiling smugly as he walked by Xander. Finley and Wyatt went over to help Luka bring him to his feet. Lona stood back a little, looking unsure if she should help or not.

"Lona!" her father called from the doorway. "Leave him be. This doesn't concern you."

Lona turned and stared at him defiantly before going over and helping Finley steady Xander's left arm.

Once he was up, Luka wrapped an arm around Xander's waist, careful not to touch any of his wounds. "You should all leave before the president says something," he told the others. "I can take him the rest of the way."

Wyatt and Finley looked at each other skeptically, but they

eventually nodded and walked out of the room. Lona stayed, though, and asked, "Are *you* alright, Luka? The president seemed to put more power into his attacks on you. You shouldn't -"

"I'm fine," he interrupted. "Just go."

Lona looked sadly at him and nodded. "I know you care about your friend, but don't forget to take care of yourself tonight, as well."

She walked out of the room then, her shirt worn backwards so it wouldn't irritate her wounded back and her coat draped over her arm.

Luka slowly and carefully carried Xander's stiff yet limp body towards the parlor.

"Did I say anything?" Xander asked quietly while they moved.

"No," answered Luka, already knowing very well what he was talking about. "You were unnervingly quiet throughout most of it."

Xander smirked as best he could.

"Was it worth it?" asked Luka with a sigh.

Xander attempted a shrug. "I guess we'll find that out when we get home."

By the time they got to the parlor, everyone else was gone. Luka laid Xander on his stomach on the couch, making sure to carefully place his head on a pillow. Mere seconds later, Atticus walked in with a glass full of a green liquid.

"Xander, drink this," he said, taking a seat by his side.

"But the president -"

"Let me deal with him," interrupted Atticus, propping up his son and pouring the liquid down his throat. Xander drank every last drop.

"Atticus, if you're quite finished, I would like a word alone with your son."

Atticus and Luka turned to see the president standing in the doorway.

"Hurry home, Luka," he ordered, stepping further into the room. "You too, Atticus."

Luka nodded, looking at Xander one last time before heading to the front door, where a wave was waiting for him, holding his shirt and coat. He put them on and slipped out quickly. Atticus stared at his son and sighed before putting down the glass and following Luka out.

President Saevus walked over to an armchair and sunk into it. "I'll give you a few moments for that medicine to set in. Though it was just meant to numb the pain, I believe."

He motioned his hand and a female wave hurried in from the direction of the kitchen, a blue salve already in hand. "Then I believe it's time you and I have a serious discussion about your future."

"Yes, Mr. President."

The wave very carefully applied the salve. Xander closed his eyes while she worked and breathed steadily, his body already beginning to tingle from the numbing medicine his father had given him, easing but not erasing the pain.

Deryn.

More than anything he wanted to leave here. To go home and check on her. To be with her.

She had seen Dakota. While she'd told Xander she'd chosen him, he couldn't help but wonder if the appearance of her first love might change that. It had been more than five years and, while the world had changed, she was becoming more and more like her old self with each passing day. What was to stop her from wanting her old life? With him.

Dakota. The simple choice. The better choice. But Xander's heart couldn't take it. He loved her too much to lose her.

Deryn.

How he longed to say her name aloud. To scream at the president and tell him how much he loved a toxic Outsider. But he couldn't do it. Not now. Not before she was safe. And free. Above all else, he wanted her to be free.

CHAPTER TWENTY-TWO

Luka's alarm went off and Deryn shot to her feet. A minute later, he came through the front door, looking shaken.

"Luka," said Bronson as he stood. "What happened?"

"I'm fine," said Luka, doing his best to stand up straight so they would be unaware of his pain. "The president's just a little pissed is all."

"Where's Xander?" asked Deryn, looking expectantly at the door.

"The president wanted to speak with him privately. It'll probably be a while."

"Is ... is he alright?" asked Deryn, her voice quivering.

Luka tried to meet her gaze but eventually had to stare at the floor. "We should probably start preparing some medicine and bandages."

Deryn's heart sank as she was suddenly overcome with the incredible urge to vomit. But she fought through it and ran to the kitchen, looking through the cabinets for any and every kind of medicine they had. While she searched, she heard soft footsteps come up behind her. Luka.

"What did he do to him?" she asked between choked breaths.

"It's not impor -"

"*Tell* me," she ordered while turning towards him with wide, red eyes.

Luka sighed. "Everyone was punished with a whipping. And Xander ... he had to endure it right along with them."

Deryn whimpered as her jaw fell open. "So he was whipped as many times as there are Guardians?"

Luka looked ashamedly to the floor and nodded.

"How many?"

Silence.

"How many times, Luka?"

He sighed again, much deeper this time. "There were twenty-nine Guardians there, including me, and I was hit three times for failing to capture Triggs. So he was hit thirty-one times."

Deryn gasped.

"Holy shit," said Bronson from the living room.

"And he's *alive*?" asked Quigley in disbelief. "Is he conscious?"

"Yes," answered Luka. "He was conscious the whole time."

Deryn turned away and began reading labels on bottles, her hazy vision making it hard for her to concentrate. *Thirty-one* lashes. In one sitting.

Luka put his hand on her shoulder. "Deryn, he's going to be_"

She fell to her knees, keeping one hand on the counter as she sobbed uncontrollably, her tears falling down her cheeks and soaking the floor. To her surprise, a pair of strong arms suddenly wrapped around her. Through her blurry vision she could just make out Luka kneeling beside her. She sank into him, burying her face in his chest as her mind became flooded with visions of Xander, wounded and writhing as he cried out in pain, trying to appear strong as he fought off unconsciousness.

She knew what it was he feared the most. That if he let the pain, the anger, the president consume him and he gave in then he might never wake up. To him death truly was the worst option, because he wasn't ready for it yet. Not until he had avenged his mother, not until Deryn was safe, not until the world was a place worth living in again. For everyone.

When Deryn opened her eyes Luka was carrying her, laying her down on her and Xander's bed and pulling up the covers.

"Go to sleep," he said, "and when you wake up Xander will be here."

She nodded, clutching the covers tightly as she tried to let sleep take over. But what if she woke up and he wasn't there? While Xander's greatest fear may have been death, hers was losing him. She wasn't ready yet. She loved him. She needed him ...

Back in the kitchen Luka was putting the medicine they would need for Xander aside, getting all of the doses ready.

"We can figure that out when he gets here, you know," said Bronson, coming up beside him. "You can just rest for a moment."

"I need to keep busy," said Luka, his eyes unblinking. Suddenly, he felt a hand grab onto his and hold it still. He looked over to see Bronson staring at him very seriously.

"What aren't you telling me?"

"Nothing," he said, crossing his arms.

"You're hiding something. Is Ruby worse than you let -"

"No," Luka said quickly. "No, nothing like that. He's fine, all things considered."

"Then what is it?"

Luka looked off to the side and sighed. "The president, he ..." He gulped. "He made me do the whipping. On Xander. Twenty-eight fucking times. And then he made his father take over while I received my punishment. I just ... I don't like torturing as it is. And when it's ... when it's someone who ... who fucking matters -"

As Luka spoke, he tried hard to fight off the tears. But he couldn't hold them in any longer and they poured out in two heavy pools, burning his cheeks. Bronson pulled Luka into his arms, letting him cry it out. Luka cringed a little when he touched his back, and tried to pull away. "I told you before that I'm not much of a toucher."

Bronson repositioned his hands so they were around his neck, but kept a firm grip on him and held him in place. "Unfortunately for you, I am. Now, in this moment I am going to continue hugging you and you're *going* to like it."

Luka stopped struggling. "I don't understand you people," he said through his sobs. "You should hate me and Xander for the things we do. We kill people, we inflict suffering, we torture our best friends, and all just so we can survive."

Bronson chuckled. "While you and Ruby are hardly innocent, it's not like you enjoy the things you're forced to do. You can give in and let the president kill you if you want, Luka, but then who would be around to help people when opportunity presents itself? Without you, Deryn would've been captured today. I saw how close that Guardian was to grabbing her. You saved her."

"Did I?"

"Yes, you did. Ruby's strong, he'll get through this. And I'm sure he would rather you were the one torturing him than one of those bastards who have it out for him. I doubt you gave it your all."

Luka smiled into his chest. "I didn't."

"There, you see? You *helped*."

Luka gave in and laughed. "You have strange logic."

"But it's still *logical*. So who cares what roundabout way I had to take to get there?"

"Hey, I fixed it!" Quigley suddenly shouted from the living room. "Looks like the Resistance is still talking."

Luka pulled away from Bronson, but Bronson grabbed his wrist. "Three lashes, Luka. Don't think for one second that I missed that. Take off your shirt and let me treat your wounds."

Luka nodded.

"Go lie down by the radio. I'll be right over."

He nodded again before walking to the living room, taking off his shirt and lying on the floor, listening closely to whatever it was those idiots in the Resistance possibly had to say.

~

"Has that medicine taken affect?"

"Yes," said Xander, carefully pulling himself into a seated position. He really didn't feel much better, but he wanted to get whatever this was over with so he could go home to Deryn. She would be worried about him, and he was just as worried about her. At least Luka would be there by now.

The same wave who had treated his wounds hurried forward, helping him back into his shirt. She then draped his coat over the couch and made a swift exit.

Xander glanced up to see that President Saevus was staring at him, sitting with perfect posture while his green eyes were serious and unblinking. Always unblinking.

"What is it you wanted to speak to me about, Mr. President?"

"I was just curious as to why you didn't let your father take over for you in there. You knew I would have let him."

"Yes, sir, I knew," said Xander. "But it was my punishment and I wanted to endure it on my own. If you didn't believe I could handle it then you wouldn't have inflicted it upon me."

"That is an interesting notion," said the president, picking up a glass of brandy from the table beside his armchair and taking a sip. He offered a glass to Xander but he declined. His mouth ached from clenching his teeth so hard, and he had no interest in swallowing anything down his raw throat.

"Yes, well, five years ago I suffered a similar punishment for my failures during the battle in Eagle Center. You called me weak back then. And a coward."

"Yes, I recall," said Saevus, putting his glass back down. Xander found himself watching the movement of his hand, his eyes landing on the gold band he wore on his left ring finger. One of the few reminders that the monster in front of him had once been human.

"That day I swore that I would better myself, make myself strong, so that I would never have to hear those words come from your mouth again. Not while directed towards me."

It wasn't a lie, but the vow had been more about keeping himself alive than being loyal. He was so young back then, so naïve. He didn't understand that the world could be better.

Xander leaned forward, putting his elbows on his knees and propping his forehead up with his fingers. "Why am I still here, sir? Have you asked me to stay because you've decided to demote me? To send me back to a lower seat?" It was much easier to sound torn up by this than he expected, when really it would have been a relief. He wasn't sure when he started being the president's favorite but he'd hated it every step of the way. And, worse, he'd dragged Luka along with him.

"No, Xander, you won't be losing your seat. Quite the contrary."

Xander's heart stopped. *No.* "What do you mean, sir?"

"With your sketchy past as a guard it hasn't been easy for me to trust you. And after learning of your mother's betrayal, someone who I believed to be a loyal servant of mine, I've been skeptical over who I let into my inner circle. Until now Elvira is the only one I've deemed loyal enough to keep my secrets. But I've decided it's time I take on another, and *you* are the one I have chosen."

There really were no words for this travesty. But Xander scrambled to come up with some. "I don't understand, sir," he said, trying hard to hide the fear he felt over what this might mean for him. "Why now, when so many of your Guardians have been working so hard to expose me as a traitor?"

Leaning back in his chair, Saevus stared straight ahead at the flames burning in his fireplace. "I'm aware of what jealousy is, Xander, and you've been known to evoke it in many people." He paused and breathed in heavily. "You've proven yourself tonight by taking your punishment. No traitor would ever endure that much pain for the one they are betraying."

They would if they had a girl they needed to get home to. Xander had learned what the president wanted a long time ago. He knew what he expected from his Guardians. To never give up until their mission was complete, even if it meant losing their life.

Saevus's hand went to his glass and Xander's eyes drifted back to that gold ring.

"What is it about my hand that intrigues you so?" asked the president, tearing Xander out of his daze.

"Forgive me, Mr. President. I was just looking at your wedding ring."

"Yes. It is a memento of my past."

"But why do you still wear it? It's been a good five years since your wife disappeared."

"Yes, I suppose it has." He paused, his eyes still focused on the flames. "Love makes people weak, Xander. Never forget that. Why, just look at what happened to your poor mother."

Xander's face grew hot as he fought hard to keep himself in control. "Are you saying you still love her, sir?" he asked in an attempt to contain himself.

The president chuckled hoarsely. "No. I do not. I never did love her, not truly. But she loved. She loved Elvira and now she is dead because of it."

Xander gulped. The president had never confessed this story before. To anyone. "Are you saying your wife is dead, sir? And Elvira is the one who -"

The door to the parlor opened and Elvira entered, carrying a large box and a bag full of supplies.

"This is all of it, Father," she said, tossing the box and bag on the floor. "His toxic slave was more than happy to assist me, since my husband wasn't exactly forthcoming." She took a small chip out of her pocket and showed it to him before tossing it in the box with everything else.

Soren slowly stepped into the parlor behind her, his eyes trained nervously on the floor. And rightfully so.

"Welcome back, Soren," said Saevus, rising to his feet. "It appears that you have purchased a lifetime supply of these pills." He stared down at the box for a moment before lifting his Element and blasting the box and bag to oblivion.

Soren winced as he watched what he'd considered his salvation destroyed. Xander's smirk finally returned.

"Father, while I do not condone my husband *or* his actions, I do believe you should be lenient with him. He's agreed to make a deal with you about our future that I know you will love."

"Oh," said Saevus, not sounding the least bit intrigued. "And what's that?"

Soren was shaking as he looked up and met the president's eyes. "When you recapture the slave, if you let me keep her, just me, then I will make sure you finally get that grandson you've been asking for since the day Elvira and I got married."

The president raised his eyebrows and glanced at his daughter, who smiled proudly at him. "And that is what you want, Elvie? I can always have him executed and you would be free to marry someone who is actually worthy." He glanced sideways at Xander.

Elvira's face dropped. "*No*, Father. I couldn't care less about Soren's obsession. Once he has his slave full-time it will only be a matter of months before he's bored of her."

Soren's downcast eyes narrowed. Clearly, he didn't agree.

Saevus was watching Soren again, contemplating this proposal. "Six months, Soren. That is what you'll get with her before she's executed."

Soren's head snapped up. "But -"

"That is the best offer you'll receive, so I suggest you take it before yours is the next death my citizens witness."

"He agrees," Elvira answered for him.

"Good," said Saevus, turning so Soren would know the discussion was over. "Xander, you may leave after giving Elvira her punishment, then you should take a few days to recuperate. We will continue our conversation once you are in better health."

"Yes, Mr. President," said Xander.

"Soren, *you* will follow me."

"Y-yes, Mr. President," said Soren as he nervously followed Saevus out of the parlor.

Once they were gone, Elvira dropped her coat and lifted her shirt, causing Xander to grimace. She turned her exposed back to him and waited for her punishment.

He lifted his Element, pressed the button for the blue flash of light and flicked his wrist, but his heart really wasn't in it.

"That was weak," said Elvira, whose knees had barely buckled from the whipping. "Just how many times were *you* punished?"

"Thirty-one," answered Xander. He put his Element away, grabbed his coat off the back of the couch and walked towards the exit.

"Where are you going? Your president said you must punish me. Do it again," demanded Elvira.

"No. If you find my punishment unsatisfactory then ask your father to do it himself."

"Just what was it the two of you were discussing?"

"My future." He glanced over his shoulder at her and smirked. "It looks like you and I will be equals now." He turned away again. "Have a good day, Elvie. And let your father know I'm taking his car home."

The car was already waiting outside for him, the president having called for it ahead of time. Xander sat hunched over in the back seat as the car moved through the city, closing his eyes and trying to focus his thoughts away from the pain.

When he arrived home, he breathed evenly as he ascended the stairs. The door was open when he reached the fifth floor and someone was standing there, calling his name, but he didn't have time to register who it was before he was falling to the floor, landing hard on his hands and knees, and hacking up blood.

"Shit, Ruby!"

Xander looked up to see Bronson and Luka hovering over him while Quigley stood behind them, looking concerned. No Deryn.

Then Xander heard a thud, followed by footsteps coming from the bedroom.

"Get me up," he ordered.

"Xander, I don't think -"

"Get me up!"

Bronson and Luka helped him to his feet and brought him inside. They had just stabilized him when the bedroom door flew open. Deryn located him with her swollen eyes and darted across the room.

"Xander!" She went to hug him but quickly pulled back, not wanting to aggravate the wounds she knew were hidden beneath his clothes.

Grabbing her shoulders sternly, Xander looked directly into

her red-rimmed sea-green eyes and said, "You are *never* going out there again. Not to the Black Market, not to Del's, nowhere. You understand?"

Deryn nodded, tears spilling from her eyes as his posture weakened.

"Good," he said, pulling her into his chest and hugging her through the pain.

Deryn carefully put her hands on his sides, barely grazing her fingers since she was afraid to injure him more.

"Where's the medicine?" she asked, turning her head towards Luka.

"I'll get it." He went into the kitchen and came back with a glass of some purple liquid and a couple of pills. The liquid was meant to heal his lashes faster and the pills would extend the numbness from the medicine his father had given him.

"Did you take any for yourself?" asked Xander as Luka handed him the glass and pills.

Luka shook his head. "But Bronson put some salve on my back."

"Lona wasn't wrong, Luka. Take care of yourself. I'll be fine."

Xander tried to hand everything back to him, but Luka shook his head again. "I'll get my own." He returned to the kitchen.

Xander's hand began to shake, so Deryn took the glass and helped him drink after he popped the pills into his mouth. "You need to get off your feet," she said, handing the glass to Quigley before draping one of Xander's arms around her shoulders. "Bronson, help me move him to the bedroom."

"Deryn, I'm fi -"

"Don't you dare finish that sentence, Xander Ruby!" she snapped. "You are obviously *not* fine."

Xander quickly shut his mouth.

Bronson came up on his other side. "I could always just carry him."

"What, like I'm some fucking damsel in distress?" Xander sneered. "I'll pass."

Bronson smirked. "I see you're just as charming as ever." He draped Xander's other arm around his shoulders, and he and Deryn helped him walk towards the bedroom.

Xander carefully climbed onto the bed, collapsing onto his stomach.

"Prop him up, Bronson. I want to get these clothes off of him."

"Fuck. No," said Xander, moving away and cringing as Bronson came towards him.

Deryn rolled her eyes. "Must you always be so difficult?"

"Yes."

"Fine," she said. "Bronson, you can go."

He nodded and left the room, shutting the door behind him.

Once he was gone, Deryn helped Xander back into a seated position. He cringed even more than before, but he somehow managed to stay like that while she pulled off his coat, followed by his shirt and pants.

Once Xander was naked and again lying on his stomach, Deryn took a moment to run her eyes over his back, taking in every last gash carved into his porcelain skin. Her eyes flooded again and, despite her best efforts to hold them in, her tears spilled over. She reached out and traced her fingers down his arm.

Xander grabbed her hand when it reached his and interlaced their fingers. "Deryn, please don't cry."

"How could he do this to you?" she asked with a whimper. "He believes you're on his side. Why would he hurt you like this?"

"He's not exactly logical. But he did have one of his wave's apply a salve so there's no need for that."

Deryn nodded and wiped her eyes. She lay down beside him, using her free hand to stroke his hair. "I can't take this anymore, Xander. President Saevus and his followers, they ... they've already taken so much. They've taken it all. My life. My family. My friends. My virginity. My mind. And today ... today they tried to take you."

"No," said Xander, shaking his head. "No, they didn't -"

"Yes they did. *Thirty-one* lashes," she spat. "You could have died. *Should* have died. I mean, even *I* was never hit that many times in one sitting." She closed her eyes and clenched her fist around a handful of hair.

Xander reached out to wipe her eyes, but she gently pressed his arm back down. "Please don't," she cried, shutting her eyes again and letting her tears fall down her cheeks. "I don't want you to hurt any more than you already do."

"They're just cuts, Deryn. Seeing you like this ... that's what hurts."

Deryn opened her eyes and looked at him sadly before leaning in to delicately kiss his lips.

Xander reached up and moved her hair out of her face, carefully tucking it behind her ear. "And you forget. *I* took your virginity. Not them."

Deryn chuckled softly through her tears and kissed him again. The two of them held hands in silence. A good hour passed before Deryn finally asked him, "What did the president want to speak to you about?"

"I'm not really sure," he said. "He's not exactly forthright. But he's deemed me loyal enough to learn more of his secrets. He says from now on I will be an equal to Elvira."

"He's bringing you closer?" asked Deryn. "So that you can become more like him?"

"Yes, it seems that way."

She took a deep breath. "No. You can't do that. You already do so much for him. Every day I see your soul becoming more torn. You *cannot* give him more of yourself."

"I don't really have a choice," said Xander, his brown eyes dark and gloomy.

"Yes, you do," she insisted, squeezing his hand tightly. "You can come with me. We can find a way out of here tomorrow and the president won't know anything until -"

"No," Xander said sternly. "I can't go with you, Deryn. It's too dangerous. Especially now that he's decided I'm trustworthy. If he finds out I'm a traitor then he won't rest until I'm found. Your safety is the most important thing to me. I won't risk -"

"But your safety is the most important thing to *me*!" shouted Deryn as she shot up. "It's *not* safe for you in Utopia! I won't leave you here!"

Xander sighed. He reached up and brought her back down. "I don't want to lose you either, you know?"

"Then why won't you come with me?" she cried, plopping her forehead against his. "I love you, you idiot. I love you."

"I love you, too."

Xander kept his eyes open, watching Deryn as she cried beside him. He hated this, seeing her cry, knowing that it would soon be over for them. But he had to do it. He had to let her go.

"Deryn."

She opened her eyes and gazed at him.

He wiped her tears with his thumb. "Deryn, I ... I want to feel you."

"What?"

"I want to feel you," he repeated. "The only way I made it through all of that torture earlier was by thinking of you, and I just want to make sure that you're really here. That I'm still alive."

Deryn chuckled and whimpered at the same time. "*Really*, Xander? *Now*?"

"No time like the present," he said with a grin.

She grinned back and stroked his lips. "I don't want to hurt you."

"I think I can suffer through a little pain for sex," he said. "Now, take off your clothes. I'm not exactly in any condition to strip you."

Deryn full-on laughed now. She stood and undressed. Then she lay back down so her body was pressed against his side. Xander cupped her cheek and kissed her softly, making sure to keep contact as she moved her hand between his body and the bed, stroking him as best she could.

"How are we supposed to do this exactly? You can barely move."

"Just shimmy under me and I'll make it work."

Deryn laughed again and shook her head at the ridiculousness of what they were doing. She lifted Xander just enough to move under him, carefully maneuvering their bodies until he was lying on top of her.

Placing his hands on either side of her, Xander lifted himself as much as he could.

Deryn leaned up and kissed his lips, using one hand between them to carefully guide him inside of her. Xander immediately moaned into her mouth.

"Yes. Definitely real," he said before biting onto her bottom lip.

Xander slowly began to move. He kept his eyes open, closely watching her as she radiated soft pleasure. She pulled away from his lips and opened her eyes so she could gaze back at him.

"Deryn ... you need to touch yourself."

"But -"

"I'm fine," he said. "We both know you won't come like this and I want to feel you. *All* of you."

Deryn nodded. She moved her hand between their bodies and gently rubbed her clit. They both kept their eyes open, only focused on each other as they grew closer to their release.

As Deryn's orgasm hit, she arched her back, causing the ring dangling from her neck to fall into Xander's line of sight. While staring at it, he remembered the place he had gone to escape the pain from his torture. Their future.

He looked beyond the ring and found Deryn's eyes back on him. Gazing into those sea-green irises, Xander immediately found his own euphoria. Deryn leaned up and kissed him through it. He took this moment to wrap his arms beneath her body and hold her close. The reward of having her there was well worth the pain.

It took them a little longer to catch their breath since their lips never parted but, once they did, Xander pulled away slowly, running one hand through her hair and never once looking away from those eyes.

"I love you," he said, completely numb to any pain but the one he felt in his heart.

Deryn smiled softly and said, "And I love you."

And then, for a brief moment, that aching feeling that had permanently made a home in Xander's chest finally released. This was *it*. That complete satisfaction he'd always wanted, always craved. Never in his life had he ever felt so complete.

Xander and Deryn remained lost in each other's eyes. What the two of them had was so much more, so much stronger than anything the president could throw at them. He could torture and take whatever he wanted from them, but he could never take this. *Love*. The strongest power in existence.

CHAPTER TWENTY-THREE

"Hold still, will you?" ordered Deryn as Xander fidgeted on the bed. She was trying to rub the last of the blue salve he'd given her that first day he brought her home on his gashes, but he was being difficult.

"You shouldn't waste that stuff on me. It's *supposed* to be for when you leave."

The faint hint of a smile crept on her lips. "I'll send Bronson to buy more." She grabbed his arms and wedged them between his sides and her thighs while rubbing the paste gently on his back. This time he gave in and let her.

Xander could see Deryn in the mirror over the dresser, and watched closely as she worked. He couldn't help but smile. "It seems we've come full circle."

"What do you mean?" she asked, her hands never stopping as she met his eyes in the mirror.

"First you gave me a cupcake, and now you're taking care of me while I'm hurt. Just add a bath to this and it's like we've gone back in time."

Deryn smirked. "Well, I was considering giving you one to clean off all of this dried blood." She scraped a bit of it off his back, trying hard not to disturb the gash it had come from.

"Really?" said Xander, raising his eyebrows. "And will you be naked, too?"

"Not if you want to complete the circle. You were very respectful that first night."

"Yes, well, I was a little afraid to get a full view of the damage. Just seeing you with your clothes on was horrid enough."

Deryn sighed. "Still. I know I didn't say it then but what you did for me that first night ... It meant a lot."

"It wasn't creepy?" he asked, cocking an eyebrow.

Deryn rolled her eyes. "No, Xander, *you're* not creepy. I was referring to the situation. I mean, what inspired you to buy me a cupcake, anyway?"

Xander attempted to shrug, but Deryn grabbed his shoulders and held them still. "I don't know. I just passed this woman in the Black Market selling them and I thought, 'Oh, right! It's her birthday,' so I bought one. I didn't realize it was going to be this big thing that you all would *never* let go."

Deryn's smile grew wider as she moved her hands along the next gash. Whatever the president had given him was healing them nicely. The smaller wounds were already closed.

Xander suddenly gulped, so she looked at him in the mirror again.

"So you saw Dakota yesterday."

"I did," she said casually as she went back to her task.

"And?"

"And what?"

He didn't answer.

She frowned. "If for some reason you think there was this magical moment of clarity where I realized that he's the one I want to be with then you'd be wrong. I made my choice and I'm standing by it."

The corner of his lips twitched.

"But that doesn't mean I felt nothing when I saw him," she added before he could get too smug about it. "Sometimes I forget how much I miss him and Talon and everyone else, but seeing him ... it was a bit of a reality check, I suppose."

Xander's smile faded.

Deryn sighed. "I'm not giving up on you, you know? I want you to come with me and I've always had a knack for getting what I want."

"Yes, you're very stubborn," he said.

"Not compared to you."

"That's debatable."

Deryn rolled her eyes again.

She climbed off of Xander and went to fill the bathtub with scorching hot water, just the way he liked it. She then helped him stand, carefully guiding his broken body into the bathroom and then the water, one leg at a time. Once he was in, she grabbed a washcloth and lathered it up, climbing onto the edge of the tub and straddling him between her legs.

"You're *really* not getting in here with me?" he asked with a pout.

"No, Xander. The point of this bath is to get you clean, not dirty."

"Says who?"

"Me."

"Well, *I* say otherwise."

Xander grabbed firmly onto Deryn's arm. She let out a loud, "Eek!" as he flipped her over his shoulder and into the tub.

Fuck, that hurt! But it was worth it to see the angry look on her face as she flipped her wet hair out of her eyes.

"Xander Ruby, you have some nerve! How dare you -"

He silenced her with a kiss. It was the easiest way to distract her, especially since he had no intention of letting her stay in those wet clothes.

Xander slowly began to unbutton her pajama top, which he was able to get off without too much protest.

"You're such an ass!" she said, shoving him away. When his wounded back touched the side of the tub and he cringed, she immediately felt guilty and began stroking his chest. "I'm sorry! Did I hurt you?"

"No," he lied, taking this moment to slip his hand into her bottoms, not even giving her a moment before plunging a finger inside of her.

It wasn't long before her bottoms and underwear were off, and she was bouncing on top of him. Xander grabbed firmly onto her hips but the act disturbed his wounds. He decided that, for now, he would have to relinquish control. But the sound of water splashing made it plenty exhilarating. Her nails tugged at his hair as she drew closer to her climax. The whole experience hurt like hell, but Xander really didn't care in that moment, because the most important part of his body felt great.

"How do you always feel so fucking amazing?" he groaned while sucking down her neck.

Deryn came first, but only by mere seconds.

Out of breath and very much satisfied, Xander looked into her eyes and smirked. "I'll bet you never thought we'd be doing *this* in a tub that first night I bathed you?"

Deryn smirked back. "Definitely not," she said, removing her hands from his hair. "I really am a terrible caregiver. All I've done is cause more damage."

"I disagree," he said. "Personally, I think you just might be the best caregiver I've ever had. Give me five minutes and I'll be able to show you my gratitude."

Deryn giggled as he kissed her neck again. But, just when he reached her collarbone, she froze. Keeping his lips in place, Xander glanced up at her.

"Xander, I think someone's at the front door."

"What?"

Tap. Tap. Tap.

"There! Did you hear that?" she asked, turning her head. "Someone's knocking." And apparently the sound of moaning and water splashing had drowned out the alarm.

"Luka can get it."

"I sent him to the Black Market to get you more medicine. I don't think he's back yet."

Xander groaned. "Oh, hell."

Deryn got out first, then carefully lifted Xander up and over the side of the tub. She hurried to the bedroom, grabbed his robe and helped him put it on.

"Walking is fucking painful," he said while slowly moving into the bedroom.

Deryn followed him, grabbed her own robe off of the chair it hung over and slipped it on. On his way out, Xander grabbed his unregistered Element off of the dresser and put it in his robe pocket.

"Don't get too comfortable," he said as he reached his bedroom door. "We're far from finished with that bath." He winked before opening the door and shutting it behind him.

Whoever was at the front door was knocking more aggressively now.

"I'm fucking coming!" he called. It took him a while, but eventually he reached the door and looked through the peephole. He groaned when he saw Elvira pacing around out there.

He yanked it open. "What the fuck do *you* want?" he asked with a sneer.

"My father sent me," she answered. "He asked that I bring you *this*." Elvira moved out of the way and motioned to a girl standing nervously on the staircase. Soren's slave.

Xander crossed his arms. "I don't want her."

"Not permanently. Just for the day. To take care of you."

"Why isn't she taking care of her own master? I can't imagine he's in the greatest condition right now."

Elvira grunted. "He's not. But my father has asked *me* to take care of my husband. So, until tomorrow, this nuisance belongs to you."

"I'm not interested," said Xander, trying to shut the door, but Elvira put her foot in the way so he couldn't.

"You don't really have a choice. These are your president's orders and you *must* obey."

"No," said Xander, kicking her foot out of the way and trying to shut his door again.

But Elvira was persistent. She slammed her hand against the door and forcefully pushed it open, grabbing Xander's shoulder and pressing her fingers into his back.

Xander cried out in agony and fell to his knees.

"Get in here," she ordered the slave, who was quick to obey. "Bring her with you when you come to the meeting tomorrow. You may have a few days off from actual work, but you will *not* miss a meeting."

"You can't order me around anymore. We're equals now."

"We'll see about that." Elvira grabbed the door handle and shut Xander and the slave inside.

When Xander tried to get back to his feet she moved to help him, but he pushed her off. "Go home. You're not wanted here." Looking at the girl, Xander could see that her eyes were swollen from crying. Not to mention her face from a brutal beating, or several.

She gulped. "But my master says I must serve you. He made it quite clear that I'm to stay with you until tomorrow."

"Aren't you worried about him?" Xander really didn't care about the answer, he just wanted her to leave.

The girl was taken aback. She obviously wasn't asked many questions. "Y-yes. Of course. I love my master. But he's ordered me to -"

"God, you're a fucking puppet. Don't you ever think for yourself?"

"I ..." She looked unsure of how to answer. "I must follow orders. President Saevus wants me here and my master wishes to please him. I am to be of any assistance to you that I can."

She blushed, causing Xander to raise his eyebrows. Then she was moving towards him, slipping her hands into his robe. Xander backed away.

"What are you -"

The girl moved with him, grabbing onto the belt holding his robe together and pulling. *Shit.*

"Get your fucking hands off me!"

"But my master says I must! He says I must assist you the same way I assist him!"

Xander grabbed her hands to stop her, but his body was still very weak and his legs gave out as he struggled, sending them both toppling to the floor.

"Ah! FUCK!"

When Xander screamed, the door to his bedroom flew open and Deryn ran out. Her eyes widened in anger when she saw there was a girl on the floor beside him. Then the girl looked up and their eyes met.

"*You!*" shouted the girl, her face livid. "You fucking bitch!"

In a flash, she was on her feet and lunging for Deryn. But Deryn grabbed her and flipped her over her shoulder like Luka had taught her. When she was down, Deryn straddled her back and pinned her arms, using Xander's Guardian shackles that she must've grabbed from his coat pocket to bind the girl's wrists.

"Untie me! Untie me and fight me for real, you bitch! Let me slit your fucking throat open like *you* slit *his*!"

Deryn pulled Xander's belt free from his robe and tied it around the girl's yapping mouth.

"What are you doing out here?" asked Xander, struggling to get to his feet while holding his robe closed.

Deryn left the girl and hurried over to help him. "I'm sorry, but when I heard you scream I thought someone was attacking you."

"She was," he said, draping an arm around her shoulders while she pulled him up. "She's Soren's personal slave. I think he told her to fuck me."

Deryn crinkled her nose. "*Gross.*"

"Whatever. We still have Chace's mind control chip. We'll just have to install it," he said, glancing at the collar around her neck. "You know her?"

"Yes. She was the slave I replaced the night I escaped. She tried to convince Soren to keep her instead, but when she called me a whore he struck and banished her. How did she end up as his *personal* slave?"

"She gave information on -" Xander stopped dead. "*Shit.* Luka."

"She gave information on Luka?" asked Deryn curiously.

"No, she -"

The front door flew open and Luka entered the apartment, not even noticing them standing there until his shoes were off.

"Th'fuck you two looking at?" he asked while removing his coat. He started to hang it in the closet, but then he noticed the girl bound on the floor. He froze. It didn't immediately register in his head how he knew her, but the moment it did was quite evident. "*You.*"

The girl's eyes widened.

Luka whipped his head towards Xander. "What's *she* doing here?"

"The president sent her to take care of me."

"I guess that explains why I saw the Tash car outside. Fucking little ..." Luka dropped his coat, stormed over to the girl and lifted her up just enough to slap her hard across the face.

Deryn gasped.

"Luka!" shouted Xander. "What the fuck are you doing?"

"This is the bitch - the *fucking bitch* who turned in Anna!"

"I know, but you can't slap a woman like that!"

"She's not a woman! She's a selfish fucking *monster*! Someone innocent is dead because *she* fell in love with a rapist!"

The girl's face fell into a horrible scowl as she attempted to yell through her gag.

Luka removed the belt and Xander quickly snatched it back, retying it around his waist.

"He's *not* a rapist, you fucking bastard!" she screamed, angry tears flooding her eyes. "He's good and kind and he loves me!"

Xander and Luka both laughed, but Deryn threw a hand over her face to hide her disgust. She couldn't even look at this pathetic girl. Thank god she'd never been brainwashed like that.

"You're all sick!" the slave continued to shout. "How could you betray him like this? By harboring *her*! The filthy whore who doesn't deserve to be breathing!"

Xander lunged forward, but Deryn grabbed his arm and held him back.

"You better hold your tongue, bitch!" he shouted.

The girl laughed.

The front door opened again and they all turned and watched Bronson enter. "What's with all the shouting?" he asked while kicking off his shoes.

They all turned back to the girl and Bronson followed their heads. His mouth fell open.

The girl blinked. "Bronson?"

"Fiona? W-what are you doing here?" he asked. "*Why* is she

tied up?"

Bronson hurried forward and reached for her binds, but Luka stepped in his way and aimed his Element. "Don't you dare release her!"

"But ... what's going on?" asked Bronson, looking at Xander and Deryn. "Why would you bring her here just to tie her up?"

They all cocked their heads and blinked.

"Bronson, what are you talking about?" asked Deryn. "She's just a slave sent here to take care of Xander."

"You mean you didn't find her and bring her here?"

More vacant blinking.

"How th'fuck do you know her?" asked Luka, keeping his Element steadily aimed.

Bronson looked Luka in the eye and said, "She's Quigley's sister. His fucking little sister! And you have binds on her! *Why?*"

"*Shit,*" whispered Xander while Deryn clutched his arm tighter.

Luka finally lowered his Element, his face falling into a frown. "Well, you might want to tell him to prepare himself, because *this* girl is fucking gone."

"What do you mean?" asked Bronson, tears filling his eyes as he tried to look past Luka to Fiona.

"Bronson." Deryn stepped forward. "She's the personal slave of the Guardian whose throat I cut to escape, and she's a little bitter about it."

"Bitter?" he repeated, knitting his brow. "But he's a sick bastard. He bought all of those pills to -"

"No!" Fiona cried out. Her eyes clenched shut and she burst into tears. "It wasn't for *her*! He would *never* run away with *her*! He would never leave me!"

"Oh?" said Xander. "And is that what you told his wife when you showed her where it was hidden along with the rest of his supplies?"

Fiona's eyes opened and she stared daggers at him. "He loves me," she said through gritted teeth.

"Fiona, what's happened to you?" asked Bronson, wiping his

wet eyes.

Before she could answer, the door opened again and Quigley walked in. They all whipped their heads towards him, Bronson and Luka moving to block Fiona from view.

Quigley looked at all of them curiously. "What are you all -"

"Mason?" said Fiona.

Shit. No one had thought to gag her again.

"Mason! Mason, help me!"

Quigley went very still as he listened to the voice. The moment it clicked in his head was very clear. "What the fuck?" he asked, running forward and pushing Bronson and Luka out of the way. "Fiona!"

"Mason!" she cried. "Mason, please! Untie me!"

Quigley reached his hands out, but Luka raised his Element and aimed it at his neck. "*Don't,*" he said sternly.

"I ... I don't ..." He turned and looked at his friend. "Bronson?"

Bronson sighed and looked ashamedly towards the floor. "Sorry, mate. But *this* isn't Fiona."

"Yes I am, you fucking pansy!"

Bronson smiled halfheartedly. "At least you still have that mouth of yours."

"As I recall, you used to get a lot of joy out of my mouth before you flipped your switch on me!"

Bronson chuckled. Noticing Luka watching him with raised eyebrows, he said, "She was my last girlfriend before I *switched* teams. Always been a bit bitter about it."

"Yeah, because you cheated on me with a *man!*"

"Hey, you're the one who said you wanted to bring another person into the bedroom to liven things up. It's not my fault you chose a man instead of a -"

"I *thought* we agreed never to talk about this in front of me!" shouted Quigley, who had turned bright crimson. "What do you mean this isn't Fiona, Bronson? It certainly seems like her."

"Because it *is* me, Mason" she insisted. "He's just been blinded by this traitorous Guardian he keeps eyeing!" She motioned her head towards Luka.

"I'm not the one who's been blinded, Fiona," said Bronson, crossing his arms. "You're the one who's fallen in love with her slave owning rapist."

Quigley went white.

Fiona laughed. "He's not my rapist, Bronson. And you know why? Because you *can't* rape the willing!"

"This is sickening," Xander whispered to Deryn. Noticing he was getting a bit wobbly on his feet, she repositioned one of the armchairs and sat him in it.

"Whose slave is she?" Quigley asked weakly, reaching out and touching a bruise on her cheek. She flinched.

"The man who Deryn slit right here," said Luka, dragging his finger across his throat. He winked at Fiona.

She went crazy trying to get to him. "You bastard! You fucking bastard! He is ten times the man you'll ever be! He's strong! He's powerful! And he loves me! Not *her*!" She motioned her head towards Deryn, who was sitting on the edge of Xander's chair with his arm wrapped around her waist. When she tensed, he tightened his grip.

"Keep telling yourself that, sweetheart," said Luka. He leaned forward and patted her on the cheek.

Fiona's nostrils flared and she spit on him.

Luka jumped. "Fucking bitch!"

He tried to lunge forward but Bronson held him back.

"Don't you hurt her, Luka! I promise this is *not* the girl I grew up with! She's been brainwashed! She's -"

"I HAVE NOT!" she screamed. Then her eyes fell back on Deryn. They narrowed. "Mark my words, I *will* kill you for what you did to him, you fucking -"

"Okay. Quiet time for you," said Bronson, pulling off one of his socks and stuffing it in her mouth. While she gagged, he tossed her over his shoulder and dropped her in Luka's bedroom, shutting her inside.

The moment she was gone, Quigley started crying.

Luka looked torn for a second while Bronson comforted his friend.

Deryn stood up and walked over to them. "Quigley, she's

just confused. When Outsiders are first made slaves they're tortured horribly. But Soren doesn't torture his slaves. She must have mistaken that for ..." She gulped, "... for love. It's fixable. It's -"

"She's *not* just confused, Deryn!" Quigley paused and took a breath. "She's fucked. Her mind is literally fucked!"

"You don't know that," said Xander, rising carefully from his chair. "Soren's at the top of my hit list. When he's gone, she might get over it quicker than you think. And now that Luka and I know who she is, we can keep an eye on -"

"Keep an eye?" snapped Quigley, cocking his head. "You're not sending her back there?"

Xander and Luka looked at each other and sighed. "We don't have a choice," said Xander. "She was only given to me for the night. I have to return her tomorrow."

"Return her? She's my sister, *not* a fucking object, Ruby!"

"Her owner would disagree."

Quigley's teeth clenched. He stormed forward and punched Xander hard in the jaw before continuing towards the balcony, fumbling in his pockets until he came out with his pack of cigarettes.

Deryn hurried to Xander's aid while Bronson followed Quigley out.

"That came out worse than I meant it to," said Xander, rubbing his jaw.

Deryn sighed and gave it a kiss. "I know. And I'm sure Quigley will realize that too, once he's had a moment to cool off."

"Well, *this* is a fucking disaster," said Luka, staring at his closed bedroom door. She had managed to get the sock out and was screaming wildly. "Seriously, out of *all* the slaves in the city, what are the chances?"

"One in a million," said Deryn as she helped Xander back into his armchair.

Luka huffed. "I hate that bitch. And I hate our small world."

Deryn looked over at the door and sighed. She couldn't agree more.

CHAPTER TWENTY-FOUR

"So you've kissed Bronson, Bronson's kissed Fiona, and Fiona's kissed Sorey. So, by association, you've *also* kissed Sorey," Xander concluded with a smirk as he and Luka sat in the basement, waiting for Deryn to finish her laps up and down the five flights of stairs.

"It doesn't work like that!" snapped Luka. "Sorey came long after Bronson, so there's been no damn crossover."

"Whatever helps you sleep at night."

"You're lucky I'm too much of a gentleman to mention *your* direct link to Soren."

Xander responded to that comment by smacking Luka hard on the back of the head. As far as he was concerned, anything that happened between Deryn and Soren didn't count.

It had been two days since the disaster encounter with Fiona Quigley and one day since Xander had returned her to Soren with Chace's mind control chip installed in her collar. He basically used it to blank her memory of the events that transpired in his apartment. If Soren asked all she would tell him was that Xander had locked her in Luka's bedroom for the night. Quigley was pretty angry about it, feeling they should have at least made her fend off Soren's future advances, but Xander refused. If she went back to him acting different in any way then Soren might get suspicious and discover the chip.

Quigley wasn't presently speaking to him.

Deryn's footsteps could be heard in the distance, growing louder until she was running into the basement, stopping in front of the punching bag Luka had gotten her as a late

Christmas present - along with all her other training equipment - and going at it for a good minute before dropping and doing ten push-ups. Then she jumped up again and sprinted for the stairs, slowing for a brief moment to give Xander a kiss.

"Work it, baby!" he called after her. He smiled proudly at Luka. "Mine."

Luka rolled his eyes. "Your love disgusts me."

"This coming from someone going on a date with a *man* tonight." Xander smirked.

"It's not a date!"

"The two of you are going out and no one else is invited. Date."

"We're just hanging out."

"Will you be dining together?"

A pause. "Yes."

"Date."

Luka snapped his head and stared at him sharply.

Xander chuckled. "You've already admitted that you like him so I don't know why you're so defensive."

"You *know* why. If my father ever found out about this -"

"He's not going to find out. You and Bronson doing things together is hardly abnormal, and in my current condition no one expects me to be there with you. It's the perfect time to go out, just the two of you, so stop whining and just take it already."

The corner of Luka's mouth twitched. "You've been surprisingly understanding about all of this."

Xander shrugged. "As long as it's not my girl I don't care who you date or fuck, or whatever else you do when you're alone. I don't like many people, but I like you and I like Bronson, so maybe that means you're a good match."

Deryn came barreling down the stairs right then, exhausted but determined as she went to town on the punching bag. After her ten pushups, she dragged herself over to Xander and collapsed in his lap.

"I am in *terrible* shape."

"Yeah, five years of slavery will do that to you," he said,

leaning down as best he could to kiss her. She met him well more than halfway.

"But you're already improving," said Luka encouragingly. "And Xander said you flipped that female Quigley bitch pretty damn well the other night. Really sorry I missed it."

"Remember, Luka, she *has* been brainwashed," said Deryn.

"Brainwashed or not, she lost my pity the moment her actions caused another person's death," snapped Luka. "She was selfish, Deryn. Maybe she was brainwashed to feel something for Sorey, but she chose to sacrifice an innocent old woman to be with him. That's bad character, *not* brainwashing."

Deryn sighed, unable to argue. "Alright, boys," she said, sitting up. "Shirts off."

Both of them raised their eyebrows. "Are we finally having that three-way?" asked Luka.

Xander glared at him. "Just because you've turned to men doesn't mean I -"

"No, you idiots. I grabbed the salve on my last run upstairs and you both need it reapplied."

"I only got three lashes," said Luka.

"Don't cut down your pain by comparing it to Xander's, Luka. You were both wounded and I will be applying this salve until you are *both* healed. Now, shirts off," she ordered, already pulling Xander's over his head.

She was silently scolding herself for accidentally breaking one of his wounds back open in a moment of passion the previous night. As spectacular as medicine in Utopia was it still had its limits, which was why she had officially called off all sexual endeavors until Xander was healed.

She meant it this time and he knew it, practically throwing a fit that morning when she avoided all of his playful attempts to get her in the tub while she bathed him and then dressed his wounds.

Deryn peeled off the bandages now, sighing as she looked at the damage done to his beautiful skin. Apparently, cuts and bruises got better before they got worse and it certainly seemed like his were at their peak. She hoped, anyway.

"Looking at that, don't you dare try and tell me my gashes are just as relevant," said Luka.

Deryn glared at him. "They are. You both matter to me and I hate seeing either of you hurt." She returned her gaze to Xander and began applying the salve. "I expect your shirt to be off by the time I'm finished, Luka."

Luka grunted but obeyed, taking off his shirt and watching Xander's face closely as he tried to mask the pain he felt.

When Deryn was finished, she gently kissed each of Xander's shoulders before moving on to Luka.

"Do I get a kiss?" he asked.

"I imagine you'll get several tonight," she answered with a smirk.

While she worked on Luka, Xander pressed his wristband to check the time. "We need to leave in ten minutes if we're going to make the tram."

Since Deryn had forbidden him from riding his hover-bike in his current condition, it was his only means of getting to the Guardian meeting in Inner City, and Luka had graciously offered to ride with him. After she pinched him until he agreed, of course. They had done the same thing the previous day with Fiona in tow and it had been one hell of a ride. She certainly was vocal for a slave who was supposed to fear Guardians.

"I'll run up to get your bandages and coats," said Deryn, applying the last of the salve on Luka's most painful gash and hurrying upstairs before either man could protest. When she returned, she bandaged them both up and helped them into their shirts and coats.

Deryn walked them to the building's exit, Xander pausing to say goodbye to her properly. Ever since his punishment had been administered, she had a hard time believing that letting him return to that place was the safest thing for either of them. She wanted to run and she wanted to do it now. But he was adamant.

"I'll be back in a few hours, Deryn. You really don't have to worry."

She whimpered but nodded, holding his face in her hands

and kissing him tenderly. Then she looked at Luka over his shoulder. "Take care of each other. I love you both and I expect you to walk back through this door in one piece."

Xander smiled and kissed her cheek. "You love me more though, right?"

She rolled her eyes and shoved him towards the door.

Of course he was right. She loved him more than anyone. With a laugh, he gave her one last kiss before walking out the door with Luka. They got a good block away before he finally showed the pain he was feeling.

"I don't know why you try to hide it," said Luka as they reached the tram stop. "She's not an idiot. She knows you still feel like hell."

"She doesn't need to know how extreme that hell is," said Xander, leaning against the closest building for support.

The tram arrived and the two of them road it to the gate to Inner City. Once they were through, they took another tram towards the president's towering home in the dead center of the city. But no public transportation went directly to it and they had to walk the last bit.

By the time they arrived, Xander was incredibly pale. Luka offered his arm as support but Xander refused it, not wanting to look weak in front of the president, though his pain was becoming significantly harder to hide.

When they got inside, Soren was the only Guardian already in his seat, looking almost as terrible as Xander. He had received twenty lashes for his betrayal. Elvira was standing beside him, looking mildly concerned, but she pulled it back quickly the moment her father entered the room.

Everyone took their seats and, despite Xander's protests, Luka helped him into his. The meeting was quick, nothing especially serious for them to discuss. The Resistance had gone quiet after the attack. Elvira wanted to use Xander as bait but President Saevus insisted that he heal properly first. Xander was mildly grateful for his concern.

When the meeting ended, Luka was the first one up and helped Xander stand.

"Xander, I would like you to stay behind. We have matters to discuss," said the president.

Every last Guardian looked at Xander curiously, but his guess was as good as theirs. They all slowly began to trickle out, with the exception of Luka.

"Why aren't you leaving?" asked Xander.

"I can wait for you."

"No. You have plans," he said under his breath.

"I think Bronson will underst -"

"Luka. Go."

Luka looked at him hesitantly and sighed.

"I will get home just fine on my own. I'm sure the president will lend me his car to get to the gate, and then it's just a short walk to the tram. I'll be fine."

He frowned but nodded. "If you need me to come back for any reason -"

"Yeah, yeah. I'll call you if I do. Now get out of here."

Luka left then, though he wasn't the last out of the room. Elvira was still in there, looking skeptically at her father.

"Elvira, this doesn't concern you," said the president. "Leave."

"But, Father -"

"Don't make me tell you again," he said, his eyes as sharp as his words.

She took a deep breath before stomping out of the room, slamming the door behind her.

"If you can control it, never have a daughter," said the president the moment she was gone. "They're far too dramatic."

"I believe yours is more dramatic than most," said Xander.

"Yes, she very well might be. Follow me."

The president turned on his heel and led Xander through a door he had never seen open before.

"How are your wounds healing?" the man asked as they walked.

"Nicely," he lied.

President Saevus glanced back at him and lifted an eyebrow.

Xander smiled. "They may still hurt slightly."

"I'll send you home with some stronger salve tonight. You may take one more day of rest but then I'm going to need you to return to your duties."

"Of course, Mr. President. Thank you."

They arrived at an elevator, a green light scanning the president from head to foot upon arrival. The doors slid open and Saevus motioned for Xander to step in first.

"Where are we going, sir?" asked Xander as the doors shut behind them.

"I told you the other day that I have deemed you loyal enough to keep my secrets, and today you will learn one of them. A secret kept in my family for generations, since our ancestors first left the underground and created Utopia."

Xander watched him curiously but the president didn't give anything away. He wasn't sure what kind of secret could have been kept for nearly two centuries, but whatever it was it couldn't be good.

The elevator stopped and the doors slid open. President Saevus stepped out first, leading Xander down a dark hallway until they reached another door. Another green light scanned the president as he walked, the door sliding upward by the time they arrived, not even having to slow their stride.

They entered a large, cool room filled with loud machines performing some task that caused air to blow Xander's hair back.

"These machines were created nearly two centuries ago as a means to pump air throughout Utopia. Without them, we would suffocate inside of our shield," explained the president, walking through the machines and towards a narrower, glass elevator in the center of the room. "When the air underground began to grow thin, the idea of Utopia first formed. While the city was being built, our ancestors' top scientists went to work testing the air, poisoned after a nuclear war in the twenty-two hundreds."

The glass elevator opened and they both stepped inside. The moment the door closed they shot upward at an incredible speed.

"Their goal was to find a way to purify the air, removing the toxins and making it breathable within our shields. But, upon inspection, they discovered something else."

A bright light blinded Xander as the elevator came to a halt, the glass door sliding open and a soft breeze hitting his cheeks. He blinked several times before he noticed the bright blue sky shining down on him, speckled with fluffy, white clouds. He gasped and backed up as far as he could into the elevator.

"Xander."

Xander's breathing grew erratic as he looked at the president, who was unconcerned that they were standing outside in the open air.

"The air was clean," the man said, slowly stepping out of the elevator.

"W-what?" asked Xander, his feet glued in place.

"No one could explain it. Research showed that the air shouldn't have been breathable for another few centuries. But, against all odds, it was." President Saevus turned and looked back at Xander. "Step out here, son. The air can't hurt you."

Xander's legs were shaking as he slowly moved forward and out of the elevator. He looked around, for the first time noticing the lush garden growing atop the high tower that was never visible through the foggy shield of Utopia. "Mr. President ... why ..."

"Have we kept this a secret?" the man finished.

Xander nodded slowly.

"It was a decision made by my great-great-great-grandfather. He asked the scientists to keep quiet about it and build the machines downstairs. He still wanted a shield to protect his citizens from future wars and they agreed it was for the best."

"Future wars with who?"

Saevus continued like he hadn't even heard him. "And then, once the city was built and the machines were functional, he had the scientists executed. Every last one of them." He plucked a red rose from a nearby bush and handed it to Xander. "He understood the importance of keeping Utopians protected. If they knew the air was clean then some of them would undoubtedly venture into the world. They would reestablish contact with other civilizations and repeat history."

"Other civilizations?" asked Xander, his eyes fixed on the rose.

"Of course. You didn't think we were the only ones to survive our ancestors' war, did you?"

The truth was that Xander had never really thought about it. He'd just assumed they were the only ones. Why else would they not be in contact with the others?

"There were four undergrounds created in America alone. In the north, the south, the east, and us, the west. But we cut off contact with them the moment we learned the air was clean. War destroyed our world, Xander, and I'll be damned if I let Godfrey Leon and his minions do it again. That is why the Outsiders must be stopped. Before they find others and real war is brought back upon us."

Xander looked up from the rose, noticing a balcony in the distance. He walked straight for it, for the first time getting a clear view of the world around him. Green and lush, snow-capped mountains in one direction and ... the ocean in another. Tears built behind his eyes but he held them back. Saevus came up beside him.

"For years my family kept Utopia safe by guarding this secret, but then my aunt Talitha married that dreadful Hayden Leon and told him everything. They chose to leave and brought others with them, ruining everything we had worked so hard for."

"I'm not family," said Xander, his eyes fixed on the damn ocean, so close yet still unreachable. "Why are you sharing this with me?"

A small smile curved onto the president's lips. "I have been aware for quite some time that Elvira is not up to the task of protecting Utopia when I'm gone. I had hoped marrying her off young would bring me a grandson I could raise properly, but I now have a hard time believing any child Soren produces would be worthy of such an important position. I had hoped when I offered to execute him she would agree but, alas, my daughter chose him for a reason. She's loved him since childhood, even looking past his obsession with that filthy slave if it meant she still got to call him husband. Really, I never should have offered him as an option, but when his parents volunteered Veli she was quick to ask for Soren instead. If only you were born a few years earlier." He glanced sideways at him and winked.

"I think I'd be as successful as Soren in producing an heir with Elvira for you. She doesn't interest me."

"Yes, and that's not what I'm asking. Marry whomever you please, produce whatever heir, I trust your judgment. What I want from you is a promise."

"A promise," repeated Xander, his breath catching in his throat. He knew what was coming, but that didn't mean he was prepared for it.

"A promise to keep this secret when I'm gone. To watch over Utopia and keep its citizens from ever venturing outside. For the greater good."

Xander looked from the ocean to the rose he still held, breathing in the clean, outside air he'd been inhaling his whole life. His heart shattered as he nodded and said, "For the greater good."

But how could keeping Utopia's citizens in a shielded prison ever be for the greater good?

CHAPTER TWENTY-FIVE

Luka walked up the stairs of their apartment building, pausing for a brief moment by Bronson's door on the third floor. He took a deep, nervous breath and continued on.

When he got to the apartment he shared with Xander and Deryn, he unlocked and opened the door, scanning the place until he found Deryn sitting at the dining room table, making some adjustments to the unregistered Elements he and Xander had been carrying around lately.

"Xander isn't with you," she said without looking up.

"The president asked him to stay behind."

"He didn't seem angry, did he?"

"No. I'm pretty sure he's officially making Xander an equal to Elvira."

Deryn sighed and put down the Element she was working on. "I don't even want to think about what that means." She glanced at him, her eyes sad for a moment before she attempted a smile. "You need to change for your date."

"It's not a -"

"*Don't* finish that sentence. It would be disrespectful to Bronson to go all wishy-washy on him again."

Luka raised an eyebrow. "Wishy-washy?"

"You *know* what I mean. You insisted that he pick you over someone who's actually willing to be seen holding his hand in public, so don't you dare change your mind on him again."

Luka sighed and took off his Guardian coat. "I won't."

"Good. I've laid out an outfit for you on your bed."

He knitted his brow as he hung his coat in the closet.

She smiled properly this time. "You should look nice tonight, Luka. While your options are limited, since the majority of what you grabbed from your father's house were shoes, I think I chose something Bronson will like on you."

"I'm not just some piece of meat putting on a show for him."

Deryn laughed. She stood and walked into Luka's bedroom with him at her heels.

The outfit she'd laid out was actually quite nice. It was his go-to date shirt, a long-sleeved, navy-blue one that brought out some green specks in his dark eyes, and she'd paired it with charcoal-gray slacks he wore every other day anyway.

"I also washed one of Xander's nicer coats so it doesn't smell like him."

"What's wrong with my coat?"

She raised her eyebrows. "You mean that old black trench coat with tears on the sleeves?"

Luka shrugged. "It's comfy. Why fix what isn't broken?"

"You're wearing Xander's coat. Now, hurry and get in the shower. I also plan to take a comb through your hair for once."

"Okay, *now* you're crossing the line."

Deryn laughed again and threw his clothes at him, which he caught. She then grabbed his shoulders and pushed him all the way to the bathroom, pulling the door shut behind him.

When she was alone, she finally had a moment to really think about what President Saevus was doing with Xander. He said he wanted to share secrets with him, but what secrets were there that they didn't already know about? Or at least have an idea about.

Deryn went back to the dining room table, but the button she was currently adding to each of the Elements was very dangerous and required her complete focus, which she simply couldn't give. So she made a cup of tea instead.

The bathroom door opened and she hurried to get a look at Luka in his date outfit. She smiled when she saw him.

"You look very nice."

"Yes, and I combed my *own* hair, thank you very much," he said with a roll of his eyes.

"I suppose there's a first time for everything." She still stepped forward and ran her fingers through his towel-dried hair, fixing one small part.

He swatted her hand away. "Stop it."

There was a knock on the front door and he quickly went rigid, his breath hitching as his skin paled.

Deryn chuckled. "Xander's coat is hanging in your closet. I'll get the door."

Luka gulped and nodded. He walked stiffly to his room while Deryn headed for the door. When she opened it, Bronson was leaning casually against the doorframe, obviously trying to play it cool in a black pea coat and dark-blue slacks.

"Evening, cupcake."

She rolled her eyes. "Didn't I already veto that name?"

"You veto all of them."

"Yes, and I'll continue to do so until the end of time." She opened the door wider so he could step inside. "He's just putting on his coat."

"Not my coat!" Luka called from the other room.

Bronson looked at Deryn curiously.

"His coat's no good so I'm making him wear Xander's. Don't worry, I washed it and spritzed it with that cologne Luka has in the bathroom.

"Luka wears cologne?" asked Bronson.

"Rarely," said Luka, coming out of his room wearing Xander's navy-blue coat, a perfect match to his shirt. Bronson and Deryn both smiled when they saw him.

"Your hair looks different," said Bronson.

Luka narrowed his eyes at Deryn. "*She* insisted I comb it."

Bronson smirked and walked over to him. He reached out and ruffled up the back of his hair a bit. "That's better." He looked over his shoulder at Deryn and said, "What can I say? I like the messy look. It's endearing."

"You two are hopeless," she said, playing with the door she was still holding open. "Don't you have a reservation you need to make?"

"Yes, Mother," said Bronson. "Look away for a second."

She obeyed.

He took this moment to lean in and kiss Luka, his hand coming up to cup his cheek. "And you're sure you want to do this? I'm really fine with staying in and cooking. Believe it or not, I really do like to cook."

Luka smiled softly. He took a breath. "We'd better hurry if we're going to make that reservation."

Bronson followed him to the door, Deryn smiling at both of them as they slipped on their shoes and left the apartment. "Have fun, you two."

Bronson kissed her cheek as he exited. "You too, cupcake." He winked and she kicked his bum, slamming the door behind him.

"Xander not back from your Guardian meeting yet?" he asked as he and Luka descended the stairs.

"No. The president asked him to stay."

"What for?"

"I don't know." Luka stopped walking for a moment. When Bronson came up beside him, he said, "No Guardian shit tonight."

"You're the boss," said Bronson, smiling and taking his hand. "Though I know very little of you, outside of what you do for a living and a mild shoe obsession. Do you have any hobbies?"

"Painting."

"Really?"

"No."

Bronson looked at him and blinked. "You make jokes! Who knew?"

The two of them dropped hands as they exited the building, doing their best to chat casually - though a bit awkwardly - as they walked to the restaurant Bronson had chosen for their night out. It was a nice place, though not so nice that it would be odd for two men to simply be dining together.

They arrived at the restaurant and Luka felt a pang of

jealousy when the hostess flirted with Bronson. But when they sat down and Bronson was smiling at him from across the table, any jealousy he felt quickly dissolved.

Bronson liked him.

He often forgot that whenever someone else touched Bronson's arm or fumbled their words around him. But it didn't matter how many people were looking at him, because he was only ever focused on Luka. He'd never had that before. With anyone.

"You alright?" asked Bronson, discretely rubbing his knee under the table.

Luka smiled - a real genuine smile - and nodded. "Yeah. Fine."

It was easy to carry on a conversation once food was involved. Bronson had many suggestions, which were really opinions, about what was best to eat there, and Luka told him just to order for the two of them. He didn't know much about fine dining. The majority of his experiences with it were Guardian family dinner parties with set menus. He'd also only ever had one girlfriend and they never went out. Every now and then he would take out a girl he was sleeping with but, even then, he tended to go for the blandest meal on the menu.

"I never eat fish," admitted Bronson when Luka asked why he hadn't picked the lobster for them since, from what he understood, it was high end. He leaned in and whispered, "Once you've had it outside fresh from the ocean, any fish born and bred in Utopia simply can't compare. Hopefully, in the future, I can cook you some real fish."

Luka looked hesitant.

Bronson rolled his eyes. "It's not toxic, Luka. One day I hope you'll realize that, when we're outside where I can feed you some proper fish." He grinned.

More hesitance. "You really think you're going to get out there again?"

"Oh, I have no doubt." Bronson paused. "It's funny. I've often thought about what would've become of me and Quigs if Fiona hadn't come back in. We'd probably be in the Resistance, which would actually be handy when this war happens. I couldn't figure out how to use an Element if my life depended on it."

Luka blinked. "You mean you haven't learned anything from working with your cupcake?"

Bronson chuckled. "Test dummy, remember? I'm a lover, not a fighter."

"You *need* to be both. I can help you learn."

"I'm not really a gun person."

"*Bronson.*"

"*Luka.*"

Luka sighed and said, "You *need* to learn. For me."

Bronson narrowed his eyes. "Oh, hell. You just *had* to play that damn 'for me' card. *Fine.* I'll learn how to use your stupid, complicated weapon. With all the moron Guardians around, I'm surprised more people don't blow themselves up."

"It's not complicated."

"There are *multiple* buttons, Luka, and you have to make sure you press the right one in the right moment or *BOOM!* You just blew up your comrade or, worse, yourself."

Luka smirked. "Muscle memory. You don't learn with active buttons."

Bronson smirked back. "I didn't know they could be deactivated."

"There's a safety switch."

The two of them took a moment just smiling across the table at each other.

When Luka started to feel uncomfortable from all the eye contact, he cleared his throat, leaned in and quietly said, "So I've been wondering, how is it that you and Quigley avoided being recruited?"

"You mean kidnapped," corrected Bronson. "And our village was farther."

Luka cocked an eyebrow. "Farther?"

"Towards the beach. And the good seafood. It was called Driftwood." That smirk was back, and the brightness of it was enough to make Luka melt. "By the time Guardians came for us we'd already received word from other villages, so everyone under the age of twenty or so was hidden. Our parents - well, not mine, but Quigley's and the others - told the Guardians there were no children in their village, something about all of them hating the rotten things, so they left."

Luka leaned back in his chair and crossed his arms.

"Disappointed we didn't get the chance to meet sooner?"

He gave a soft shrug. "I don't think you would've liked me very much back then. Teenage Luka was even more of an ass than twenty-something Luka."

"Twenty-three!" Bronson said proudly, picking up his glass of whiskey after the waitress, who was eyeing him, put it down. He didn't even notice. "Twenty-four in two months and ten days." He put down his glass. "I like it when you smile."

Luka pulled back his smile. He hadn't even realized he was doing it.

"Now, now, Luka. Put it back on. You smile so little but you're just such a cute little cherub." Bronson reached across the table and tapped his cheek.

Luka narrowed his eyes. "*Cherub?*"

"So does that mean *none* of the people I date, real or fake, like my nicknames?"

Luka smiled again. Then he pulled it back. *Damn.*

"You're too cute."

Their first course came shortly after, followed by their dinner. Bronson was very passionate about how Luka should eat his meal. When Luka joked about just swirling it all together and eating it as one glob Bronson nearly had a heart attack.

While their date wasn't without it's momentary awkward pauses, it wasn't nearly as bad as Luka was expecting. He'd often questioned if perhaps the only reason he liked Bronson was because of all the attention he received from someone so highly desired, but that really wasn't it. He just liked him. Because he made him smile in a world that held such little joy. While he enjoyed going out and drinking with Xander, they rarely ever laughed together. But whenever he was around Bronson he laughed a lot.

After dessert, which Bronson graciously let Luka pick for himself, the two of them went to a nearby bar for drinks. A table of women kept looking at them, trying to get their attention, but while Luka noticed them, he found that he had no interest in even contemplating whether any of them were attractive or not, and Bronson didn't notice them at all.

When they were each two whiskies in, they left the bar for a nearby alley to smoke a cigarette.

"Have you ever shotgunned anyone?" asked Bronson as he took a drag.

"Don't think so. What is it?"

"I'll show you."

He inhaled deeply and took Luka's face in his hands, kissing him hard and blowing the smoke into his open mouth. When they came apart, Luka blew what smoke remained into the cold, damp air. They smiled at each other.

"And now you know," said Bronson. "It actually works better with something stronger than a cigarette, but really I was just looking for an excuse to kiss you."

An then Bronson went in again, pressing Luka against the nearby wall as he ran his hands through the short but messy hair. He could feel Luka's body tremble beneath his, his arms shaking as they wrapped around him. It was several minutes before Luka fully sunk into it, his hands gripping Bronson's hips tightly as the other man pressed his body against his, kissing him with more fervor than anyone ever had before.

When Bronson finally pulled away, he let out a deep sigh against Luka's cheek, simultaneously warming him and sending chills down his spine.

"God, I like you," said Bronson, kissing his jaw. "I like how cute you are." Then his cheek. "And that you taste like whiskey and cigarettes."

"So you like that I taste like you?"

Bronson chuckled softly. "It tastes much better on your tongue." He ran his up Luka's lips. When Luka crinkled his nose, Bronson chuckled again and pressed their foreheads together, staring into the other man's dark eyes. "Your eyes have some green flecks in them. I like that, too."

Luka tried to smile, but his dark eyes with green flecks quickly filled with sadness. "I like you, too."

"And why do you look so bummed about that?"

"Because if my father ever finds out about this, that I'm spending my time with someone other than a marriageable women capable of producing an heir, he wouldn't hesitate to have you killed."

"Slight mood killer," said Bronson, though his grip on Luka didn't waiver.

"I'm serious, Bronson. My girlfriend Helena, the one I told you about, she ..." Luka gulped. "My father's the one who assigned her to the mission she died during. It was a suicide mission. He knew it was. Her family lived in Outer City and she only ever became a guard to support them. They died of 'toxic poisoning' shortly after. That's why I haven't dated anyone ... not since ..." He paused and took a breath. "I like you more than I liked her, I know I do, and her death ... it broke me."

Bronson's smile had faded but his eyes were still on Luka's. He took a deep breath and kissed him softly. "Would you believe me if I said you were worth the risk?"

"No."

His smile returned. "I didn't think so." Then he slowly breathed into his mouth, "But you are," and kissed him hard.

The two of them stayed in the alley, glued to each other until the sound of the bustling street reminded them that curfew was approaching. They walked back to their apartment building side by side, Bronson having to fight the urge to grab Luka's hand.

It wasn't long before they were home and standing outside Bronson's door, glued to each other once more.

"Curfew's coming," said Bronson, putting a hold on their kissing.

Luka opened his eyes and gazed at him hungrily.

"Quigley's over at his ex's tonight. Do you want to stay over?"

Luka gulped. Of course he and Bronson had been staying

together almost every night for nearly a week now, but he understood the implication in Bronson's voice. Without another thought, he found himself nodding.

"Are you sure?" asked Bronson, stroking his cheek.

Luka nodded again. "I've never been more sure of anything."

Bronson smiled and kissed him again. He fumbled with his free hand until he found the door handle, pushing it open and dragging Luka into his apartment with him. Luka slammed the door behind them.

CHAPTER TWENTY-SIX

After Xander left the president he fell into a daze. He knew he took the man's car to Middle City's gate, but he didn't remember much after that. Presently, he was sitting on the ground in an alley. It must have been raining at one point because his clothes were damp, and somehow he had ended up with the small radio he had confiscated from Sable Bai in his hand. He'd been keeping it at Del's but had no recollection of going there.

Everything he had ever believed was a lie.

The air outside was breathable. It had been breathable for a long time. Long enough for his mother to have seen the beach, to have felt the breeze on her face and the sand between her toes. To discover whether the water was cold or warm.

A tear fell down Xander's cheek.

A part of him felt like he should really do it. Keep playing the part and take over for President Saevus. Then, maybe, he could change things. Tell Utopians the truth about the air they breathed in every day and let them decide what to do with their own lives. Remain secure in their bubble, never seeing the world, never really living, or to venture outside and help rediscover what and who was out there. But another part, the bigger and more selfish part, wanted to run. Run outside with Deryn and experience the world together.

Without thinking, Xander twisted the knob that turned on the radio. Static. He switched to another channel. Static. Then another. Static. Then -

"- room with the telecommunication system should always be your

starting point."

"Really, Talon? Always? *Why* always? *There's nowhere else for us to go around there."*

"The old notes we found clearly state that there are several hidden passageways where -"

"Talon Leon," said Xander, pressing a button on the side.

Silence. With a little bit of static.

"Who -"

"This is Xander Ruby." Only now did he realize that this was what he'd wanted. To speak to Talon. That was why he'd grabbed the radio from Del's. It had to be. "And I want to talk to you alone."

More silence. But there was no click, and Xander knew there would be a click if someone went off the channel. How did he know that? Del must have told him when he grabbed it but he truly couldn't remember.

"I know you're still there. Get rid of the other person. I would like to discuss the thirty-one lashes I received because, for some reason, the Resistance chose to target me specifically." A pause. "Dakota Triggs saw her. He told me. *She* told me. I could properly identify the disguise she was wearing that day. Isn't it time you sat down and listened to me?"

"Talon, I'm getting off," said the other voice, which Xander now recognized as Nita. *"But I'm coming back on in five minutes, Ruby. That's all you get, so make it count."*

Click.

"Sounds like it's just you and me," said Xander.

Silence

"Why do you keep toying with us, Ruby?"

Xander frowned. "That was never my intention. I thought telling your stupid friend that she was alive would give you peace of mind. But, apparently, it only made you more enraged."

"If you know where she is then why haven't you returned her to us yet?"

"Easier said than done. While I may be able to walk right out the front door, I can't exactly bring a fugitive with me."

Another pause.

"I don't trust you, Ruby."

"Clearly."

"There could be other ways you knew that information about her. Maybe she has escaped, but you already found her and are using the information you witnessed to manipulate us."

"Maybe I am. But I'm not."

This pause was a little longer.

"Oh, great and wise Talon Leon, please, tell me what I can do to earn the trust I so desperately desire?"

"Stop being a smartass, for one." Talon sighed through the line. *"Meet me tomorrow in Deryn and Dakota's place. If you really have her trust then you can ask her where that is."*

"That's all fine and dandy, but I wasn't joking about the thirty-one lashes. I'm in no condition to travel outside."

"In one week then. Noon. I'll make sure Dax isn't there and you make sure to either come alone or with Deryn."

"And will you be alone?"

"Of course not. I'm not an idiot."

"No, you just work with them."

Click.

"Looks like our five minutes are up. I'll see you in one week, Talon Leon."

Xander clicked off before Talon could respond.

And then he was just sitting in a dirty alley again. Alone.

He sighed and checked the time on his wristband. A hovering clock told him he had a half hour until curfew. It was a struggle to stand but, somehow, he managed it. A quick glance out of the alley and into the street let him know that he was in the Shopping District, mere blocks from Del's hideout. He wobbled to the nearest tram stop - his back really hurting after sitting with it pressed against a wall - and took the tram home.

When he stepped off, he struggled to walk the last few blocks to his apartment, but was goaded by the approaching curfew. He arrived, unlocked the doors and stepped inside, nearly collapsing when he reached the stairs. But the urgent sound of approaching footsteps motivated him to stand. He used the railing to get to the second floor, where he was met by a worried looking Deryn.

Staring up at her, he found her familiar green eyes and, suddenly, everything he had just learned came rushing back to him. His whole existence was a lie. Guardians were meant to be protectors of its citizens, but all this time they'd been protecting them from something that didn't exist.

"Xander ..."

Hearing his name on her lips, knowing that she lost so many years of her life - in quarantine, in guard training, as a slave - all because President Saevus wanted to protect the lie, Xander couldn't stop himself. He burst into tears, thankful that her arms were there for him to collapse into.

"I'm sorry," he said over and over again with no further explanation, and she didn't ask for one.

When the alarm went off, signaling the start of the curfew, Deryn helped him stand and practically carried him up the stairs. They made it inside mere seconds before midnight.

Deryn managed to get his weak body to the bedroom where she undressed him, pausing momentarily when she found the small radio in his coat pocket but putting it aside for now.

Her radio was presently switched on, Talon and Dakota speaking at the top of the hour, like they always did.

"Deryn, I love you. I'll be waiting for you for as long as it takes, at our _"

She switched it off.

Seeing the moment for what it was, Xander asked, "Where is your place with him?"

Deryn sighed and sat on the bed beside him. "Just these old ruins we used to go to when we were children. West of Redwood. We liked to play hide and seek in some of the old stone buildings that were still partially intact."

Xander nodded. So that was that.

The president had given him a salve that would work to keep his wounds closed, so she took off his bandages and applied it, followed by a soothing paste she had sent Bronson to get that would cool and numb his wounds.

"Will you please tell me what happened?" she asked, lying down beside him once she was finished and gently stroking her fingers through his hair.

"It's a lie. All of it," he answered with a sniffle.

"What is?"

"The air. President Saevus showed me machines. Machines that have been around since the creation of Utopia. They ..." He gulped. "They're used to pump in air from the outside, so we can all breathe in our fucking bubble."

Deryn's hand froze in his hair. "What?"

"That's why your grandmother left when she married Hayden Leon. Because she *knew*. She knew and she told her husband, so they left Utopia knowing it was safe outside." And then he told her everything else. About the president's reasoning for keeping everyone trapped, about the other people who might be out there rebuilding the world.

"My dad never told me any of that," said Deryn, her eyes nearly as sad as his. "But he has to know. My grandmother must have told him at some point." She sighed. "I'm so sorry, Xander. If I'd have known -"

"It wouldn't have changed anything," he said reaching his hand out, needing to touch her in some way. "My mom still wouldn't be able to see the beach."

Deryn brought her hand out of his hair and stroked his wet cheek. "But you can. Don't you see, Xander? This is the universe telling you that you need to leave Utopia. Come with me. Please."

Staring into her sea-green eyes, Xander took a deep breath. "Deryn ... I can't. Now that he's decided I'm to be his successor, if I leave he won't stop until he hunts me down. I won't risk your life like that."

"You won't be risking my life. Together, with the Resistance, we're going to destroy that son of a bitch. Do you hear me? You will *never* be his successor. I won't let him drag you down any further than he already has, even if I have to kill him with my bare hands."

Xander smirked through his tears. "It's really hot when you talk like that."

"*Don't* get any ideas. There will be no sex of any kind until you're fully healed. Understood?"

He nodded and pushed his face forward just enough to brush his lips against hers. "I don't know what I'd do if you weren't here."

"It doesn't matter because I am here," she said, kissing him a little harder. "I love you, Xander, and I will protect you. I promise."

"I love you, too." He gave her one more soft kiss, then closed his eyes. "Could you hold my hand while we sleep?"

She smiled and reached down, interlacing her hand with his. She kept the covers low since she didn't want them irritating his back and watched him until he fell asleep, his breathing even but tears still falling from his eyes. Her heart ached for him. He had so wanted to believe that all of the bad he had done wasn't for nothing, but now that he knew the truth she didn't know what was going to happen to him. No matter what he said, she needed to get him out. Before his soul was shattered beyond repair.

CHAPTER TWENTY-SEVEN

Over the next few days Xander didn't do much. Seeing the state he was still in physically, President Saevus had given him permission to take more time off. He still had to attend meetings, but the president's personal car ventured all the way to Middle City to pick him up then brought him back home each day.

He spent the majority of his time sitting on the balcony, just staring up at the damn bubble they were trapped in, not even caring enough to light a cigarette. Deryn tried to sit with him but it was like he didn't even see her.

"Xander." She took his hand in hers, stroking the back of it with her thumb as she stared up at him from her spot on the ground. "Please don't do this to yourself. Come back to me."

He closed his eyes and took a breath, giving her hand a soft squeeze. "I haven't gone anywhere. I just ... I need time, Deryn. To process."

She nodded. "Alright. I'm going to the basement to do my training. Will you come down in a bit?"

"Of course."

She stood, leaned in and kissed the top of his head, relishing the scent of his soft hair for a moment. "I love you, Xander."

A soft smile spread across his lips. "I love you, too. I promise I'll be okay."

She nodded again, hurrying back inside before he could see the tears in her eyes.

Instead of heading straight down to the basement, she stopped by Bronson and Quigley's apartment first, walking right in without knocking. Both were home, Bronson making their breakfast in the kitchen while Quigley was reading one of Deryn's books on the couch.

He looked up when she entered. "How's he doing?"

"No better," she said, her words feeling heavy on her tongue.

"I'm leaving for the Black Market for you just as soon as I eat," said Bronson, poking his head out of the kitchen.

"No rush," she said, going over and sitting beside Quigley. "I wish I could go myself, but I promised Xander I wouldn't leave the apartment anymore and I really don't think this is the time to push his buttons."

"Or maybe it's exactly the time to push his buttons," said Quigley. "If he's that out of it he might not even notice you're gone."

Deryn laughed halfheartedly. "He'd know. He always knows."

"If it makes you feel any better, Luka's not doing so great either," said Bronson, hurrying out of the kitchen with a protein shake he had made for her. Their new routine before her morning workouts.

"That doesn't make me feel better," said Deryn, taking a sip, still unable to hide her hatred for the taste. "Worse, actually."

"They were raised to believe something, as ridiculous as it was, and they used that belief to justify their actions against Outsiders," said Quigley, flipping a page. "I'd be torn up too if I found out I no longer had an excuse for murder."

"Quigs! I know you're angry about Fiona, but just fucking don't, alright?" snapped Bronson.

Quigley slammed the book shut and huffed. "And what exactly am I supposed to do? I know where she is but I can't *do* anything! And the Guardian who always swore he'd help me isn't *doing* anything! He's ... he's fucking sulking over something he should've realized a long time ago. The president is a liar! He's a fucking liar and the fact that he's pumping 'toxic air' all throughout the city so us bubble people can breathe shouldn't be such a shocker!"

Deryn reached over and put her hand on his. "He and Luka are going to help Fiona, Quigley. You know they are."

"I know, it's just ..." He rubbed his free hand down his face. "That girl wearing Fiona's face the other night was so fucked in the head. The longer she's with *that man* the worse it's going to get."

"It won't be much longer. I promise. We just need to figure it out first."

"She *has* a mind control chip installed. Why don't we just go get her?"

Deryn sighed. "You know it's not that simple."

Quigley didn't agree or object.

She hugged him before finishing her drink and standing. "If I'm still downstairs when you get back, Bronson, please come get me."

"Will do, cupcake," he said as she headed out the door, not even bothering to criticize the nickname.

"Dunno why she worships him so much," said Quigley, returning to his book. "Sending you out on special errands just because he feels bad about something obvious."

"Yes, that. Not to mention the thirty-one lashes he received that she feels guilty about. He was raised to believe there is a linear way of thinking, you can't blame him for being upset."

"I can blame him for letting Fiona go back to a fucking rapist."

"No, you can't. Because if he didn't return her there'd be an investigation into why and then we'd all be fucked. Just be happy that we know where she is now."

Quigley sighed and put his book down again. "I don't feel happy about anything right now."

Bronson frowned. "I know. Maybe you should go upstairs to Xander and join the club."

"At least he has Deryn." There was a small hint of sadness, and perhaps jealousy in Quigley's eyes.

"I think that's the only reason he hasn't completely lost it," said Bronson, heading back into the kitchen. "After we eat you're going up there."

Quigley grunted but he didn't argue. He knew someone needed to make sure this depressive Xander didn't jump off the damn balcony. Not that any of them truly believed he would without getting Deryn out of Utopia first. But even the strongest people had moments of weakness.

~

When Bronson arrived back home several hours later he went straight down to the basement. Deryn had finished her workout and was now practicing evasive techniques with Luka. She had her Element fastened to her hip and was currently dodging what was meant to be a surprise attack, whipping it out and aiming.

"Already a vast improvement," said Bronson, leaning against the wall and smiling.

It was true. She had only been working with Luka since just after Christmas and he could already see her arms and legs beginning to tone, not to mention the swiftness of her movements.

"Determination, Bronson," she said, giving her Element a spin before putting it back in its holster. "I refuse to be the weak girl Xander found on a street corner any longer, and I was never a terrible soldier. Not the greatest, but that was only because I had little desire to kill anyone back then. Now I have a list."

"And I don't envy anyone on it."

"Bronson is going to start training with us soon," said Luka, flashing him a smile.

"I think that's wise," she said. "You should at least learn how to handle an Element."

"I'm going to be honest, I don't have a lot of desire to kill anyone either, like mini cupcake. I haven't been through anything terrible enough to give me that drive."

"What about when the president had your village destroyed and Quigley's parents were killed?" said Luka.

Bronson sighed. "Yeah, you're right. That was terrible. But I didn't see it happen, I don't know who was involved, and while I want the president dead I don't particularly want it done by my hand."

Luka stared at him with hard eyes. "But, if it comes down to it, would you do it?"

Bronson shrugged. "I suppose I'd have to."

"Then you're learning," said Luka. "You and I can start now before you have to leave for work, since I'm sure Deryn plans to abandon her training now that you're back."

Bronson smirked and held up a bag he was carrying. Deryn smiled and went over to him, taking off her holster and fastening it around his waist.

"Have fun, you two." She took the bag and winked, walking and not running up the stairs since her muscles were terribly sore from her earlier workout. Not to mention Luka flipping her a few times when she failed to evade him properly.

When she got upstairs, Xander and Quigley were on the balcony sharing a cigarette. While she did not condone smoking in the least, she was still happy Xander was taking a few drags. Maybe that meant he was starting to feel like himself again.

As she approached, Quigley glanced at her. "Guess my shift is over. And look! He didn't jump or anything!" he said with a smile.

Xander rolled his eyes. "If any of you actually believe I'd do something that stupid then you really don't know me at all."

"Yeah, yeah. You have too many people counting on you, blah, blah, blah. Just keep reminding yourself about that." Quigley put out his cigarette and left.

"Nothing like spending a few hours with someone who's clearly still pissed at me," said Xander, staring back out at the street.

Deryn ducked down and sat in her usual spot on the ground. "Then why didn't you come downstairs and watch me like you promised?"

"Sorry," he said with a sigh. "I just ... If you haven't noticed, I'm a bit out of it."

"You don't say."

Xander moved his gaze to her, a small smile tugging at his lips. Then it faded again. "You know I wouldn't ever off myself

_"

"Xander, I know," she said firmly. "I didn't send him up here. Bronson probably did. They're just worried about you. Quigley may be angry but he still loves you."

Xander nodded. "You've been using that word a lot lately. Love."

"Yes, well, when two people I care a great deal about got hurt because of me it put a lot of things in perspective." She looked at him and smirked. "Don't worry, I still love you the most."

He half-smiled.

Deryn held out her arms. "Xander, come here."

He went to her without hesitation, sitting beside her and happily letting her embrace him. One hand stroked his hair while the other clung to the back of his neck. He loved the way she held him.

"So I had Bronson pick something up for me," she said after a while of just sitting there. "It's something I've always wanted to do and I'm hoping you'll do it with me."

Xander pulled back a bit so he could look at her. "He picked you up something you can *do*?" he asked, cocking an eyebrow. "You officially have my interest. Also, if this is some sort of sex act, the answer is always yes."

"Devil's three-way?"

"Except *that*."

Deryn laughed. "I hate to disappoint you, but what he picked up for me has nothing to do with sex. I said we're waiting until you're fully healed and I meant it." She grabbed the bag she had placed beside her and pulled out some metal contraption, shaped like a gun but with a thousand tiny needles on the end.

Xander looked at her skeptically.

"It's a tattoo gun," she said, playing with the screen attached to it. "I designed something for us. Granted, I'm no artist, but I think it turned out pretty well."

She showed him the screen. It was two blackbirds flying towards each other.

"This one is mine," she said, pointing to the smaller bird flying to the right. "And this one is yours." The bird was mildly larger and flying left. "I thought we could put them on our fingers. You gave me your symbol of commitment." She palmed the gold ring around her neck. "And now I want to give you mine."

Xander lifted his hand and stroked the little birds. "It's beautiful, Deryn. But I can't get that on my finger. Someone will see and question it."

"Already thought of that," she said, going back into the bag and coming out with a plain gold ring. "You'll get it on your middle finger and this is wide enough to cover it."

He smiled softly and took the ring, trying it on both middle fingers and deciding it fit best on his left hand. Then he took it off again and readied the chosen hand.

Deryn giggled and said, "You really trust me with this?"

"Guess so."

She took his hand and gave it a kiss before positioning the tattoo gun just right. She clicked on his bird so it became centered on the screen and pressed the only button. Xander didn't even flinch as the needles pressed into him. When it was finished, she took away the gun and they both admired the small blackbird now imprinted permanently on his middle finger.

"Your turn," he said, taking the tattoo gun and switching the screen to the other bird. They chose Deryn's right middle finger and positioned the gun. Once it was in place, he pressed the button.

Deryn did her best not to flinch either. When it was done she smiled proudly as she looked at her small bird, placing it beside his. "They really look quite nice," she said.

Xander put the gun aside and tried on the ring, making sure it covered the bird completely. It did. He then took it off and pocketed it, pulling her close so he could kiss her. "I still don't think I deserve you. But, fuck, I love you."

She smiled softly, then reached up and stroked his cheek with her tattooed hand. "Just two blackbirds flying home together. Hopefully forever."

"Yes. Hopefully."

Deryn's smile faded and she pinched him. "*Forever*, Xander."

He finally smiled and said, "Alright. Forever."

Their lips entangled and their hands entwined, the two small birds on their fingers flying towards each other as they kept warm during that cold night. For the first time Xander actually appreciated Deryn's no sex rule, because it meant he got to hold her just like this, and feel the warmness of her tongue pressed against his. Sometimes he needed these moments to remember that it wasn't just the physical part of their relationship that he loved, it was her. All of her. The taste of her breath, the beat of her heart, the way she held him like she never wanted to let go.

He hadn't realized it before she came into his life, but he had once been as dead inside as she was. Alive but not actually living. He'd given up. And he had almost done it again. But his blackbird always knew how to bring him back, and together they were going to fly away from the hell bubble they were trapped in and find a way to be together. Forever.

For the first time in his life he saw the future. Not just some fantasy he created to survive the pain, but the real future. And she was it.

CHAPTER TWENTY-EIGHT

Xander walked through the forest west of Redwood, still wearing his gasmask and nervously glancing over his shoulder every few steps. He had told President Saevus that he wanted to see the beach and the man had been fine with that, even encouraging him to breathe the salty air, saying there was nothing else like it. *He* had breathed the salty air. Yet his mother never would. It hardly seemed fair.

He wanted to take off his gasmask, he really did, but every time he started to he imagined he heard a noise and panicked. He knew, deep down, that no one was following him, but he didn't understand what was holding him back.

The air was clean.

It had been clean for a long time and he had been breathing it his whole life.

So why couldn't he just take off the mask?

Xander stopped walking and pressed his hand against the closest tree, taking several deep and even breaths. He could do this. It was the same air. *No one* was following him.

He brought his free hand up to his gasmask, pausing as his middle finger touched the release button in the back of it. It was the finger with his blackbird tattoo, presently covered by gloves meant to protect him from the *toxic* air.

Closing his eyes and thinking of Deryn, he pressed the release.

The mask opened and he pulled it off slowly, holding his breath and closing his eyes for a moment. When he opened them again he waited for the world around him to become clear before taking his first breath. He blinked and looked up at the bright blue sky. This was it. The outside world without the haze of a mask in front of his eyes.

Xander gulped as he took in the trees towering over him, a soft breeze waving their branches and hitting his face. It wasn't until he felt a chill that he realized his cheeks were wet. He closed his eyes again and let the tears fall willingly, whimpering as he fell to his knees, tearing off his glove so he could run it through the grass beneath him. He plucked a small yellow flower growing nearby and gave it a whiff. Not especially aromatic but he still tucked it in his pocket to give to Deryn later.

Getting back to his feet, the gasmask now hanging from his belt, Xander wiped his cheeks with his bare hand, gave his small tattoo a rub and continued on. At first his breathing was a bit off but, eventually, it evened out, inhaling this air as he would any other. Because it was the same.

Before long Xander came across a heavy slab of stone, the edges too smooth to have been made by natural causes. He brushed his fingers through his hair as he entered the ruins Deryn played in as a child, suddenly feeling nervous that he was here to meet the brother of the girl he loved. After all their years knowing *of* each other, he and Talon had never actually met before. He didn't come out of hiding much and Xander hoped to find out why. One would think he'd be first in line to rescue his sister, but on every raid the Resistance had ever made he was never there.

Xander left the thick patch of trees he'd been walking under and entered a more open part of the forest littered with stone buildings, some still towering higher than the trees around them but looking terribly unsafe. Others had caved in or collapsed long ago and only left small pieces in their wake.

He had never seen anything like it before. Deryn told him she used to have books with pictures of ancient cities but he hadn't had another chance to go to Redwood and search for them. He stared up at the tall buildings and shattered windows with branches growing out of them, and wondered what this place had once been like. Before the world went to shit. He bet it was beautiful.

Hearing something hidden in the trees, Xander took his Element out of its holster, placed it on the ground and stepped away.

"Unarmed," he said, holding up his hands. "As promised."

Someone stepped out of the trees wearing a green coat that blended well with its surroundings. Talon Leon walked forward, his shaggy hair pushed out of his eyes so he was able to stare coldly at Xander without any obstacles. He held a gun at his side, but there was no need to aim it since Xander was well aware that there were three -

A leaf crunched behind him.

- *four* other people scattered around the ruins, their weapons trained on him.

Talon stopped walking a good five steps away from Xander and scanned him up and down. His eyes stopped on his face, investigating it for a moment before he realized what wasn't right.

"Where's your gasmask?"

Xander smirked and pointed to where he had attached it to his belt.

"Why aren't you wearing it?"

"The very same reason I decided it was time to contact you." Xander lowered his arms to his sides. "The president shared something with me recently. A Saevus family secret, if you will. So answer me honestly, Talon Leon." He paused and gulped. "All this time. Did you know?"

Talon blinked. It took a moment but, eventually, Xander's words hit and understanding entered his eyes.

"So you did know," said Xander with a frown. "A vital piece of information to help *your* cause, yet you chose to keep it to yourself."

"You really believe any of *your* people would listen if I told them -"

"A week ago I wouldn't be standing here in front of you like *this*!" spat Xander, pointing at his bare face. "Not everyone

would have believed you, but some would have. *I* would have."
He crossed his arms and breathed heavily. "Deryn didn't
know."

Something sparked in Talon at the mention of his sister. His
eyes - *her* eyes - lit up with a brief moment of hope, and Xander
found himself staring into them, the small bit of her in there
keeping him from pouncing on this man for being such an
idiot.

"What are you looking at?" asked Talon.

Xander didn't answer. Just kept staring.

Talon knitted his brow. "The hell, Ruby? You falling in love
with me, or something?"

Xander couldn't stifle his laugh. "If you were only so lucky. I
was just noticing the Leon eyes are brighter than the Saevuses."

"My gran said it was the sunlight," said Talon, a hint of
sadness in his voice. "Don't think there was much merit behind
it."

"How long have you known?" asked Xander, point blank.

"I thought we were here to talk about Der -"

"Humor me."

Talon huffed and glanced up to where one of his comrades
stood. Even in baggy clothing, Xander knew that figure. Small
yet muscular with curvy hips.

Nita nodded.

"Five years and change," he answered. "I'm sure you can
guess when my dad decided to share that information with me.
And I haven't come forward with it because he told me not to.
He thought exposing the president's lies like that while Deryn
was in his possession would be a foolish move."

"At least it would have been a move. Do you really believe
she's been better off these last five years than if she'd just been
executed right at the beginning?"

Talon tensed, all color draining from his tan face. If it
weren't for his golden skin he and Deryn would actually look
quite a bit alike, but it really made all the difference.

Xander cocked an eyebrow. "Don't tell me you were under
the impression she was treated well all these years? Because, I

assure you, she wasn't."

With a clenched jaw, Talon asked, "*Why* are you here, Ruby? To remind me what a terrible brother I am? Because I don't *need* the reminder! You said you wanted to speak to me so why don't you shut up and tell me what's so damn important you couldn't just say it over the two-way."

"Is that what it's called?" asked Xander, genuinely curious. "Huh. I've just been calling it a radio."

"Yes, a *two-way* radio. Our ancestors used them."

"Fancy." He smirked. "You forget that you're the one who asked me to meet *you* here. And I came because, judging from what I overheard between you and the missus on the *two-way*, you're looking for another way into Utopia."

"Of course we are."

"Then do me a favor and don't fucking waste it trying to take me prisoner this time. I have Deryn in my possession. I'm admitting it. She escaped four and a half months ago on her own and I came across her shortly after. So when you find your way in contact me and get her out. Before *anything* else. I don't care if you have some other fucking agenda to take care of, you get her first. And I mean *you*."

Talon blinked. "Why?"

"Why you?"

He nodded.

"Because, as of right now, she's refusing to leave Utopia, and I believe you or your dad are the only ones capable of convincing her to go. And since he's been missing in action for the past five years, that leaves one. Though you haven't exactly been running into the line of fire."

Talon's nostrils flared. "I'm sure Dax could convince -"

"No, he couldn't."

He could tell Talon wanted to question that statement but, for whatever reason, he kept his mouth shut and glanced at Nita again.

"Why do you keep looking at her? You're in charge, aren't you? You shouldn't need someone else to make your decisions."

"I've never exactly been in a situation like this before," said Talon. "And I don't understand why Deryn would ever choose to stay in Utopia if she had an out."

Xander stared down at the ground and sighed softly. "She doesn't want to leave me there alone. But the reason I'm here now without a gasmask, the reason the president shared a family secret with me is because he's chosen me to continue his legacy. If I just up and vanish one day he won't stop searching for me until I'm dead, along with anyone who helps me. If there was ever a chance for me to escape I've already missed it."

Talon closed his eyes and started massaging the bridge of his nose, clearly fighting off the urge to look at Nita. "I can't believe I'm saying this, but I think you're telling the truth." He opened his eyes and walked forward, grabbing Xander's jaw and holding it still so he could look properly into the man's eyes.

"Now who's falling in love -"

"Shut it, Ruby. I need to figure this out." Talon stared into Xander's eyes for a good, long while, grunting every now and then as he tried to read something behind them. "I want to speak to her," he finally said, releasing Xander's jaw but keeping eye contact. "Tonight. I want to hear her voice before I make any decisions."

Xander clicked his tongue. "That's a little complicated."

"Why?"

"She doesn't exactly know I'm here, and she'll be fucking pissed when -"

"I don't care. Get her on the two-way tonight or no deal."

Xander grunted. "Fair enough. But, like I said, she's going to be fucking pissed and she already doesn't want to go, so there's a fairly good chance she won't speak."

Breaking their eye contact, Talon fisted something in his pocket. Xander was going to make a joke about it until he saw the flash of sadness pass through the other man's eyes. He reached into his pocket and pulled something out, holding open his palm so Xander could see. It was a bracelet, clearly a home craft adorned with various pieces of rubble used as charms.

"Deryn made this for me ..." Talon paused and gulped. "... a long time ago. She used things she found here, our ancestors objects." He touched a small black piece. "This was a piece of a record that was unsalvageable." Then a small wheel. "This was from a toy car. She gave it to me and I laughed at her, thinking it was the ugliest thing I'd ever seen. Two days later I was *recruited* and she stuffed it in my pocket before I was taken away." A tear slid down his cheek as he shoved it into Xander's hand. "I'm going to need that back. But just ... show it to her. And ..." Another gulp. "And I was *always* there. I promised my dad I would never be in the line of fire, but I was there on every last mission we had to try and rescue her. Do you know how fucking heartbreaking it is to have to wait outside in the shadows while others follow your plan for rescue? Your *failed* plan? Every single time I failed."

"Then I trust you'll be sure not to fail this time." Xander glanced at the bracelet before slipping it into his pocket beside the flower he'd picked earlier. "You'll get this back when you get your sister, and I trust you'll take a moment when that happens to thank her for making you something from the heart." He smirked. "I should be able to get to her by nine tonight, so make sure you're tuned in. It's been a pleasure doing business with you."

Xander held out his hand. Talon stared at it hesitantly before giving in and shaking. He backed away slowly as Xander reached for his Element. While he was down, one of the trio of onlookers who weren't Nita jumped down and hurried over to him. Once Xander was up straight, the stranger clapped him on the back.

Xander cried out in agony, falling to his knees as the pain he still felt from his healing gashes shot through him.

"What the hell are you doing?" demanded Talon, hurrying over and shoving his comrade.

"He said he was whipped and I wanted to know if he was lying. I told you to *demand* to see them," said the man, his voice sharp and full of malice. "He could be acting now."

"You bastard!" Xander jumped up and swung his fist, knocking the man to the ground, his gasmask going crooked and revealing part of a face he thought he recognized.

With a grunt, Xander dropped his coat and lifted his shirt, showing the red and scabbed marks that were finally healing.

"My punishment for *your* stupidity, you fucking twat." He lowered his shirt and grabbed his coat and Element, making sure to give the man on the ground a hard kick in the side as he passed him.

"You are a fucking twat," he heard Nita say as she jumped down, appearing aggravated as she helped her comrade to his feet. Then she lifted her mask and sprinted after Xander.

"Dammit, Neetles!" shouted Talon, running after her.

"Hey!"

Xander whipped around when he heard her voice, his eyes flaming. She tossed something to him and he caught it. A small, clear bottle with a yellow liquid.

"I know Utopian medicine is supposed to be way more advanced than ours and everything, but your cuts look damn angry. Put that in your bath tonight. It's all natural and should calm them."

"I hate to break it to you, but my cuts are lacking emotion."

She chuckled. "You're funny. I don't remember you being funny back in Eagle."

"Young Xander was fucking hilarious." He put the bottle in his pocket, which was getting fairly full. "Thanks."

"For what it's worth, I told Dax his whole plan to kidnap you was beyond stupid, but orders are orders." She glanced over her shoulder and gave Talon - who was standing only two steps behind her - a sharp look. "I'll personally make sure he's in no way involved in this mission."

"Smart girl," said Xander, looking past her to Talon. "Hold on to this one. Get rid of the fucker who doesn't follow orders."

"He's on my team," admitted Nita. "And, believe me, he and I are having a long and brutal discussion tonight that'll have him begging for a new captain." She grinned.

"I like you," said Xander. "Makes sense that you and Deryn were friends. I'll bet you raised hell together."

"*Are* friends," she corrected. "And yes, we did." She smiled sadly. "And, to be clear, if we don't get Deryn or Talon's bracelet back, and you betray us in any way, I'll be second in line to kill you. Talon's first."

Xander raised his eyebrows. "Fair enough. Though, I should warn you, I'm not an easy target."

"And I never miss."

The two of them shared a smile. Xander nodded at Talon and walked away, already trying to come up with the best way to tell Deryn about this meeting. She'd be angry. There was definitely no avoiding that. There never was.

CHAPTER TWENTY-NINE

Xander checked the clock on his wristband as he stepped through the door to his apartment building. Less than five minutes until nine o'clock.

He'd been right about the time he would get home, which meant he had very little time to explain everything to Deryn before her brother would expect to hear her voice.

He sighed and headed up the stairs. As he reached the fourth floor he heard his front door open. Deryn was waiting for him at the top.

"You're later than expected," she said as he approached, holding out her arms. "Has the bastard decided to share more secrets with you?"

"No," said Xander, reaching her arms and happily walking into them. He wrapped his around her waist and nuzzled his cheek into her bosom. "I went outside."

Deryn tensed in his arms. "Did you take off your -"

"Yes. A breeze feels nice." He took the small yellow flower out of his pocket and pulled away so he could hand it to her properly.

Deryn smiled as she took it. "Did you go to the beach?"

"Not today," he said, his eyes lowering to the floor. "Let's get inside."

She knitted her brow, knowing immediately that something was off but not questioning it just yet.

He took her hand and the two of them walked inside. Once his shoes were off, he sat her down at the dining room table and told her to wait there. She did as instructed, twirling the flower between her fingers nervously while she waited for him to return.

When Xander came back he was carrying the two-way radio she had found in his pocket the day President Saevus shared his stupid secret with him. She had been meaning to bring it up again but wanted him to be in a happier, stable state of mind first. He wasn't quite there yet.

Xander pulled one of the chairs around and sat beside her, placing the two-way on the table. "Do you know what this is?" he asked.

She nodded. "My dad had one. It was how he and his comrades communicated with each other when they went out exploring."

"Right. And now your brother uses them."

She stiffened, all color draining from her already pale cheeks. "Xander, you ... you didn't ..."

"The night Saevus told me everything I used it on a whim and he was on the other end, communicating with your friend Nita who's back in the underground trying to find another way in."

"And did you -"

"Yes."

Her body began to shake. Whether from anger or fear, she didn't know but it wouldn't stop. "You spoke to him. Without asking me first."

"I didn't need your permission -"

Her head whipped towards him, her eyes flaming. "Yes. You. Did," she said through gritted teeth. "The last time you tried talking to the Resistance you were nearly killed!"

"Which is why I was careful about it this time. Dakota wasn't allowed anywhere near our meeting."

"Your *what*?" she snapped, rising from her chair and slamming her hands on the table, nearly crushing the yellow flower. "Are you insane?"

"Apparently," he said. "But I'm fine, Deryn. I took off my mask and put down my weapon. We had a very pleasant conversation."

"Ha!" she spat. "You're lucky you weren't killed!"

"No, I'm lucky your brother isn't as big of an idiot as your boyfriend."

She smacked the back of his head. "Stop that! Why would you call him that now? What's wrong with you?"

Xander sighed and rubbed the spot she had hit. "Sorry," he said. "But I knew if I told you ahead of time you would've forbidden me to go and I have a hard time saying no to you. Now please sit and let me explain."

While she did as he instructed, she certainly didn't look happy about it.

"Deryn, you know it's not safe for you here anymore. It never was but it's getting harder and harder to hide you with each passing day. Other Guardians are watching my every move, the president has such faith in me that when it's shattered all hell will undoubtedly break loose, and I love you too much to ever risk you being recaptured and used as a tool against me. So your brother and I made a deal. As soon as they find another way in their very first task will be getting you out. *Just* you."

Deryn felt as if she'd been punched in the gut, all air leaving her lungs and catching in her throat.

"Nita believes they'll be in within the next couple of weeks."

Tears fell from Deryn's eyes, but her body was so numb she didn't even feel them. "No," she whispered, the only word she could manage to speak in that moment.

"Talon wants to speak to you, to know for certain that you're really with me."

He picked up the two-way radio and turned it on. Deryn immediately snatched it from him and turned it off.

He sighed again and took it back. "I know you're angry but he's your brother. You love him and you miss him. Don't tell me that you don't."

She said nothing as he turned it back on and pressed the button on the side. "Hello."

There was a bit of static, and then a voice on the other end. *"I'm here."*

Xander glanced at Deryn, who had her watery eyes fixed on the two-way, her body shaking as she took deep breaths.

"She's going to need a minute," he said, putting the two-way on the table in front of her.

More static. *"Alright. I'll wait,"* said Talon's cracking voice. Even through the bad connection it was obvious he was holding back tears.

Deryn just kept staring at it, her arms crossed over her chest as her heavy breathing continued.

"Deryn, please."

She snapped her head to look at him again, her eyes seething.

Xander sighed and reached into his pocket, removing the bracelet Talon had given him. Deryn's face softened when she saw it, her mouth falling open as she reached out to take it from him.

"He's kept this with him all these years. Ever since the day he was recruited and you stuffed it in his pocket."

"He told me it was the ugliest thing he'd ever seen," she said, fiddling with the dangling pieces on the bracelet.

"To be fair, it isn't exactly beautiful."

"I thought it was." She whimpered and touched a piece of clear plastic. "This one makes rainbows when you put it in the sunlight."

"Ruby, are you still there?"

Deryn glanced at the two-way again, her tears falling heavily now. She wiped them on her sleeve.

"He also told me that he was always there."

She glanced sideways at him. "Where?"

"Every rescue attempt the Resistance ever made to find you. He led them all, he just couldn't go in because he promised your dad he wouldn't. But he instructed everyone from the shadows."

Deryn blinked, gaping down at the radio as Talon spoke again, sounding panicked that no one was responding.

"Ruby! Ruby, you promised me! Where -"

Deryn lifted the two-way and pressed the button on the

side. "Talon."

Silence. Then static. A whimper. *"Deryn?"*

She closed her eyes and took a deep breath. "Yes, it's me. How refreshing that none of you almost got Xander killed this time for simply relaying a message. I appreciate it, big brother."

Talon laughed softly. *"While I can tell you're really angry with me, I'm relieved you still have that attitude."*

"Yes, well, if you spoke to me five months ago I'm afraid you would've been very disappointed." Deryn clicked her tongue. "Here's the deal, Talon. You can find your way into the city all you want, but the only way you're getting me out of here is by dragging me unconscious through the streets, because I'm not leaving without Xander. Got it?"

Silence. Static. *"Umm ..."*

"We're a package deal."

"Deryn, we can't bring a Guardian into our base."

"No, you can't leave someone fighting for *your* side here to die!" she shouted. "Which is exactly what you'll be doing if you don't get him out of here, too."

"I ..."

"Figure it out and do *not* contact me again until your conscience catches up to you." She threw the two-way down on the table and stormed into the bedroom, slamming the door behind her.

Xander picked it up. "Told you she'd be angry."

"Yes, you did. Still."

"I'll check in with you on your progress in a week. Same time."

Silence.

"Alright?"

A click, and a pause. *"Yeah, I ...Ruby ..."*

As Talon began to whimper, a new voice appeared. *"I believe what he's trying to say is thank you, Ruby,"* said Nita. *"We'll speak to you in a week."*

Xander turned off the two-way and stared at his closed bedroom door. He waited a moment before following her.

The door wasn't locked, he knew it wouldn't be. The room

was dark and he could just make out Deryn's silhouette on the bed. She was lying in the fetal position with her back to him. He lay down beside her, hugging her from behind.

"I hate you," she said, placing her hands on top of his.

He kissed her cheek and said, "I know. And I love you. That's why I did this."

"If you really loved me then you'd want to be with me always."

"I do want to be with you always. But I'm trying to be realistic here, Deryn. No matter how much I love you and want to be with you, that doesn't change the fact that being with me is a risk. A *dangerous* risk I can't let you take."

"You don't make my decisions for me. If I want to take the risk -"

"Deryn, stop, alright? Just stop!" he finally snapped, squeezing her tighter. "You didn't survive five years of slavery to give up your one chance at freedom for a fucking Guardian!"

She tensed in his arms.

"You're going to leave here to be with your family outside and I'm going to stay. But don't for one second think that you leaving means I'm going to stop fighting. I am *never* going to stop, Deryn. I'm going to expose the president for the lying bastard he is and one day I'm going to join you out there. But not *now*. I've worked too fucking hard for too many years to bring that man down to leave now and risk the lives of everyone I care about. If I leave, not only will he come after me and you, he'll come after Luka, and Bronson and Quigley!"

Deryn gulped. "We can all run together," she said softly.

Xander laughed, though there was no amusement behind it. "Your brother won't even consider housing one Guardian. What do you think will happen if you show up with two? And Quigley and Bronson won't go anywhere without Sorey's fucking slave."

She whimpered and turned in his arms, grabbing his face and looking at him with her sad eyes. "Xander, please. Being with you is the only happiness I know anymore. Please don't make me leave you behind."

He grabbed her hand and kissed its palm before moving his lips to her wet cheek. "You won't be leaving me behind. Even though we'll be separated we're still both going to be fighting. Until we're together again. You and I ... we're forever. Alright?"

She nodded and wrapped her arms around his neck, holding him as tightly as she could while crying into his hair. "I'm holding you to that."

As she continued to hold him, something hard in his pocket pressed against her thigh. "Is that a bottle in your pocket, or are you just happy to see me?"

"Both, actually," he said, pulling away so he could reach into his pocket and pull out the small bottle. "Your friend Nita gave this to me for my gashes. She said they looked angry and needed something natural."

"And why exactly did she see your angry gashes in the first place?" demanded Deryn.

"One member of their little group wanted to prove that I was lying about being whipped so he smacked my back. Don't worry, I hit him quite hard for it."

"Good," she said, taking the cap off the bottle and giving it a sniff.

"I'm supposed to put it in a bath."

"I'll draw it for you," she said, sitting up slowly.

"You don't have to."

She rolled her eyes. "Obviously. But I want to."

"And will you be joining me?" he asked with a wicked grin.

"We're *not* having sex, Xander. You're still not healed."

"I know. But when I get to choose between naked Deryn and clothed Deryn, I'll choose naked every time."

She wished she could be offended but she very much preferred naked Xander, as well. "Yes, I'll join you," she said, taking the bottle to the bathroom.

Xander waited for the water to start running before standing, wanting to give her a moment alone. He glanced at the nightstand, saw Talon's bracelet and sighed. Loving this girl sure was complicated sometimes.

When he got to the bathroom, Deryn was sitting on the

edge of the tub. Her hand was under the tap like she was testing the water, but her eyes were glazed over.

"Deryn."

She blinked and glanced at the level of the water. Deeming it high enough, she turned the knob to off then carefully dumped in the contents of the bottle. While Xander undressed, Deryn dipped in her feet, not voicing it though obviously testing the water to make sure it wasn't poisonous. She sighed in relief when nothing happened.

"How come I'm the only one who's naked?" asked Xander as he stepped into the tub.

Deryn smiled softly. She stood and undressed quickly before joining him, the natural medicine even soothing her glossy pink scars that never healed. Sometimes she forgot that she was living in constant pain.

She made Xander sink all the way in and carefully rubbed his back, making sure the water got into his wounds. When that was done he leaned against her, using her breasts as a pillow while she hugged her arms tightly around his neck.

They didn't say anything, just stayed like that, silent tears running for Deryn's eyes as she feared that their time together was coming to an end.

Yes, they would both fight even when apart, but Xander was in so deep she was starting to believe that it wasn't possible for him to come out of this alive.

"Please come with me, Xander," she said quietly, kissing his cheek and hugging him tighter. He turned so he could meet her lips with his, the two of them kissing softly for a long while. The bath water went from hot, to lukewarm, to cold, and still they stayed there, lips and arms entangled, and Xander never answering, since he knew he couldn't tell her the words she so desperately wanted to hear.

CHAPTER THIRTY

"So how's Bronson's training going? Has he learned much tossing you around, or is he only good at that while naked?"

Xander smirked as he stood beside Luka in President Saevus's parlor, waiting for their Guardian meeting to begin.

"Funny," said Luka, rolling his eyes. "For someone so muscular he lacks strength, but he's getting pretty good with an Element. At least he hasn't shot his toe again since that first day."

"So you like them muscular then?"

"I'm not against punching you in the fucking face right here and now, so I suggest you watch your tone."

"You certainly are *testy* today." Xander laughed.

"Shut your fucking mouth or I'll gladly tell you exactly what Bronson and I do while alone in enormously graphic detail. And I do mean *enormous*."

Xander shut his mouth immediately.

Luka smiled triumphantly. "That's what I thought."

"Hi, Xander. I heard you're officially back to work tomorrow," said Lona, walking up to them. "How are you feeling?"

"I've been better," he admitted.

"I can imagine." She smiled, reached into her bag and pulled out two thermoses, handing one to each of them. "I made this for you. It's an old healing remedy of my mother's. Really just an herbal tea but it made my cut feel better. Of course, I only got one strike so I can't exactly compare."

Xander opened the thermos and gave it a whiff. "Swear you're not poisoning us?"

"Only if my father put something in there."

He cocked an eyebrow.

Lona laughed. "Don't worry. He was nowhere near it."

"Still not speaking to him?" asked Xander, taking a sip. Luka was still looking at his thermos uncertainly.

"Yes, but it proves very difficult when he won't stop trying to speak to *me*."

"Lona!" Arron Von called from the other side of the room.

She grunted. "See what I mean?"

Lona ignored her father and stayed with Xander and Luka until President Saevus arrived. They all went into the conference room and sat at the large table, Xander right next to the president and smiling smugly at Elvira just across from him. She practically growled as she pulled up that day's agenda on her portable computer.

The meeting went as usual. There was nothing new or particularly exciting to report, other than the president's official announcement that Xander would be taking on a much larger role in the organization. No one looked particularly pleased by this information. Though, Xander did note that Mathis Fender was missing and, therefore, unable to scowl at him properly.

When the meeting ended, Xander had barely gotten out of the room when someone was grabbing his arm. He turned to see his father. Atticus was a bit shaky and his face looked more worn than the last time he saw him.

"Were you punished for giving me that medicine?" asked Xander, realizing that his father, who was old and not presently in the president's favor, would not have been offered the same healing remedies as him.

"Of course I was," answered Atticus. "I was hoping we could have a moment to speak. Just the two of us. I have been trying to find some time with you for awhile, but you always seem to be previously engaged."

"Yes," said Xander. "And I am now. So, if you'll excuse me." He tried to pull out of his father's grip, but Atticus only clutched him tighter.

"Xander, it's important."

"I'm sure it is," said Xander, seizing his father's wrist and yanking him off of his arm. "But I really have no interest in -"

"Mr. President!"

Everyone turned their heads to see Mathis running through the hallway. He was carrying something in his hand and waving it around frantically. Xander squinted to see it was a wristband. A broken wristband.

His heart stopped.

Shit.

But it couldn't be ...

Mathis pushed him and his father apart and entered the conference room.

"Th'fuck is that about?" asked Luka, coming to his side.

"Mr. President, I've found my son's wristband!"

"And what interest does that hold for me, Mathis?" asked the president coldly.

"Sir, I know my son holds little interest with you, but his disappearance was so close to the escape of the Leon slave. I've thought since the beginning that it was too much of a coincidence."

Luka went stiff beside Xander. He glanced sideways at him and noticed how pale his friend had become. "You didn't," he whispered.

Xander's throat went raw. He gulped. "He had her. I had no choice."

"I've been trying to find some sign of him around the city since he first disappeared. I finally found his body with his detached and broken wristband two weeks ago in a dumpster," continued Mathis, "and I've waited to bring this news to you until I had something!"

President Saevus relaxed his stance and said, "Go on."

Mathis sighed in relief. "I took the wristband to the Government Lab. They were able to find out exactly when it was deactivated and I have acquired the security footage of the area around the alley at that time. It was downloading when I headed here and should now be available to view."

Luka grabbed Xander's arm and slowly backed them out of there. He didn't stop until they were in the parlor.

"What are they going to see?" he asked, leaning in close and speaking softly, by the chance that someone decided they had no interest in Mathis's discovery and tried to leave.

"I used Deryn's knife to kill him," confessed Xander. "He'd dragged her into the alley and I heard her scream. My hood was down. My hood was definitely fucking down!"

Xander's fists clenched. He lifted one and slammed it against the wall.

"Stop that," snapped Luka, grabbing his arm. "And keep your voice down." He glanced down the hallway and bit his lip. Then he looked back at Xander and sighed. "Go. Get her out of here. Right now."

"But what about you -"

"I'll hold them off here for as long as I can." Luka let go of Xander's arm. "When Leon asks you to go with her you need to do it."

"What?" said Xander, his voice cracking. "Luka, that would be insane. I could never just go like that. He'd find me. And I would never leave you here to deal with this on your own."

"I'll be fine," said Luka, moving towards the hallway. "Mind control, remember?" He lifted his wrist and winked. "Now *go*. You're wasting time."

Xander nodded and ran towards the door, the president's car already waiting to take him home. As he jumped in and urged the driver to move, Luka walked through the hallway leading to the conference room. Atticus was still standing outside the door, turning as he heard footsteps and noticing that Luka had come back alone.

"Where's Xander?" he asked.

"Previously engaged, remember?" said Luka, walking into the conference room. Mathis had just pulled up a hologram of the security footage for viewing. Atticus didn't follow Luka. His eyes were still focused on the hallway his son had disappeared down.

Inside the conference room, Luka watched nervously as the security footage outside of the alley began to play.

It started out simple enough. First nothing, then two hooded figures were walking towards each other. Even without seeing her face, Luka knew the smaller figure was Deryn by the way she carried herself. Dougal tried to speak to her but she carried on. Then he grabbed her and slammed her against the wall in the alley. President Saevus had Mathis change the angle of the footage so they could see what was happening, but it wasn't a very clear view.

"What do you think, brother?" asked Veli, smiling at Soren. "Is that your slave he's got there?"

Soren tensed but continued to watch the footage with great interest.

President Saevus smiled wickedly. "We already know it was. Speed it up."

Mathis nodded and quickened the footage.

"Maybe next time you should watch it first and actually find something of interest, instead of bringing us such boring surveillance footage," said an irritated Elvira.

Mathis narrowed his eyes. "When we find something of interest, and I know we will, I didn't want to have to wait until the next meeting to bring it to the president's attention. And since he refuses all private meetings with me -"

"On with it, Mathis," said the president, growing visibly impatient.

It wasn't long after Mathis sped up the footage that a third person ran into the camera's line of sight. Even when he paused and zoomed, the face wasn't visible, but everyone agreed that it was a man with blond hair. He entered the alley and soon the three figures were all in deep enough that they were out of view. The president had Elvira add to her notes that all alleys would need cameras installed in the future. A good ten minutes passed before two people were exiting the alley, and Dougal Fender wasn't one of them.

Mathis paused and zoomed in again, the room going silent when they were all faced with someone very familiar.

Suddenly looking very angry, President Saevus scanned the room. "Where's Xander?"

Everyone else followed suit. A few Guardians walked out of the room to go looking for him.

While they were gone, Elvira moved closer to the hologram. Xander may have been clear but the person with him was buried in shadow from their hood. "They're holding hands," she pointed out. "Dear husband, could you tell us whether or not this is your slave whore he's with?"

"Why would you assume it was, *dear wife*?" asked Soren through clenched teeth.

"Who else would Dougal seize like that?" she spat. "Now come look."

Soren grunted but stood. He got close but couldn't see much. While he had spent many nights memorizing every curve of her body, it was hard to tell in the long coat she was wearing.

But then he saw something. A small tuft of hair hanging out of her hood. Mahogany-brown, the light hitting it in a way that showed a streak of red when Mathis moved the footage forward a bit. He had often twirled that hair around his finger while she slept, getting lost in the softness of it.

"Why did your face change?"

Soren blinked and moved his eyes to Elvira standing beside him. She spotted the recognition in them immediately.

"It's her," she said, her face growing white. "Father! Father, did you hear that? It's *her*! With Xander! It's the slave!"

"*Where* is Xander?" President Saevus repeated louder this time. When no one could answer, his eyes moved to Luka. "*You*."

Luka only had a moment to be fearful before he was pulling out his Element and shooting a blast at Mathis Fender. In less than a second he was as dead as his son. Then Luka went for Soren but, before he could strike, someone was shooting at him. He ducked.

Out of the corner of his eye, Luka watched as Finley slipped out of the room, then he noticed Lona and Wyatt looking horrified.

Another blast came at him. He rolled out of the way.

Then another.

"Don't kill him! Stop him!" ordered the president.

Luka made a run for it passed his two friends, knowing that they were too frozen to do much of anything. He had barely made it into the hallway when someone successfully hit him with a blue string of light. Luka fell to the floor, screaming in agony.

Then his eyes opened and he was rolled onto his bleeding back. The president standing above him. "*Where* is Xander?"

Luka said nothing, playing the part of mind controlled puppet very well.

"I'll search his apartment, Mr. President!" shouted Veli, running towards the front door.

"Elvira, track his wristband and if he's at his apartment send others," the president commanded. "I will take care of our Luka here."

Luka barely had a moment to look into the smug eyes of his father, who was standing behind the president, before another streak of blue light was whipping towards him. Then another. And another. Something knocked him hard in the head. Then harder. And before he had any chance to fight it, the entire world went black.

CHAPTER THIRTY-ONE

Xander only took the president's car as far as the gate to Middle City, knowing very well that as soon as they figured out it was him who had killed Dougal they would track his wristband, and he had no interest in being trapped in a car when that happened. Since Deryn had forbidden him from riding his hover-bike while healing, it wasn't their waiting for him, but Luka's was and he had access.

As he rode Luka's bike home, he started to panic about the fate of his friend. How would they know about the mind control chip? Would they even think to check for something like that? Whether they did or not, Luka would still be in deep shit for the time being. And suddenly Xander couldn't believe he had left him there to deal with this on his own. What had he been thinking?

And then he remembered.

He had been thinking about Deryn. They both had. That was why Luka had stayed behind, to at least create a minor distraction so she would have a chance to get out.

Xander took deep breaths to stop the tears from forming behind his eyes, silently thanking and praying for his best friend at the same time.

Luka would be fine. He had to be.

It didn't take Xander long to get home, abandoning the bike on the curb and sprinting inside. Once in his apartment, he began frantically calling Deryn's name. It figured that this was the one time she wasn't waiting for him at the front door. It only took a few seconds for her to come running out of the bedroom.

"Xander, what's wrong?"

"Get your things," he ordered.

Her face fell. "What?"

"Get your fucking things! We have to get you out now!"

She took a few steps towards him. "But why? What happened?"

"We always knew this day would come, Deryn, now go and get your fucking things!"

Deryn's heart was racing as she stared at Xander, who was both determined and frightened as he breathed heavily.

This was real.

She turned quickly and ran back into the bedroom.

Xander went to the closet and took out her coat and shoes, tossing them onto an armchair. Then he went into the kitchen and grabbed anything he could find that might be useful. Medicine, herbs, food, everything.

Deryn came back out holding her rucksack, her smaller bag already strapped to her hip. Xander grabbed it from her and began stuffing everything inside.

"Let's go," he said, swinging her rucksack over his shoulder and heading towards the door.

"Where exactly am I supposed to go?"

"I don't *fucking* know, Deryn!" he snapped, pausing for a moment to rub at his temples and think. "To Del's. Just until the Resistance finds that way in."

She bit her lip. "Xander, there ..." She gulped. "There is another way."

He turned and furrowed his brow. "What do you mean?"

"I met two people at the Black Market who can help. They have a ... business of sorts, getting people out of the city who are trapped here."

Xander grew still, his eyes drawing towards hers. "How long ago did you meet them?" he asked hoarsely.

"Last month, just before Christmas," she answered honestly. "They found me when I went to the Black Market with Luka." Deryn sighed and took several steps forward. "Xander, please come with me. I've already packed for you. I've been taking your clothes for weeks."

Well, that explained the missing sweaters. But Xander still kept her gaze as he shook his head slowly. "I can't."

"Why not?" she shouted with angry tears in her eyes.

"It's too dangerous -"

"That's bullshit! That's fucking bullshit and you know it!"

"Deryn, please," said Xander, closing those last few steps between them. "You *need* to go."

"Not without you!" she cried, throwing herself into his arms. "You say you love me, Xander, but if you truly did then you'd come with me! You'd come! So that ..." She gulped. "So that we could continue to keep each other safe."

"But me staying behind ... *that* is what will keep you safe. Please ..."

"No."

"*Please!*"

Just then, the alarm went off, signaling someone entering the building. Not Luka. Xander pulled away from Deryn in a panic.

"You need to go!"

"No!"

"Go!"

"I am not going without you, Xander!"

"Then fucking hide! Please, do something!"

"No, I won't! I will *not* hide! Not anymore!"

There was a bang as someone tried to force the door open, but Xander had locked it immediately after entering. But the person outside of it somehow had access and the door swung open. They both took out and aimed their Elements. Xander put his arm on Deryn and moved her behind him just as his father stepped through the doorway.

Atticus stared at his son as he shut the door, noticing the cold, determined look in his eyes. Then his gaze drifted to the girl standing behind him. The one he hadn't seen since the fateful day his wife, and almost his son, had been taken from him. And she was looking back at him now with that same fear in her eyes that still gave him nightmares.

"Xander, what have you done?"

"Whatever do you mean, Father?"

Atticus's eyes moved back to him. "You killed Dougal, didn't you? That's why you're here."

Xander didn't acknowledge his question. "Deryn, get your shoes and coat on."

Deryn kept her head low as she looked nervously at Atticus, her nostrils flaring as she slowly began to move towards the armchair where Xander had put her things. He moved his body so it was in front of her the entire time.

Deryn slipped on her shoes and fastened her coat, pulling up the hood so her face would be hidden. Then she walked back over to Xander. "You can't fight from the inside anymore. Not if they know you killed Dougal. So come with me," she said, ignoring Atticus's presence.

Xander looked at her, his lips quivering as his eyes finally began to tear. "I can't -"

"Come with me!"

"Xander, don't!" pleaded Atticus. "If you go then the president will not rest until he's found you! You have to stay!" He looked at Deryn. "I have one of those mind control chips. I stole it right after I found out about their existence. You can install it in his wristband! If you do then we can lie to the president! We can tell him Xander had it installed the entire time! He'll be safe!"

Deryn's nostrils flared. "Is that what you call the condition Xander's been in since New Year's? Was he *safe* when your president had him whipped thirty-one *fucking* times!" she shouted. "He's *not* safe here!"

"At least if he's here then he'll still have a chance at life!"

"This is no fucking life!" Deryn spat, her fists clenching as she burned with rage. Her entire body convulsed as she stared at this man she hated. He didn't look the least bit like Xander because *he* was a monster. "What father would ever want this life for his son?"

Atticus's bottom lip fell as he looked ashamedly towards the floor.

"Deryn, please."

Deryn turned to see Xander looking sadly at her.

"He's right," he said. "Please. Install it."

A huge crack formed on Deryn's heart and it slowly began to shatter in her chest.

"Deryn, you have to do it."

"No," she cried. "Xander, please don't make me."

"You need to stay safe. This ..." He gulped. "... is the only way."

Deryn was shaking.

"Do it."

She whimpered.

"Please, love."

Her eyes widened as he called her that. *Love.* A single tear dripped down her cheek. "I'm not ready to let you go."

Atticus's mouth dropped as he watched the performance in front of him. Xander reached up and slowly wiped her tear, tracing his fingers down her cheek.

"Xander, no. Not *her*," said Atticus in disbelief.

"Don't you dare judge me, you fucking *rapist*!" shouted Xander, turning back towards his father with flaming eyes. "I hate you." His voice was quivering and full of disdain, and Atticus knew his words were true.

"Xander, it ... I ... I didn't want -"

Before Atticus could find his train of thought, the alarm went off again. While Atticus and Deryn looked at the door, Xander looked at her.

Deryn.

Milky, soft skin. Plump, pink lips. A few light freckles scattered across her face. And those eyes. Those sea-green eyes he could never get enough of. They moved and looked back at him, wet and beautiful, and Xander realized that he was not ready to let her go either.

Before he knew what he was doing, had any time to second guess himself, Xander grabbed her hand. Her sea-green eyes looked down at their clasped hands, and then back up at him.

They brightened.

The front door was blasted open and Veli stepped through, his eyes widening.

"*You!*" he shouted, looking angrily at Xander and Deryn. "I fucking knew it was you, *traitor* -"

Xander didn't give him the chance to finish before he was raising his Element and blasting Veli into oblivion - not the usual blast of an Element but one Deryn had created that was ten times more powerful.

Deryn grabbed Xander and pulled him behind the couch with her, but Atticus was not prepared for the blast and flew backwards, his face and clothes now covered in Veli's gory remains, his left leg pouring blood as part of the broken door lodged itself in it. An arm flew by and smacked him in the head.

And the rest of the apartment was not in the greatest of conditions either.

Atticus shot back up and looked at his son in disbelief.

"The next time you and I see each other, Father, we will be enemies," said Xander, tossing his Element aside. He grabbed his unregistered one out of Deryn's rucksack and put it in his holster.

"Xander, Son, please, no!"

Xander closed his eyes and turned away from him. "Deryn, let's go!" he ordered.

Deryn nodded, squeezing his hand tighter.

"No!" shouted Atticus, scrambling to his feet until an excruciating pain shot through his injured leg.

Xander and Deryn ran to the door. Deryn turned to him at the last moment, smiling viciously before vanishing from sight, his son disappearing right along with her.

"*Xander!*"

CHAPTER THIRTY-TWO

"Father!" Elvira ran into the hallway where an unconscious Luka was still being dealt with. "There was interference on Xander's wristband! No matter what I tried I couldn't locate it, so I've been following Veli's tracker and it just vanished! Right after he got to Xander's apartment!"

"Vanished," repeated President Saevus. "How can it just vanish?"

Elvira glanced sideways at her husband and took a breath. "It can vanish if someone destroyed it. Or him."

Soren looked to the floor and bit his cheek, trying unsuccessfully to stop himself from laughing.

"Atticus Ruby's tracker is presently on the premises but he doesn't seem to be moving," continued Elvira.

The president let out a loud growl. "Barath, get your son locked up in the basement! Wenton, get to Xander's home immediately! Soren, Elvira, Eamon, you get underground! Take as many guards as you need to swarm the place! Everyone else, get out there and *find him!*"

"Do you want us to take the emergency hover-bikes?" asked Elvira.

He nodded and she began ushering everyone to their location. All of the bikes were designed like her father's car. Untraceable and able to fly high into the air.

"We *will* find him, Father. I promise you," said Elvira, taking the president's hand.

Saevus scowled and said, "See that you do." He pulled away

and left his daughter standing there alone.

~

Deryn ran through the streets, pulling Xander with her as she went as fast as she could to Cherish Lane. She had located it on a map shortly after re-meeting Neo and Odette, and had memorized the quickest route to get there while avoiding the main roads.

It wasn't far, only three blocks, and upon arriving she immediately knew which house was the oldest one on the block. The only one not made of metal. Old, wooden and decaying, she understood why they'd used such an unimpressive place as an entryway to their hidden tunnels.

She took the key out of her coat's inside pocket, where she kept it, and unlocked the front door.

"Deryn, where are we going?" asked Xander as she yanked him through the doorway, then locked the door behind them.

"Through a bookshelf," she answered, walking into the room to their left. The bookshelf was against the far wall, the only thing not covered by dusty sheets. She went over and pushed it aside, locating the hidden tunnel behind it.

"But who did you meet at the Black Market?"

"You'll see when we get there."

They both stepped through the passageway. Xander pushed the bookshelf closed again while Deryn stood behind him, pulling a flashlight out of the rucksack he still carried.

"What happened tonight, Xander?" she asked as they walked through the dark tunnel with only their small splash of light, hand-in-hand. "How'd they find out about Dougal?"

"His father found his broken wristband and discovered the exact time it was deactivated," answered Xander. "He brought security footage from outside the alley for everyone to view and I bolted."

"And Luka?"

Xander's hand tensed in hers. She tried to look at him but it was impossible in the darkness.

"Luka, he ..." He took a deep breath and Deryn knew he was fighting back tears. "He stayed behind, hoping to buy us more time."

Deryn gulped, her heart slowing as she thought of Luka, undoubtedly being tortured that very moment. *Shit.*

"He'll be alright," she said encouragingly, giving Xander's hand a squeeze. "He has the mind control chip installed. They'll find it."

She did her best to sound convincing, but it was hard considering she didn't know if she believed the words she was saying. How would they find it if they didn't know to look?

It wasn't long before they reached the hover-bike Odette had promised would be there. "We take this to the end of the tunnel," explained Deryn, waiting for Xander to mount it first. As much as she wanted to learn to drive one of these things, she realized now was not the time.

Xander looked at it skeptically. "Why aren't you telling me who it was you spoke to?"

"Maybe you don't know them," she said, motioning to the bike.

"If I didn't then you'd just tell me."

"Get on the bike, Xander."

"Not until you tell me -"

"Time is limited and you'll find out soon enough. I'll drive if you won't."

As soon as she began to mount the bike, Xander pulled her off. He grunted and sat first, handing her the rucksack and waiting for her to climb on before starting it.

"Just because we're currently on the run and a time crunch, don't think for one second when I find out who it is I won't scream at you."

Deryn smiled and pressed her cheek gently against his still-healing back, breathing him in as she realized he was really here, running with her. "It wouldn't be us if you didn't."

Xander was happy the darkness hid his smirk as he rode off into the dark tunnel.

It was a long ride, a good ten miles at least, probably farther. When they reached the end of the tunnel, there was a short ladder that led to an escape hatch. Xander insisted on going up first, by the chance that there was a group of Guardians waiting for them at the top. The fact that she wouldn't tell him who they were meeting had him thinking the absolute worst. If this was a setup then whoever was behind it would pay with their life. He would make sure of that.

But the hatch didn't lead anywhere exciting. Just onto some tram tracks with an opening to an inside compartment that was empty. Once safely inside, he took the rucksack from Deryn and tossed it aside before pulling her up. Only a few seconds passed before the door to the compartment was thrown open, a familiar face blinking and then smiling when he and Xander locked eyes.

"Hello, Xander," said Neo Boyce.

"Oh shit, is it time?" asked Odette, coming up behind her husband and shoving him inside. She shut the door behind them.

Xander slowly began to turn his head towards Deryn, his eyes widening as he did so. "*These* are the people who sought you out?"

"Yes," said Deryn with a shrug. "So?"

"No offense," said Xander, looking coldly at Neo, "but I think we'll find our own way out." He pulled Deryn towards the door, but she yanked him back.

"Xander, no!" she shouted. "We wouldn't even know where to begin to get out of Utopia! They were *your* friends. Why don't you trust them?"

"Do *you*?" asked Xander.

"For the right price I do," she said, reaching into the small bag strapped to her hip and pulling out an envelope of money. She handed it to Neo. "Five-hundred coin. It's all there, but we're sort of short on time so I'd appreciate it if you counted later."

Neo smirked. "I have a hard time believing the Outsider princess would scam us. I trust you." He put the envelope in his pocket. Then he looked at Xander. "Good to see you again, old friend."

Xander scowled at him. "What are you doing here, Neo? I

have a hard time believing you've been helping others when the two of you were so quick to show your cowardice after the president won against the Outsiders."

"People can change," said Neo.

Odette smirked and gave Xander a onceover. "Clearly. Who knew the notorious Guardian Xander Ruby had a soft spot for Godfrey Leon's precious daughter?" She moved her gaze to Deryn. "I really never believed you'd get him here."

"Are we fucking doing this or not?" demanded Xander. "If you didn't notice by our dramatic entrance, we're on a bit of a tight schedule."

"Yeah, yeah, don't get your panty's all in a twist," said Neo. "We're just waiting on one more."

Deryn raised her eyebrows. "One more?"

"Yes, our third," said Odette. "We'll need all three of us to get you out."

"And if you're here I imagine she's only minutes behind you," said Neo.

Xander crinkled his forehead. "What does that -"

Just then, the compartment door slid open and someone in a Guardian coat entered. Their hood was up, so Xander and Deryn couldn't see their face, but they weren't particularly tall.

"Did anyone follow you?" asked Neo.

"No," said a familiar woman's voice. "No one even noticed me leave." She pulled down her hood, revealing the sharp but pretty face of Finley Scout. "Hello, Xander."

Xander and Deryn immediately raised their Elements.

"What the fuck is this?" he demanded.

"Relax," said Neo. "Finley's been helping me and Odette since the beginning."

"You're a traitor?" asked Xander, looking wide-eyed at Finley.

She smirked. "You're one to talk. Harboring Leon, Xander? *Really?*" She moved her eyes over to Deryn and stared at her coldly. "Luka put on quite a show for you. Killed Mathis. Almost got Soren too, barely missed before everyone started firing at him."

"He has a mind control chip installed," said Xander. "You'd better make sure -"

"I'll let the president know," she said.

Xander's nostrils flared. He turned to Deryn. "Are you sure you want to trust these people?"

Deryn scanned them, her eyes stopping on Finley for a moment. As much as she hated the woman, she couldn't convince herself that she was lying about being a traitor. Luka had told her once how Finley was forced to become a Guardian by her father, just like him. And if Finley was anything like Luka ...

"We don't have much of a choice," said Deryn. "I took a chance when I let *you* help me and I think I have to do it again."

Xander took a deep breath and forced himself to nod.

"So we're going then?" asked Neo.

"Yes," said Xander.

"Alright! Let's get this party start -"

"Hold on," said Finley, whose eyes were still on Deryn. "I want to talk to Leon." Then they moved to Xander. "*Alone.*"

Xander sneered and stood protectively in front of her. "Like hell you will!"

"It's important," she said. "I'm not going to hurt her."

"Fuck no -"

"Xander, it's fine," said Deryn, putting a comforting hand on his arm. "We're wasting time here, so just let her talk to me and then we can be on our way."

Xander held his hand out to Finley. "Give me your Element."

Finley rolled her eyes but still obeyed. Then she motioned for Deryn to step out of the compartment first. Deryn did just that, making sure to shove hard into Finley's shoulder as she passed her.

"You're as insufferable as I remember," said Finley, following her out and shutting the compartment door behind them.

"What do you want, Scout?" asked Deryn, turning towards her and crossing her arms.

Suddenly, Finley's entire face changed. She looked pensively towards the floor and sighed. "Look, I ... I wanted to apologize for what I did to you all of those years ago. When my ..." She gulped. "When my father owned you."

"Apologize?" repeated Deryn, her throat instantly growing raw.

Finley looked up. "Yes. I was young back then. I know it's no excuse but I really didn't understand that it wasn't your fault. My father ... he's a pig. I see that now. A filthy, disgusting, greedy pig, and I've made a point to defy him in any and every way that I can."

"I see," said Deryn, her arms falling to her sides.

"Becoming a Guardian, it changes people. Mostly for the worst, but not always."

Deryn nodded, and glanced towards the door Xander was behind. He had definitely changed for the better.

"Lift your shirt."

Deryn's head whipped back towards Finley. "*What?*"

"Lift your shirt, Leon. Those scars I gave you from the black flames, I've been working on a cream to heal them." Finley reached into her pocket and came out with a small container. "It's not perfect yet and it isn't instantaneous, but if you apply it now then they'll begin to heal like regular scars."

Deryn's lip quivered as she tried to nod her head, unsure if she did it successfully. She moved her coat aside and lifted her shirt with shaky hands. Finley opened the cream and stepped forward, rubbing it generously on Deryn's marked skin.

"Tell me the truth," said Finley as she worked. "Was it you who sent me that email?"

Eyes still focused on the scars, Deryn nodded and quietly said, "Yes."

Finley smiled lightly. "I thought at the time that it didn't sound like him, but I just couldn't figure out who else would have gone to the trouble." She glanced up and raised an eyebrow. "Jealous?"

Deryn chuckled. "Far less than you are now."

Finley bit her cheek. It wasn't long before each scar was

covered with the cream, instant relief spreading throughout Deryn's body even though Finley had said it would take a while. Her body was healing. She could feel it.

Finley closed the cream and looked sadly at her. "Sorry you had to have those for so long."

Deryn bit her lip to hold back her tears and nodded. Finley handed her the small container and she slipped it into her pocket.

"Apply it every twelve hours for as long as it takes. Now come along, we don't have much time," said Finley as she reopened the compartment door. "We're ready!"

"Excellent," said Neo. "That just leaves one last thing to take care of." He, Odette and Finley all looked at Xander. His wrists, specifically.

Neo reached out and took off his citizen wristband. Once that was gone, Xander stared down at his guard wristband.

"I suppose they're already tracking me."

"No," said Finley, walking over to him. "But they're trying." She pressed something on his wristband. A small chip popped out and she held it up. "When activated, this chip makes you disappear off the radar for a good couple of hours. I installed it while you were sleeping that first night you came to my place, and I activated it the moment it became clear you were the one who killed Dougal."

"Why the fuck would you install that?" demanded Xander. "You didn't know what I was up to back then."

"No, but I was being cautious. I installed one in Luka's wristband while we were out drinking together a couple weeks ago. Wyatt and Lona too, in case there's ever a time where any of them need to run."

Xander stared at the small chip and froze. "But you just took it out. Won't that make it so -"

"The Black Market, as well as all of our secret passages, have tracker blockers installed, so the moment you decided to come to us you've been in the clear. But I'm afraid the same can't be said the moment you step outside," explained Odette.

They all looked at Xander's wristband again. He lifted his

arm and clutched onto it. "So what do you propose?" he asked.

"We're removing it," said Neo as his wife pulled something out of the pouch she had strapped to her hip.

Xander went white. "What?"

"Don't worry, it'll only hurt for a second," said Odette, holding up a strange device with a needle poking out of it. "Finley, go grab one of our decoy's from the other compartment."

Finley ran out of the compartment, returning a few seconds later with a plain metal wristband. "You'll wear this one while your wrist heals. The shaved bone will obviously never grow back but you'll be able to survive without it."

"And what of the poison that's supposed to kill me the moment it's removed?" asked Xander.

"That's what the needle's for," said Odette, grabbing his wrist and poking her tool against it. "It will inject the antidote into you the moment the wristband is removed. Unfortunately, you'll still get a few of those black marks on your veins. But not Soren bad or anything."

Xander grimaced.

"It's not so terrible," said Finley. "Easy enough to cover with makeup, at least."

She lifted her wrist and wiped the area just above her wristband, revealing a black vein poking out of it. When she caught Xander's eye, he gulped.

"We needed a test subject and I was the only one available."

Deryn placed her hand in Xander's free arm while Odette readied the device. He clenched his eyes shut as something poked into him, his wrist stinging as raw flesh was exposed to the air for the first time in years. When Deryn's hand tensed he opened his eyes, staring down at bone and black veins halfway up his forearm. He only got to look at his wounded wrist for a moment before Finley was clasping on the decoy wristband.

"We'll dispose of this one properly later," said Odette, handing off the old wristband to her husband, who made a face at the dried blood on the inside and tossed it along with the citizen wristband into a corner.

Neo then went to the wall at the back of the compartment and shoved it until a doorway opened. "Let's go!" he ordered, stepping out first. Odette followed him.

Xander turned to Deryn and put an arm around her waist. "Are you alright?" he asked, glancing sideways at Finley.

Deryn nodded and smiled. "Let's get out of here."

He nodded back and kissed her forehead. Finley tried not to stare as Xander took Deryn's hand, but it was hard not to. It was one thing to suspect a relationship between the two of them, but seeing it happen with her own eyes was something different entirely.

Xander then came up beside Finley and grabbed her wrist. He pulled up her sleeve, looking closely at the black veins covered by makeup that traveled halfway up her arm. It was obvious he was wondering how he'd missed them the many times he'd seen her naked, pre-Deryn.

"You've *really* been doing this for years?" he asked, pressing down on one of the veins.

"I have," she answered, pulling her arm away. "You've hidden your betrayal by staying close to the president's side, while I've hidden mine by being as insignificant as possible. He and the other Guardians have no idea where I am right now and, what's more, none of them care. Sometimes it's best just to stay hidden in the shadows."

"Are you all coming?" asked Odette, poking her head back inside.

Finley nodded and ran over first, and she and Odette disappeared outside. Xander grabbed their rucksack and tossed it over his shoulders. Then he and Deryn followed after them.

Neo had a trapdoor open a few feet away on an unused tram track. He ushered everyone inside, just a few feet to drop, then followed after, pulling the door shut behind him.

Inside the dark passageway they were submerged in, Odette led the way to a simple stone wall. She looked back and smiled at Xander and Deryn. "It's a bit of a maze down here. Hope you're ready for it."

She pushed the wall and opened another doorway. Neo

hurried through first, followed by Odette and Finley.

Xander and Deryn followed but hung back a little, both glancing around skeptically. Xander clutched his unregistered Element tightly, keeping it steadily aimed at Neo, Odette and Finley's backs.

"Honestly, Xander, we were friends for years and you really trust me so little?" asked Neo, glancing back at him.

"I don't trust anyone," answered Xander.

Neo frowned. "What a sad way to live."

Xander eyed the hand that was not holding onto Odette's, noticing the gold ring he was wearing.

"When did you two get married?" he asked.

"Last year," said Odette, smiling brightly as she looked over her shoulder. "It was a small ceremony. Just Finley and two others. We just wanted to make it official." She looked dotingly at her husband and kissed his cheek.

Xander grunted in disgust.

"No need to be so verbal, Xander. We already know *your* opinion on marriage," said Neo.

"You know, my sister really is out of your league," said Odette, looking back at them again.

Xander scoffed and squeezed Deryn's hand tighter. He was pretty sure he'd already obtained the best girl out there, and if he could get her then no one could possibly be 'out of his league'.

"I'm not against marriage," he said.

Neo, Odette and Finley all looked at him and raised their eyebrows. Deryn stared at the ground and blushed, but Xander was not afraid to meet each and every one of their gazes.

"I am against *arranged* marriage. And marriage during a time of war. If the war ever ends then I have every intention of getting married."

Deryn smiled and glanced at the spot on her chest where she could feel the ring grazing her skin.

"So, how long have you two been, umm ... together?" asked Neo.

"You escaped in September, right, Leon?" asked Odette.

"Finley, isn't that what you said?

Finley nodded slowly.

"Xander found me three days after I escaped," answered Deryn. "The night before the curfew began."

"Not exactly what I was asking," said Neo. "How long have you two been -"

"November fifth," they both answered before he could finish.

"Oh, that's sweet. They both remember the exact date," said Odette. "So what was November fifth, then? First kiss? First fuck?"

Deryn blushed again and quickly began inspecting the walls they were passing.

Neo smirked. "First fuck it is then."

"Are you always this chatty with the people you help escape?" asked Xander with a sneer.

"I was only trying to catch up with an old friend," said Neo, rolling his eyes. "Can you honestly say you're not the least bit curious about my life these last few years?"

Xander paused. "Mildly."

"Ah, I knew it! I knew you missed me!"

"I've been perfectly fine without your presence in my life, Neo," said Xander. "But, I admit, I've checked before to make sure you were alive."

"And?" asked Neo, cocking an eyebrow.

"You were, so I left it at that."

"No hello?"

Xander looked at him very seriously and said, "It was better for you that I didn't."

Neo looked forward again and they all continued to walk in silence.

When they hit what looked like a dead-end, Neo announced, "We're here!" He took three black devices out of his pocket and handed one to Odette and another to Finley. He kept the third.

"What are those?" asked Deryn, looking at them curiously.

"Two-ways you can install in your ear," answered Odette. "We've taken many of the Resistance's ideas and made them better."

The three of them pressed a button on the small devices, placed them in their left ears, and tested that everything was in working order.

"Once we head through this wall we'll be in the underground," explained Neo. "It's overrun with S.U.R.G.E.'s and probably guards at this point, since your escape doesn't exactly appear to be a secret."

"It definitely isn't," said Finley.

"Odette and I will go ahead of you to scout out the best possible route to get out of here. You two will stay with Finley. She has a satellite to keep the S.U.R.G.E.'s away."

Finley lifted a small gun with a cone shaped barrel, a smaller version of the guns the Resistance used to take the S.U.R.G.E.'s down. "It throws off their radar and sends them in the opposite direction," she explained.

"Finley will stay with you until you get to the deep underground where the water supply flows, which is also where Odette and I will meet back up with you. I'm going to explain this next part now, in case we don't have time later," said Neo. "In the event that there are too many S.U.R.G.E.'s and guards running around for you to just walk out of here, there's one much quicker but riskier exit.

"Outside of the room we'll be meeting in is the water supply, which is, essentially, an indoor river. This is our Plan B. *Your* out. If this becomes our course of action, when you get there you will follow the water as long as you can. The flow is pretty rough and there's a good minute where you'll have to hold your breath. The president knows people have used the water supply to escape Utopia before and I have no doubt he'll send some of his guards down there to search for you. You need to be prepared because you *will* be spotted, so when you reach the water jump like your goddamn life depends on it, because it does."

"But don't worry about being followed," said Odette. "The moment you're through the grate down there, I'll be standing by to switch the water's direction. Whoever follows you will be sent to the deeper underground of our ancestors and down a large waterfall. They *won't* survive."

"So if the president knows people have used the water supply to escape before, I can assume correctly that he'll know exactly where we'll arrive outside," said Xander, scowling.

"Yes, but by the time he gets there you'll be long gone," said Neo. "Don't know why you'd dilly dally during an escape."

Xander shook his head. "But what about cameras or S.U.R.G.E.'s? I doubt he's stupid enough to keep the area unpatrolled."

"He has both, but we reprogrammed the two S.U.R.G.E.'s down there ages ago. They see what we want them to see, and the camera is on a constant loop. It never sees anything of value," explained Neo. "Don't worry so much. We have our shit together. We'll try to take the longer way out but, like you said, we're on a time crunch here."

"Our usual clients aren't so high profile, or pursued," said Odette. "But we're always ready for a challenge. So, shall we?"

Xander grunted. "*This* isn't going to be a complete disaster." He glanced sideways at Deryn, who was standing there stiffly, her eyes unblinking.

"Well, it really would have been better if you came to us *before* you were found out," said Neo, "but what's done is done. No use fretting over it."

"If it were anyone else I might worry, but the two of you have gotten out of some rather sticky situations in the past. You'll be fine," said Odette. "Just move fast and don't hesitate to kill."

There was a pause.

"We need a moment," said Xander, pulling Deryn a few feet back.

He took both of her hands in his, but noticed the other three were still watching them. He twirled his finger and they all turned to face the opposite direction.

"Are you sure you want to do this?" he asked once they were as alone as they were going to get. "We could always just go back and hide with Del. Take some time to figure things out."

Deryn bit her lip and thought about this for a moment. But she eventually shook her head. "We can't put them at risk like that. If the Guardians don't see us leaving then they'll know we're still hiding in the city. They'll put up more borders, making it impossible for us to ever escape. This is our one-shot and I think we should take it."

Xander's hands tensed in hers, his expression unreadable.

"It's time, Xander," she said, trying hard to smile as she gave his hands a squeeze.

He nodded slowly. "You're right."

"Are you regretting coming with me already?" she asked, looking at him sadly.

"No. But it would be easier for you to get out if I gave myself up."

"That would *not* be easier. If you gave yourself up then I could never just leave."

Xander smiled. "I know. I've called you on your stubbornness before."

Deryn smiled back. "You're worse."

"If I were worse then I wouldn't be here right now."

"I was going to cave and install that chip," she admitted.

"I know. But I'm happy you didn't." He leaned in and kissed her softly. Then he pulled her body against his and breathed her in. "Are you ready?"

She nodded.

"Okay, Neo," said Xander, pulling away from her and retaking her hand.

Neo, Odette and Finley all turned back around.

"Well, this is it," said Neo, half-turning towards the wall. He paused and looked back at Xander. "I'll say good luck now. Maybe, if we're all still kicking when this war is over -"

"We'll have a drink like the good ol' days," said Xander with a smile. "Just as long as you don't sing that fucking song I made up. Luka tried to bring it back recently." He sighed as he thought of Luka, truly hoping he was all right.

"Oh, you mean this one?" Neo cleared his throat. *"Oh Utopia, only trains those, heroic, loyal and stunning. While the wine and the whiskey flows, we flee Eagle without the running!"*

"Shut it," Xander said sternly.

Neo laughed and turned the rest of the way towards the wall. He gave it a shove, revealing a much wider and darker tunnel. "Alright, ladies and gentleman. It's go time!"

CHAPTER THIRTY-THREE

Neo ran through the opening first.

"See you on the other side!" said Odette before following him.

Xander and Deryn looked at Finley and waited for the go-ahead. She was quiet for a moment, but once they heard mumbling coming from her ear, she looked at them and said, "Let's go."

They all walked through the open wall, Finley in the lead. It shut automatically behind them. Xander and Deryn's nerves finally hit as they realized they weren't hidden anymore. They were out in the open, and the underground was a dangerous place. Anyone could be lurking in its depths. Enemies. Allies. Though, at this point, it was hard to differentiate between the two.

"*Finley, avoid the east tunnel. There is a swarm of maybe twenty S.U.R.G.E.'s over here and they're spreading out quickly. Over,*" said Neo's voice through Finley's headset.

"Okay," she answered. "Odette, how does it look to the west? Over."

"*No good. Stick north for now. I'm circling back around to check it out. Over.*"

Finley turned on the light on her citizen wristband as the tunnel got narrower and darker. She held her arm out in front of her, showing three tunnels heading in different directions. She went for the one straight ahead.

"*About three S.U.R.G.E.'s from the swarm are headed that way, Fin. Be prepared. Over.*"

Finley picked up her pace. Xander and Deryn hurried after her, but he was still in a great deal of pain from his lashes and not moving so well.

"Are you alright?" asked Deryn. "Do you need me to carry the rucksack?"

Finley slowed and glanced back at them.

"No," he said. "I'll be fine. Lona gave me some tea with natural herbs in it earlier and it's actually helped with the pain."

"Lona," repeated Deryn, glancing sideways at him.

"For me *and* Luka," he said. "She was just being nice."

"Mmhmm," she said, now glancing elsewhere.

Xander frowned. "Oh, come on. You're not going to be jealous over a little tea, are you? You know she only gave it to me because she wanted to give it to Luka. I'm not the one she slept with."

"*Lona* slept with *Luka*?" said Finley, turning around as her mouth fell open. "Don't tell Odette. She'll *kill* him."

"It's not jealousy," said Deryn, ignoring Finley. "I just don't like the way she's attached herself to you. *Or* him."

"Why not him?" he asked.

"He's taken."

Xander cringed. "Not exactly -"

"He's *taken*, Xander," she said sternly. "And it's really time for you to accept that."

Xander grunted.

"Luka's taken? By who?" asked Finley, cocking an eyebrow.

Before anyone could answer - or not answer, since neither Xander or Deryn planned on giving her a straight one - a weird whistling sounded up ahead. Finley whipped back around and held out her wrist. They could all just make out three black robots with silver wings fluttering towards them, a blue light emerging from each and scanning the area in front of them.

Finley held up her small gun with the cone shaped barrel and aimed for the center S.U.R.G.E. The gun created blurry waves in the air that caused the robot to immediately turn in the opposite direction. The other two quickly followed suit.

When they were gone, Finley turned back towards Xander

and Deryn, who were both staring at her wide-eyed.

"Who made that?" asked Xander.

"I did," said Finley. "With some assistance from two traitors who work in the Government Lab. I won't give names."

Xander shrugged. "Wasn't going to ask." He paused. "How long have you been doing this?"

"I don't know," said Finley, turning back around and walking on. "It was Odette and Neo's idea. They just asked me if I wanted in and I said yes. Is that *really* so hard to believe?"

"Yes," he answered truthfully.

Xander and Deryn were walking fairly close to Finley now and, even in the dark, he could see that she looked hurt.

"I hate being a Guardian, Xander. You *know* that."

"I do," he said.

"Personally, I think *you* betraying the president and fucking Leon is a bit more shocking."

Xander smirked. "Well, you know me. I *live* to shock."

"Finley, stop heading north!" said the frantic voice of Odette in her ear. *"Guards have entered the underground led by fucking Soren! Over."*

"The east is clear now," said Neo. *"There will be a few S.U.R.G.E.'s up ahead but nothing you can't handle. Over."*

"Got it. Over."

Finley looked at Xander and Deryn.

"Soren is here with guards."

She darted to the right wall and felt along it until she found a small button disguised as a bolt. She pressed it to reveal a narrow opening. The passageway was so thin that Xander had to take off his rucksack, and they shimmied through it sideways, the opening shutting behind them just as voices started to echo down the tunnels.

"We shouldn't talk anymore," whispered Finley as they moved through the narrow space. "Not if guards are here."

They came out in a small cavity where several men sat around a heater, warming their hands. Xander and Deryn stopped and froze, but Finley walked right past them.

"Hey, Fin! What you bring us tonight?" asked one of them.

"Nothing tonight, Rees. On a mission." Finley beckoned the couple forward. "No need to worry. They're just tunnelers."

Xander and Deryn slowly stepped out of the passageway.

"We got a couple of wanted criminals tonight, boys, so guards and S.U.R.G.E.'s are on full alert. Make sure you keep it down," she ordered.

The men all laughed.

"*Really*? These blokes?" said Rees. "I could snap the girl in half with just my thumb and the blond, angel boy doesn't look like he'd take much effort."

"*Angel boy?*" repeated Xander with great offense. "I'll have you know that I've been one of the top Guardians for -"

"Xander, he's not worth the effort," said Finley, grabbing his arm and pulling him and Deryn along.

"One of these days you're going to give in an' marry me, Fin!"

"Keep dreaming, Rees!"

"Finley, the east is all clear. If you hurry, you might be able to make it out before more guards head this way. Over," said Neo.

"We're coming through now. Over," responded Finley.

They headed through another narrow passageway and came out in tunnels that looked exactly like the ones before. As Xander returned his rucksack to his shoulders, he had to wonder how his old friends never got turned around in this place.

Finley began running, staying close to the wall to their left. The tunnels ahead were lit with a faint light. Then shadows appeared on the walls in the shape of several peoples silhouettes. Finley grabbed Xander and Deryn, hurried back a few steps and shoved them into a small crevice in the wall. A few seconds later, several guards walked around the corner laughing.

Finley took a deep breath and confidently stepped forward. "Excuse me!"

All of their heads snapped in her direction.

"What's with all the poppycock?" she demanded.

"M-madam," one of the guards mumbled. "We weren't

doing nothin'."

"Clearly," she scoffed. "The president would not be pleased to hear you were down here gallivanting around when we're in the middle of a time crunch! *Get moving!*" she ordered.

"Y-yes, Madam," they all said before running off.

"And make sure to separate yourselves!" she called after them. "We need to cover as much ground as possible!"

"Yes, Madam!" they all called over their shoulders at her.

Once they were gone, Finley sighed in relief and pulled Xander and Deryn out of their hiding place.

"Their numbers are growing. We don't have much longer to get you out of here before escape becomes impossible."

Xander and Deryn nodded.

They took off running again, their legs carrying them faster than before and Xander doing his best to ignore the pain. Finley guided them to the end of the tunnel but, instead of leading them down another one, she pulled open the wall with the dim lights, revealing a tall staircase.

The three of them ran inside and Finley shut the wall behind them. They ran up the stairs, not stopping, not slowing, even after they got to the top.

"We're up! Over!" she said into her headset.

"All's clear up here," said Odette. *"But guards are beginning to swarm near the water supply. Over."*

Finley kept running, urging them forward, twisting and turning down every corner until they came to a door. Just a regular, everyday door that she pulled open.

Xander and Deryn stopped the moment they entered this new room, glancing around in awe at the amazing sight in front of them. This was no ordinary room. There were computers, large screens, panels housing thousands of buttons, something Deryn recognized as ancient telephones scattered around.

Odette and Neo were standing in the center of the room. Finley hurried over to them but Xander and Deryn stood frozen.

"What is this place?" asked Deryn, staring at a large whiteboard almost as long as the wall. covered with faded handwritten notes. Several countries were listed, dates and status updates written below each one.

"It's our ancestors' communication room," said Finley, looking over her shoulder at them. "They used it to speak to the other bases around the world."

"Does any of it still work?" asked Xander, noticing many of the notes written on the board had been smudged so they were illegible.

"No, but if someone knew what they were doing I'm sure they could get it going," said Neo. "The Resistance visits this room a lot. We think they're trying to replicate the technology."

"As fascinating as I'm sure this is, we don't exactly have time to pause," said Odette, hurrying over to a door at the far end of the room. "There are too many guards. We have no choice but to go with Plan B."

"I have to say, this is the most exciting mission we've ever had," said Neo as he followed his wife and they both took off their headsets, stuffing them in their pockets. Finley did the same.

Odette opened the door to reveal a closet, and hanging inside were two steel-blue trench coats with Saevus's crest on the sleeves. They took them out and slipped them on, Odette also putting on a blonde wig over her dark hair. Neo had a small hat that the guards were allowed to wear on cold nights to cover his face a bit.

"Finley, you go first," ordered Neo.

Finley nodded before looking back at Xander and Deryn. "This is goodbye then. Good luck. Both of you."

She hurried towards the only door to their left. Xander bit his cheek, looking torn for a moment before locking eyes with Deryn. She sighed and nodded towards Finley.

Xander grunted. "Finley, wait!"

She stopped and turned.

Xander let go of Deryn's hand for the first time since they entered the underground and stepped forward. "Look," he said. "Sorry, for, uhh ... Well, for being such an ass to you, I suppose. It just comes so damn naturally."

Finley smiled softly. "I know. And don't worry." She glanced at Deryn. "I get it. We've all done things we're ashamed of."

He nodded. "Be careful. The president knows that you're loyal to me."

"I will," she said. "And don't worry. I'll take care of Luka."

He nodded again.

"You better get the fuck out, Xander. I don't really feel like mourning your death anytime soon."

Finley gave him one last smile. Then she turned back around, opened the door and shut it quietly behind her.

"Get to the water and just fucking jump," said Neo. "Keep out of sight as long as you can, then kill whoever gets in your way."

Xander nodded. He stepped forward and held out his hand. "Thanks, Neo."

Neo smiled, took Xander's hand and shook.

Xander squeezed hard and pulled him close. "If something happens out there," he whispered, "and I have to give myself up, you make sure she gets out. Don't let her come back for me."

"Got it," said Neo, giving him a pat on the back.

"There are also some Resistance members, six of them, hiding out in the city. They've been trapped since the curfew began. They're at an abandoned building in the old section of the Shopping District. One of the only brick buildings with an apartment above it. If you can, get them out. You'll recognize one of them and you'll want to question her, but you have my word that she's trustworthy. Understood?"

Neo smirked. "I gotta hand it to you, Xander. Being the president's top dog all this time. You even had me fooled."

"That was the point," said Xander, smirking back at him.

Deryn suddenly came up beside him and retook his hand.

"Xander, it's time for us to go. We've delayed this for long enough," she said, her palm sweating against his.

"Right." He took one last deep breath. "This is real. Are you ready for this?"

"No," said Deryn truthfully. "But when will I ever be?"

"If you two want to kiss for good luck we won't stop you," said Odette, watching them with a fixed fascination. Neo looked just as intrigued.

"You two are fucking creepy," said Xander. But, still, he ignored them and leaned forward, giving Deryn a soft kiss and pressing his forehead against hers. He just stood there for a moment, breathing her in before he finally said, "Let's go."

CHAPTER THIRTY-FOUR

Xander tugged Deryn forward before either of them had a chance to be frightened and pull back. They stayed hidden in their black hoods as they stepped through the door, pressing themselves firmly against the wall as they moved in the shadows.

Up ahead they could already see several guards running around while a Guardian with their hood up barked orders. Another Guardian walked up, several inches shorter than the first. They whispered back and forth, but then Finley went up to them. They directed her upstream and she ran off.

The water was there. So close but untouchable from where they stood.

Xander and Deryn walked to the very edge of their narrow hallway, their Elements held at their sides, still covered in shadow while one step forward would put them in the light. As long as no one looked their way all they had to do was wait for a chance to make their move.

Finley appeared again with two guards in tow. She said something to the two Guardians and somehow managed to usher them the in direction she'd come from, glancing nervously towards the dark hallway where she knew they stood.

This was it. Their one chance to go.

And they took it.

Without another thought Xander and Deryn left the safety of the shadows, sprinting downstream and towards the water.

"There they are!" someone shouted from above. They both glanced up to see several guards on hover-bikes, flying much higher than protocol normally allowed.

"Shit!" said Xander, picking up his pace and dragging Deryn along with him.

The bike zoomed in their direction and they both slammed to the ground before the guard could grab either of them. When it came for them again, Xander rolled and jumped to his feet, grabbing the guard by the coat and yanking him off of the bike. The bike kept zooming forward, crashing into a guard unfortunate enough to be standing close by, killing him instantly.

Deryn was up again and latching back on to Xander's hand. The water was so close. Only a few hundred feet away.

Glancing over her shoulder, Deryn saw another guard with an Element pointed towards them. She grabbed Xander and pulled him out of the line of fire just as a loud and powerful blast shot by.

"Do *not* kill Xander Ruby!" a familiar voice ordered. "My father wants him alive! Do whatever you want to the girl but Xander is off limits!"

Deryn turned in that moment and aimed her Element at the voice, her eyes locking with Elvira's for a brief moment before she was shooting a blast at her. The woman barely had time to duck. Soren was standing beside her, frozen in place as he watched Deryn move her Element to him. She fired.

Elvira shoved his legs so he landed hard on his back. "Fucking idiot!" she shouted, leaping to her feet and darting towards Deryn.

Deryn wanted to try again but Xander pulled her away before she could.

"Give up the slave, Xander! Give her up now if you want a chance to live!" shouted Elvira from behind them. She motioned to a nearby guard on a hover-bike to come to her. When he did, she shoved him off and took his place, ascending into the air. Now above them, she sent a blast down at their linked hands.

Xander and Deryn dodged in opposite directions, but quickly scrambled to get back to each other. They rolled together to dodge another blast from somewhere above and Deryn shot up, aiming her Element and stunning the guard who had shot at them, sending her and her bike crashing down.

The two of them were back on their feet and running while the guards on the ground surrounded them. Finley was among them, shooting a stunner that shot right by Deryn's ear, 'accidentally' hitting the guard directly in front of them.

Elvira landed her bike, her body burning with rage as she jumped off and marched towards Xander, her Element raised. He shot a blast at her. She had a shield up before it even left his gun.

She fired a stunner at him and he dodged it, having to let go of Deryn's hand again. While plummeting towards the ground, he aimed his Element. She hadn't been expecting it. Not mid-fall. And, against all odds, his blast hit her right hand.

Elvira's Element shattered into a million pieces, the metal protecting her hand but not her fingers. She fell to her knees in pain, a guard immediately coming to her aid and applying pressure to her fingerless and bloody nub.

Xander would have loved to fire again while she was down, to finish her once and for all, but several guards were already shielding her.

With a grunt, Xander jumped to his feet. When he turned back around, Eamon Graham had suddenly appeared and grabbed Deryn from behind. He lifted his Element to save her but, before it was necessary, she had a lock on Eamon's arm and flipped him like Luka had taught her. When he was down, she shot a blast at him, close enough in proximity that there was no escaping alive. "Fucking bastard!" she shouted, giving her dead rapist a hard kick.

While Deryn was distracted two guards tried to come at her from both sides. Xander shot two blasts at them and, when they dodged, he grabbed Deryn's hand and pulled her as fast as he could towards the water.

"Xander!" called a familiar, deep voice that was steadily becoming closer. President Saevus.

Xander turned his head and saw it was coming from an

approaching S.U.R.G.E.

"Stop running! Return to me now and I will spare the slave!"

His running slowed.

"Xander, no!" shouted Deryn, pulling hard on his hand as they finally reached those final fifty steps to the water.

A flash of blue light shot out of a nearby Element, aimed at Deryn. Xander shoved her out of the way and took the lash against the left side of his face.

"Xander!" screamed Deryn as he fell hard to the ground. She tried to run back for him but someone grabbed her. "No!"

A new rush of adrenaline hitting her, Deryn grabbed the handle of her knife in the holster on her wrist and whipped it out. She twisted herself free from the woman who held her and jammed the blade right into her jugular vein, letting her collapse to the ground. Another hand gripped her arm. She spun on her heel, yanked her arm free and planted the tip of the blade on her new attacker's neck. She froze when their eyes met, hers drifting downward until she was staring at the scar along his throat, and then back up. Soren Tash.

Deryn gulped, her heart filled with such hatred for this monster in front of her. With narrowed eyes, she coldly said, "This time I won't miss."

She pulled her hand back, finally ready to strike and finish Soren once and for all. But there was a scream. The scream of a wife who, for some reason, loved her bastard of a husband. And even while Elvira faded into unconsciousness, her hand bleeding out, she still managed to start an unmanned hover-bike and send it hurdling towards Deryn and Soren.

Both were knocked down and sent rolling, Xander grabbing Deryn's right hand as she spun by him, slowing her descent as she dropped her knife and flipped into the water. The rucksack flew off his shoulder while they slid and plopped into the water with her, continuing to flow downstream.

Deryn gasped as she came up for air, struggling to hold onto Xander's hand and keep herself afloat.

He wasn't in the water. He was still on the edge, lying on his stomach and struggling against something.

"Xander, get in!" she shouted, unable to see what was holding him back.

"Deryn, I ..."

He grunted and seemed to be trying to pull his leg away from something. She bobbed up as best she could, now able to see that the bike that had crashed into her had stopped on top of his leg.

"Pull it out!" she screamed, still bobbing and trying to yank him into the water with all her might. She sunk down, using everything she had to get him to budge. But he didn't. Not even a little. She came back up for air, sobbing as her eyes met his.

"Deryn, let go!" he demanded.

She shook her head. "No! Two blackbirds flying home together, remember?"

Tears filled his eyes. "Deryn, please!"

"No!"

"*Please!*"

Xander's eyes darted all around, finally stopping on something to his left. He used his free hand to grab it. Deryn's eyes widened as he lifted her knife, and she stared at him for one final, world-shattering moment.

"I love you," he said.

"*No!*" she cried one final time.

Xander brought down the knife, stabbing through her hand so she was forced to cry out and let go, the water rushing her downstream and through a grate, something clicking behind her. The last thing she saw as she was pulled under the rushing water was the distant figure of Xander being swarmed by guards.

CHAPTER THIRTY-FIVE

Deryn gasped for breath as she slid out of a pipe and into a shallow pool of water. She stayed on her back until she stopped flowing, turning her head to cough out the water that had lodged deep in her lungs. The moment it passed she was up, running for the pipe and searching frantically for a way back up.

"No!" she screamed, slamming her fist against the damn thing. "Xander!"

She cried as she backed up a few steps, staring at the tall outer walls of Utopia.

She was outside. Something she'd been dreaming of ever since she was taken from her home eight years ago. But Xander wasn't with her. Deryn's body might have been outside but her heart was still trapped inside, forever with the man she loved. She couldn't be free without him.

Deryn collapsed to her knees, her hands landing in the mud as she wept. Her wet eyes stared down at the bleeding gash on her right hand, a mere inch lower than her blackbird tattoo, the mark that tied them together. Forever. That was what they had said.

"Forever," she whispered, refusing to believe that this was it. They had promised each other forever, and she wasn't going to fail him now.

A S.U.R.G.E. flew in front of her, scanning a blue light over her crouched figure. She froze, unsure if she should run or -

"Leon, it's Odette," said a voice speaking through the robot. *"This S.U.R.G.E. is going to lead you somewhere safe. Stay there and I'll*

be down as soon as I can. Should take me about an hour."

"Where's Xander?" demanded Deryn, tears dripping down her cheeks. "What's happening to him."

There were several heavy seconds of silence. *"The president arrived. He ordered Xander to be bound and taken to his home. Neo's tailing them as best he can. I should have an update from him by the time I reach you."*

"Is he hurt?"

This time the silence was accompanied by a static sigh. *"They removed the bike from his legs. From where I was, it didn't look like anything was broken but he's not in the best of conditions. We can talk about this later, Leon. You aren't doing Xander any good by staying out in the open like that. Get into hiding, wait for me and when Neo or Finley has news we'll plan our next course of action. Understood?"*

Deryn nodded, though she wasn't sure if Odette could see her. "Understood," she finally said, climbing to her feet. She searched the area until she found her rucksack, throwing it over her shoulder and following the S.U.R.G.E. as it zoomed off.

It led her away from Utopia and into the trees, eventually stopping near a vine hanging from a branch. Per the robot's urging, she gave the vine a tug and was quickly pulled up and into a large tree, coming to a stop on a wooden platform. She walked to the edge of it, a perfect view of the circular city of Utopia.

Deryn tossed her rucksack aside, sat down and brought her knees to her chest, staring at the tall building in the city's center that rose high above the protective shields, the only light in the dark night. President Saevus's home. Xander was on his way there now, and she had never felt more terrified.

She was still sitting like that an hour later when someone landed on the platform behind her. Without looking back, Deryn asked, "Any word?"

"Not yet," answered Odette, taking a seat beside her. "Neo couldn't follow them any further than the end of the underground. He's on his way here. Now we just wait for word from Finley."

"You won't leave him -"

"No, of course not." Odette crossed her arms and sighed. "You paid us for a service and it hasn't been met yet. We *will* get Xander out. Or die trying."

Deryn nodded, her eyes still focused on the center of Utopia, silently wondering what hell was waiting for Xander inside that tower.

CHAPTER THIRTY-SIX

Bronson and Quigley walked quickly through the streets of Middle City, sent home early from the restaurant they worked at when it was overrun with guards. Every place was overrun with guards, all marching around, instructed by various Guardians and searching for something.

Someone.

A feeling of dread had formed in the pit of Bronson's stomach the moment the guards arrived, and it was growing steadily larger. He kept calling Luka but there was never any answer. Something was wrong. Terribly, terribly wrong.

He tried Luka on his wristband again. Nothing.

"Stop calling him, Bronson. Obviously he's busy with something," said Quigley, glancing around at the chaos.

"He's answered me while working before. Something's not right, Quigs. Who else would they be going this crazy for, if not cupcake?"

"Her brother," answered Quigley. "Her father. Her former lover. Yes, all people associated with her, but not necessarily *her*. Our cupcake is fine, Bronson. You'll see when we get home."

Bronson nodded, trying hard to believe him but still picking up his pace. He needed to see her. To see Xander. And to see ...

Luka.

His face flashed in Bronson's mind, covered in red as they turned the corner onto their street. The president's car was outside of their building. Waiting.

Bronson and Quigley froze.

More red flashed through Bronson's mind.

As the door to their building opened, Quigley pulled Bronson into the shadows, both of them watching as a man was carried out of there, crying out in pain as blood poured from his leg.

"Dammit, Wenton! Tell me what's happening," Atticus Ruby demanded as two guards carried him towards the car. The Guardian Wenton Pace was walking just behind him.

"Just getting an update," said Wenton, who seemed unconcerned with his comrade's injury. He suddenly smiled. An unnerving, wicked smile that made Bronson's blood run cold. "Looks like we're going to the president's house where your son will soon be joining us."

Bronson and Quigley barely glimpsed the look of utter terror on Atticus's face before he was stuffed inside the car.

The moment it was gone, flying high in the air and towards Inner City, Bronson was running, entering their building and not stopping until he was five floors up. He halted and gasped at the sight of Xander's demolished apartment.

There was blood on the walls and -

"Shit, is that an *arm*?" screeched Quigley from behind him, cringing but still approaching the thing. "It's definitely a man's arm."

When he noticed Bronson tense, he grunted and unhappily pulled the sleeve that was still attached to the dismembered arm back a bit.

"You can relax. It's not Luka. Luka's all smooth and this man's all hairy."

"He's not completely smooth," said Bronson with a faint chuckle as tears poured from his eyes. "He gets this cute little stubble on his chin but he has to shave it off before Guardian duties."

Quigley sighed and stood up straight.

Bronson readied his wristband in front of him, but before he could try Luka again Quigley was gripping his wrist.

"*No*," his friend said sternly. "Do not call him, Bronson.

Clearly something's happened here and if Xander's been caught I imagine Luka was dragged right down with him. We can't be part of this. What we need to do now is go downstairs and act like we never saw this, never cared enough to come up here and check on them. Understand?"

Bronson gulped.

"The president may consider sparing his favorite minions, but he'd have you and me executed without a second thought. You know that, right?"

He sighed and nodded.

"We're no good to anyone if we're dead." Quigley released his friend, taking one final and heartrending look around the apartment they had spent so much time in. Then he headed for the stairs. "Let's go."

Bronson followed him, his heart aching as he thought about the three people who lived in that shattered and bloody apartment. The three people he had come to love like no other but Quigley. To love like family.

Xander, who had such a good heart buried under that asshole exterior.

Deryn, who had been torn down and broken so many times but kept rising back up. Always fighting, even when all seemed hopeless.

And Luka, who Bronson had grown to feel so strongly for in such a short amount of time. The man who had somehow seeped into him when he'd always figured himself incapable of true feelings.

He hadn't loved Fiona when his mind told him that he should. He'd always assumed it was because she was a woman, but no man had ever come close to touching his heart the way she had. Until now. With Luka. Who not only touched his heart but dug even deeper until he was gripped around his soul. He couldn't lose him. Not now. Not yet.

They had only just begun.

CHAPTER THIRTY-SEVEN

Xander was tossed into a dark cell deep below President Saevus's tower, the guards who put him there making sure to rough him up a bit before exiting. It must have been very exhilarating to hit and kick someone who'd been their boss until just moments earlier.

Really, the roughing up was completely unnecessary. His face still bled from the lash he'd taken for Deryn and his right leg ached where the stupid hover-bike had landed on it. It didn't appear to be broken but it still hurt like hell.

Xander cringed as he pushed himself to an upright position, pulling up his pant leg to get a better look at the thing. Bloody and bruised but no bones were poking out at funny angles.

His head fell back against the wall behind him as he finally let it sink in.

He'd been so close, so *fucking* close to freedom with Deryn!

She should have been able to kill Soren, to get her revenge, and they should have escaped together. But that bitch Elvira, practically bleeding to death and still able to get her way.

"Shit," he whispered into the dark, realizing that this was it for him. The end. And why? Because he was selfish. Because he couldn't bring himself to let her go just yet.

And now he would never see her again.

The tears had just begun to fall when Xander heard a groan. His head shot to the side, only now noticing the still figure lying in the cell beside his.

"Luka!"

He rushed over to his friend, reaching through the bars and

stretching as far as he could, just able to grab Luka's shoulder and drag him closer.

Luka's head was already plopped to the side, his eyes opening slightly. Xander bent down, the light in his friend's eyes faded as he stared vacantly at Xander. He blinked once, a tear dripping down his cheek as he finally realized what he was looking at.

"Is ... is she ..."

"Yes," said Xander, taking his friend's hand through the bars. "Yes, she's out."

"Good," said Luka with a soft sigh, his heavy eyes closing once more.

And then he was gone, drifting back to unconsciousness. Perhaps the last safe place he would ever experience.

The president had said nothing to Xander after arriving in the underground, just stared at him, emotionless, unreadable. Of course he was angry, that was a given, but it went so much deeper than that.

President Saevus had trusted Xander. He had shared secrets with him and planned on naming him his successor. And Xander had made a fool of him.

Xander would die for this. He knew he would.

He squeezed Luka's hand, sighing in relief when he felt a faint squeeze back. What he needed now was to focus on the silver lining. Deryn was out. Deryn was free. And even though he would die, Deryn would live.

Xander wasn't sure how long he'd been down there when he heard the shouting, but it had to have been a good hour at least. When the door at the end of the hall swung open, he let go of Luka's hand and moved far away from him.

Several figures stormed towards him, one walking with an obvious limp.

"You cannot keep my son down here, Mr. President, when he is clearly not in his right mind!"

Xander smirked. His stupid father, still trying to fight for him like it wasn't hopeless.

The president scoffed. "And how exactly do you propose he

received this *wrong* mind, Atticus?"

"There is no mind control," said the voice of Soren. "He isn't even wearing either of his wristbands! We checked the one he has on. It's a fucking fake!"

"Calm down, Soren," ordered the president.

"But, sir, we all *know* the truth, so why are we even down here humoring him?"

"Because of Luka, you fucking idiot!"

Xander's heart skipped a beat. Finley.

Suddenly, the four of them were standing before him and behind them was Barath, looking the smug bastard he always was, and even further ... Lona and Wyatt, frightened out of their wits but hanging near Finley.

"How could you?" screamed Finley, slamming her fist into the bars as tears fell down her cheeks. "How could betray us, Xander? How could betray us and bring your best friend down with you? You bastard!" She turned and found a guard standing nervously at the end of the hall. "Open this!" she ordered.

The guard waited for a nod from the president before rushing forward. The moment the cell door was open Finley was inside, smacking Xander hard across his already marked and bleeding face.

"What the hell do you have to say for yourself?" she spat, gripping the collar of his coat with both hands and giving him a private and remorseful look.

Xander couldn't help it. He smirked. Then he gripped her wrists and shoved her back a few steps, still smiling as she regained her balance. "You're right," he said, holding up his arms. "No mind control. But I suppose I can't let someone innocent go down for my misdeeds." He nodded towards Luka. "Check his wristband. I stole a mind control chip shortly after I found out Veli had acquired some and installed it in Luka." He then looked past Finley to Soren. "So sorry about your brother, by the way. Such a tragic loss."

Soren didn't even react. Not about his brother. But he did step forward, moving slowly and keeping his gaze on Xander. "Did you fuck her?"

Xander's smirk grew even wider. "You know I did. And, what more, she fucked me. *Willingly*, at that."

Soren lunged but was quickly halted by President Saevus.

"Not yet," he ordered, staring at Xander through the bars, his eyes still unreadable. "Xander will not be touched until I come up with a proper punishment for his actions."

Atticus whimpered. "Mr. President, please -"

"Get your leg treated, Atticus. I want to make sure you're standing when it comes time for your son's sentencing." He turned to leave. "Ms. Scout, check young Luka's wristband. If there's a chip in there take the appropriate action and report back to me later. Soren, *you* will follow me."

"Yes, Mr. President," said Soren, giving Xander one last venomous look before following Saevus out.

Atticus made no move to leave, watching Finley closely as she left Xander's cell and had the guard open Luka's. Then his eyes moved to Barath, who was presently staring at his son's unmoving figure with a smile.

"You sicken me," spat Atticus.

"I sicken *you*? In a moment my son will be out of here and on his way to healing while yours will be left behind to rot until the day of his execution. If this is what Luka needed to get back on the right track then so be it."

"It's here," said Finley, holding up the small chip for everyone to see.

"And my heir lives on," said Barath, grinning at Atticus. "Yours will not." And with that, he turned on his heel and marched out of Saevus's personal dungeon.

Lona, who'd been standing against the wall, released a small whimper. She and Wyatt hurried into the cell and crouched down beside Luka, neither having the courage to glance over at Xander.

Lona was the one to reach out and check his pulse. "He's alive."

"Yes, but barely," said Finley. "Lona, head upstairs and find an empty bedroom. Wyatt, you carry him. And *be* gentle. I'll send for a doctor and find him some medicine to hold him over until they arrive."

They both nodded, Lona running ahead of Wyatt, finally braving a glance at Xander but unable to hold it for long before the sadness took over and she was running faster.

Wyatt carefully lifted Luka. Not wanting to irritate the lashes on his back, he put him over his shoulder. Luka dangled, his body appearing lifeless as Wyatt carried him out of there. He never glanced at Xander, though his eyes were visibly wet.

Finley shut the cell door as she exited and the guard locked it, as well as Xander's. As she left the dungeon, she and Xander shared one last knowing glance. If his father hadn't still been there watching him he would've at least tried to thank her, but the meeting of his and Finley's eyes was enough to put Atticus on alert.

Leaning his head back against the wall, Xander sighed and said, "Leave me, Father. You and I are finished. We have been for a long time."

"Xander, please. You have to fight this."

"I have no will and no way. It's over."

"I can explain about the Leon girl. I can! I didn't want to -"

"I don't fucking care what you did or didn't want to do!" he shouted, his eyes falling back on Atticus's. "You *raped* her! There is no excuse, no reasoning you could give me that will ever change the fact that you hurt the girl I love in an irreparable way! Now leave me and don't you dare come back!"

Atticus gulped, his eyes haunted and wet. But he left. It would perhaps be the last thing his son ever requested of him and he granted it.

~

Finley sat beside Luka's bed, holding his hand and struggling to keep her eyes open. His breathing had become steadier but he still looked awful.

Lona was curled up in a chair nearby, fast asleep while Wyatt lay sprawled on the floor at her feet. Finley had to feel slight pity for the girl. She really did seem to like Luka but, from what Deryn and Xander had said, he was taken. By who, she couldn't imagine. Luka had always seemed to be even more afraid of commitment than Xander. Probably because of his home life. It's hard to imagine understanding love when you've never experienced it. At least she'd had her mother, but Luka's mother had dies giving birth to him. He had no one.

Just as her eyes began to flutter closed, Finley heard a faint voice say her name. They shot back open and found Luka staring at her.

"W-where ... where am I?" he asked.

"In the president's home. In one of the guest rooms," she answered, running the back of her hand across his forehead. "How do you feel?"

"Fucking awful," he said, looking down at his bruised arms. "What happened?"

"You don't remember?"

Luka shook his head.

"You were tortured and stunned when they found out you knew about Xander and Deryn Leon."

"Deryn Leon?" asked Luka, looking up at her. "What does she have to do with anything?"

Finley knitted her brow. "Don't you know?"

He shook his head again.

"She was living with you and Xander. For quite some time, I believe."

"I'm living with Xander?" he asked. "Why th'fuck am I living with Xander?"

Finley's breath hitched. "Luka, what is the last thing you remember?"

"I don't know, I ..." He closed his eyes and thought hard. "Clearly?"

"Yes."

"I remember my father convinced the president to have my mind swept. To find out if I was hiding about Xander."

Finley closed her eyes and rubbed the bridge of her nose. "Luka, that was nearly two months ago. We're halfway through January now."

Luka's eyes widened. "W-what? But I -"

"Please, just close your eyes and get some sleep," she said. "We'll figure this out in the morning, alright?"

Luka nodded slowly. He closed his eyes but Finley could tell he wasn't resting. She continued to hold his hand, her eyes glazing over as she fell deep in thought. There were rumors about this sort of thing happening. That was why mind control chips were still in testing stages, because test subjects kept losing their memories. The degree of it varied, but it sure as hell seemed like Luka was on the crappy end of the scale. She had hoped she could confess everything to him, and that together they could come up with some way to get Xander out of there. But Luka ... poor Luka truly didn't have a clue.

"Shit," she whispered into the dead room.

What the hell had she gotten herself into? And all for a man who was never going to love her back.

CHAPTER THIRTY-EIGHT

Xander didn't know how long he lay in that cell, the air around him completely silent as he awaited his impending doom.

The gash on his face had clotted and his leg still hurt like hell, but it didn't really matter. Nothing mattered, because in the near future he would be dead.

The only thing that frightened him about the thought was that he would have to die without ever seeing Deryn again. They hadn't gotten a last moment together, not like he'd wanted. Instead in their last moment he'd stabbed her, the woman he loved, in a desperate attempt to get her to leave him behind.

But he knew she wouldn't leave him behind. Not completely. Even now he was sure she was out there, trying desperately to find a way to come back for him instead of enjoying her newfound freedom. Which was why he hoped the president would get this over with. The sooner the better. So Deryn could start moving on.

His heart ached at the thought but it was what she needed to do. To find someone who actually deserved her love and give them her whole heart. To forget about him and the thousands of ways he had failed her.

His cheeks were wet though his tears were silent. He lifted his hand, tearing off the ring he wore so he could stare at the small tattoo on his finger.

Just two blackbirds flying home together.

That was what Deryn had said, with a promise of forever.

But their forever was being cut short.

For years Xander had spent every day fearful that it might be his last. Now he embraced his imminent death, as long as it meant she got to live.

"Deryn, please stay away," he whispered to the small tattoo. "Please."

The door to the hall of cells burst open, several sets of footsteps heading towards him. Xander slipped his ring back on but stayed lying down.

It was only two lowly guards, there to transport him somewhere else. Perhaps to his torture, which would undoubtedly come before his death. It would be Saevus's last attempt to break him. But he would not break.

Once bound, the guards guided him limping down the hall and up several flights of stairs. One was rough, kicking him every time his limp slowed him down, but the other kept giving him secret looks of sympathy.

They entered an elevator and rode it to one of the top floors. It was one he'd never been on before. Of course, that wasn't saying much. He hadn't been to the majority of floors in the president's home. The first floor was where they had their meetings, the third through sixth floors were all bedrooms. The president's room took up the entire seventh floor. No one had ever been in there, as far as he knew. They tortured people on the thirteenth floor. Kept them prisoner in the basement, often more appropriately referred to as the dungeon. Three floors worth of cells. And then he'd been to the top, floor one-hundred he believed, only to take another elevator to the roof above the fucking bubble. But that was it.

This was floor ninety-two. He hadn't the faintest idea about what happened on floor ninety-two. The guards guiding him didn't seem to have a clue either as they stepped off the elevator, looking around hesitantly before approaching a single room with windows on all four sides. Elvira was standing in the center of it, looking quite pale and mighty pissed.

Xander smiled as he entered. "Hello, Elvie. You don't look well, like maybe you've experienced an immense amount of blood loss recently. Shouldn't you be resting?"

Elvira sneered, sending the guards away with the wave of her wrist, which just happened to be attached to a metal hand. Xander's smile grew.

"Well, would you look at that. Right hand, just like your mother."

The little color left in Elvira's cheeks vanished at the mention of Del.

"What? You never guessed there were people out there who knew about your failed order from your father? Kill your mother. That was it, right?"

"Shut up!" she shouted, stomping towards him and slapping him with her metal hand.

He flinched as little as he could. "Don't know why you're so upset. I think it's sweet that you still love your mommy."

Elvira grabbed him by the coat and pulled him close. "Listen here, you fucking traitor! Pretty soon you will be dead, and you can go knowing that Soren will have his hands all over your whore for months before she joins you in the afterlife, and I will make sure any moment she's not with him is spent in pure and utter agony. Mark my words, she will suffer for your treachery."

Still smiling, Xander simply said, "Mark *my* words, by the end of this Deryn will have your head."

The doors to the room swished open. "Elvira, drop him."

Elvira stiffened at the arrival of her father. She released Xander and stepped back, obediently awaiting further instruction.

President Saevus moved so he was in Xander's line of sight, the faint hint of a smile on his lips that made Xander uneasy. "Please, Xander, have a seat."

Xander followed his hand to a single chair in the center of the room. He shrugged and sat, fully ready to embrace whatever it was this man planned to throw at him.

They all waited there for a moment, Xander watching curiously as the area outside of the glass room filled up with every last Guardian, except for one. Luka was nowhere to be found, and he imagined he wouldn't be for quite some time after the torture he'd endured before the mind control chip was discovered. He hated that he was the reason his friend had been inflicted with so much pain, but he was incredibly grateful that Luka was at least alive.

It took all his effort not to shoot Finley a glance, desperate to receive some sort of sign that Luka was indeed alright. But he couldn't risk it. Instead he found his father, who was staring at him desperately but didn't seem to have any inkling about why they were all standing out there, staring in at Xander.

"Gang's all here!" exclaimed Xander, smiling at the president.

"Yes, indeed," said Saevus, smiling in return. "I do find it amusing that you're not even attempting to fight for your life."

Xander shrugged. "What's the point? As you've already confirmed, I have no mind control chip installed. I could claim I was brainwashed, but reconditioning after such a thing hasn't really been mastered yet, so I don't know what good I'd do you."

"I could install a mind control chip in you now. Make you cooperate and hunt down that whore of yours," said the president.

"You know, it's funny. You all keep calling her a whore, yet it's your Guardians who were never able to keep it in their pants whenever she was around. Especially *your* husband." He moved his eyes from father to daughter. "Isn't that right, Elvie? Hell, some might even say that Sorey's the whore."

She pounced and, this time, punched him with her metal hand. He just laughed in response, spitting blood from his mouth and onto her shoes.

"Relax, Elvira. Now, more than ever, you should not let Xander get such a rise out of you. Look at the position he's in. He's already lost." The president smiled wider.

"My girl is out. I call that a win," said Xander.

"Yes. *Your* girl," repeated the president, that creepy smile not wavering.

"To think, if it had all worked out you and I really could

have been family. What is she to you again? Second cousin?"

"First cousin once removed, I believe," corrected Saevus. "But blood does not make family, Xander. As I'm sure you're well aware." He motioned to Elvira, who left the room and went to a small computer console just beside the door, pressing several buttons. Before long, the room changed, and suddenly Xander realized what this room was. It was a viewing room for surveillance footage, where video could be seen with life-size images when it needed to be analyzed closely.

A hologram of a man on a table appeared in front of him. Several people in lab coats were scattered around the man, a horrific scream echoing through the air. It was a voice he knew.

"Luka."

"Yes," said the president. "While Mr. Voclain claimed to not remember anything from his time under mind control, I still had his mind swept to make absolutely certain. Turns out he was telling the truth. He remembers nothing."

Luka's screams continued. Xander stood so he could see properly. A metal contraption was strapped to his friend's head, transmitting something onto a monitor while the people around him poked needles inside his skull.

"It really is a shame such a thing was necessary so soon after Luka's last mind sweep," said Saevus, still smiling away. "They say having it done more than once a year can be terribly damaging on the psyche. He's resting now, so we can't be certain if there will be any everlasting affects or not just yet, but our Luka is strong. I'm sure he will persevere."

Xander glared at the man. "He found Deryn Leon at my apartment one evening. I didn't have a choice."

"Oh, but we always have a choice, Xander."

Another earth-shattering scream echoed in the small room. Luka panted as he struggled to breathe through the pain.

"You can turn it off, Elvira," the president called to his daughter. The image vanished. "Now, sit, sit." He motioned to Xander, who obeyed. "I have something even better to show you."

Elvira reappeared holding a collar similar to what slaves

wore. Soren still wore the one that helped him speak, though he rarely used it anymore. His voice was still quiet and harsh but it was improving, to Xander's annoyance.

Xander didn't even struggle as Elvira strapped the collar to his neck, smiling wickedly before exiting again.

"This memory is a personal favorite of mine and I feel utterly blessed that it happened in my home, where all rooms are properly monitored. So I can watch it again and again."

The room was overcome again with holographic images, but before Xander's eyes even had a chance to focus on the surveillance footage, there was a scream. A familiar, terrified, resonating scream that he knew, that he had awoken to many times over the past five months.

His face paled as the figure in front of him came into focus. *Deryn.*

He and the president were now surrounded by a faded version of the parlor downstairs, Guardians scattered around, drinking and laughing joyously as Elvira tossed Deryn to the floor and whipped her with a flash of blue light from her Element.

Xander cringed.

She was already bruised and bloody, but her face was smooth, free of the many scars she had accumulated throughout her years of suffering. Her eyes were fearful as Elvira pulled her up by the hair.

"Your family has left you behind, cousin," spat Elvira, forever smirking. *"Your boyfriend has left you behind. And now you belong to us."*

Deryn tried to push her off, so Elvira gripped harder, forcing another scream out of her.

"You disgust me."

Elvira spit on her before tossing her back to the floor.

Xander fidgeted in his chair uncomfortably. This was it. The day Deryn had been taken hostage after the Outsiders' attack on Eagle Center. It was the day everything in both their lives had gone to complete shit.

And he was about to see her nightmares played out in front

of him.

"Atticus, step forward," ordered President Saevus's hologram, who was sitting in an armchair very casually and sipping on a glass of brandy.

Xander's eyes drifted sideways at the movement. The hologram of Atticus, who had been sitting on the couch with his head in his hands, slowly stood and walked towards the president. *"Y-yes, Mr. President?"* His eyes were red and puffy, his voice raw and weak as he obviously mourned the recent loss of his wife.

"I am very disappointed in your family, Atticus," said President Saevus, taking another sip of his drink. *"First, your son betrayed us by not fighting, and then it turns out your wife was the one who instructed him to do so. What do you have to say for yourself?"*

"My son is young, sir. He didn't understand the seriousness of his actions. And my wife -"

"Your wife has already been judged, and her penalty was given," said President Saevus, smiling affectionately at Elvira. *"The current matter at hand is what to do with young Xander."*

Xander's breathing grew shallow as he scanned the glass walls around him until he found his father, his eyes dark and hair disheveled as he stared down at the floor, refusing to watch the scene in front of him. Feeling Xander's gaze on him, he glanced up for just a moment, his breath hitching as a single tear slid down his cheek.

"Please, Mr. President," pleaded Atticus's hologram, echoing a memory the present Atticus did not want to relive. *"Please, I beg of you, spare my son. Pardon him this once for his lack of action. He will never betray you again. He watched his mother die, he knows better now."*

"Tell me, Atticus, how far would you go to ensure Xander's survival?"

Atticus's hologram, who'd been whimpering, suddenly sucked it all back. In a very serious and clear voice, he stated, *"I would go to hell and back."*

President Saevus's holographic lips curved into a wicked grin, the present Saevus standing beside him and mimicking the action. *"Good."* The hologram put down his brandy and stood from his seat. *"Elvira, bring us the girl."*

Elvira grabbed Deryn by the hair again, dragging her towards Saevus and Atticus. She threw her at their feet. Deryn landed hard, catching herself on her bound hands but her wrist twisted at a strange angle.

"Take her, Atticus."

In that moment, everything inside of Xander shut down. He could not move, could not breathe, his heart stopping and head spinning as the truth, something he should have realized a long time ago, may have realized deep down but didn't want to admit, suddenly came to light.

His father was the first.

Atticus's hologram, who had been staring down at Deryn, suddenly brought his head up to look at his president. *"S-sir ... what -"*

"I said take her," repeated Saevus. *"Right here, right now. Show this filthy excuse for a human what happens when you choose poison over logic."*

Xander's heart fell hard into his stomach. Half of it was still stopped while the other half was beating at an incredible rate, all of his heart feeling as if a hand was crushing the life out of it. The president's hand.

He stood from his chair and took several steps back. He was too close. He was too -

"You see, Luka. These are the gifts that are given when you join the president."

Xander's head spun again. The air around him became icy as he saw Luka and Barath's holograms out of the corner of his eye, watching. Hearing and seeing everything.

Luka *knew.*

"Sir, please. My wife -"

"Is dead," the president said coldly. *"Don't make me tell you again."*

Atticus looked down at Deryn once more. She was staring up at him with frightened eyes.

"No!" she screamed as he leaned down to grab her. *"Please, no!"*

Atticus pulled her to her feet and pushed her towards the

closest table. As they moved, Xander heard a crash of thunder echo through the large room. He only now remembered it had poured that night while he buried his mother with his bare hands, thunder and lightning flashing above him. The thunder sounded again, Deryn wincing as a new fear awoke inside of her.

Atticus tossed her on top of the table. He closed his eyes for a brief moment and took a deep breath. Deryn tried to struggle but he easily overpowered her.

"No!" she screamed louder. *"Please! Please, stop!"*

But Atticus didn't stop. His eyes glazed over as he began to undo his zipper.

"Please ..." she repeated much quieter this time. Atticus stood very still. His eyes focused and looked at the frightened girl beneath him. *"I ... I'm a virgin."*

The little life still inside of him vanished in that moment. His eyes darkened as a single tear dripped down his cheek, much like the one the present Atticus had shed mere moments ago.

"What is this?" sang Elvira as she overheard the weeping girl. *"A virgin!"* She cackled and everyone joined in.

"Do it, Atticus," ordered President Saevus, who was far less amused than the others.

"No!" screamed Xander from where he stood, feeling so completely helpless. He could not stop this, because it had already happened. This was old security footage. Just a memory, and memories could never be changed. "Stop this now!"

Atticus's hologram blinked his eyes. They stopped on Deryn one final time, and he slowly mouthed the words, *"I'm sorry."*

The current president had obviously never seen that part before, because his angry eyes shot to Atticus through the glass walls.

Tears poured down the young Deryn's cheeks as she realized all hope was lost. Atticus closed his eyes as he began to remove her pants.

Xander tried to cover his ears but the sounds were too

strong, and the moment Deryn's innocence was stolen from her was made painfully clear by the horrible cry she let out.

He clenched his eyes shut as Deryn's screams grew louder, both her cries and the thunder resonating in his ears, but a strong jolt of electricity shot through him from the collar he wore. His body jerked into the air and he fell hard on his back, squirming until the pain stopped.

The president's wicked face appeared above him. "If you ever close your eyes for longer than two seconds then that will happen. Again and again. But don't worry. It will stop when you lose consciousness, so it cannot kill you. But the moment you wake up you will watch the *girl you love*, yes I heard you tell your father earlier -" He smirked. "- lose her innocence to him, and many others shortly after. Again and again," he repeated. Then he turned on his heel and headed for the door. "Your execution will be in two days, Xander. Until then, enjoy the show."

The moment the door was open Xander was on his feet, darting for it and shoving the president aside as he lunged for Atticus.

He had barely touched his father before the electricity was shooting through his body again and he was falling. The moment he stilled, he looked at Atticus and said, "You should've let me die."

Xander stared straight up at the ceiling, unable to feel anything as he was dragged back into that room. Deryn had lied to him. She'd told him she didn't remember who the first was, and he'd let himself believe her. Because the truth, something he had always known deep down, was far worse than the lie. Her hatred for Atticus delved so much deeper than him raping her. She hated him the most because he was the first. The one to hurt her in the worst way imaginable. By taking something she could never get back, no matter how much she and Xander tried to pretend.

Finally, her screams died down. Xander's head turned just in time to see his father's hologram stepping away from her while redoing his pants.

"Well done, Atticus," said President Saevus as he stepped up behind him. *"It's been a long time since you've had someone so young. Tell me, was hell everything you imagined it would be?"*

His father didn't answer.

"Would you like to have her? Perhaps she could keep your wife's side of the bed warm, since she won't be there to heat it for you."

Atticus gulped. He stared down at Deryn, crying and curled into a ball as she tried to cover herself. One look at the blood on her thighs caused Atticus's face to contort in what most would view as disgust. But Xander was not fooled. He knew it was pain.

"No," said Atticus. *"I will not be having her again."*

Tears slid sideways down Xander's cheeks and onto the cold floor. His father had the chance to take her in, to keep her safe. But he didn't take it. He left her to the wolves.

"Was it really that terrible?" asked President Saevus with a laugh. *"Would anyone else like to judge for themselves?"*

Several Guardians moved forward, but it was Soren who got to her first, his eyes filled with lust as he began to touch the beaten girl on the table.

Beyond the holograph Xander could see the president through the glass wall, watching him with a look of triumph plastered on his cruel face. He knew he had won. "Two days, Xander."

Saevus turned and left right then, all of his Guardians filing out behind him. Atticus was the last, looking back at his son with so much regret. But it wasn't enough. It would never be enough. Not unless he could change the past.

"Leave," ordered Xander, his mouth filling with bile as Soren touched the girl beneath him like what he was doing to her was something intimate. Something out of love and not hate. But Xander knew better. Because he did love her and he would never hurt her like that.

He pointed his eyes upward, staring at the white ceiling as Deryn's screams continued to echo around him. Somehow, deep down, he had been able to convince himself that maybe this wasn't the end. That there was still a chance Finley would get him out, or someone else would come for him, but now he didn't even care. Because he had failed Deryn all those years ago. She suffered because of something he had done. And there was no forgiveness for that.

He would never deserve her.

CHAPTER THIRTY-NINE

Deryn sat on that platform in the tree without rest, the sun now rising and her eyes never leaving the center tower in Utopia as she waited for word, *any* word on Xander.

Last they had spoken to Finley he was imprisoned in a cell in the basement, untouched from what she had claimed. Aside from the wounds he had received during their escape attempt. His leg was bruised but not broken and his face had a terrible lash across it, but he was fine.

Which meant the president was planning something horrible.

"Deryn."

Deryn glanced over her shoulder at Neo, who was carrying an apple and some slices of bread. She sighed and faced the city again. "I already told you I'm not hungry."

"But you need to eat."

"Anything I eat right now will only come right back out, so what's the point?"

Neo huffed. "Okay. Then how about some water?" He plopped down beside her and handed her a thermos.

She took it though she didn't drink right away. Mainly, she just wanted something to fidget with. "No word?" she asked.

"Not about Xander."

She gulped. "Then Luka?"

They had already heard that he'd been brutally tortured after killing Mathis Fender, but also that his mind control chip had successfully been discovered and removed. But when Deryn had heard that he woke up with no recollection of anything, not since long before she came into his life, her heart broke. It had been his greatest fear that he wouldn't remember, and Xander always promised him that he would. And now he didn't even know. He didn't know about the small family they had become and that he was loved.

"The president ordered his mind swept. Finley tried to go in with him but she wasn't allowed, and when he came out he was ... well, he was worse. Fading in and out of consciousness."

Deryn sucked in a breath, tears falling from her eyes as she thought of Luka, a friend she had never expected but loved all the same.

And then she thought of Bronson and Quigley. They had surely seen their apartment by now and were probably terrified.

"I had my mind swept in the beginning," she admitted. "Multiple times and only days apart, in case they missed something." She rolled her wet eyes. Everyone knew mind sweeping wasn't real. Just another form of torture. "Luka's strong. He'll be alright."

Neo nodded. "You do understand that when we go in getting one person out will be tough, but getting two will be -"

"*Don't* say impossible," she snapped. "If it's money you want-"

"No, of course not," said Neo, looking mildly offended. "But I just ... I don't think we can. They'll be kept far apart. You know they will."

Deryn nodded. "But you'll try?"

He smiled softly. "Yes, we'll try."

Just then, the vine that hung to the ground made a swishing noise. They both looked over their shoulders as Odette appeared and stepped onto the platform. She didn't look well.

"How did things go with the tunnelers?" asked Neo.

"What?" Odette paused and thought. "Oh! Fine. Well ... you know, the usual. Most ignored my very existence but Rees has agreed to help and he's dragging two others along with him."

"You have news about Xander," said Deryn, understanding the ominous look in the other woman's eyes.

Odette nodded, glancing nervously at her husband, who silently urged her to continue. "His execution has been scheduled. We have two days to get him out."

"That's it?" asked Neo.

She nodded again, still avoiding Deryn.

"Odette," called Deryn, her voice desperate. "Please tell me what you know."

Odette finally looked at her, releasing a heavy sigh. "The night you were first taken prisoner, do you remember it?"

Deryn stiffened but nodded.

And then Odette went on to tell her about the cruelest form of personalized torture President Saevus had come up with yet. Xander had to watch it. That first night, her virginity, taken from her by his father only hours after his wife was killed. Something she had never been able to admit to him no matter how hard she tried.

And then there were the others.

Deryn hung her head low and sobbed, knowing very well that Xander would find some way to blame himself for something that was out of his control. Like he always did.

"Two days," Neo muttered to himself. "How the hell are we going to infiltrate that fucking tower in two days with only five men?"

"Six," corrected Deryn with a hiccup.

"What?" asked Odette.

"Six men," she repeated. "Don't think for one second you're going back in there without me."

Odette and Neo exchanged a look. "Deryn, we just got you out," said Odette. "We cannot allow you to -"

"You will *not* tell me what I can and cannot do!" snapped Deryn, rising to her feet. "I have had no control over my life since I was fifteen years old and it ends now! This is my choice and I'm going in there whether you *allow* it or not!"

Odette sighed but conceded.

"Even so," said Neo, continuing his train of thought. "*Six* men isn't nearly enough. Not for the plan I've been playing with in my mind. We need more."

Deryn thought. Then she remembered something. "What if I could get you five more? Would that be enough?"

Neo cocked an eyebrow. "And just where exactly are you getting these five?"

"The Resistance."

Odette and Neo exchanged another look. "The moment we inform the Resistance of your escape they'll be scooping you up and locking you in a room somewhere to make sure they don't lose you again," said Odette.

Deryn shook her head. "Not if we do it right."

~

Talon had been sitting alone in his room when his two-way radio started crackling. At first he ignored it, but then he'd heard the faint voice coming from the other side. A voice he'd only heard once in the past five years but was permanently ingrained in his mind.

He'd stumbled over himself to get to that damn radio, stretching to grab it from where he'd fallen on the floor and pressed the button before he was even back on his feet. "Deryn?"

And then his sister's voice proceeded to tell him the two words he had been waiting for over five years to hear. *"I'm out."*

She wanted to meet him alone at the ruins. He'd immediately gone to Nita, who insisted that she and her team accompany him, though she'd promised they would hang back so as not to scare Deryn off. She had been a prisoner for five years and was bound to be a bit skeptical of everyone she encountered.

Deryn had also insisted that he tell no one about this, especially Dakota. He didn't understand why she wouldn't want Dakota knowing about her escape but he agreed, nonetheless, and sent his friend off on a fake mission so he wouldn't have the opportunity to wander to the ruins and destroy Talon's one chance at reuniting with his sister.

As he sat atop a large stone that used to be a piece of a towering building, he found himself reaching into his pocket where his bracelet was normally kept. He was so used to fidgeting with it that he felt incomplete without it. With nothing else to fidget with he ran his hand through his hair, glancing around anxiously for any sign of Deryn.

He had gone to see his father before he left, though the man barely registered his presence. While he'd wanted to tell him where he was going and who he was bringing back with him he didn't want to get his hopes up. Not again.

And then Talon heard it. A rustle of leaves, steps breaking rotting twigs on the ground. Everything he'd been trained to listen for. He snapped his head in the direction of the noise, fixing the hair he'd messed up and waiting for someone to emerge from the trees.

His heart raced as a figure came into view, his breath clogged somewhere in his throat. He gulped to relieve it though it didn't do much good.

And then, there she was. Standing there, looking up at him, was his little sister, her eyes still bright and her hair mahogany-brown with faded streaks of red.

"Deryn." He jumped down, fighting off the urge to run to her and take her in his arms. He'd dreamed of this moment. Every night for five and a half years.

But Deryn wasn't moving.

Talon took a step closer. Then another. And -

Before his third step touched the ground, she turned on her heel and took off running. Talon immediately reacted, taking off after her.

"Deryn! Deryn, please! Come back!"

But she didn't come back. She darted through the trees with all the skill she had as a child, back when she used to mimic the animals they chased, specifically the deer.

As Talon approached a clearing, he caught sight of her in the center of it, skidding to a halt and turning to face him.

He entered the clearing, freezing at the scene in front of him.

Nita was on her knees beside Deryn, her hands bound behind her back, flinching as his little sister pulled a knife out of her sleeve and pressed the tip to Nita's neck. Nita's team were there too, all three of them bound with weapons held to their backs. There were five people with Deryn, three he didn't recognize and two who looked vaguely familiar. Children of Guardians who attended Eagle Center, if he remembered correctly.

"So when I asked you to come alone, you thought that meant bring four armed soldiers with you?" asked Deryn, her brow furrowing as she stared across the way at Talon.

Talon met her eyes and gulped. "Yes, well, sometimes being the son of Godfrey Leon means people want to ambush me. Experience has taught me to be cautious."

"So you thought I'd ambush you?"

"You *are* ambushing me," Talon pointed out, still not exactly sure what to make of his current situation.

"Beside the point."

Talon glanced down at Nita, who sighed and shrugged. "Deryn, what are you doing?" he demanded, his eyes raising back to her.

"Negotiating," she answered. "After our conversation last week, I got the impression you weren't willing to do so."

"Negotiate what? You're *out*!" he shouted, unable to think rationally in that moment. His sister, his *little* sister who he had been crying over, fighting for, dreaming about for all these years was here in front of him, and she was holding a knife to his girlfriend's throat.

His girlfriend who didn't look terrified in the least ...

And then he understood what Nita was silently trying to tell him. Deryn wasn't off her rocker, which was where his mind had gone.

"As you may recall, I told you that Xander and I are a package deal, yet here I am, outside without him." Deryn's eyes were wet as she spoke, and Talon had to fight off the urge to move forward and comfort her. "Saevus discovered his deception and while we tried to get out together he didn't make it. His execution is scheduled to take place in two days. And we're going to get him out."

Talon's eyes widened. "*We?*"

"We have the six of us here and one person on the inside," explained Deryn. "It's not enough. But eleven should just about do it."

Talon glanced at Nita and then the three members of her team, only one of them expressing any displeasure in the request. The others remained neutral.

"I can't send my men into a death trap for a Guardian," he said, looking back at Deryn.

"Why do you label him like that?" she demanded. "He's a person, just like you and me, and he needs help!"

Talon ran a hand through his hair. "Even if we somehow manage to get him out, what the hell are we supposed to do with him? We can't bring a Guardian to the base."

"*Person!*"

"He may be a person, but he's still a fucking Guardian, Deryn!" shouted Talon, unable to stop himself from snapping. She was being completely unreasonable. "I can't let him in."

"Then he and I will leave!"

Talon's heart dropped. "What? No."

"You don't want us to stay! You don't want us to leave! Make up your damn mind!"

"I want *you* to stay!" snapped Talon.

"Package deal," she repeated with a sneer. "He protected me. He took me in and protected me when *you* failed to do so!" Deryn removed the knife from Nita's neck and pointed it forcefully at Talon. He flinched, and then immediately regretted it when he saw the sadness in her eyes. "Fine." She bent down and used the knife to cut Nita's binds. "We'll do it without you."

Talon went white. "No."

"You say that a lot. But I'm going back for him whether you help me or not."

Deryn waited a moment but when Talon didn't speak she moved to leave, the other members of her group already releasing Nita's team.

She took a step away from him. And then another. And -

"Alright!" he shouted, stumbling forward and falling to his

knees.

Deryn glanced over her shoulder at him. "What did you say?"

Talon climbed back to his feet, tears streaming from his eyes as he stared at his sister. "I said I'll do it! I'll do anything! Just, please ... please don't leave."

Deryn's tough exterior melted in that moment, her shoulders bobbing as she cried. "I didn't want our reunion to be like this but -"

"Don't explain. There's no need, alright? Just ... just please, let me hug you now."

Deryn gave a small smile and lightly lifted her arms. Talon lunged forward and scooped her up, crying openly as he hugged her as tightly as he could. They both laughed through the tears as her arms linked around his neck, neither wanting to ever let the other go.

And for a brief moment in time it felt like maybe everything was going to be okay.

But the real war was just beginning.

L. Stoddard Hancock is the bestselling author of the Cruel and Beautiful World series - Broken Wings, Sunken Eyes, and Arise. A California native, Laura currently lives in Oregon with a self-help guru for a roommate and a cat named Milo who runs both their lives.

www.lstoddardhancock.com
www.facebook.com/lstoddardhancock

Printed in Great Britain
by Amazon

11508901R00214